THE FAMILY
JENSEN

THE FAMILY
JENSEN

William W. Johnstone
with J. A. Johnstone

PINNACLE BOOKS
Kensington Publishing Corp.
www.kensingtonbooks.com

PINNACLE BOOKS are published by

Kensington Publishing Corp.
119 West 40th Street
New York, NY 10018

PUBLISHER'S NOTE
Following the death of William W. Johnstone, the Johnstone family
is working with a carefully selected writer to organize and complete
Mr. Johnstone's outlines and many unfinished manuscripts to
create additional novels in all of his series like The Last Gunfighter,
Mountain Man, and Eagles, among others. This novel was inspired
by Mr. Johnstone's superb storytelling.

All Kensington titles, imprints, and distributed lines are available at
special quantity discounts for bulk purchases for sales promotions,
premiums, fund-raising, educational, or institutional use. Special
book excerpts or customized printings can also be created to fit
specific needs. For details, write or phone the office of the Kensington special sales manager: Kensington Publishing Corp., 119 West
40th Street, New York, NY 10018, attn: Special Sales Department;
phone: 1-800-221-2647.

ISBN-13: 978-0-7860-2130-7
ISBN-10: 0-7860-2130-6

First printing: May 2010
Eighth printing: May 2013

16 15 14 13 12 11 10 9 8

Printed in the United States of America

Prologue

The temperature in the small, stone-and-log cabin climbed steadily during the afternoon. The single room was about twelve feet by twelve feet. There were no windows, and the door was closed and barred. The only light and the only air came in through gaps between the logs where the mud chinking had fallen out . . .

And through the loopholes that had been carved in those logs so men who had to fort up in the cabin could fire rifles at their enemies.

Shots blasted occasionally from outside, but the bullets stood little if any chance of penetrating the thick walls. Lead smacked harmlessly into stone or logs.

The three defenders fired even less often. They stood at the loopholes, two at the front wall and one at the back, sweat trickling down their faces, and waited patiently for a target to present itself. When they had a good shot, they took it quickly, without hesitation.

The oldest of the trio, manning a loophole in the rear wall, squeezed the trigger of a heavy-caliber Sharps rifle. The weapon's boom was deafening in the cabin's close confines. The acrid smell of burned powder already hung in the air, and that latest shot added to the sharp tang.

"Got that son of a buck," the old man said with satisfaction. "That'll learn him to stick his ear out where I can see it."

"You blew his ear off, Preacher?" one of the younger men asked.

The old-timer turned his head and spat on the hard-packed dirt floor as he lowered his Sharps and started reloading the single-shot rifle. "Damn right I did." He paused and then added slyly, "O' course, since his brain was right on t'other side of his ear, I reckon that ball went on through and messed it up a mite, too."

That brought grim chuckles from the other two men, but the respite lasted only a moment before one of them warned, "Hombre coming up on your side, Matt."

A wicked crack came from Matt's rifle, and he said, "Not anymore. Obliged for the heads-up, Smoke."

Smoke Jensen grinned and gibed, "Somebody's got to watch out for you, youngster."

Preacher snorted. "You're a fine one to be callin' anybody youngster. You ain't much more'n a kid yourself, Smoke. Why, it don't seem like it's been more'n a year or two since I first come on you and your pa, down on the Santa Fe Trail."

"That was nigh on to fifteen years ago, Preacher," Smoke said.

The old man snorted again. "When you get as old as I am, the years flow by like water in a high mountain crick." He grinned, revealing teeth that were still strong despite his age. "The years are as sweet as that water, too, and I still drink deep of 'em."

"I believe that," muttered Matt Jensen, who was the youngest of the three men.

They had been holed up in the cabin since a little before noon. It was around two in the afternoon, and the sweltering cabin would just get hotter as the day went on. With the coming of night, the temperature would cool off fairly quickly at that elevation. Smoke, Matt, and Preacher weren't looking forward to the darkness. It also meant the small army of gunmen that wanted them dead could get close enough to toss some torches onto the roof. When that happened, they could either stay inside and die from the smoke and fire . . .

Or they could go out that door with guns in their hands, fighting to the end, dealing out blazing death to their enemies.

Not a single one of the three had to ponder the question. They *knew* what they were going to do . . .

Unless they could figure out some way to turn the tables on the gunslinging bastards who had forced them to take shelter there.

Preacher ran his fingers through his tangled white beard. He was dressed head to foot in buckskins and had a broad-brimmed leather hat thumbed back on thinning white hair. An eagle feather was stuck in the hatband. He had a Colt .44 holstered on his right hip and a sheathed Bowie knife on his left. This was his eighty-first summer, but somewhere along the way, he had become as timeless and ancient as the mountains, weathered slowly but hardly weakened. He could ride all day, he could whip men half his age, and he could drink just about anybody under the table. He'd been naught but a boy when he went west, and he had been there, by and large, ever since, for more than six decades.

He was a mountain man, one of the last of that hardy breed.

He was also something of a surrogate father to Smoke Jensen, having taken the boy under his wing when Smoke's own father Emmett had been killed. Smoke hadn't been known by that name then; he'd been given the name Kirby Jensen when he was born. Preacher was the one who had dubbed him Smoke that long-ago day when Kirby, Emmett, and Preacher had been ambushed by a Kiowa war party. Maybe it was because of the powdersmoke that filled the air when Kirby Jensen received his baptism of fire, or maybe it was because his ash-blond hair was almost the color of smoke, but whatever the reason, the handle stuck, and from that day forward he'd been Smoke Jensen.

He wasn't a boy any longer, but rather a man in the prime of life, just over six feet tall with shoulders as broad as an ax handle. Down in Colorado, he had a damn fine ranch called the Sugarloaf and an even finer wife named Sally. He had a reputation, too, as a man who was fast on the draw, maybe the fastest on the entire frontier. Smoke had no desire to live the life of a gunfighter, though. He drew the walnut-butted .44 on his hip only when he had to . . . but as many men had learned, to their short-lived but final regret, he didn't cotton to being pushed around.

Just as Preacher had helped Smoke out when he was orphaned, so Smoke had taken in Matt Cavanaugh, who had lost his family at an even younger age. That was back in the days before Smoke had settled down, when he was still searching for gold in Colorado. He had found it, and since Matt helped him work the claim, Smoke felt that Matt deserved an equal share in it. He had also taught Matt everything that Preacher had taught *him* about how to survive on the frontier, and more importantly, how to live his life as a decent, honorable man.

When the time came for Matt to strike out on his own, as a tribute to the man who had become like an older brother to him he had taken Smoke's last name, and ever since he'd been known as Matt Jensen. It was a name that was becoming more widely known, as Matt was drawn to danger and adventure like a moth to flame. He wasn't reckless, but he didn't back down when challenged.

So the three men who waited in the stifling cabin in the Big Horn Mountains shared not a drop of common blood . . . and yet they were family. Bonds stronger than blood held them together, bonds forged by love, respect, and shared danger. Most of the time, each of them went their own way, especially Preacher and Matt, both of whom tended to be fiddle-footed, but distance didn't mean anything to such men. When one needed help, the others would come a-runnin'.

At that moment it looked like the three of them might well die together.

Preacher squinted over the barrel of his Sharps through the loophole and said, "Those hombres must not have the sense God gave a badger! Here they come again!"

Whoever had built the cabin back in the old days had known what he was doing. The area around it was cleared of trees and brush for a good fifty yards. No one could sneak up on the place unseen. Some thick stumps remained, where trees had been chopped down, and as some of the hired gunmen charged out of the trees, they threw themselves behind those stumps and opened fire, aiming at the loopholes they had spotted from the powder smoke that gushed through them from time to time.

"Son of a gun!" Matt exclaimed as slugs chewed splinters from the log wall all around the loophole he was using. He was forced to draw back momentarily. So were Smoke and Preacher.

"More coming out of the trees!" Smoke called. He saw men dart out from cover, race past their companions who were firing from behind the stumps, and then dive behind other stumps. "They're leapfrogging at us, blast it!"

It was true. As soon as the second wave of attackers had gone to ground, *they* opened up on the cabin, allowing the first ones to advance past them.

That wasn't the only trickery going on. "Circling to your left, Matt!" Smoke said. Matt twisted in that direction, thrust the barrel of his Winchester through an opening, and began firing as fast as he could work the rifle's lever.

Smoke bit back a curse as he spotted some of the gunmen running to his right, trying a flanking move in that direction. He wished one of his friends, Sheriff Monte Carson or the gambler and gunhawk Louis Longmont, was there to cover the fourth side, although he wouldn't have wished them into such a predicament as the one in which he, Matt, and Preacher found themselves.

There was only one thing to do. He leaned his Winchester against the wall, threw aside the bar that kept the door closed, drew one of the long-barreled .44s he carried in his holsters, and yanked the door open. Palming out the other Colt he leaped outside, landing on his belly.

Both six-guns began to roar. Firing in two directions at once was a tricky, almost impossible thing to do, but in the hands of Smoke Jensen, guns could do almost anything. He could make them sing and dance if he wanted to, folks said.

His guns sang a melody of death.

His left-hand gun slammed bullets into the bodies of the men charging at the cabin head-on. The right-hand Colt bucked and roared as it tracked the gunnies who were trying to circle in that direction. Men cried out and stumbled or spun off their feet as Smoke's lead ripped through them.

From the corner of his eye, Matt had seen Smoke's daring play, and he jumped into the doorway, using his rifle to mow down the men going to the left. At the back of the room, Preacher threw down his empty Sharps and snatched up another Winchester. With deadly accurate fire he held off the men attacking from that direction.

For thirty seconds, it sounded like a small war as the thunderous gunfire echoed back from the peaks surrounding the beautiful little valley where the cabin was located. Then the hammers of Smoke's guns clicked on empty chambers. With Matt covering him, he scrambled to his hands and knees and dived back through the doorway. Matt hurried after him, slamming the door closed and dropping the bar in its brackets again.

"You give them ol' boys what for?" Preacher drawled.

"I reckon we did, Preacher," Smoke said as he sat with his back against the wall and reloaded his Colts. "The last I saw, they were skedaddling back to the trees."

"The ones who could still move, that is," Matt added.

The other two knew what he meant. They had turned back the attack and done considerable damage to the enemy force.

As silence fell again, they heard the pathetic moans of wounded men. Not one of the defenders wasted any sympathy on those varmints. The gunnies had known what they were getting into.

"It was a mite of a hornet's nest in here," Preacher said. "Plenty o' slugs flyin' around." He touched a gnarled finger to his cheek, and the tip came away bloody. "Felt like one of 'em kissed me, and sure enough it did."

That little bullet burn on Preacher's cheek was the only injury they had suffered. They had been very lucky so far, and they knew it. Luck would only last so long. They knew that, too.

"Bannerman must be paying those boys pretty well," Matt commented. "That many gun-wolves don't come cheap."

Smoke said, "If there's one thing Reece Bannerman has, it's money, and plenty of it."

"Then why's the dang fool want more?" Preacher asked. "Why's it so all-fired important that he steal this valley from Crazy Bear's people?"

Smoke had finished reloading his guns. He picked up his rifle again and took his place at the loophole. As he peered out at the silent trees where the gunmen were hidden, he said, "I guess some men never get enough, no matter how much they have."

"Well, I ain't gonna let it happen," Preacher declared. "We're gonna get outta this fix somehow and show Bannerman he can't get away with it. I owe Crazy Bear a whole heap o' thanks for what he done for me. That's why I come a-runnin' when I heard he was in trouble."

"Crazy Bear's a good man," Smoke agreed. "I was glad to help out when I got your letter, Preacher."

"And it's a good thing I was visiting Smoke at Sugarloaf at the time," Matt added, "because I want to be in on this, too."

"You just want to see Crazy Bear's daughter again," Smoke said with a smile.

"I won't deny that," Matt said.

Preacher snorted. "You young fellas may be fond o' Crazy Bear, but I owe the ol' rapscallion my life. I ever tell you that story, Smoke?"

"I don't think so," Smoke said, although as a matter of fact, Preacher *had* told him the story before. It was a pretty good yarn, and they needed something to pass the time while they waited for Bannerman's hired guns to attack again.

So as the three men stood and watched, and the heat grew worse in the cabin, Preacher drawled, "It was about thirty years ago, I reckon. I was on my way through this same valley. Weren't no ranches nor towns hereabouts in those days. 'Twas still mighty wild country, and it might cost a man his hide if'n he didn't keep his eyes open . . ."

BOOK ONE

Chapter 1

An eagle soared through the vast blue sky overhead. The tall man in buckskins saw it as he rode along the edge of the trees, just as he saw the chipmunk that raised its head from a burrow in the clearing fifty yards to his left and the squirrel that bounded from branch to branch in a pine tree off to his right. He saw a dozen moose grazing half a mile ahead of him, and he saw the wolf slinking toward them through tall grass. A bear lumbered across a hillside nearly a mile away, and Preacher saw it, too.

But he never saw the man who shot him.

He didn't hear the heavy blast of the rifle echo across the landscape and up the canyons that cut through the mountains until after the slug smashed into his body and drove him forward in the saddle, over the neck of the rangy gray stallion. He tried to grab on to something and stay on the horse, but his whole body seemed to have gone numb from the bullet's impact. His muscles refused to work the way he wanted them to. He managed to kick his feet free of the stirrups just before he fell. As the horse shied, Preacher toppled from the saddle.

Even though his body wouldn't cooperate, his mind still worked. He didn't think the horse would bolt, but he hadn't had the animal all that long and didn't have complete confidence in him yet.

Preacher wasn't completely numb. He felt the jolt as he landed heavily on the ground. Somehow he kept the fingers of his right hand clamped around the long-barreled flintlock rifle he'd been carrying across the saddle in front of him. He had a couple of those newfangled Colt Dragoon revolvers that he'd picked up in St. Louis tucked behind his belt, too. If he could get to cover, he knew he could give a good accounting of himself.

Making it to cover was not easy. Feeling began to flow back into Preacher's body, but it brought waves of paralyzing pain with it.

Preacher knew how to deal with pain. If a man wanted to live, he learned how to ignore it. Whether it was in body or spirit, hardly a day went by without something hurting. The trick was not to give in to it.

Still clutching the rifle, Preacher rolled to his right, closer to the trees. It was a good thing he moved when he did. Another shot sounded and a heavy lead ball smacked into the ground where he had been lying a heartbeat earlier. Preacher kept rolling. Every movement sent fresh bursts of pain stabbing through his body.

When he was within a few feet of the trees he came up onto his hands and knees, got his feet under him, and launched into a dive that carried him to the edge of the pines. Vaguely, he heard another shot and felt a ball tug at his buckskin shirt as he flew through the air. He slammed into the ground again, the impact softened slightly by the carpet of fallen pine needles on which he landed.

More shots sounded, coming close enough together Preacher knew there was more than one bushwhacker. He scrambled around to the other side of a thick-trunked pine and rested his back against the rough bark. He tried to take a deep breath, but that made the pain in his left side worse.

All right, he told himself, he had a busted rib, or a cracked one, anyway. Probably just cracked. If it actually was broken, all that falling, rolling, and jumping around surely would have plunged the jagged end of a bone into his left lung and he'd be drowning in his own blood. So, he decided, the rib was cracked. It hurt like hell, and could still break easily if he wasn't careful.

His left side was covered with warm, sticky wetness. He thought he might bleed to death if the hole wasn't bound up soon. Any time a fellow was shot, he had to worry about the wound festering. There were all kinds of ways to die on the frontier.

Holes—more than one—he corrected himself as he gingerly poked around on his side. The rifle ball had struck him in the back, on the left side, glanced off a rib, and torn its way out the front of his body. He was lucky the bone had deflected it outward, rather than bouncing it through his gut. He really would have been a goner then.

Breathing shallowly through clenched teeth, he pulled up his buckskin shirt and used the heavy hunting knife that was sheathed on his hip to cut two strips from his long underwear—not easy to do, because his left arm was still partially numb. He managed to wad one of the pieces of woolen fabric into a ball and shove it into the exit wound. Since he couldn't reach the spot with his right hand, he gritted his teeth and forced his left arm to reach around his back to where the bullet had entered. The few minutes it took seemed more like an hour, but finally he pushed the wadded-up cloth into the bullet hole.

That helped slow down the bleeding. He knew if he lost too much blood, he would pass out. If that happened, chances were he would never wake up again. His enemies would slip up on him and cut his throat.

He didn't know how many there were. The shooting had stopped, but from the sound of the volley a few minutes earlier, he figured five or six.

Nor did he know who they were. He had spent five decades on the earth, testified by the leathery skin of his face and the numerous silver strands in his dark hair and beard.

Few men lived that long without making enemies. Preacher had probably made more than his share, although he had left many of them dead behind him, either in shallow graves or out in the open for the scavengers and the elements to take care of. It depended on how put out with them he'd been when he killed them.

There were still plenty of folks carrying grudges against him, and obviously he had just crossed trails with some of them . . . unless the bushwhackers were no-good thieves who wanted to kill him and take his outfit.

He had a good horse, a sizable batch of supplies on the pack horse he'd been leading, and some fine weapons. No pelts yet; it was too early in the season for that. Those days, not many people would bother stealing furs. The mountains weren't trapped out yet, far from it, but the fur trade wasn't what it used to be. The last great rendezvous had been eight years earlier, in '42. A lot of the mountain men had gone back east to be with their long-neglected families. Others had headed west to look for gold in California.

Preacher had no intention of leaving the mountains for good. When his time came, he intended to die there.

He listened intently. The woods were quiet. The shooting had scared off all the animals. If the bushwhackers started skulking around, he would hear them.

He was disgusted with himself for letting somebody shoot him in the back. He didn't know where they'd been hidden or how carefully they had concealed themselves, but he didn't care. He should have known they were there, lying in wait for him.

Was a time when he would have known, because Dog would have smelled the sons of bitches, and Horse probably would have, too. But the big wolf-like cur was gone, and so was the gray stallion that looked a lot like Preacher's current mount.

Over the years, Dog had tangled with outlaws, savages, grizzlies, panthers, and lobo wolves. He had gotten chewed up, shot, half-drowned, and mostly frozen. None of that had killed him, but time had. The years always won in the end.

Horse, at least, was still alive as far as Preacher knew. He had left the stallion in Missouri with an old friend who had promised to make Horse's final years as comfortable and pleasant as possible. Preacher wasn't sure he had done the right thing. Being put out to pasture was a hard destiny. Maybe he should have brought Horse back to the mountains with him one last time.

If he had, he woudn't be sitting there with a couple of bullet holes in him, he told himself. Because Horse's keen senses would have alerted him there were enemies nearby.

Off to his left a ways, something rustled in the brush.

A grin that was half-grimace drew Preacher's lips back from his teeth. He reached to his waist and drew out one of the Dragoons. It was a fine weapon, well balanced, with a seven and a half inch octagonal barrel and a cylinder that held six .44 caliber loads, although Preacher always left one chamber empty for the hammer to rest on. Engraved on that blued steel cylinder was a scene of Texas Rangers battling Comanches. Preacher figured it was based on the fight at Bandera Pass a few years back. Captain Jack Hays, who'd been in command of the troop of Rangers involved, had told Preacher all about that ruckus one time when he was down in San Antonio de Bexar.

Yes, sir, a mighty fine gun. It shot straight and true, and between the two revolvers and the flintlock rifle, he had eleven rounds ready to go. More than enough to kill every one of those damn bushwhackers.

Of course, they'd probably kill him, too, Preacher reflected, but they wouldn't live to brag about it.

Another rustle, to his right that time. They had him surrounded. They were so confident they had him trapped, one of them was bold enough to call out, "We're gonna kill you, old man, if you ain't dead already. You got anything to say?"

Preacher didn't respond, except to draw his other Dragoon.

His left arm was still weak, but he was able to hold the revolver fairly steady.

"You should've minded your own business back at that trading post, old man. You must be soft in the head. Who in his right mind would kick up such a fuss over a damn Indian whore?"

So that was why they wanted him dead, Preacher thought. They had trailed him all the way out there, a week or more, over some fracas at a trading post? He supposed that the fellow whose guts he'd spilled on the ground meant something to them. A friend or maybe kinfolk. Even so, the man had been a sorry son of a bitch, hardly worth dying over. Seemed like they were bound and determined to do just that, though.

"Shut up, Riley," another voice, older and harsher, said. "That's enough. Let's get this done. You boys ready?"

Preacher was ready. He braced his back against the tree trunk and raised both Dragoons in front of him, as a cry rang out through the trees. A half laugh, half scream, jagged, nerve-scraping sound that was one of the craziest things Preacher had ever heard.

Chapter 2

The eerie cry made some of the bushwhackers let out surprised yells. Getting ready to charge Preacher had drawn their nerves pretty tight, and that shriek startled them into pulling triggers. Shots blasted through the woods, but the wail continued. It didn't sound human.

Bullets whipped through the branches and thudded into tree trunks, but none of them came close to Preacher. He spotted a muzzle flash off to his right and reacted instantly, angling the Dragoon in that direction and dropping the hammer. The heavy revolver roared, smoke and flame erupting from its muzzle. Somewhere in the woods, a man screamed. Preacher didn't know if his shot had found its target, or if whatever was making that unholy noise had gotten hold of the man.

With his back against the tree to brace himself, Preacher pushed to his feet. He didn't know exactly what was going on, but there was a good chance he would die right there. If that turned out to be true, he planned to go out standing on his own two feet with shooting irons in his hands.

"What the hell is that?" a man shouted. There was a great thrashing in the brush. "Look ou—*yahhhhh!*"

The howl of pain made the bushwhackers shoot again. A grim smile tugged at Preacher's mouth again. If they kept it up, they'd all ventilate each other and save him the trouble, he thought. That would be just fine with him.

The older voice he'd heard giving orders earlier bellowed, "Head for the horses! Let's get the hell out of here!"

Preacher aimed at the voice and thumbed off two more rounds from the Dragoon. He figured the chances of him hitting anything in those thick woods were pretty slim, but it wouldn't hurt anything to try. There were still so many guns going off, the bushwhackers likely wouldn't notice two more shots.

The gunfire died away, but Preacher could hear men crashing through the brush. He let them go without sending any more lead after them. Blood still oozed from the holes in his side, and he was starting to get a little dizzy. Best to let those varmints take off for the tall and uncut, he decided.

Once he got his strength back, he might try to track them down. He didn't cotton to the idea of letting anybody get away with shooting him.

There was also whatever kind of wild creature had made that sound, he reminded himself. He might have to deal with it, too.

The swift rataplan of hoofbeats drifted through the woods to his ears. The bushwhackers had reached their horses and were putting some ground behind them. The hoofbeats faded into the distance until he could no longer hear them and silence settled once more over the valley.

Preacher felt his legs weakening underneath him. His head spun, and each of the guns in his hands seemed to weigh a ton. It was all he could do to hold them up. When he felt himself slipping, he tried to stiffen his legs, but it didn't work. He'd lost too much blood, and his strength had leaked out of him along with the crimson fluid. Slowly, inexorably, he slid down the tree trunk until he was sitting on the ground at its base again.

He heard a crackling in the brush. Something was moving

toward him. Something big, from the sound of it. The thing came closer, stepping around trees and pushing brush aside.

A gray veil seemed to have slipped down over Preacher's eyes, making it difficult for him to see. He could make out the massive, looming shape, but that was all. The Dragoons had sunk to his lap, his thumbs still looped over the hammers. He struggled to lift the weapons. If he could manage to raise the guns, when the thing stooped to reach out for him with its clawed, misshapen paws, he would blow a couple of fist-sized holes in it. Anything that big had to be a grizzly bear, his fevered brain decided . . . but he had never heard a griz make that kind of a noise.

He was wrong. The looming shape finally came to a stop directly in front of him, and as Preacher gazed up at it, his vision cleared enough for him to realize that it wasn't a grizzly bear after all.

It was the biggest, ugliest Indian Preacher had ever laid eyes on . . . and the last thing Preacher saw as consciousness fled from him. He didn't feel a thing when his head fell back against the tree trunk with a solid thud.

The aromatic smell of woodsmoke filling his nostrils was the first thing Preacher recognized as awareness began to seep back into his brain. Then, not surprisingly, he heard the crackle of flames and felt warmth on his face. After a moment he figured out he was lying on something soft, near a fire.

He kept his eyes closed and his breathing regular. Although he had just come to, his instincts were already working. Since he didn't know where he was or what was going on around him, the smart thing to do was to not let on that he was awake.

He moved a hand slightly and felt something soft yet bristly. A thick fur robe of some sort, he decided. He sniffed the air and under the woodsmoke smelled bear grease and something else, a faint musky scent.

A woman. She began to sing softly to herself, under her breath, confirming Preacher's guess.

All those sensations were intimately familiar to him. He had spent many winters with various tribes, sharing a lodge or a tepee with a comely squaw. Sometimes when he visited those tribes again a few years later, he found little ones trailing after those squaws who'd wintered with him. He never tried to be a pa to those kids. He'd always figured that a restless varmint like him, who would probably come to a bad end, didn't have any business trying to act like a father. Might as well ask the wind to be a good parent. It wasn't going to happen.

As he lay on the fur robe Preacher thought about what he remembered from earlier and decided that the big, ugly Indian must have taken him to a village rather than kill him. He kept his eyes closed, shifted his body a little, and realized he had bandages wrapped tightly around his torso. His side felt stiff and hot where the rifle ball had torn through it, but whoever had tended to the wounds had packed each of them with a healing poultice. Preacher knew that with time and proper care, he would heal.

Of course, it was possible the redskins were trying to save his life so they could kill him in their own way, in their own sweet time. He knew such things happened.

Preacher hadn't gotten a very good look at the beadwork and decorations on the big Indian's buckskins, but he thought they indicated the man was a Crow. The Crow got along with white men about as well as any of the tribes did, and better than some. They didn't hate everybody with a white skin, as the Blackfeet did, nor were they devoted to war like the Sioux. Preacher had always gotten along well with the Crow, and he hoped the impression he'd gotten from that brief glimpse was correct.

The woman stopped singing. He heard her moving around, and then she was beside him. He felt the cool touch of a wet cloth on his skin as she wiped his face with it. He thought he might as well go ahead and take a chance.

He opened his eyes.

The woman drew back with a little gasp when she saw that he was awake. In her own tongue, she said, "He lives."

"I do live," Preacher replied in the same language, which he had recognized instantly as Crow. He was fluent in the lingo. "Thanks to you."

The woman shook her head. She was young, probably no more than twenty summers. She had a round, pretty face, with dark eyes. Her hair, as black as a raven's wing and slick with bear grease, was parted in the center and pulled into braids on each side of her head.

"You live because of Crazy Bear," she told Preacher. "He is the one who brought you here."

"You bound up my wounds?"

She nodded. "Yes, after packing them with moss and herbs that will heal them."

"Then I owe you a debt of gratitude as well. How are you called?"

The woman hesitated, then said, "Bright Leaf."

"Thank you, Bright Leaf. I am called Preacher."

She leaned back again. Her breath hissed between her teeth. "Ghost-Killer," she whispered.

He saw fright in her big, dark eyes and shook his head, wanting to reassure her. The movement made his surroundings spin madly around him for a few seconds. "That is one of the names the Blackfeet know me by," he said. "But I have never been an enemy to the Crow."

Early in his career as a mountain man, he had mastered the art of slipping undetected into a village, cutting the throats of some of the warriors, and getting out again without anyone knowing he had been there until the bodies were discovered the next morning. That demoralized his enemies and made them regard him with the respect they would give a supernatural creature. Many of the tribes thought he was special because the story had spread about how he had talked all day and all night to save himself from being burned at the stake. That incident had given him the name of Preacher.

Despite his words, Bright Leaf scooted away from him and stood up, backing around the fire ring in the center of the tepee. "I will go and tell Crazy Bear that you have returned to life," she said. "Stay there. Rest."

Preacher sighed. There wasn't much else he could do except follow her orders. He felt as weak as a newborn kitten. Even if he could make it to his feet, he doubted he could walk across the tepee, let alone go outside and wander off.

"I will stay," he told Bright Leaf.

She nodded, then bent over and pushed aside the flap of hide that covered the tepee's entrance. Preacher was able to look outside for a second. He saw darkness, edged with the flickering glare of a fire. Night had fallen. Since it had been the middle of the afternoon when he was shot, he reasoned he had been unconscious for several hours, at the very least.

A tide of weariness washed over him. He lay there struggling to keep his eyes open. He knew if he closed them, he would fall asleep. He wanted to stay awake until Crazy Bear got there, so he could talk to the man.

Only a couple minutes passed before the hide flap was swept aside, this time by a muscular arm as big around as the trunk of a small tree. The warrior who came into the tepee had to stoop low to make it through the entrance. When he straightened to his full height, he stood near the center of the tepee, so his head wouldn't poke against the sloping hide wall.

In the glow of the fire, Crazy Bear didn't seem quite as ugly as he had in broad daylight. It softened the harsh planes and angles of his face, made the scars less noticeable, and the broken, crooked lump of a nose didn't dominate his features quite as much.

Bright Leaf came into the tepee behind the man and peeked timidly around his massive form at Preacher.

The Crow warrior regarded Preacher impassively for a

moment and then said, "Bright Leaf tells me you are the one called Ghost-Killer."

"This is true," Preacher said, then continued, "But as I told her, the Crow are not my enemies." He thought for a second that he saw a smile play over the man's twisted lips.

"This is good. Our village will not have to fear you."

"Nope," Preacher agreed. "You got nothin' to fear from me. I'm plumb friendly."

The warrior hunkered on his heels beside the fire. "I am called Crazy Bear. I lead this band of my people."

So he was a chief, Preacher thought. That wasn't surprising, considering the elaborate decorations on his buckskins and the beads tied into his braids.

"Thank you for saving my life."

"I did not save your life," Crazy Bear said. "The Ghost-Killer cannot die."

"You saw how much blood I lost, Crazy Bear. If you hadn't helped me, I would have died. Believe me. But even before I could bleed to death, those men would have killed me. Thank you for stopping them." Preacher paused. "I suppose it *was* you who made that terrible noise?"

The massive Indian definitely smiled. "You call the laugh of Crazy Bear terrible?" He folded his arms across his broad chest and shrugged. "There were six of the white men, and I was alone. I thought it best to make them afraid, in hopes that they would flee."

"You were right about that. You got hold of at least one of them, didn't you?"

"Two had broken arms when they fled."

"You should've broken their necks," Preacher muttered.

"We will kill them another day, eh, Ghost-Killer?" Crazy Bear extended his hand, white man fashion, as if to seal the agreement.

Preacher didn't hesitate. He reached up, grasped the man's hand, and said, "You got a deal, Crazy Bear. We'll kill them another day."

Chapter 3

As it turned out, Bright Leaf was Crazy Bear's cousin. She was a widow, her husband of less than a year having been killed in a rockslide several months earlier. Preacher understood a little better why Crazy Bear had taken him back to the Crow village. If Bright Leaf's late husband had had a brother, he would have taken Bright Leaf as one of his wives. Since that wasn't the case, Crazy Bear felt like it was his job to find his cousin a new man.

If she nursed the wounded white man back to health, then out of gratitude to her, and to her cousin Crazy Bear, surely the man called Preacher would take her as his wife. Nature would run its inevitable course.

Preacher had something to say about that. He wasn't anywhere near ready to settle down.

Although, that verdant valley in the Big Horn Mountains would have been a nice spot to do so. Its green meadows and towering pines were watered by several creeks that ran clear, fast, and cold. Rugged gray peaks mantled with snow formed its borders, and over all of it arched the achingly blue and beautiful vault of the sky. Wildlife was abundant. A man would never lack for good hunting there.

When Preacher had gained some of his strength back, he sat outside most of the day and enjoyed his surroundings. The women and children avoided him, casting nervous glances at him from a distance. Despite the fact that he seemed harmless, he had a reputation as a bloody-handed murderer of men.

Some of the warriors stopped by to talk, and soon Preacher had a number of friends among the band. Elk Runner, Tall Tree, Paints His Face, and the others were all older men, bearing the scars of their years, much like Preacher himself. They told many stories, their powerful voices rolling out while their hands glided and swooped through the air, describing visually what had happened. With such friendships to occupy his time, the days drifted by pleasantly for Preacher.

Bright Leaf was a good cook, and the savory stew she prepared for him did much to help him regain his strength. She changed the dressings on his wounds twice a day, applying the poultice she made each time. The fever left the bullet holes and they healed, becoming puckered scars to go along with other such marks scattered around Preacher's body, including knife scars, and the claw marks from the time he'd fought with a grizzly.

Sometimes when she changed the dressings, Bright Leaf let her fingers stray over the map of pain and trouble etched into his pale-skinned torso and murmured, "How is it you are still alive? You should be dead a dozen times over, Preacher!"

"I'm just too ornery to die, I reckon," he told her with a grin.

Eventually, after he had been in the village about two weeks and the wounds in his side were almost completely healed, the moment arrived that he'd been expecting. Bright Leaf came into the tepee one evening wrapped in a buffalo robe instead of wearing her usual buckskin dress. She stood before him and let the robe slide off her shoulders so that it fell around her feet. Underneath it she was all smooth coppery skin and firm flesh. She lowered her eyes, shy but proud, as Preacher's gaze played over her body.

"I would not be a good husband to you, Bright Leaf," he

told her, his voice hoarse. "You will wake up one morning, and I will be gone. I will not be here to hunt meat for you."

"I know," she whispered. "Crazy Bear has told me I should keep looking for a husband. But I want you, Preacher. If only for tonight . . . I want you."

He reached up to her and drew her down next to him. As long as she knew what sort of man he was, he would not deny her.

"Ghost-Killer," she said later, as they were making love. "Ghost-Killer!" Then she clutched him tightly and breathed, "You have slain my ghosts."

Preacher hoped that he hadn't slain Crazy Bear's friendship with him at the same time.

Judging by the solemn, even angry expression on Crazy Bear's face when he walked up to the log where Preacher was sitting the next day, Preacher thought the chief must know what had happened between him and Bright Leaf the night before. That hunch grew stronger when Crazy Bear sat down beside him and said, "The time has come for us to talk."

Preacher nodded slowly. "All right, Crazy Bear. We will talk."

Crazy Bear surprised him by saying, "Those white men who tried to kill you . . . why did they seek to take your life?"

Preacher answered the unexpected question with a question of his own. "Why do you ask this?"

"Because soon you will be strong enough to go after them and settle the debt for what they did to you. I would like to know the sort of man whose life I saved, and the best way to know a man is to know his enemies."

Preacher thought that over and nodded. Crazy Bear was right, true enough. He said, "Do you know Boadley's place?"

"The white man's trading post on Antelope Creek?"

"That's right," Preacher said. The fortress-like trading post had been built at the height of the fur trade by an Englishman named Boadley, who erected his establishment at the southern end of the Big Horns about a week's ride from the valley. It was still there. Men who ventured into the mountains in search of pelts usually stopped at the trading post to replenish their supplies before continuing.

"I was at Boadley's," Preacher went on. "No one else was there except the old man, his wife, and another Indian woman who was a lot younger."

Crazy Bear made a face. "One who sells herself to the white men?"

Preacher shrugged. Everybody had to do something in life, and he'd never been one to sit in judgment of the decisions made by other folks, as long as they didn't cause him any trouble.

"Seven men rode in," he continued. "I didn't like the looks of them, but I wasn't hunting for trouble. I had stew, a bowl of beans, and a jug, so I stayed where I was at a table in the corner and let those fellas come stomping in like they owned the place."

"There are some men who feel they own every place they happen to be," Crazy Bear said.

"That's right. They were that kind. They yelled orders at Boadley, and they yelled some more when he didn't jump fast enough.

It made the old man mad. He's an Englishman, but he's still got some bark on him. He didn't say anything, though. There were seven of them, after all, and his wife was there."

Crazy Bear nodded. "And it was not your fight."

"Seven to two ain't much better odds than seven to one."

Crazy Bear snorted, as if to say when one of the two was Preacher, it changed things.

"Anyway, I hoped they'd bluster around for a while, get the supplies they were after, and leave. But then they saw the young woman, and I hate to say it, but they didn't figure on riding out until each of them had a turn with her."

"That is why she was there," Crazy Bear said, his voice hard as flint.

"True," Preacher agreed, "and if they'd all been gents about it, I reckon that would've been the end of it. But I heard the others talking, and from what I heard, I knew that one of them, a man they called Axel, liked to treat his women rough. They told him he had to wait until last, because by the time he got through with the woman, no other man would want to lay with her."

Crazy Bear made a noise deep in his throat, a growl that reminded Preacher of an actual bear.

"Yeah, I didn't like it, either," Preacher said. "But I kept telling myself it was none of my business. I sat there for a long time trying to convince myself to stay out of it. Must have been, oh, three or four whole minutes." Preacher looked off into the distance. "Then I got up and told Boadley I was gonna go tend to my horses."

"But you did not tend to your horses," Crazy Bear said.

Preacher shook his head. "Nope. I went around to the back of the place, to the little cabin next to the barn where the woman took the men. It was dark by then, and they had all been out there except Axel. He was waiting in the trading post for the last one to come back, so he could take his turn. I stayed in the shadows until the fella went inside, and Axel came out."

"You struck him down from ambush?"

"No, I wouldn't do that, even to a skunk like this Axel was supposed to be. Anyway, there was a chance that the things the other men said were just empty talk."

Crazy Bear nodded. Some men were as full of hot air as a sweat lodge.

"It didn't work out that way," Preacher said. "I waited to see what he'd do. He hadn't been in that cabin more than a couple minutes when I heard his fist striking that girl. She cried out and begged him not to hurt her, and he just laughed at her."

"So you stopped him."

The memory was still vivid in Preacher's head. Kicking the door open, lunging into the room lit by a single candle, seeing

Axel's hulking shape looming over the young Indian woman whose face was already bloody, her nose flattened by one of the first blows to fall. Axel's ham-like fist was lifted over his head, poised to descend again. Before it could, Preacher's fingers wrapped around Axel's wrist, stopping it cold. Preacher's rangy body possessed incredible strength, and he threw Axel against the log wall so hard that the man's eyes rolled in their sockets.

Axel then made the mistake of getting up. Preacher let the man make it to his feet, then chopped blow after savage blow to his face, breaking his nose just like Axel had done to the young woman. Axel's face was raw and bloody when he finally collapsed onto his knees and pitched forward onto the floor.

That should have been the end of it. Preacher had thought Axel was out cold when he picked the woman up out of the crude bunk, and wrapped the blanket around her. She was Shoshoni, he saw, and he spoke her language. He told her to go out and hide until the men were gone. She scurried away into the darkness.

Content to leave Axel there to sleep off the beating Preacher left the cabin. His horse was saddled, he had already loaded the supplies he'd bought onto his pack animal, and it would have been the easiest thing in the world for him to slip away into the night.

But Axel wasn't unconscious. The strength in his brawny body allowed him to shake off the thrashing Preacher had given him and struggle to his feet while Preacher was still halfway between the shed and the trading post. Axel had pulled the knife from the sheath on his belt and charged after Preacher, bellowing like a maddened bull as his long legs covered the distance in just a few fast strides.

Preacher had time to whirl around. Starlight glinted off the blade of the knife in Axel's hand. Instinct sent his own hand flashing up as the blade swept down. Preacher grabbed, twisted, shoved . . . and Axel screamed as he suddenly found himself with twelve inches of cold steel buried in his belly.

Preacher's fingers were still wrapped around the wrist of the hand that clutched the knife. The muscles in his arm and shoulder bunched under the buckskin shirt as he ripped the knife across Axel's midsection. The keen blade sliced deep, opening up a huge, gaping wound. Axel kept screaming as coils of guts spilled out over his fingers.

Those dying shrieks brought Axel's companions bursting out the back door of the trading post. Light from inside the building spilled over the gruesome scene.

Preacher was already moving. He could have shot it out with them then and there, and on reflection, maybe he should have. But he hadn't set out to kill anybody on that particular night. He wanted to be left alone. Moving swiftly like a shadow, he reached his horse, jerked the reins loose from the hitch rail, and swung up into the saddle.

All sorts of yelling was going on behind him as he hit the trail. He heard men shouting Axel's name, and then muzzle flame bloomed redly in the darkness behind him. They didn't have a hope in hell of hitting him. He was gone.

The mountains rose in front of him, part of the frontier that had been his home for decades.

"You did not think they would be able to follow you," Crazy Bear said as he and Preacher sat on the log.

"I didn't think they'd bother. They didn't seem all that fond of Axel. But I reckon I misjudged them. They came after me."

Crazy Bear looked at him for a long moment. "It must have been hard for a man like you to leave instead of fight."

"When a man gets to be my age, there are times when he's tired of killing."

"I have not seen as many summers as you, my friend, but enough so that I know what you say is true," Crazy Bear said with a nod. "But now that they have come after you, you will go after them."

Preacher nodded. "They had their chance to let it go. Now it's my turn."

Chapter 4

Preacher didn't go after the men immediately. He wasn't quite in good enough shape to do that. Instead, he remained in the Crow village another week, resting and recuperating. Bright Leaf shared his blankets every night. If Crazy Bear knew about that, the chief didn't say anything, and Preacher was grateful. He didn't want to be enemies with a man who had saved his life.

In talking with Crazy Bear, he discovered the chief had been out hunting by himself that day, as he was in the habit of doing. Crazy Bear had a certain loneliness about him. He had risen to his position of leadership because of his great physical strength and his cunning as a warrior, but his size and freakish appearance made him something of an outcast even in the tribe he led. All the other warriors had great respect for him, but that didn't necessarily make them his friends. And the women of the village, who might normally wish to marry a chieftain and bear his children, were a little afraid of Crazy Bear.

So Preacher felt some sympathy for him and spent a lot of his time talking to the chief. Preacher had had many adventures during his life on the frontier, and Crazy Bear seemed to enjoy hearing about them.

They were sitting on rocks outside the tepee Preacher

shared with Bright Leaf when shouts from the other end of the village drew their attention. Crazy Bear rose to his great height and said, "There is trouble." He strode off, his long legs carrying him quickly toward the source of the commotion.

Preacher went after him and caught up by the time they reached a group of warriors and women clamoring around someone. The crowd parted when Crazy Bear demanded in a loud voice to know what had happened. Preacher frowned when he saw a young warrior in blood-stained buckskins lying on the ground. An older woman, probably the boy's mother, was on her knees beside him swaying and wailing.

Crazy Bear knelt on the young man's other side and slid a big hand under his shoulders. The wounded warrior was still breathing. He opened his eyes as Crazy Bear gently lifted him and propped him up in a sitting position.

"What happened to you, Anteater?" Crazy Bear rumbled. "Where is your brother?"

The young warrior struggled to speak. He managed to gasp out, "Storm Cloud . . . is dead. White men . . . shot him . . . the same white men . . . who shot me."

Crazy Bear lifted Anteater's shirt to check the wound. Preacher saw a red-rimmed bullet hole on the right side of the youngster's chest, where the ball must have penetrated Anteater's lung. He couldn't have long to live. Sheer stubbornness and the desire to bring the news of what had happened to the village had kept him hanging on.

Crazy Bear leaned closer. "Where were these white men?"

"Near . . . Owl Rock . . . Storm Cloud and I were . . . hunting there . . . We did not see them . . . until they opened fire on us . . ."

"How many?"

Anteater gave a tiny shake of his head. "Not sure . . . As many as . . . the fingers of both hands . . . maybe more."

Crazy Bear glanced up at Preacher. "The men from Boadley's place?" he asked.

"Could be," Preacher said. "There were only six left when I rode away from there, but they could've joined up with some other fellas."

Crazy Bear turned his attention back to the wounded Anteater and said, "Did you fight them?"

"No," the young warrior said. "We never . . . had a chance . . . to fight back. They just . . . shot us and then . . . laughed about it. I heard them . . . while I lay in the grass . . . unable to move . . . They thought I was dead . . . They said . . . killing redskins was . . . great sport."

Preacher's jaw tightened in anger. Fury burned inside him. He told Crazy Bear, "That sounds like the same bunch, all right. No-good polecats, every damn one of 'em."

Anteater went on, "I did not understand . . . all their words . . . but I heard them say . . . they would wait there . . . for the wagons. Then when they were no longer . . . looking at me . . . I crawled away and hid . . . and rested until . . . I could come back here."

"You are certain that Storm Cloud was dead?"

Anteater lifted a shaking hand and touched a finger to the center of his forehead. "One of their bullets . . . hit him here."

Crazy Bear nodded grimly. No one could survive a wound like that.

"I had to come back . . . to tell our mother . . . what happened," Anteater gasped out. That brought another wail from the woman. The young warrior tried to reach out toward her, but his hand stopped suddenly and his arm fell at his side, limp in death. His last breath came out of him in a long sigh.

Crazy Bear lowered him to the ground again and stood up, stepping back to let the women of the tribe take over. They would tend to the body and to the grieving mother.

The warriors gathered around Crazy Bear, their faces taut with anger. Tall Tree said, "We must do something about this."

"We must find the white men who did this and kill them," Elk Runner added.

"I will find them," Crazy Bear declared. "Ghost-Killer and I will find them." He looked at Preacher, who jerked his head in a curt nod. "But we will go alone."

That brought protests from the other warriors, who wanted to help avenge the wanton murder of the two young men, but Crazy Bear wouldn't be swayed from his decision. The village was not a large one, with only two dozen warriors, and despite the fact that they would outnumber the white men, at least according to what Anteater had seen, a pitched battle against a better-armed force might not leave enough men to defend the village if the Blackfeet or some of their other enemies were to attack. It was good strategy on Crazy Bear's part, Preacher thought, and would help to insure the continued safety of the rest of his people.

Of course, the two of them going up against five-to-one odds—or worse—was a mite reckless. Preacher already knew that Crazy Bear didn't intend to take on the killers directly. The chief was too smart for that.

The warriors weren't happy about it. Grumbling, the crowd broke up, and Crazy Bear and Preacher walked back toward Preacher's tepee.

"It will not be easy, two against ten or more," Crazy Bear said.

"Yeah, but we'll be able to take 'em by surprise," Preacher said. "They don't know that we know they're at Owl Rock."

He had seen that landmark several times in the past. It was several miles east of the village, on the eastern edge of the Big Horns, a tall column of rock with some rounded bulges on the top that made it look a little like an owl.

"What are these wagons they spoke of?"

Preacher shook his head. "I don't know. There's been some talk back in the settlements about trying to establish a trail up the east side of the Big Horns, an offshoot of the Oregon Trail that would lead to the Montana country. Damn fool idea if you ask me. Too many Sioux and Cheyenne up there to ever settle that territory for good. But somebody could be tryin' to take a wagon train in that direction." Preacher rubbed a hand over his grizzled jaw as he thought. "If a bunch of outlaws was to hide at Owl Rock, they could ambush any wagons that came along. If that's what they've got planned, I'd sure like to put a stop to it."

Crazy Bear grunted and said, "I care nothing about any white settlers. Their wagons wear great ruts in the earth. Their numbers crowd the land. They should all go back and leave this country to the real people."

Preacher understood why Crazy Bear felt that way, and to tell the truth, he wasn't sure but what he agreed with the Crow chief, at least for the most part.

Preacher had seen the crowded cities back east and knew that more and more people wanted to leave their squalor and journey west, where there was plenty of land free for the taking—for anyone who could grasp the opportunity and hold it. That westward tide wasn't going to stop any time soon, and in the end, trying to oppose it was just as futile as attempting to stop a real tide. Preacher was pretty sure it couldn't be done.

So he didn't argue with Crazy Bear. He just said, "Right or wrong, the people with the wagons don't deserve to be robbed and murdered. But when you and I kill those white men, chief, it will be to avenge the deaths of Anteater and Storm Cloud, not to protect any settlers."

"You are well enough to travel, and to fight?"

Preacher nodded. "Just let me get my gear together."

Crazy Bear had brought Preacher's saddle mount and pack animal back to the village with him, the day he had saved the mountain man from the ambush. In the three weeks since, the horses had been grazing nearby, growing fat and lazy. They would have to start earning their keep again.

Preacher's guns and supplies were in the tepee. When he walked up, Bright Leaf was standing there, a worried look on her face. She said, "Some of the women told me what happened to Anteater and Storm Cloud. They say you are leaving, Preacher."

She had stopped calling him Ghost-Killer, which was fine with him. He nodded and said, "Yes, Crazy Bear and I are going after the men who killed those young fellas."

"These are the same men who hurt you?"

"I don't know," he answered honestly. "They could well be. Or they might belong to a different bunch. I won't know until I lay eyes on 'em."

"Either way, they are bad men. Cruel. Violent. Ruthless."

"I don't reckon there's much doubt about that."

"You are not well enough—" Bright Leaf began.

Preacher stopped her by putting his hands on her shoulders. "Thanks to you, I am well. Or close enough to it that it doesn't matter."

Bitterness edged into her voice as she said, "Then I wish I had not taken such good care of you. I wish you were still too weak to throw your life away like this."

"I don't intend on throwin' anything away, especially my life," Preacher told her with a smile.

"But you do not know what will happen."

"Nobody does. That's one of the things that keeps life interestin'."

"Life is safer when it is not interesting."

Preacher couldn't dispute that. Safer, maybe . . . but a whole hell of a lot more boring.

"I have to get my things," he said.

She stepped aside. "I will not stop you." As he started past her, she added, "When you have killed the men you seek . . . will you come back to our village?"

Preacher hadn't thought about that. He was well enough that once the grim errand he and Crazy Bear were about to set out on was done, he could go on with his plans. One more season of trapping was as far ahead as he ever thought. He could spend that season there. Beaver were still plentiful in the area.

But . . . if he spent the season in the valley, then wintered there as well, it might be too easy to stay on for good. He might grow too accustomed to having his belly filled with Bright Leaf's cooking. He might get too used to waking up with her body snuggled warmly against his. If that happened, he would grow soft and fat.

Was it truly better for a man to be cold and hungry and lonely? All he knew was he had spent much of his life in just such circumstances, and he was still alive. The edges of his entire being were still honed to a keen sharpness. If he ever lost that, there was no telling what might happen to him.

Bright Leaf was still looking at him, waiting for his answer. Preacher met her gaze and said, "I might come back . . . someday."

"But not now."

"No," he said. "Not now."

She nodded, then glanced away, obviously unable or unwilling to look at him any longer. He knew he had hurt her and wished he had been able to avoid that. But the only way would have been to turn her away when she first came to him, and that would have hurt her, too. At least they had had a few days and nights of happiness.

Preacher went into the tepee. When he came out wearing his old buckskins that Bright Leaf had cleaned and mended for him and his broad-brimmed beaver felt hat, he carried his rifle and had his pistols tucked behind his belt. His hunting knife was in its sheath, and his saddlebags were slung over his shoulder.

Bright Leaf was nowhere to be seen. Preacher didn't look for her. He went to find Crazy Bear so they could get their horses and set out on their mission of vengeance.

Chapter 5

"Are ten or twelve men enough to stop and rob an entire wagon train?" Crazy Bear asked as he and Preacher rode through the Big Horn Mountains toward Owl Rock, following trails that were well known to both the Crow chief and the white mountain man.

"Depends on the size of the wagon train," Preacher replied. "I've seen some with a hundred or more wagons, and no, I don't reckon a gang that size would attack such a big train. But maybe this is a smaller group of wagons. If those renegades know the wagons'll be passin' by Owl Rock, they must know how many are in the train. They could shoot the driver on each wagon and bring the whole train to a stop. Then it would just be a matter of pickin' off the outriders and killin' one of the lead oxen in every team. That'd bog the wagons down so they couldn't move for sure." Preacher shrugged. "The pilgrims who were left could either surrender or try to fight it out. Either way, they wouldn't have much chance, stuck out in the open like that."

"Perhaps if they surrendered, those men would take their goods and let them go," Crazy Bear suggested.

Preacher shook his head. "You really believe that, after the way they murdered Anteater and Storm Cloud just for the sport of it?"

"No," Crazy Bear said. "I do not. These are men who enjoy killing. They would slaughter everyone on the wagon train before they were finished."

"I'm afraid you're right," Preacher said. "Of course, we don't know yet that there is a wagon train, or when it's gonna get here. All we got to go by is what a mortally wounded boy overheard."

"Anteater was a clever young man. I trust his words."

"That's good enough for me, then," Preacher declared.

He was listening for shots in the distance but so far hadn't heard any. That was a good sign, he told himself. The wagon train may not pass by Owl Rock for days yet. He and Crazy Bear might be in plenty of time to keep the settlers from being attacked.

When Preacher saw a column of black smoke rising into the sky several miles to the east, his hopes were dashed. "Son of a bitch," he muttered. "Look yonder."

"I see it," Crazy Bear said. "The wagons Anteater spoke of?"

"More than likely." Preacher heeled his horse into a faster pace and tightened his grip on the pack animal's reins. "Come on."

The two men rode hard toward the smoke. Leading Preacher's pack horse slowed them down a little, but not much. When they reached the foothills of the mountain range and left the more rugged terrain behind them, they were able to go faster. Owl Rock rose in front of them. The towering formation loomed over the prairie that bordered the hills.

They topped a ridge and pounded down the far slope. The burning remains of a dozen covered wagons came into view. The flames were beginning to die down as the canvas coverings and the boards were consumed, leaving only the iron wheels and framework of the wagons, but a considerable amount of black smoke still billowed skyward.

A few dead oxen lay in their traces, but most of the animals were gone. The raiders must have gathered them up and driven them away. They could use some of the oxen for meat and trade the others to the Indians for pelts.

The ground around the wagons was littered with bodies. Preacher's face hardened into a grim mask as he saw them sprawled in attitudes of death.

"We are too late," Crazy Bear said.

"Yeah. They must've attacked the wagons not long after they shot Anteater and Storm Cloud. We never had a chance to stop them. The wagons probably came along before we'd even left the village."

Preacher saw one small ray of hope. "The bastards haven't been gone long. They took their time about lootin' the wagons and then settin' 'em on fire."

They rode up to the first wagon and reined in. Preacher recognized right away that it wasn't actually the lead wagon. Marks on the ground told him that several others had been driven away from there.

Preacher pointed out the tracks to Crazy Bear and said, "They moved everything they wanted from the other wagons into the first two or three and burned the others. Then they rode off and took their loot with them."

He swung down from the saddle and moved to the nearest of the corpses. Rolling the man onto his back, Preacher saw that he'd been shot several times. Lifeless eyes stared up at the late afternoon sky.

"We'd better check 'em all and make sure they're dead," he told Crazy Bear.

"Should we not pursue the men who did this?"

"We will," Preacher said. "But with those wagons full of loot, they won't be able to move very fast." He glanced at the western sky, where the sun was sinking lower toward the Big Horns. "There are only a couple hours of daylight left. They'll have to make camp, and that's when we'll catch up to them."

A faint but savage smile curved Crazy Bear's lips. "Then Ghost-Killer will strike," he said.

Preacher didn't say anything to that. He had moved on to the next body, searching futilely for a sign of life. He and Crazy Bear continued checking the sprawled corpses, Preacher noting with anger that there were a number of older women and children among the bodies.

No younger women, though, or girl-children older than ten or twelve. Preacher took note of that as well, and his face grew even bleaker as he realized what it meant.

The renegades had taken prisoners with them.

He pointed that out to Crazy Bear, who nodded in agreement. "They will sell the women and girls as slaves to the northern tribes," he said. "Sometimes Blackfeet and Sioux will deal with white men if it means bringing misery to other whites."

"Yeah, I know. Them havin' prisoners is gonna make our job harder. Those skunks won't hesitate to use the women and girls as hostages."

"Perhaps we should have brought more of my warriors with us."

Preacher shook his head. "Nope. This is still a two-man job . . . as long as it's the right two men."

Suddenly he heard a groan that came from somewhere nearby. As he spun around, he saw one of the blood-soaked figures on the ground move an arm. Instantly, Preacher sprang to the man's side, knelt, and carefully turned him over.

The wounded man was a stocky old-timer with a bald head except for a fringe of gray hair around his ears. His homespun shirt was blotched with crimson, testifying to the fact that he'd been shot several times. His eyelids fluttered and then opened to reveal watery blue eyes filled with agony.

"Who . . . who . . . ?" he gasped.

"Take it easy, old-timer," Preacher said as he propped the man's head on his leg, much like Crazy Bear had with Anteater earlier that day. "We're friends."

The old man's pain-wracked gaze moved past Preacher to

Crazy Bear, who stood there looking down at him. "That . . . that's an Injun!"

"He won't hurt you," Preacher told him. "He's a friend of mine. I'm Preacher, and he's Crazy Bear. What's your name?"

"I'm . . . John Spaulding. I'm glad . . . you're a preacher, mister. I'll need somebody . . . to pray over . . . my grave."

Preacher didn't bother to correct the man's mistake. He said, "Don't worry about that, Mr. Spaulding. You're gonna be fine. Can you tell us what happened here?"

"Those damn . . . Mayhews."

"You know who did this to you?" Preacher asked, frowning in surprise.

"Yeah . . . Clint Mayhew and his brothers . . . and probably some other . . . no-good scoundrels."

Preacher thought that describing men who would carry out such a massacre and kidnap a bunch of women and girls as "no-good scoundrels" was being too kind to them.

"How did you know them?"

"They were supposed to . . . come with us to Montana . . . but they kept . . . causin' trouble . . . Lee DuBusk, our wagonmaster . . . made them and their friends leave the train . . . 'fore we ever veered off from the Oregon Trail." Spaulding's tongue came out and moved over his lips. "Have you got . . . any water? I'm mighty . . . dry."

As shot up as the old man was, water wasn't going to help him and might just make things worse, Preacher knew. But it was hard to deny such a request. He glanced up at Crazy Bear and said, "Can you get the canteen off my horse?"

The Crow chief nodded and went to get the water.

"Are you . . . sure you can trust that redskin?" Spaulding asked.

"He saved my life a few weeks ago," Preacher said. "So now I'd trust him with it." He thought of something else. "These Mayhew brothers you mentioned . . . is one of 'em named Riley or Axel?"

"Yeah, both. There were . . . five of 'em . . . Clint, Riley, Jord,

Walt . . . and Axel. Now that I . . . think about it, though . . . didn't see Axel in the bunch that . . . jumped us today."

That was plenty of proof for Preacher. He could see how it all laid out. The five Mayhew brothers and a couple companions had been kicked out of the party of immigrants heading for Montana. After that they'd decided to ride ahead of the wagons and ambush them, or maybe they had come up with that plan after running into some other outlaws up in the Big Horns. Either way, they had gotten sidetracked a little by their visit to Boadley's trading post, where Preacher had killed Axel Mayhew. After bushwhacking Preacher they had carried on with their plan to waylay the wagon train.

"Do you know how many there were?" Preacher asked as he heard Crazy Bear move up next to him with the canteen.

"Not sure," Spaulding said. "All hell broke loose . . . there was so much shootin' . . . Had to be . . . at least a dozen of the bastards. Maybe more."

"When they left, they took prisoners with them, didn't they?"

"Y-yeah. They took everybody's money and valuables . . . and piled 'em in a wagon. Then they . . . got the women and girls . . . and made 'em get in a couple other wagons. I heard 'em yellin' orders . . . heard the woman screamin' and cryin' . . . but I couldn't see much. I was already . . . shot to pieces." Spaulding licked his lips again. "Can I get some o' that . . . water now?"

"Just a minute," Preacher told him. "The Mayhews and their bunch headed north?"

"Yeah, I . . . I think so."

Preacher knew the dying man couldn't tell him anything else that was important. He took the canteen from Crazy Bear, pulled the cork with his teeth, and held the neck of it to Spaulding's mouth.

"Here's the water. Drink as much as you want."

Spaulding gulped greedily at the cool liquid. When he had swallowed quite a bit of water, he licked his lips again and sighed. "That's better," he said, his voice slightly stronger. "Are you gonna go after them?"

"We are," Preacher said. "We'll do everything we can to rescue those women and settle the score with Mayhew and his bunch."

"How many of you . . . are there?"

Preacher smiled. "Just the two of us."

"Just . . . two? You can't—"

The old man's voice broke off abruptly as his face twisted in pain and a spasm shook him. His hands moved to his bloody midsection. He gasped, said, "Oh . . . Lord!" and then died. Preacher saw the light go out of his eyes and the lines of agony on his face ease.

"There was nothing you could do for him," Crazy Bear said. "He was dead before we got here, only his body did not know it yet."

"Yeah, I know," Preacher said as he eased Spaulding's head to the ground. "Maybe I should've lied and told him there's more than two of us. He might've gone out with a little more hope that we'd be able to help those women."

"The two of us will have to be enough."

Preacher gazed off to the north, his eyes following the tracks of the wagons.

"Those captives'll have to hope so, anyway," he said.

Chapter 6

There were twenty-eight bodies scattered around the burned-out hulks of the wagons. Preacher and Crazy Bear couldn't take the time to dig graves for all of them, or even a mass grave big enough to hold all the luckless pilgrims. But Preacher had noticed a ravine in the foothills with a lot of loose rock on its sides. It would have to do, since the only other option was to leave the bodies for the scavengers and he wasn't going to do that.

He unloaded the supplies from his pack animal, then draped a body over the back of each horse and led them to the ravine. While Preacher was doing that, Crazy Bear found the corpse of the young warrior Storm Cloud and covered it with rocks to protect it until men from the village could retrieve it and take it back to be placed in a tree in the proper Crow custom.

It took ten trips to transport all the corpses from the wagon train. Once they had been rolled down to the bottom of the ravine, Preacher picked out a likely looking rock. He and Crazy Bear put their shoulders to it and shoved. It took some grunting and straining, but the boulder finally moved and began to roll down the slope. It picked up speed and knocked other rocks loose, and soon there was a miniature avalanche of rocks and dirt sliding down the side of the ravine. The debris came to rest with a rumble and a roar, and when the dust cleared, Preacher saw that all the bodies were covered.

"One hell of a way to lay folks to rest," he muttered as he gazed down at the immigrants' final resting place.

"It is not the Crow way," Crazy Bear said, "but I think they would have chosen it over being left where they fell."

"Yeah, I expect you're right." Preacher looked up at the mountains looming to the west. The sun was touching the tops of the peaks. "We'd better get on the trail. We've got a little light left. Those wagons will be moving slow enough that we can shave off a lot of the lead they have on us."

The two men followed the tracks left by the wagon wheels until it was too dark to see anymore. They stopped to let their horses rest and to talk over the situation.

"If those ol' boys are dumb enough to build a fire, we can probably find them tonight," Preacher said. "If they're not, we may have to catch up tomorrow and follow them just out of sight until nightfall again. I'd just as soon not have to do that. The longer those women and girls are in their hands . . ."

His voice trailed off. He didn't have to go into detail about what he meant. Crazy Bear understood as well as he did the risks that the prisoners faced. It was possible that some of the captives had already been assaulted. But the longer the outlaws had them, the worse it would be.

"If we go ahead in the dark, we risk losing their trail," Crazy Bear pointed out.

"If we do, it ought to be easy enough to pick up again in the morning. They've been runnin' parallel with the mountains all the way from Owl Rock."

The wagons were staying on the prairie, about half a mile from the edge of the foothills, and heading in a generally northward direction, curving gradually to the west to follow the Big Horn range. There weren't many places for them to go. The mountains were too rugged for the outlaws to take the wagons across them.

A couple more days of travel in the same direction would put them in the Montana country, where they could rendezvous with the Blackfeet or the Sioux. The Mayhews and their companions were running a considerable risk. It was possible the Indians they encountered would kill them, scalp them, and take the prisoners and the goods from the wagon train.

Unless the men the Mayhews had joined up with had some sort of previous arrangement with the hostiles, Preacher mused. For years there had been certain white men who traded guns and whiskey with the Indians. He figured trash like that wouldn't mind expanding their enterprise to slaves and stolen goods.

He and Crazy Bear discussed the possibility for a few minutes, and the Crow chief agreed it might be true. He said, "I think we should go on and try to find their camp tonight."

"That's what I think, too," Preacher said. "We'll take it slow and easy, so they won't hear us comin'."

After resting the horses for a short time longer, the two men mounted up and rode northward again. The stars had come out, and the millions upon millions of pinpricks in the night sky cast enough illumination for them to see where they were going. The Big Horns loomed blackly on their left.

Preacher and Crazy Bear weren't in any hurry. The worst thing they could do was ride right into the middle of the enemy camp without knowing it was there. That wouldn't accomplish anything except get them dead in a hurry.

Their eyes constantly searched the darkness for the light of a campfire. There was nothing like that to be seen, so their other senses came into play. It was Preacher's nose that warned him they were getting close to their quarry. He caught a faint whiff of wood smoke in the air, along with the smell of tobacco. He reined to a halt and put out a hand to signal Crazy Bear to do likewise.

The Crow chief was already bringing his pony to a stop. "I smell it, too," he whispered. "But I see nothing."

"They probably stopped just before dark and built a fire to cook their supper, then put it out," Preacher replied, his own voice quiet enough that it couldn't be heard more than a few feet away. "They've got their pipes goin', too, but those don't give off enough light for us to see them."

"We should go forward on foot now."

"Just what I was thinkin'."

Since it was likely the outlaws had made their camp at the edge of the foothills where there was more wood for a fire, Preacher and Crazy Bear dismounted and led their horses toward the hills. When they reached a small grove of slender trees, they tied the animals there and worked their way along the line of hills that curved to the northwest.

Preacher and Crazy Bear moved in almost complete silence. Like shadows flitting through the darkness, they followed their noses toward the enemy camp. The smell of wood smoke faded, but the aroma of tobacco drew them on. As it grew stronger, they dropped to the ground and proceeded on their hands and knees.

The sudden sound of voices nearby made them sink to their bellies in the grass and lie motionless. A man said, "Jord, leave that gal alone. I think she's had enough."

"Damn it, Clint," another man responded. "You and Walt had your turns with her. Now I oughta get a chance."

"Take one of the others," Clint Mayhew responded. Preacher recognized his voice as the one that had given the orders the day they had ambushed him three weeks earlier.

"All right," Jord Mayhew said. "I'll see if I can find one nobody's got at yet."

His brother Clint grunted. "You do that."

Anger burned brightly in Preacher as he listened to the conversation. The idea that those skunks talked so casually about assaulting women made him wish he could just stand up and empty his Dragoon Colts into the varmints. But there were too many outlaws for him to do that. He couldn't hope to kill them all before they killed him and Crazy Bear. If that happened those prisoners would be as bad off as they were.

He took his hat off and lifted his head so that he could look over the grass. His keen eyes spotted three wagons parked at the edge of some trees that grew down the slope of a foothill to the plains. A dark mass off to one side was the oxen and saddle horses belonging to the outlaws. He looked for guards posted around the camp. Those men would have to be taken care of first, and quietly.

Preacher watched as a man grasped the arm of a woman who'd been lying on the ground and jerked her to her feet. He marched her over to one of the wagons and told her, "Climb inside for now." From the way she was weeping, Preacher knew she was in pain or terrified. Probably both.

Another man followed, a swagger in his step. He leaned into another wagon and said, "You there. Get out here." When the prisoner didn't respond quickly enough to suit him, he reached into the wagon. A scream came from the woman as Jord Mayhew pulled her out of the wagon by her long, dark hair.

The scream cut off abruptly as he threw her on the ground. When she fell silent Preacher thought for a second she had been knocked out by the fall. But she bounded to her feet and a torrent of angry words spewed from her mouth in a language he didn't recognize. It wasn't any Indian tongue he had ever heard, although there were certain similarities.

Whether he understood the words or not, he could tell from the tone of the woman's voice that she was giving Jord a good cussin' out. When a few English obscenities slipped into the flow, he was sure of it. Jord laughed and reached for her, but she slipped away, darting out of his reach with a graceful agility.

"Damn you, gal, come back here," Jord said and lunged after her. Laughter came from some of the other men gathered around the camp as she eluded his rush with apparent ease and he stumbled as he grabbed for her and missed.

Being laughed at made Jord angrier. "You're gonna be sorry you gave me trouble," he warned the woman. "You're just makin' it worse for yourself."

She spat more curses at him in that unknown tongue.

Jord charged her again, and Preacher had a feeling she would have continued to avoid him if one of the men sitting nearby hadn't stuck a leg out without warning and tripped her. With a cry of dismay, the woman went down hard, tumbling to the ground and rolling over. Jord pounced on her.

A second later, he let out a yell and leaped back up. "Look out! The bitch has got my knife!"

Preacher heard a soft grunt from beside him, then another, and realized that Crazy Bear was laughing. "The white woman has much spirit," the Crow chief whispered. "She will make them pay for whatever they do to her."

Preacher heard admiration in Crazy Bear's voice and understood why he felt that way. Preacher couldn't help but admire the woman himself. As the outlaws jumped to their feet and began to shout in alarm over the fact that one of their prisoners was armed, several of them grabbed at her but had to jump back to keep from being slashed by the blade she held. She whirled and leaped and danced, keeping her captors at bay with the flashing knife.

Clint Mayhew strode up and leveled his arm so that the pistol in his hand pointed straight at the woman. "Drop it," he ordered, "or I'll kill you."

"Don't shoot her, Clint," one of the other men objected. "She's the prettiest one of the bunch!"

"Yeah? Well, what good's that gonna do you if she's liable to geld you if you get anywhere near her? All these bitches better learn right now, they don't have any say in what happens to 'em!"

The woman with the knife didn't drop the weapon. Instead, she backed away and directed her curses at Clint.

"Blast it, I mean it," he told her. "I'm gonna kill you."

A hundred yards away, Crazy Bear whispered to Preacher, "We cannot allow him to harm her."

"I can drop him from here with a rifle shot," Preacher said, "but that's gonna make it a lot harder to get her and the rest of the prisoners free."

It was a difficult decision, balancing the life of one woman against the lives of all the other captives. Preacher and Crazy Bear guessed there were probably a couple dozen women and girls being held in those wagons.

At that moment, the sound of hoofbeats made itself heard in the night air, and they didn't have to make the decision. The pounding rumble meant many horses, and the large group seemed to be coming straight toward the camp. Some of the outlaws turned toward the sound and lifted their rifles.

The newcomers distracted the woman with the knife, too. One of the men was able to get behind her. He tackled her, wrapping his arms around her waist as he drove her off her feet. "I got her, Jord!" the man shouted.

Jord Mayhew leaped forward and brought a booted foot down on the knife, pinning the blade to the ground. He leaned down and took hold of the woman, then dragged her to her feet. She fought against him, but he slammed the back of his hand across her face, stunning her. She slumped in his grip. Still holding her, he turned with the others to watch as the large group of riders came loping up to the camp.

One of the outlaws stepped forward and raised his voice. "Welcome, Red Moccasins!" he called.

Preacher heard Crazy Bear's breath hiss between his teeth. "Red Moccasins," the Crow chief repeated. "He is a Sioux war chief. We are too late to save the prisoners from being handed over to them!"

Chapter 7

Even at that distance, Preacher could tell an atmosphere of tension filled the camp as the dust from the arrival of the Sioux warriors settled. The darkness made it impossible to get an accurate count, but he estimated that the newcomers numbered about thirty. The white men were betting their lives the Indians would abide by whatever bargain had been struck with them.

"Greetings, Lupton," one of the warriors said in English. "What do you have for us this time?"

"Great bounty, Chief. Fifty oxen, and nearly half that many female slaves."

Red Moccasins made a curt gesture with the lance he carried. "Oxen!" he said with disgust in his voice. "What need do the Sioux have of oxen when there are more buffalo on the plains than there are stars in the sky?"

"You don't have to hunt these critters, chief, and risk having some of your warriors caught in a stampede. You can slaughter one for meat any time you need to."

Red Moccasins shook his head. "A true warrior fills his belly and the bellies of his family with his own skills! Only a woman would do as you say!"

The tension in the air grew worse. Preacher wasn't surprised by Red Moccasins' reaction to Lupton's proposition.

The Sioux war chief regarded it as an insult. One more such spark might set off an explosion of violence that would leave the outlaws dead and their captives in the hands of the Sioux. That might not be such a bad thing—it would cut down the odds against Preacher and Crazy Bear—except for the fact that some of the women and girls might be killed in the fighting.

"I apologize, Red Moccasins," Lupton said. "I know better than to make an offer like that to a man such as yourself. We will keep the oxen, but the slaves are yours. We ask only safe passage through your lands, and a dozen buffalo hides."

"And all the loot they already stole from the wagon train," Preacher added in a whisper to Crazy Bear. The Crow chief spoke little English, so Preacher had been keeping up a running translation for him.

Crazy Bear nodded and said in his own tongue, "The Blackfeet would have taken the oxen as well as the prisoners. Those white men were ready for whichever tribe they encountered."

Preacher agreed. The man called Lupton must have traded with the Indians before. He probably made a regular business of smuggling guns and whiskey to the various tribes, as well as preying on immigrant trains whenever he got the chance. He had slipped for a moment there with his Sioux customers, a mistake that had come close to getting him and the others killed, but that moment of danger seemed to have passed.

"You have a jug?" Red Moccasins asked.

"Of course," Lupton replied.

The chief gestured with his lance again. He and his men began to dismount.

Lupton said to one of his men, "Build a fire. The chief and I are going to parley."

There would be a lot of talk before Lupton and Red Moccasins settled the details of the deal they were striking. The parley might last until morning. The rest of the Sioux and the other outlaws would share the whiskey the white men had brought along, and most likely share the women as well. It would be a long, ugly night.

But it could pay some dividends for him and Crazy Bear, Preacher thought. By morning a lot of their enemies would be drunk and less alert.

The two men put their heads close together. "We cannot kill all of them," Crazy Bear said. "Not even Ghost-Killer could do that."

"You're right," Preacher agreed. "And we can't drive off in those wagons, either. That would be too slow We'll have to slip in before dawn and take the women out of there on foot. Then we'll stampede the horses through the camp and scatter them. Maybe that'll give us time to get the women into the hills and hide them."

Crazy Bear nodded. "It is not a good plan . . . but with two against fifty, it is all we can do."

The Crow chief was right about that. They'd likely wind up getting themselves killed, Preacher thought, but there was no alternative.

The white outlaws had kindled a fire and they heaped wood on it until the flames leaped high and cast a garish light over the camp. In that glare, Preacher and Crazy Bear got their first good look at their enemies.

The man called Lupton, who sat down to negotiate with Red Moccasins, was tall and rail-thin, with a jutting spade beard. Preacher recognized the Mayhews from his encounter with them at Boadley's trading post. They were all brawny, fair-haired men. Clint Mayhew, the oldest and the leader of the clan, sported a silvery beard. The rest of the outlaws were typical frontier scum, some dressed in homespun and whip-cord, the others in buckskins.

They were heavily armed. Preacher saw lots of rifles and pistols around the camp, although all the pistols seemed to be single-shot flintlocks. He didn't spot any of the new Colt revolvers, just Dragoons like he carried or the earlier model Patersons.

After a while, Lupton stood up, went over to the wagons, and said, "Climb out of there, ladies. Make it quick now." Evidently, Red Moccasins demanded a look at what he would be getting if he dealt with the white men.

As the women climbed out of the wagons and lined up like terrified sheep, Preacher looked for the woman who'd given Jord Mayhew so much trouble earlier. It was impossible to tell which one she was. He didn't see anyone who had dark hair as long as the woman who'd grabbed Jord's knife had. Maybe it was braided and put up.

Red Moccasins walked up and down the line of prisoners, leering at them. He stopped to grab one woman's hair and jerk her head up so that he could glare into her face. When he came to one with large breasts, he pawed them and laughed. Finally he turned to Lupton and nodded, signifying that he would take the captives in trade.

A faint rustling sound to Preacher's left caught his attention. He turned his head in that direction and frowned. The noise continued. It seemed to be about twenty feet away. He tapped Crazy Bear on the shoulder and nodded in that direction. Crazy Bear returned the nod. With less sound than a snake would have made, Preacher crawled through the grass toward the rustling. A wild idea had leaped into his head, and he wanted to see if he was right.

When he was in position, he lay still and let whoever was skulking through the grass come to him. The growth parted near him. He heard panting and knew it came from both exhaustion and fear. He waited until the woman was right beside him to make his move. She seemed to have no idea he was there, and he knew the ordeal she had gone through had drawn her nerves so tight she would try to scream as soon as he touched her.

He made sure that when his left hand shot out in the darkness, it closed tightly over her mouth. At the same time, he wrapped his other arm around her and threw himself on top of her so she couldn't move.

She bucked underneath him, struggling frantically, but she was no match for his strength. His hand over her mouth prevented her from making any sounds other than a couple of muffled squeaks that wouldn't travel more than a few feet. Keeping her pinned down, Preacher put his mouth next to her ear and whispered urgently, "I'm a friend! Stop fightin', lady. I'm here to help you."

He repeated it several times before the words finally penetrated her frightened brain. Her struggles eased and then stopped. He went on, "Don't try to get away, and don't make a sound. You understand? I'll let go of you, but you got to promise you won't yell or jump up."

A couple seconds went by, and then the woman nodded.

"All right," Preacher said. "I'm gonna take my hand away from your mouth. If you make a racket, you'll get us all killed, understand?"

He moved his hand away. She didn't cry out. She just lay there panting as she tried to catch her breath.

Then she whispered, "Thank you." The English words were understandable enough, but they had a heavy accent.

"I'm gonna get off of you now." Preacher slid to the ground beside her. While he was lying on top of her, he had felt the long hair that hung down her back. "You're the gal who grabbed the knife earlier and almost cut Jord Mayhew, ain't you?"

More words in that foreign tongue tumbled out of her mouth. Preacher figured she was cussing Jord again. He let her go on for a few seconds before he stopped her.

"I don't understand what you're sayin', but I know you're upset and I don't blame you the least little bit. Did any of those varmints hurt you?"

"No. Not yet. That big ugly one, Jord, he was the first who tried."

"I'm glad you speak some English, 'cause I don't understand that other jabberin' you were doin'."

"Romany. It is the language of my people. We are . . . how you say . . . gypsies."

Preacher understood. He had seen gypsies on some of his trips back east in St. Louis and Philadelphia. With their dark hair and eyes and swarthy skin, they reminded him a little of Indians. He had never been around them enough to learn their lingo, though.

"I'm called Preacher," he told her. "What's your name?"

She hesitated, as if still unsure whether to trust him, then said, "Mala."

"Mala. That's a mighty pretty name. You got any kinfolks in those wagons?"

"My brother's wife, Nadia. I was traveling with her and my brother Gregor, and my father and grandfather." Her voice caught a little as she added, "They . . . they are all dead now, except for me and Nadia."

"I'm sorry," Preacher said, knowing what she said was true. All the men with the wagons had been wiped out, even the old-timers. "My friend and I saw the wagon train. We know what happened. We've been trailin' that bunch ever since."

"You followed us? Why?"

"To help you ladies who were captured, and to settle a score with the Mayhews and the rest of those varmints they're with. They killed some young men from the village where my friend lives."

"Your friend . . . he is a savage?"

"He's a Crow chief," Preacher said. "But he won't hurt you. He hates the Sioux, and he hates the Mayhews and them others. We're gonna try to get all the gals away from 'em."

Mala asked the same question the dying John Spaulding had asked earlier in the day. "How many men do you have?"

Preacher gave her the same answer he had given Spaulding. "The two of us."

She exclaimed quietly in her native tongue. "There are

forty men in that camp, all of them killers. There is nothing you can do against such odds!"

"We'll see about that. First we'll get you somewheres safe that we can leave you—"

"No," Mala said. "If you are going to try to rescue the others, I will help you."

"You were tryin' to get away," Preacher pointed out.

"And I am ashamed that I abandoned my brother's wife and the others. It seemed there was nothing I could do. So when Jord Mayhew let me go when the Indians came, I slipped away and hid in the brush while the other men weren't looking. Then I crawled out here. I . . . I knew that even if I got away, I would probably starve to death or be eaten by a wild animal, but I thought that was better than being a slave to savages." She reached out to clutch Preacher's arm. "But now . . . now that I have a chance to fight . . . now that I can kill some of those terrible men before I die . . . I would go back."

Preacher thought it over for a second and then nodded. Having Mala along might make it easier to get the other women away from the wagons. They would trust her, where they might not believe what he told them.

"Come on," he told her. "Stay low and be as quiet as you can. I'll take you to Crazy Bear."

"Crazy Bear? I thought you said your friend was an Indian."

"That's his name," Preacher explained. "He is kind of big and, well, ugly like a bear."

"I do not care, as long as he will help me kill some of those evil men."

"We're gonna have to kill a lot of 'em if we're gonna have any chance of gettin' out of here," Preacher said.

Chapter 8

As Preacher and Mala crawled back toward the place he'd left Crazy Bear, Preacher lifted his head enough to see what was going on. The flames of the campfire still leaped high in the air. The women had been herded back into the wagons, and the white men and the Sioux were passing jugs of whiskey back and forth in celebration.

That was a risky thing to do—you could never tell what an Indian would do when he'd guzzled down enough who-hit-John—but Red Moccasins' warriors had demanded the fire-water. They would fall into a drunken stupor sooner than the outlaws would, so as long as Lupton's bunch and the May-hews were careful not to start any ruckuses, they would prob-ably be all right.

When Preacher and Mala crawled up to Crazy Bear, the Crow chief had his knife in his hand in case he needed to fight. Preacher whispered, "It's all right. I brought one of the women back with me. She's the one who tried to carve a hunk out of Jord Mayhew."

Crazy Bear grunted. "For a woman she is very brave, or perhaps very foolish."

Preacher was glad they were talking in the Crow tongue, not in English. He suspected Mala would take offense if she knew Crazy Bear had said she might be very foolish. She'd certainly seemed to have a fiery nature when she was going after Jord and the other men with that knife.

"She wants to help us rescue the other women, so I'd say she's very brave."

"But she was fleeing and abandoning them."

"She was scared and didn't know what else to do."

Crazy Bear thought about it and then shrugged. "How is she called?"

"Her name is Mala."

"Mala," Crazy Bear repeated. "It is a good name."

"What did he just say about me?" Mala asked in English.

"He said you were very brave," Preacher told her, which was only stretching the truth a mite.

"Give me a weapon, and I will show you how brave I am."

Preacher chuckled. "Yeah, I remember. Here." He drew a narrow-bladed dirk from a sheath he'd slipped into the top of his left boot and pressed the grip into her hand. "I reckon you know how to use it."

"Let me at that damned Jord Mayhew. I will carve off his man parts."

"Yeah, that sounds mighty entertainin'," Preacher said. "I reckon his squallin' while you did it would wake up the whole camp, though, so if you do have to use that blade on one of the varmints, try to cut his throat instead. That way he can't make any noise."

Mala nodded. "Yes. What you say makes sense. I will remember. When will we go to the camp?"

"Not for a while yet. We need to let them Sioux warriors get good and drunk first."

"So we wait, while God knows what happens to Nadia and the other women?"

"I don't like it any better than you do," Preacher replied to her angry question, "but we don't have any choice if we want to save their lives."

Mala waited in silence, but Preacher could sense her

fuming. Crazy Bear leaned toward him and said, "She is full of spirit, as I told you."

"Yeah, she's full of somethin', all right. I just hope she can keep it under control until it comes time for us to make our move."

Hours dragged by. Preacher was used to waiting, motionless and silent. So was Crazy Bear. A man learned to do that when he was hunting wild game, or else he went hungry a lot.

Mala didn't have that ability. She shifted around in the grass. She muttered to herself, sometimes in English and sometimes in the strange language she'd called Romany. Preacher wanted to tell her to hush up and be still, but he figured it wouldn't do any good. As long as she didn't cause enough commotion to alert the men in the camp that somebody was hidden in the tall grass, he supposed her fidgeting and muttering wasn't hurting anything.

It was damn annoying, though.

From time to time, a woman's cry floated over the prairie. The sounds made Mala more upset. Preacher understood and told her in a whisper, "Hold on. We'll get 'em out of there as soon as we can."

The stars wheeled through the sky overhead. Preacher lifted his head occasionally to check the camp, and each time he saw fewer men moving around. Many of the Sioux had passed out from the whiskey, and some of the outlaws were drunk and either asleep or only semi-conscious. Preacher had a strong hunch Lupton posted sentries and those men would still be awake and alert.

Finally, when the faintest tinge of gray appeared in the eastern sky, Preacher told Mala, "All right. It's time." He said the same thing to Crazy Bear in the Crow tongue. Switching back and forth between the languages so that both of his companions understood, he went on, "We'll split up. Mala and I will circle to the left and head for the wagons to get the women out. Crazy Bear, you go around to the right and close in on the horses. Any sentries you come across, kill 'em as quiet as you can."

Crazy Bear nodded. "Signal me when you are ready for me to stampede the horses."

"I'll howl like a panther," Preacher said. He grinned in the darkness. "I can make it sound real, and that'll spook them horses even more. We'll head up into the foothills with the women just as fast as we can. I seem to remember there's a canyon up there that might be a good place to hide 'em. It's narrow, and one man could hold off quite a few."

"I know the place," Crazy Bear said. "I will come there when I have killed as many of the enemy as I can."

"Don't be too stubborn about it and stay too long," Preacher said. "We'll have a better chance of gettin' those gals outta here if we're both still alive."

Crazy Bear turned to Mala. "May the spirits smile on you, valiant one," he told her.

"What did he say?" she asked Preacher.

"He was wishin' you luck."

"Oh." She looked at the Crow chief. "Good luck to you, too, Crazy Bear."

He gave her a curt nod, then crawled off into the grass, disappearing quickly.

"He is big," Mala said, "but not really that ugly."

"You ain't seen him in broad daylight yet," Preacher said.

He motioned for her to follow him and started crawling to his left. He didn't hurry, but he didn't waste any time, either. When they reached the trees that covered the slope, Preacher stood up in the thick shadows and reached down to take Mala's arm. He helped her to her feet and put his mouth next to her ear.

"As much as you can, try to step where I step. Let your weight down easy. Keep your balance all the time, and don't let that pigsticker bang against anything."

"I will be careful," she promised. Her breath was warm against his ear as she spoke. He felt the warmth of her body near his, as well, but didn't think anything about it. She was an ally in a desperate fight, that was all. The fact that she was also a beautiful young woman didn't even enter his thoughts, the way it might have if he had been twenty years younger.

Like the ghost the Blackfeet considered him, Preacher glided silently through the shadows under the trees. Each of his senses was operating at peak efficiency. He heard a faint movement up ahead at the same time he smelled unwashed flesh.

A sentry leaned against a tree trunk. In the darkness, Preacher's cat-like eyes were able to make out his shape. He had his hand wrapped around the barrel of his rifle and the weapon's butt rested on the ground beside his feet. At that late hour of his shift, the guard was struggling to stay awake.

Preacher drew the long-bladed hunting knife at his waist. Striking with the swift, silent deadliness of a viper, he slid his left arm around the sentry's neck, jerked him back, forced his head up, and slashed the blade across the luckless outlaw's throat, slicing deep into it. Hot blood spurted from the severed artery. The man let go of his rifle and started to struggle, even though he was already doomed. Preacher didn't want him thrashing around and making a racket, so he drove the heavy brass ball at the end of the knife's grip against the man's temple. The blow was enough to stun him. He sagged in Preacher's grip and finished bleeding to death in silence.

Carefully, Preacher lowered the corpse to the ground. He wiped the blade on the man's shirt and straightened. Touching Mala's arm to let her know she should follow him he cat-footed his way toward the wagons again.

She moved more quietly than he had expected her to. She seemed to have a natural talent for that sort of thing, he thought. Gypsies had a reputation for being sneaky. In Mala's case it seemed to be deserved, at least as far as being able to slip unnoticed through the shadows.

Another guard stood near the wagons. Preacher waited

for a long moment, studying the camp. The fire had burned
down some, but still provided enough light for him to see
Lupton and Red Moccasins sitting beside it, talking. Most of
the Sioux warriors were sprawled around the camp, snoring
in their whiskey-induced slumber. Some of the white men
were asleep, too. A few were still passing a jug back and
forth. None of them seemed to think they were in any danger
whatsoever. Their confidence bordered on arrogance.

On the frontier, arrogance could get a man killed pretty
damn quick-like.

Preacher didn't see any of the women or girls around the
camp, which meant they were all in the wagons. Good. The
guard posted near the vehicles moved back and forth, trying
to stay awake. Preacher slipped into the thick shadows between the wagons and waited until the guard passed just outside the shrouding darkness.

The man was one of the Mayhews. He let out a long, weary
sigh . . . and that was the last sound he ever made. The next
instant, Preacher's left hand clamped like iron over his mouth
and pulled him backward across the wagon tongue into the
shadows. At the same time, the knife in Preacher's other hand
drove into the man's back. The mountain man guided it with
practiced ease between a couple ribs so that the razor-sharp
blade penetrated the guard's heart. It paralyzed the man, and
in a couple seconds he went limp.

Preacher lowered the body, then turned and whispered to
Mala, "Come with me."

They slipped along the side of a wagon that was away from
the fire. Preacher cut the ropes that held the arching canvas
cover over the vehicle and pulled it away from the sideboards.
Then he told Mala, "You do the talking. Tell them to come
with us. But be mighty quiet about it, all of you."

"I understand," she said. She stuck her head and shoulders
through the opening Preacher had made and hissed to get the
attention of the captives. "Wake up! Wake up, we must go!"

Several of the prisoners exclaimed in surprise, but others

were already crying and whimpering so Preacher hoped the sounds wouldn't be noticed. The gypsy woman quickly hushed them up, saying, "It's Mala! I have come back for you. Be quiet now, we must go."

Preacher held his breath, hoping the women would understand and realize their lives depended on swiftness and silence. After a moment, Mala backed away slightly from the wagon and held the canvas up so one of the captives could climb out of the vehicle. From the size of the dim shape, Preacher figured it was a girl, not a full-grown woman.

The escaping prisoner was followed by another and another. "This is Preacher," Mala told them. "He is a friend and will help us get away. Do as he says."

Preacher pointed into the hills and whispered, "Head that way as fast as you can. Be careful. Don't make any more noise than you have to. Watch out for each other and give a hand to whoever needs it. Keep movin' no matter what you hear goin' on back here."

The women and girls were clearly terrified, but they understood it was their only chance of escaping the awful fate planned for them. They moved off into the darkness in ones and twos as others continued to climb out of the wagon.

When the first wagon was empty, Preacher and Mala moved on to the second one. No one seemed to have missed the guards Preacher had killed. There hadn't been any uproar yet. Preacher cut the canvas loose, then whispered, "Let's get these other women out."

The second part of the rescue operation went off without a hitch. When all the women were out and moving up the hill through the trees, Preacher said to Mala, "All right, you'll have to look after 'em now. It'll be light soon, so you ought to be able to find your way into the foothills. Keep an eye out for that canyon Crazy Bear and I were talking about. That's where we'll rendezvous with you in a little while."

"What are you going to do now?" she asked.

"Improve the odds as much as I can," Preacher said. "Get goin'."

"Preacher . . ."

"No time," he said as he glanced at the lightening sky. "Go!"

Mala went, hurrying up the wooded slope after the others. Preacher waited until she was out of sight, then he turned to face the camp. He sure as hell hoped Crazy Bear was ready to stampede those horses.

Preacher pulled both the Dragoon Colts from behind his belt, looped his thumbs over the hammers, stepped out from behind the wagons, threw back his head, and let out a scream that sounded just like the cry of a blood-crazed panther.

Chapter 9

Men leaped to their feet, outlaws and Sioux warriors alike, shouting curses and confused questions. A few were so drunk they continued to snore, even with all the racket going on. Most of those on their feet were disoriented from the whiskey they'd consumed and from being jolted out of sleep.

Before anyone could do much more than look around bleary-eyed, the shrill cry of another panther ripped through the night. It came from a different direction and was followed instantly by a rumble like thunder.

Crazy Bear had slipped among the white men's horses and the Sioux ponies and removed their pickets and hobbles. Spooked by the animal-like cries, the herd bolted just as Preacher planned. The horses charged through the camp, pounding their hooves on the ground, trampling anything in their way. Men screamed as they were caught in the stampede and knocked down. Hooves slashed and hammered at them, breaking bones and pulping flesh.

Lupton and Red Moccasins leaped aside, barely avoiding the charge. Others scattered and got out of the way, too. Preacher was ready for them. The guns in his hands roared as he thumbed off shot after shot, firing with both hands. Each time flame gouted from the muzzle of a Colt, either an outlaw or a warrior fell, downed by a .44 caliber ball. Preacher tried for head shots, the hardest to make but the most effective. No man was going to get up after one of those .44s bored through his brain and exploded out the other side of his skull.

Preacher emptied both guns, killing eight men with ten shots in approximately six seconds. One man had a shattered shoulder and was out of the fight. He would most likely bleed to death. Another man writhed on the ground and tried to howl in agony, but Preacher's shot had broken his jaw and torn half of it away. All he could do was make a pathetic, bubbling moan.

There was no time to reload. Preacher jammed the Colts behind his belt and drew his knife. As he sprang forward, he snatched up a tomahawk that had been dropped by one of the trampled Sioux warriors. With the knife in his right hand and the 'hawk in his left, he plunged among the stunned survivors and slashed back and forth. Blood spurted and bone cracked as he laid into them.

Preacher wished Dog could have been there. The big, wolf-like cur had loved a good fight. His shaggy shape would have been tearing through the enemy, sharp teeth flashing as he ripped out throats.

That wasn't to be. Preacher had to handle the killing himself. Gore splattered both arms to the elbows as he wreaked havoc among the outlaws and the Sioux.

He heard a deep, powerful voice chanting and knew that Crazy Bear had arrived and was singing a death song. Whether it would be death for Crazy Bear or just for his enemies didn't really matter. Many spirits had already departed the realm, and more were on their way.

Preacher spotted the giant Crow and hacked his way toward him. Several bodies were scattered around Crazy Bear's feet, the heads twisted at unnatural angles on the necks. As Preacher reached his side, Crazy Bear grabbed two more men and slammed their heads together with such force their skulls split wide open like melons. Crazy Bear tossed the corpses aside.

Shots began to roar. Preacher heard the hum of a lead ball pass his ear. Some of the men had taken cover behind the empty wagons and were shooting from there. The campfire was out having been scattered to glowing embers by the stampeding horses. Nobody could see very well.

"Come on!" Preacher said. "Let's go!"

"There are more to kill!" Crazy Bear protested.

"You'll get your chance later, I reckon!"

The gunmen were just as likely to hit their own allies as they were Preacher and Crazy Bear, even more so after the mountain man and the Crow chief turned and ran deeper into the darkness, away from the camp.

Preacher let his instincts guide him. He nearly always knew where he was and which direction he needed to go. Within moments, he and Crazy Bear reached the timber on the slope and began to climb above the camp. A lot of futile shooting and yelling still went on below.

"It will not take them long to discover we are gone," Crazy Bear said. "Then they will come after us."

"Yeah, but there ain't nigh as many of 'em as there was a while ago," Preacher said. "I reckon we wiped out more'n half of 'em."

Even so, he knew they were still outnumbered. The survivors wouldn't let them get away with what they had done. Dawn was less than an hour away. Once it was light enough, the men would come looking for them.

Preacher hoped he could have a warm welcome waiting for them when they did.

They were about a mile away from the camp when Mala suddenly stepped out from some brush and motioned to them. "Preacher!" she called softly. "Crazy Bear! Over here!"

They veered toward her. As they came up to the gypsy woman, Preacher asked, "Are the others all right?"

Mala nodded. "A few tripped and turned their ankles or

scratched themselves on the brush while they were running in the dark, and a few are still in bad shape from what happened to them earlier, but we can all move quickly if we need to."

"Did you find that canyon I told you about?"

Mala turned and pointed toward the Big Horns. Although the sun was still below the horizon, the first reddish-gold rays of the new day were starting to touch the mountaintops. There was enough light to see the black mouth of the canyon about a hundred yards away.

"Is that the one you mean?"

"Yeah," Preacher said. "Are the others hidden inside it?"

"Yes. I stayed out here to wait for you and Crazy Bear."

It hadn't been necessary for her to do that, but Preacher didn't say anything except, "All right, you can head back there now." He added in Crow, "Crazy Bear, you go with her."

Crazy Bear nodded, but as Preacher started off in a different direction, Mala said, "Wait! Where are you going?"

"I need to get our horses," Preacher explained. "There's not much time. We're liable to need the ammunition that's on my pack horse."

"Then Crazy Bear should go with you, to help you."

Preacher shook his head. "Nope, I'd rather he stayed here with you ladies. If anything happens to me, he'll get you out of this mess."

"But I cannot even talk to him!"

"He savvies a few words of English. I reckon you can make him understand if you work at it. Anyway, I won't be gone long."

Without looking back, Preacher loped off in the direction of where he and Crazy Bear had left their horses the night before. He didn't see any sign of the enemy as he moved swiftly through the timber. It took him only fifteen minutes to find the horses, which were right where they'd been left. He moved slowly as he led the animals back toward the canyon, making as little noise as possible. He didn't want to increase the odds of drawing unwanted attention.

A little less than an hour after leaving Crazy Bear and Mala, he reached the canyon. He made a bird call, knowing that Crazy Bear would recognize it. An answering signal came back indicating that everything was all right and Preacher should come ahead.

The mouth of the canyon was narrow—about fifty feet wide—and its sides were sheer. It opened up a little as he went deeper into it, until the walls were a hundred yards apart. The canyon penetrated about a quarter mile into the mountainside before it took a sharp turn and ended abruptly against a rock wall. The floor of the canyon was littered with rocks and brush and scrubby trees, which provided cover for anyone trying to defend it.

The women and girls were gathered just around the bend. Crazy Bear and Mala came out to meet Preacher.

"Any trouble?" the mountain man asked.

Crazy Bear shook his head. "The men who are left have not found us yet, but they will. These women gave no thought to concealing their trail."

"Don't reckon most of 'em would know how to, even if they'd thought about it," Preacher said. "That's all right. Let those sons o' bitches follow us. We'll be ready for 'em when they get here."

"What do you plan to do?"

The sun flooded the canyon with light as Preacher pointed up to a narrow ledge that ran along one wall all the way to the canyon mouth, ending at a tall, narrow spire of rock. "I'm gonna climb up there and be waitin' for 'em when they come chargin' in. You and Mala will be down here with rifles, puttin' up just enough of a fight so they'll think you and I are both trapped in here with the women. As soon as they're right under me, I'm gonna drop that tall rock on 'em. The ones it don't get, I'll introduce to Mr. Samuel Colt." He patted the butts of the two Dragoons.

Crazy Bear thought for a moment, then nodded. "This plan might work. But how will you budge that rock?"

"I figure I can snap it off at the base if I get my feet on it and my back against the canyon wall."

"I hope so. I am not sure we can kill all of them otherwise."

"We'll kill as many as we have to," Preacher said.

Mala looked puzzled and was starting to look impatient. Preacher explained the plan to her in English. As soon as she heard it, she shook her head.

"What's wrong?" Preacher asked.

"You cannot move that rock by yourself. It's mad!"

"I don't see any other way to do it."

"You and Crazy Bear both go up there," she suggested.

"I need Crazy Bear down here to handle one of the rifles. I'm countin' on you to use the other one."

Mala turned and pointed to the women. "One of them can use the other rifle. I'm sure that someone among them can fire a gun."

Preacher rubbed his jaw. "Well, it'd be easier with both of us up there, I reckon—"

"Wait here," Mala interrupted. She went to talk to the women.

Crazy Bear said, "She likes to give orders."

"You understood what she said?"

The Crow chief smiled. "No, but I know when a woman is telling a man what to do."

"Yeah, yeah, I guess," Preacher muttered. He had seen the open admiration in the eyes of Crazy Bear and Mala as they looked at each other, and he thought it was a good thing. Evidently she didn't care that the big galoot was ugly as sin. But if it was going to amount to anything, they all had to get out of there safely first.

Mala returned with a middle-aged woman who had a weathered face and strands of gray in her brown hair. "This is Mrs. Harris," Mala said. "She can shoot a rifle."

"I was raised on a farm in Ohio," the woman said. "I could

knock a squirrel out of a tree at fifty yards by the time I was ten years old."

Preacher grinned. "I don't doubt it a bit, ma'am." He got Crazy Bear's flintlock from where it was slung on the back of the chief's pony and handed it to her, along with powder horn and shot pouch. "There you go."

He gave Mala his rifle and ammunition, then reloaded his Colts and stuffed his pockets full of caps, balls, and powder charges. Crazy Bear slung a bow and a quiver of arrows on his back. The two of them waited until Mala and Mrs. Harris had taken positions behind some rocks where they could cover the canyon mouth, then Preacher and Crazy Bear began to climb the rugged wall that formed the back end of the canyon.

It wasn't an easy ascent, and became harder when they reached the level of the ledge. They moved sideways along the canyon wall toward the ledge, searching out handholds and footholds that sometimes were nothing more than narrow cracks in the rock. Preacher wondered if Crazy Bear's fingers would support the weight of his massive body, but somehow Crazy Bear managed to cling to the rock and keep moving.

Preacher reached the ledge first. After hauling himself onto the ledge he stretched out a hand to grasp Crazy Bear's wrist and pulled the chief onto it. When they both had solid rock under their feet again, they worked their way along the ledge toward the canyon mouth and the rock spire.

Once there, they hid behind the towering rock and waited. The sun was high enough to heat up the ledge and sweat trickled down Preacher's face and back.

They didn't have to wait very long. Preacher spotted movement on the hillside below the canyon and silently pointed it out to Crazy Bear. The chief nodded. Men were working their way through the trees. He and Preacher crouched lower and didn't move again.

With eyes narrowed against the sun's glare, Preacher recognized Clint Mayhew, one of his brothers, the outlaw called Lupton, and Red Moccasins. The four of them were accompanied by four more outlaws and half a dozen of Red Moccasins' warriors. Fourteen in all, Preacher thought as a grim smile touched his lips. The stampede and the battle the night before had wiped out more of the enemy than he had realized.

When the men were hidden behind trees close to the canyon mouth, Red Moccasins called sharply to two of his warriors. They hurried forward, carrying flintlock rifles, and started through the opening.

A rifle cracked from inside the canyon, and one of the warriors stumbled and clutched at his side. That was good shooting, Preacher thought. A second shot roared, but that bullet whined off harmlessly.

"Go!" Lupton shouted. "Get in there before they can reload!"

The men sprang out of cover and charged toward the canyon opening, confident they could overwhelm the defenders.

It was time to spring the trap.

Chapter 10

Preacher and Crazy Bear lodged their backs against the stone wall and lifted their feet so they were braced against the rock spire. They put all their muscles into the task of toppling the rock.

As Preacher felt how unbudging the rock was, he knew he never could have broken it off by himself. Mala had been right. With Crazy Bear's incredible strength coming into play, they at least had a chance. Grunting with the effort, the two men continued to push, pitting their strength against the timeless majesty of the rock.

Down below, the howling warriors were almost at the canyon mouth. Right behind them came Lupton, Mayhew, and the other white killers.

Preacher heard a crack and felt the rock shift slightly under his feet. That inspired him to even greater efforts. Although he didn't have the immense strength of Crazy Bear, his rangy form packed plenty of power. Together, the two men pushed against the rock . . .

And suddenly the spire was gone.

Like a tree toppling in the forest, it fell away from them, causing both of them to drop to the ledge. Preacher grabbed hold quickly to keep from falling off. Beside him, Crazy Bear scrambled for purchase as well.

Below them, the rock spire slammed down in the canyon mouth with a huge crash. Preacher heard snatches of several men screaming before the thunderous roar drowned them out. A cloud of dust billowed into the air as he made it back to his feet and reached down to help Crazy Bear rise as well.

Preacher drew his Colts and waited for the morning breeze to carry the dust away. He saw that the spire had shattered into a thousand pieces when it landed. Men stumbled around the debris in a daze, and as the echoes of the crash rolled across the hills, he heard screams again. Some of the attackers had been caught under the falling rock, just as he'd hoped.

He began firing methodically at the men still on their feet. Beside him, Crazy Bear had the sturdy bow in his hands and sent arrows whistling down into the canyon mouth. Preacher knew it took a lot of strength to pull it, the sort of strength only Crazy Bear possessed. The arrows went all the way through a man to the fletching, the head and nearly a foot of shaft standing out on the other side of the man's body.

"You son of a bitch!" Lupton bellowed. He had a pair of flintlock pistols in his hands. One of them roared, sending a ball whistling past Preacher's head to splatter on the canyon wall behind him.

Before Lupton could fire again, Preacher's right-hand Dragoon blasted. The shot drove into the outlaw's chest and knocked him back on his ass. Gasping in pain and shock, Lupton tried to raise his second pistol, but he didn't make it. The weapon slipped out of his fingers, and he toppled sideways as death claimed him.

Red Moccasins threw his lance at Crazy Bear. It was an awkward throw because of the angle, and Crazy Bear knocked the lance aside with his bow. He dropped the bow, let out the gibbering laugh that had given him his name, and leaped off the ledge, as he yanked out a knife. Crazy Bear crashed into Red Moccasins, and both men went down.

Preacher was busy trading shots with Clint Mayhew.

"Preacher! You bastard!" Mayhew shouted as he fired a pistol. "I should've known it was you!"

Preacher felt the ball's passage through the air only inches from his ear and ducked in the other direction. Mayhew fired the pistol in his other hand and got lucky. The ball creased Preacher's upper right arm, ripping the buckskin shirt and plowing a shallow furrow in the flesh. The impact was enough to numb Preacher's arm and knock him back a step against the canyon wall.

Mayhew grabbed up a pistol that one of the wounded men had dropped and lined the sights on Preacher's chest. With hate contorting his face, he pressed the trigger, but even as smoke and flame gushed from the barrel, a shot from Preacher's left-hand gun smashed into Mayhew's body and threw off his aim.

At the same instant, a rifle cracked behind the man and a ball struck him in the back. The two impacts coming together from opposite directions held him upright for a long moment as blood gushed from both wounds. Then his knees unhinged and he fell straight to the ground. Preacher saw Mala standing behind Mayhew with a rifle at her shoulder. Smoke still curled from the barrel.

Before Preacher could call down his thanks to her, she lowered the rifle and rushed forward. Preacher saw that Red Moccasins was on top of Crazy Bear and about to plunge a knife into the Crow chief's chest. Preacher couldn't fire because Mala was in his way.

Mala reversed the rifle and grasping it by the barrel, swung it like a club. The stock slammed into the back of Red Moccasins' head, knocking him forward. As his knife swept down, the blade dug into the ground next to Crazy Bear's head instead of burying itself in his chest.

Crazy Bear's hands shot up and locked around the Sioux chief's throat. With a heave, Crazy Bear rolled over and put Red Moccasins under him. Red Moccasins flailed and thrashed but was no match for Crazy Bear's strength. Crazy

Bear's hands twisted one way, then the other, and Red Moccasins' neck snapped with a crack like that of a breaking branch.

The shooting had stopped. Preacher's right arm still hung numb at his side, but he tracked his left-hand gun from side to side of the canyon mouth, his eyes searching for more threats. All the attackers were down, either dead or mortally wounded.

Crazy Bear lumbered upright, leaving the body of Red Moccasins at his feet. Mala ran to him. For a second Preacher thought she was going to throw her arms around Crazy Bear, but she stopped herself and stood looking up at him.

"You are all right?" she asked in English.

Somehow he understood. He nodded and smiled. He was still ugly as hell, Preacher thought, but the smile helped a little.

"I hate to intrude," he called down to them, "but I'm shot and somebody may have to help me down."

The feeling came back quickly to Preacher's wounded arm, so it hurt right smart when Mala used some of the outlaws' whiskey to clean the furrow and then bound it up.

They gathered up all the rifles, pistols, and ammunition from the dead outlaws and armed the women. "Reckon you could hold off an army for a while now if you needed to," Preacher told Mala, "but I don't think you'll have to worry about that. Shouldn't be anybody else around to bother you before Crazy Bear and I get back."

He was glad he could use his right arm when he and Crazy Bear got on their horses and rounded up the animals they had stampeded that morning before dawn. By midday they had driven enough mounts to the canyon so the women could ride instead of walking.

Once they returned with the horses, Preacher and Crazy Bear dragged off the bodies. There was no question about what would be done with them. The scavengers would feast. Some varmints didn't deserve buryin', to Preacher's way of thinking.

They rode out that afternoon, leaving the grisly scene behind them, and made camp that night several miles away.

The question remained: what were they going to do with twenty-five women and girls who no longer had families and found themselves hundreds of miles from civilization?

"Seems to me there's only one answer," Preacher said to Crazy Bear and Mala as they sat beside their campfire that evening, having made a meal on the supplies they'd found in the outlaws' saddlebags. "I'll take y'all back down to the Oregon Trail. There are wagon trains comin' along there every week or so at this time of year, so it shouldn't be long before you can catch on with one of them and head on west. I think you'll like Oregon better'n you would have Montana, anyway. It's a lot more settled."

"You will not guide the women alone," Crazy Bear replied when Preacher had translated the plan into the Crow tongue. He looked at Mala. "I will come with you."

Preacher shrugged. Crazy Bear had his own people to lead, back in the Big Horns, but he supposed the village could get by without him for a while longer.

Mala explained everything to the other women, who were happy to go along with the idea. Some of them would have a hard time putting their ordeal behind them, but a new life in Oregon would be a start.

The whole party left the next morning, riding south. Preacher wouldn't have been surprised if they ran into more trouble along the way, but for once, that didn't happen. They reached the North Platte River and the landmark known as Independence Rock a week later. Preacher looked at the deep wagon ruts alongside the stream and knew it was only a matter of time until more immigrants came along.

Crazy Bear stayed that night, but the next morning he went to Preacher and said, "It is time for me to go."

Preacher nodded. "I know. You have responsibilities you need to take care of."

"But I will not be going alone."

Preacher glanced toward the spot where Crazy Bear's pony waited. Another pony stood beside it, with Mala holding the reins.

"She's goin' with you, is she?" Preacher grinned. "I can't say as I'm surprised. I've seen the way you two been lookin' at each other right along. Learnin' how to communicate, are you?"

"Yes," Crazy Bear said solemnly. "Very well."

"She won't mind livin' in a Crow village from now on?"

"She says she wants to be with me, and I want to be with her. What more is there in life?"

"I reckon you're right about that." Preacher held out his hand. Crazy Bear had saved his life, and they had fought side by side. Those things created a bond that could never be broken. As they clasped hands, Preacher went on, "If you ever need my help, Crazy Bear, let me know and I'll come a-runnin'."

"And the same is true for you, my friend," the Crow chief said.

Mala ran over and threw her arms around Preacher's neck, hugging him tightly in farewell. "Thank you for everything," she said. "Without you, none of us would be here."

"You held your own in that fight," Preacher told her. "Reckon you did even more'n your share. You'll make a good wife for a warrior, right enough." He paused, then added, "I just hope the young'uns take after you when it comes to their looks, not their pa."

The mention of children brought a blush from Mala, which surprised him a little. He would have thought she was too bold to blush, but he had long since learned that gals were an infinite source of surprises.

"I meant what I said, Crazy Bear," Preacher called as his

friends mounted up. "If you need me, put the word out. It'll find me."

Crazy Bear lifted a hand. "Farewell, Preacher."

"So long." Preacher stood and watched them as they rode away, adding softly, "Live a happy life."

Interlude

"I reckon that's just what they've done, for the most part," Preacher said in the heat of the little cabin where he was holed up with Smoke and Matt. "Had a little trouble from time to time, the way most folks do, but they're still together all these years later."

"That's right," Smoke said. "I can vouch for that."

"So can I," Matt added.

Smoke watched the trees in front of the cabin. He couldn't shake the feeling that Bannerman's hired guns were going to try something again. Waiting for nightfall made more sense, but while he was shooting it out with them during the last attack, Smoke had caught a glimpse of a man he recognized. Lew Torrance was a top man with a gun, one of the best on the frontier. He had been pointed out to Smoke once in a saloon in Santa Fe, though they hadn't met. Smoke wasn't surprised that Bannerman had hired a cold-blooded, efficient killer like Torrance.

Torrance had a flaw, though: he was impatient. When he took on the job of killing someone, he wanted to get it done as quickly as possible. That impatience had come close to getting Torrance killed a time or two. Smoke didn't believe that the man would be content to wait for the sun to go down.

That last attack should have taught the gunmen they

couldn't charge the cabin in the open and expect to win. The first attempt had cost them some lives. The same thing would happen if they tried again.

Movement in the trees caught Smoke's eye. He knew whatever they were up to wasn't anything good.

"Those varmints are stirring around again," he told Preacher and Matt.

"They ain't nothin' goin' on back here," the old mountain man reported.

"It's quiet on this side, too," Matt said.

Smoke's eyes narrowed. He muttered, "What the hell . . . ?" Something big loomed in the trees. It came into view through a gap in the growth and looked so odd for a second Smoke couldn't figure out what he was looking at.

Then he recognized it as a flatbed wagon that probably had been fetched from Reece Bannerman's ranch. Someone had built a wall on the front that rose a good six feet straight up behind the driver's seat and extended from one side of the wagon to the other. Rifle barrels protruded from three holes that had been cut in the wall.

The wagon didn't have a team hitched to it. The tongue had been lifted and tied to the wagon it wouldn't gouge into the ground in front of the vehicle. It began to move, which meant men were behind it, pushing it slowly but steadily toward the cabin. Powder smoke spurted from the rifles as the gunmen concealed behind the wall opened fire.

"What's goin' on?" Preacher asked as the shots began to ring out and bullets thudded into the cabin's thick walls.

"The damnedest thing you've ever seen," Smoke replied. "They're bringing their own cover with them. They've made a rolling wall out of a wagon."

He cranked off several rounds from his Winchester. Splinters flew from the places where the slugs struck the boards, but he doubted if any of them penetrated. He figured that wall was several layers thick.

Matt went to one of the loopholes in the front wall and took a look for himself. "Holy cow!" he exclaimed. "How in blazes are we going to stop a thing like that?"

"I don't know," Smoke said. Between his pa Emmett and Preacher, he'd been raised to never give up, never back down. But it seemed likely that at least one man with a torch would be riding on that fortified wagon. Once it was pushed close enough, they'd be able to throw the torch over the wall and onto the top of the cabin. They could finish off Smoke, Matt, and Preacher at almost point-blank range when the resulting fire forced them out.

The wagon was sort of like an old medieval siege engine, Smoke thought, recalling the history books he had read that described such things being used to breach the walls of castles. Immediately something else occurred to him.

"Preacher, get out of the line of fire of the door!" he called to the old-timer. "Matt, cover me! That blasted thing can't move without somebody pushing it!"

"You got it, Smoke!" Matt said, his keen mind instantly grasping what his adopted brother had in mind. Together, they grabbed the bar holding the door closed and tossed it aside. Smoke went low, throwing himself onto his belly at the threshold, while Matt fired around the edge of the door, pouring lead at the hidden riflemen to keep them distracted.

From that angle, Smoke could look *under* the wagon and see all the way to the legs of the men who were pushing it. He snugged the rifle's stock against his shoulder and began firing from his prone position. Men yelled in pain as his accurate bullets smashed ankles, shattered shins, and tore through calves. Smoke's shots knocked their legs right out from under them, and the wagon lurched to a halt. It had covered only half the cleared distance between the trees and the cabin.

As busted legs spilled the men behind the buckboard onto the ground, Smoke had even better targets. He kept firing. His bullets drove into the bodies of the fallen men, killing some of them instantly and wounding others. One of them shouted to his companions, "We can't walk! Get us out of here, damn it!"

Men rushed from the trees to come to their aid, but Matt's rifle fire drove them back. The wounded men began shooting back with handguns, but the range was too great for much accuracy. Smoke's jaw tightened as he drilled another gunman through the head while the hombre tried to drag himself to safely on his bullet-riddled legs. Killing men like that was pretty cold-blooded, but they had called the tune, he thought. They could damned well dance to it.

Or rather they couldn't, he reminded himself with a faint, grim smile, because he had shot their legs out from under them.

But any man he spared might be the one who killed him or Matt or Preacher later on. Even worse, the hired guns might launch another attack on Crazy Bear's village and murder more women and kids. Smoke wasn't going to lose any sleep over killing snakes like that.

The four men who'd been standing in the wagon bed gave up the fight. They leaped from the vehicle and made a dash for the timber. Matt winged one of them, shattering his elbow from the looks of the way the man's arm jerked and flopped, but they all made it into the cover of the trees. That left the wagon sitting there empty, with the four men who'd been pushing it sprawled behind it, dead.

Smoke rolled out of the doorway and into the cabin as bullets from the trees began to kick up dirt not far in front of his face. Matt slammed the door and dropped the bar back into place.

"Well, that didn't work out too well for 'em," Preacher said with a dry chuckle. "That was mighty fast thinkin' on your part, Smoke, firin' under the wagon like that."

"It was the only way to get at any of them," Smoke said as he got to his feet. He took a handful of .44-40 cartridges from a pocket and began thumbing them through the Winchester's loading gate.

"What do you reckon they'll do next?" Matt asked.

Smoke shook his head. "There's not much telling. We've managed to whittle down the odds considerable. They'll be a little more careful from here on out, even with Lew Torrance egging them on."

"Torrance?" Matt repeated. "I've heard of him. He's supposed to be a really bad hombre."

"He is. I don't know if Bannerman has him bossing that bunch, but it's possible. Or maybe Torrance is just one more gun-wolf. Bannerman seems to have plenty of 'em."

Preacher snorted in disgust. "Varmints like that put me in mind of flies buzzin' around a big steamin' pile o' buffalo dung. There's always more where they came from."

"Which would make Reece Bannerman that pile of buffalo dung, I suppose," Matt said with a grin.

"You said it, youngster, not me." Preacher spat on the hard-packed dirt floor of the cabin. "Hard to fool a fly, though."

Smoke ran his tongue over dry lips. None of them had mentioned how thirsty they were, nor would they. Their canteens were on their saddles, their horses somewhere in the vicinity. Before taking shelter in the cabin they had turned the animals loose, swatting their rumps and yelling so the mounts would gallop off, out of the line of fire. Smoke knew that he, Matt, and Preacher wouldn't have any trouble finding them later.

All they had to do was get out past the guns of those hardened killers first.

To get his mind off how cotton-mouthed he was, Smoke said, "I recall the first time I met Crazy Bear. You had told me about him, Preacher, but just hearing about him doesn't really prepare anybody for meeting him in the flesh."

Preacher chuckled again. "Ain't that the truth. But you run into his boy first, didn't you?"

"That's right," Smoke said with a nod. "Not far from here, in fact, over in Buffalo Flat. That's where I met Sandor. It was years ago, a mighty bad time in my life . . ."

Book Two

(Note: The events in this section take place between the novels *The Last Mountain Man* and *Return of the Mountain Man*)

Chapter 11

Hatred filled the heart of the young man who rode a big Appaloosa into the settlement of Buffalo Flat, Wyoming Territory, at the southern end of its main street. Sometimes that hatred burned so hot, it seemed on the verge of erupting, like flames from his brown eyes. At other times it was a cold hate, like ice had coated the expressionless face and it would never thaw again.

The important thing about that hatred was it didn't leave room inside him for the pain he would otherwise feel.

Richards . . . Potter . . . Stratton. Those were the names of the men Smoke Jensen intended to kill. The men who had taken away everything that meant anything to him. The men responsible for the deaths of Smoke's wife Nicole and their son Arthur, as well as the baby's namesake, the old mountain man called Preacher. They had taken it all from him, and he would take everything from them. His only regret was that the worst he could do was kill them.

Smoke rode straight in the saddle like a cavalryman. His brown, broad-brimmed Stetson was pulled low over his face. Ash-blond stubble sprouted on his jaw. He had already cropped his hair close to his skull, and was thinking about growing a beard to change his appearance even more. After all, he was a wanted man. There was a $10,000 reward on his head because those lying bastards had made *him* out to be an outlaw and killer when in reality they were the ones who were evil.

Bounty hunters were already after him, and they didn't care whether they brought him in dead or alive. In fact, most of them would probably prefer to kill him. It was easier to handle a dead body than a live prisoner, especially one as dangerous as Smoke Jensen.

So, as he slowly, methodically, made his way through Wyoming toward Idaho and the town of Bury, where he knew he would find the men he was looking for, he considered the best way to stay alive would be to leave his true identity behind. He needed new clothes instead of the fringed buckskins he wore. As much as he loved the Appaloosa he called Seven, the horse was mighty distinctive. He might have to change mounts. Hell, Smoke had thought a few days earlier, it might even be a good idea if he started calling himself by another name, although he was damned if he could think what it would be. He had been Kirby Jensen, then Preacher had given him the nickname Smoke. Those were the only names he had ever known.

Those were things he mulled over, but he wasn't in any hurry. He had all the time in the world. His hate for Richards, Potter, and Stratton would always be there.

In the meantime, he could use some supplies, and might pick up some new duds while he was in Buffalo Flat. He reined Seven toward a hitch rail in front of a big, false-fronted building with a sign that read HAMMOND'S EMPORIUM.

Before he could get there, the door opened suddenly and a man burst out, running onto the high porch that also served as a loading platform. Smoke realized an instant later the man was being *forced* to run. Right behind him, gripping the back of his belt and his coat collar another man was shoving him forward.

When they reached the edge of the porch, the man doing the pushing stopped short and gave his hapless victim an extra shove. The fellow's mouth opened in an alarmed yell as he flew off the porch with his arms and legs windmilling frantically, which didn't do him a bit of good.

He crashed into the street, splattering a pile of horse apples underneath him. His face drove into the dirt with stunning force. His fingers scrabbled at the ground, he drew a leg up, and dug the toe of his shoe into the street as he tried to lift himself onto his hands and knees. He didn't have the strength and after struggling for a moment, he let out a groan and slumped back down on his belly, grinding the horseshit into his coat even more.

Smoke had reined Seven to a halt when he saw what was happening, to prevent the horse from stepping on the man who'd been thrown out of the general store. He sat there impassively as two more men emerged from the building and joined the one who'd done the throwing.

"Funniest thing I ever saw, Mitch!" one of them whooped as he smacked the palm of his hand against the black chaps on his thigh. "I swear, that Injun looked like he was tryin' to fly, the way he was flappin' his arms around!"

"Didn't do him no good did it?" his thickset companion added, also with great amusement. "He still done belly-flopped right in that pile o' horseshit!"

A short, slender middle-aged man with a massive mustache drooping over his mouth edged out of the open door onto the porch and said in a tentative voice, "Uh, he hadn't quite got around to payin' me for that new suit yet, boys, and I reckon it's ruined now."

The two spectators instantly lost their air of joviality and turned to the store's proprietor. "What're you botherin' us about, Hammond?" demanded the stocky one in the steeple-crowned white hat.

The man who wore a black leather vest over a red shirt and a black hat to go with his black chaps, crowded the aproned storekeeper and poked him in the chest with a rigid forefinger.

"Yeah, you best run on back into your hole like the little rat you are!" he scolded.

Smoke's eyes took in the fact that all but the shopkeeper wore low-slung guns. He had seen the likes of them many times since coming west with his pa. They were hardcases who considered themselves badmen. Maybe they really were tough . . . but chances were, they weren't nearly as tough as they thought they were.

The first man, who was tall, lean, and hatchet-faced, carried himself with the air of a leader. He turned, took a bill from the pocket of his whipcord trousers, stepped past his companions, and tucked the money into the top of the storekeeper's apron.

"There," he said in chilly tones. "There's your payment for the damned suit, Hammond. Mr. Garrard always pays his bills, and so do the men who work for him." The man spat near Hammond's feet. "It's more than you deserve for letting a filthy redskin shop in your store."

"He . . . he's got just as much right to come in here as anybody else," Hammond said, surprising Smoke by his willingness to speak up when he was surrounded by three gun-hung gents who were also considerably bigger than he was.

The hatched-faced man smiled, but there was no humor in the expression. "He's got a right to come in, and we've got a right to throw him out on his ass."

"I say we throw ol' Hammond here on his ass, too," the man in the black chaps suggested. "Throw him right down there in the shit next to that redskin."

Smoke glanced around the settlement. Quite a few people had stopped on the boardwalks or come out of the buildings onto the porches to watch what was going on, but nobody had made a move to step in. His instincts told him that nobody would. He didn't particularly care what happened to the storekeeper or the young man who'd gotten thrown in the street, but he had things to do and this business was holding him up. He was getting a mite impatient.

Quietly, he said, "I'd be obliged if you'd leave that man alone."

His voice was deep and powerful and carried well despite the fact that he hadn't raised it. The three hardcases turned to look at him with surprise on their faces. Obviously, they weren't used to anyone interfering with whatever they wanted to do.

"What the hell did you say, mister?" asked the man in the big white hat.

"Said I'd be obliged if you'd leave him alone," Smoke drawled. "He looks like he runs the store, and I need to buy some supplies."

The hatchet-faced man eyed Smoke's well-worn buckskins and said, "What hole in the woods did you crawl out of?"

Smoke ignored the question. He lifted the reins in his left hand and nudged Seven closer to the hitch rail. When he got there, he turned the Appaloosa alongside the rail so that Seven was between him and the men on the porch while he swung down from the saddle. No use in giving them too tempting a target. Smoke stepped up to the horse's head, whipped the reins around the wooden rail, then moved out into the open. Every nerve, every muscle, was ready for blinding action if any of the men tried to hook and draw.

The hatchet-faced man suddenly smiled. "Stranger's got a point, boys," he said.

"What?" the man in the black chaps asked. "You gonna let him get away with talkin' to us like that, Mitch?"

"Can't interfere with the workings of commerce," Mitch said. "That wouldn't be right at all. Come on. Let's go up the street to the Birdcage. I'm buying."

His two companions didn't like it, but a free drink was a free drink, and not something to be refused. They cast dark, murderous glares at Smoke, then went to the end of the porch, down the steps, and started along the boardwalk toward the saloon. The hatchet-faced man ambled after them, keeping an eye on Smoke as he did so and never quite turning his back until he was well away from the store. The last Smoke saw of his face, he was still wearing that smirk.

Smoke knew what had happened. Mitch had recognized the stance and attitude of a fellow gunfighter and wasn't ready to challenge him . . . yet. But it might well come to that unless Smoke mounted up and rode out of Buffalo Flat *pronto*.

He wasn't going to do that. He wasn't in the habit of running from trouble and sure as hell wasn't going to start.

Hammond came to the edge of the high porch. With his Adam's apple bobbing in his stringy neck, he asked, "You don't know who those fellas are, do you, mister?"

"No, and they don't know who I am, either," Smoke said, "so I reckon we're even."

Another groan came from the man who'd been tossed out of the store. Smoke had gotten a pretty good look at him while the man was flying through the air, even though the glimpse had been a brief one. The man was young, probably no more than twenty, and even if the hardcases hadn't mentioned him being an Indian, Smoke would have known it from the black hair and eyes, the high cheekbones, and the coppery skin.

Since it wasn't common to find an Indian wearing a town suit, a white shirt with a stiff collar and a tie, and store-bought shoes. Smoke felt curiosity stirring inside him. He stepped over to the young man's side and reached down to take hold of his arm.

"Let me give you a hand, friend."

Smoke's broad shoulders in the buckskin shirt were a good indication of how strong he was. He lifted the young man to his feet without much effort. The youngster was unsteady and would have fallen if not for Smoke's hand on his arm.

Smoke wrinkled his nose. "You're gonna need a change of clothes, because that suit may have to be burned." He looked up at Hammond. "You have another one like it?"

The storekeeper nodded. "Yeah."

"Bring it out the back. You probably don't want this fella going through the store the way he is now."

Hammond rubbed his jaw in thought and then nodded. "Yeah, that's a good idea. But I got to get paid this time."

"You got paid for this suit," Smoke pointed out. "I saw that hombre called Mitch give you the money. This fella must have the cost of a suit with him, or he wouldn't have been buyin' one in the first place, now would he?"

"No, I reckon not. What you say makes sense, young fella. I'll meet you around back in a few minutes if you'll help Little Bear back there."

Smoke nodded. "Come on," he told the Indian.

They went along the alley beside the store, the young man still stumbling some. He muttered under his breath.

Smoke either didn't quite catch the words, or else the man was speaking some strange language that Smoke had never heard before, because he didn't understand a thing the fellow was saying.

When they reached the back of the store, Smoke saw several empty crates on the ground. He upended one and told his companion, "Here, sit down before you fall down. Are you hurt? The way you keep stumbling around, maybe you busted something when you landed in the street."

"I—I'm all right," the young man replied in a trembling voice. "I just . . . just . . ." He pawed at damp eyes with the back of a hand. Smoke realized those weren't tears of pain. The youngster was crying because he was so mad. It was fury that caused him to shake.

"Better take it easy," Smoke advised. "Hammond called you Little Bear. Is that your name?"

Before the young man could answer, heavy footsteps sounded in the alley and a harsh voice said, "Hey!"

Smoke turned in that direction. A barrel-chested man strode toward him, glowering angrily. A lawman's badge glittered where it was pinned to his vest.

Chapter 12

Smoke's hands moved toward the twin .44s holstered on his hips. He was a wanted man, whether the charges were justified or not. He managed to stop the instinctive reaction, and hoped the lawman hadn't noticed it. He didn't want to get in a shootout with the small-town star packer. That would give his status as a fugitive some legitimacy.

"What can I do for you, Sheriff?" he asked.

"It's marshal," the man said. He had a good-sized gut hanging over his belt, but despite that, he didn't look particularly soft. "Marshal Thad Calhoun. I'm the law in Buffalo Flat. What's this I hear about a run-in you had with Mitch Thorn, Earl Ballew, and Gus Harley?"

"It wasn't much of a run-in," Smoke said. "I asked them to leave the storekeeper alone, and they did it."

"Thorn's killed men for less, damn it!"

Smoke shrugged. "He didn't try to kill me."

"Well, you're just damn lucky," Marshal Calhoun blustered.

"Somebody is, anyway."

Calhoun's forehead creased in a frown. "What do you mean by that, mister?"

Before Smoke could answer, the back door of the store opened and Hammond came out, a fresh suit of clothes draped over his arm. He stopped at the top of the steps leading down to the ground and said, "Hello, Marshal."

"What the hell do you think you're doin', Luther?" the lawman demanded.

"Why, doin' business, of course," Hammond replied, looking and sounding genuinely puzzled.

Calhoun pointed at Little Bear. "With *him*?"

"His money spends just as well as anybody else's. I'm sorry, Marshal, but there ain't no law saying I can't sell a suit of clothes to an Indian."

"Well . . . maybe not. But you had to know it'd annoy the hell outta Thorn and his cronies if they caught that redskin in your store."

"Listen, Thad," Hammond said. "The only ones who set out to cause trouble here are Mitch Thorn and those other two hardcases who work for Garrard. If you've got a problem with anybody, it ought to be with them."

Calhoun glared and hitched up his gunbelt, although it sagged right away again with the weight of his big belly pressing down on it. "Don't try to tell me how to do my job," he huffed.

"And don't try to tell me how to do mine," Hammond shot right back at him. Smoke found himself liking the little banty rooster of a storekeeper.

Calhoun blew out his breath and shook his head in exasperation. "You been warned, Luther," he said, then turned to Smoke and went on, "As for you, mister, I sure as hell hope you're just passin' through Buffalo Flat, because you ain't wanted here."

Actually, he was, Smoke thought wryly. Ten grand worth of wanted, in fact. But he said, "I just stopped to buy some supplies."

"Fine. When you've bought 'em, you'll ride on, if you know what's good for you."

With that, Calhoun turned and stomped back up the alley, heading for the street. Smoke watched him go.

Hammond came down the steps, saying, "Take those filthy clothes off, Little Bear. You got the money to pay for these?"

"Yes," the young man said sullenly. "And my name is Sandor."

"Oh, yeah, I forgot. Your ma calls you one thing, and Crazy Bear calls you another. Reckon you're Little Bear in the Crow village and Sandor here in town, is that it?"

The young man nodded as he stripped off the soiled coat. He dropped it on the ground at his feet and began unbuttoning his shirt. It wasn't as filthy as the coat and trousers were, but it stunk of horse droppings, too.

He looked over at Smoke and nodded. "Thank you." He wasn't so mad that he was crying and shaking anymore, but his dark eyes were still deeply troubled. "There's no way of knowing what those men might have done if you hadn't intervened."

Hammond laughed, then said, "I'm sorry, Little Bear . . . I mean, Sandor. It's just that I'm not used to hearin' an Indian talk like that."

"My mother made sure that I learned to speak English properly, as well as her native Romany."

"Romany," Smoke repeated, recognizing the name. "You're part gypsy."

Sandor nodded. "My mother is Rom, my father is Crow. Though my mother lives as a Crow woman would live, she has never forgotten her heritage. I was named after her father."

"Folks need to remember where they come from," Smoke said.

Sandor put on the clean clothes. Hammond looked down at the pile of filthy ones and sighed. "I suppose burning's the best thing for them," he said. "Seems a shame, but I don't reckon I could ever get that smell out. Just leave 'em there for now, and I'll tend to 'em later." He turned to Smoke. "You said you needed some supplies?"

"That's right."

"Soon as Sandor here pays me, I'll be glad to help you."

Sandor pointed toward the building. "My money is inside, in my pack."

"All right, fine."

They entered the store through the rear door. The inside was like dozens of other frontier emporiums Smoke had seen, with shelves of goods along the walls and in the center of the main room, as well as a counter in the back where Hammond could pack supplies in boxes and tote up bills. A lot of the lumber had a raw, new look to it, and Smoke realized the walls looked the same way. That was true of the rest of the settlement as well.

"This town hasn't been here very long, has it?" he asked Hammond.

"Only about six months," the storekeeper replied. "It's growin' by leaps and bounds. Fella named Bannerman brought a herd of cattle up from Texas and started a ranch not far from here. That prompted other stockmen to give it a try, and as they came in, the town followed. I heard about it, brought three wagonloads of goods up here, and set up my store in a tent, startin' out." He waved a circling hand to take in the sturdy building around them. "You can see how it's grown since then. Whole town's the same way. Things really took off when Jason Garrard started runnin' stagecoaches between here and Casper. Nothing like a line of communication with the outside world to make a town grow."

Sandor had taken some money from a beaded buckskin pouch. He laid it on the counter in front of Hammond. "This is for the suit," he said.

"Much obliged," the storekeeper said as he picked up the bills and raked the coins into his other hand.

"Garrard," Smoke mused. "That's the name of the fella those three troublemakers work for, isn't it?"

Hammond nodded. "That's right. Gus Harley and Earl Ballew are shotgun guards on his coaches. Mitch Thorn's what you'd call a troubleshooter, I guess. It's quite a ways from here to Casper, across a lot of open country where bandits could stop a stagecoach without much trouble. Thorn rides along sometimes to make sure the coach gets through."

Smoke scraped a thumbnail along the beard-stubbled line of his jaw as he frowned in thought. He turned to Sandor and said, "Your pa's name is Crazy Bear?"

"That's right," the young man said.

"And he's a Crow chief?"

"Yes."

"I think I've heard of him," Smoke said. "An old friend of mine once told me about meeting up with a Crow chief called Crazy Bear. Said he was one of the biggest hombres he'd ever seen."

Sandor smiled. "That is my father. Your friend probably said he was one of the ugliest men he'd ever seen, too."

"Well, now that you mention it . . ."

"I take no offense at such a description. My father *is* ugly, in the physical sense. But he is also the best man I have ever known. What is your friend's name?"

"He was called Preacher."

Recognition lit up Sandor's dark eyes. "Preacher!" he repeated. "Of course. I have heard my father speak many times of him and the way they rescued my mother from the bad men who had kidnapped her." The young man frowned suddenly. "Wait a minute. You said he *was* called Preacher?"

"He crossed the divide a while back." Smoke didn't want to talk about it. Preacher's death was still too recent, too painful, to dwell on.

"I'm sorry. My father always spoke very highly of him. Perhaps you could ride by the village and tell him the news when you leave Buffalo Flat."

"Why can't you tell him about it?" Smoke asked.

"Because I am going the other way. I'm catching the next stage for Casper, and from there I will make my way on to Denver and eventually back east to college. My mother wishes me to have a white man's education."

"Is that a fact?" Smoke and Preacher had known some educated Indians, although most had no interest in accepting the white man's ways, and even less in going to school.

"Yes. Why do you think I needed this suit of clothes?"

Smoke smiled. "I'll admit, I hadn't spent a lot of time wondering about it. No offense, Sandor, but I've got my own chores to take care of." He paused, then went on, "I reckon I could take the time to ride by your father's village and tell him about Preacher."

"Good. It's about ten miles northwest of here in the mountains."

"Not far from Bannerman's Circle B spread," Hammond put in. "There's a road out there now, so it ain't hard to find, Mister . . . ?"

Smoke hadn't mentioned his name to anyone in Buffalo Flat so far, and he thought it would be a good idea to keep that up. He thought quickly, glancing down at his buckskin shirt as he did so, and then said, "Just call me Buck."

"All right, Buck," Hammond said, and his smile made it clear he knew that wasn't the name Smoke had been born with. But that was common on the frontier. A man might use half a dozen different monikers in the course of his life. "You said you needed some supplies?"

"Yeah. Flour, salt, a little sugar if you've got it, some Arbuckle's."

"How about some jerky?"

"Sure," Smoke agreed. "Usually comes in handy havin' some jerky tucked away in the saddlebags, in case you run into a stretch where you can't find any game for fresh meat."

"I'll start puttin' the order together," Hammond said. "Be ready in half an hour or so. Are you ridin' on out today, like Marshal Calhoun told you to?"

"That depends. Is there a good hotel in town?"

"Well, there's a hotel. Can't say as to how good it is. The Garrard House, couple blocks up the street."

Smoke raised an eyebrow. "Garrard? Same one who runs the stage line?"

"One and the same. He's got the livery stable, too, not surprisin' since he had to have a barn and corrals for his stage teams. I got a feelin' he'd like to spread out into even more businesses."

"Sounds like he's trying to take over the whole town."

"You didn't hear that from me, Buck," Hammond said. "I don't cotton to bein' pushed around, but I still got to live and work here. Between Thorn and his cronies and Marshal Calhoun, Mr. Garrard usually gets pretty much whatever he wants."

"The lawman's in his pocket, eh?"

Hammond shook his head, but he wasn't disagreeing with Smoke's assessment. "You didn't hear that from me, neither."

Smoke turned to look at Sandor. "When's that stage you're gonna take to Casper supposed to get here?"

"Two days from now, if it's on schedule," the young man replied.

"You plan to stay in town until then?"

"I do. I've already said my farewells to my mother and father. I'd prefer not to go through that again."

"Then I think I'll hang around Buffalo Flat for a while, too," Smoke said.

Sandor frowned. "You don't have to stay here to protect me. I know it didn't look like it out there, but I can take care of myself, you know. My father is a Crow warrior, after all. The blood of fighting men runs in my veins."

"Mine, too," Smoke said, thinking of how his father had spent four years fighting for the Confederacy in the War of Northern Aggression. "But I've been on the trail for quite a while. I wouldn't mind sleeping in a bed for a change."

"Well, in that case . . ." Sandor shrugged. "Anyway, I can't tell you what to do. Just be careful if you run into Thorn and his friends again. Thorn is very fast with a gun, and while the other two can't match his speed, they are killers, too."

"The boy's right," Hammond added. "You don't want to have any more trouble with those hombres."

"No trouble," Smoke agreed. "I'm a peaceable man."

Chapter 13

When he checked in at the hotel, Smoke had to stop and think again before he scrawled a name in the register for the clerk. He had already established himself as Buck with the storekeeper, Luther Hammond, but he needed a last name to go with it. One name was as good as another, he supposed, since it was a lie anyway. He thought about the points of the compass. Buck North? Buck South?

Sure as hell not Buck East.

Buck West sounded pretty good, Smoke thought with a smile. He wrote the name in the register.

The balding clerk read it upside down and asked, "Do you have any bags, Mister, uh, West?"

"Only my saddlebags," Smoke replied. They were already slung over his shoulder, and his Henry rifle was in his left hand. "You have a corral or a stable out back?"

"No, sir, but you can take your mount right down the street to the Garrard Livery. Mr. Garrard owns it, too, so you get a break on the price, seein' as you're a guest in his hotel."

Smoke nodded. "How about a dining room?"

"No, I'm afraid we don't have one of those, either. But Clancy's Café across the street has pretty good food."

"Clancy's, eh? Garrard doesn't own it, too?"

"No, sir. Not yet, anyway."

Smoke looked at the clerk, but the man appeared to just be making conversation. His comment didn't have any particular significance.

The clerk slid a key across the desk. Smoke picked it up, nodded, and said, "Obliged." He had already given the man a five dollar gold piece, which would pay for the room for a week. He didn't really intend to stay that long, but it was easier to pay in advance and get some money back when he left. He wasn't broke, although he was a long way from rich and had gotten in the habit of watching what he spent.

"Room 3. Turn right at the top of the stairs."

Smoke nodded again and went up. Like everywhere else he'd been in Buffalo Flat, the hotel had a lingering scent of raw wood about it, although there he could smell fresh paint, too. The lobby had a curiously empty look about it, as if Garrard hadn't finished furnishing it yet.

As long as the bed in his room was comfortable, it was all Smoke really cared about. He found room 3, opened the door, and tossed his saddlebags on the bed, then bounced the mattress up and down with his hand. Passable, he decided. He leaned the Henry in a corner and looked around. Other than the bed with its iron bedstead, the room contained only a small table with a basin of water on it, a single ladderback chair, and a ceramic thunder mug peeking out from under the bed. The floor was bare wood, with not even a rug. The single window overlooked the street and had a paper shade that could be pulled down instead of a curtain.

It was a simple, utilitarian place, good only for sleeping, but since Smoke didn't plan on doing anything else there, that was all right with him. The afternoon light had begun to fade as the sun lowered toward the Big Horns to the west, so he left the room. He wanted to tend to his horse before night fell.

As he closed the hotel room door, he bent and stuck a small piece of broken matchstick between the door and the jamb. If it was lying on the floor when he came back, that would tell him that he'd had a visitor while he was gone. A wanted man could never let his guard down. Somebody might recognize him from one of those damn reward posters and try to collect the bounty on his head.

He went out through the lobby to the street. Seven stood at the hitch rail where Smoke had tied him a short time earlier, after leaving Hammond's store. As Smoke untied the reins, he wondered briefly where Sandor had gone. He'd left the young man at the store.

That was none of his business, of course, and yet Sandor was one of the reasons he had decided to stay on in Buffalo Flat for a few days. If the young man was going to hang around the settlement until the stagecoach arrived, it was possible he would wind up in trouble again. If his path happened to cross that of Thorn, Ballew, and Harley, trouble was more than possible. It was highly likely.

Nobody appointed you that fella's guardian, Smoke told himself as he led the Appaloosa toward the livery stable. *You got business of your own waitin' for you in Idaho. Killin' business. Revenge business.*

But it wouldn't bring Nicole and Arthur back. Nothing would do that. Smoke found himself wondering if a man who lived only for hate could be considered truly human. Didn't there have to be a shred of something else left, a reminder, small though it might be, of the man he once was?

With a little shake of his head, he pushed those thoughts out of his brain. Time enough to ponder questions like that once his work in Bury was done—once Richards, Stratton, and Potter were all dead, along with any gunmen they had working for them.

The stable was a large barn with a sign on it that read GAR-RARD LIVERY. Next to it was a smaller building that housed the office of the Garrard Overland Stagecoach Company, according to a sign on it. This fella Jason Garrard was a mite fond of the sound of his own name, Smoke mused. He led Seven past the stagecoach office and through the open double doors of the barn.

"Hello?"

A man came through a smaller side door and greeted Smoke. "Howdy. I was just over talkin' to the boss. Need to put up your horse?"

"That's right," Smoke said. "I was supposed to tell you that I'm staying down at the hotel, too. Clerk there said something about that getting me a break on the price."

The hostler looked Seven over and let out a low whistle of admiration. "Mister, I'd give you a break on the price just for the privilege of havin' a fine-lookin' Appy like this in my barn."

"I thought this was Garrard's place."

"Well, yeah, it is," the man said with a shrug. "What I mean to say is, I'd give you that break if I owned this stable. What I can do is give you my word that I'll take mighty fine care of this big fella."

As the hostler moved forward and raised a hand to pet Seven on the shoulder, Smoke advised, "Best be careful. He can be a mite touchy."

The hostler drew his hand back. "One-man horse, eh? Well, I'll handle him cautious-like, but he'll still get the best care he can get in Buffalo Flat."

Smoke felt an instinctive liking for the stocky, middle-aged hostler. He smiled and said, "Thanks. My name's West, Buck West." It wouldn't hurt to practice using his new name a little, he thought.

"Pleased to meet you, Mr. West. I'm Hoyt Dowler. How long you plan on stayin' in these parts?"

"I'm not sure. Probably two or three days."

Dowler nodded. "Gimme a dollar and a half. That'll cover the bill for three days, seein' as you're stayin' at the hotel. If you stay longer, you can pay more then."

"Take two dollars," Smoke said as he passed over a couple coins.

"Sure." Dowler pocketed the silver. "Anything else I can do for you?"

"You look like a man who enjoys a good meal."

Dowler grinned and patted his ample belly. "You could say that."

"I'm told Clancy's is a good place to eat. What do you think?"

"Seamus whips up a hell of a good Irish stew."

Smoke nodded. "That'll do me, then. See you later, Hoyt."

"So long, Buck."

Smoke turned toward the double doors, where he saw three figures standing in the opening, silhouetted by the fading light. With the glare of the setting sun behind them, he couldn't make out their faces, but that didn't matter. He recognized them by their shapes.

"Oh, hell," Hoyt Dowler said under his breath.

Quietly, Smoke said, "Hoyt, take my horse and put him in a stall. Then you'd better head back out that side door. You can unsaddle him and rub him down later."

"But . . . but Mr. West—"

"Just do as I say," Smoke told him. "It'll be all right."

Dowler swallowed hard, grabbed Seven's reins, and led the horse away along the aisle that ran down the center of the barn.

Thorn, Ballew, and Harley sauntered a few steps into the building. Thorn was in front, with the other two a step back and flanking him.

"West, is it?" Thorn asked. "That's your name?"

"Buck West," Smoke said. He was getting more practice than he'd really expected.

"Well, I never heard of you, *Buck West*," Thorn said, letting scorn drip from his use of the name. "And I reckon I've heard of just about everybody west of the Mississippi who's slick on the draw."

"I never said I was slick on the draw," Smoke pointed out.

"You act like you think you are. It rubs me the wrong way."

"Why should you care?"

Thorn's upper lip curled in a sneer. "Because I'm the

fastest gun around here. Maybe in the whole territory. And my friends here are almost as fast."

Smoke felt anger welling up inside him. He struggled to tamp it back down. Normally, he would let loudmouthed assholes like those three say what they had to say and then kill them, if they were bound and determined to draw on him. But he didn't want to draw any more attention to himself. His reputation was big enough already. He didn't want it to interfere with his mission of vengeance.

"Well, that's good to know," he made himself say as he heard Dowler scurry out of the barn through the side door.

"Don't you want to find out if it's true?"

Smoke shook his head. "Not particularly."

He saw Thorn stiffen and knew that he'd made a mistake. His apparent lack of interest was even worse than a challenge to the gunman. Thorn took it as an insult, a sign that Smoke thought he was insignificant.

"You don't have a choice, mister," Thorn snapped. "We're gonna settle this right here and now."

Smoke sighed. It looked like he was going to have to kill them after all.

"Hold it!"

The sharp voice came from behind Smoke and to his right. He almost whirled in that direction and slapped leather, but he realized that if he took his eyes off Mitch Thorn, the man would go for his gun. Instead Smoke stood there, steady as stone, while another man strode into the barn through the side door that Hoyt Dowler had used earlier.

The newcomer wore a brown tweed suit. He was short and wide and had a shock of graying red hair. He demanded, "What's going on here, Mitch?"

"Nothing you need to be concerned with, boss," Thorn replied. He looked irritated by the interruption.

"I think it is," the man who had to be Jason Garrard replied. Smoke supposed that Dowler had darted across the narrow gap between the livery stable and the stage line office to alert his employer that there was about to be a shootout in the barn. Garrard went on, "I think you're about to kill this man, and we've had a talk about that."

"Damn it, Mr. Garrard—"

"Buffalo Flat is a growing town," Garrard went on as if he hadn't even heard Thorn's attempt to protest. "A lot of it is my town already, and more of it will be. But it'll stop growing if it gets a reputation as a place where a man can get shot for nothing."

"It ain't nothing!" Thorn burst out. He gestured with his left hand toward Smoke. "This son of a bitch horned in earlier and stuck up for that damn redskin when the boys and me threw him out of Hammond's store. And now just look at him, standin' there like he thinks he's some sort of gunslick!"

"You let me worry about Hammond," Garrard said. "Once my store's established, he won't be around here for very long, anyway. A man's got a right to bring his horse in and stable it. You can't shoot him just because you don't like his looks."

"Well, then, what *can* I do?"

Garrard looked Smoke up and down for a moment, then shrugged and said, "There are three of you and only one of him. Why don't you just give him a good beating and let it go at that?"

Before Thorn could respond to that suggestion, Smoke said, "Reckon I'd have something to say about whether or not any beatings are handed out."

"Really?" Garrard smiled, and Smoke knew he didn't like that man. Not one little bit. "What are you going to do about it?" Garrard went on. "If you go for your gun, my men will kill you. Even if you should happen to survive, you'd be dangling from a hangrope by morning. We've got a good tree for it, right at the edge of town. The marshal and the judge would see to that."

"So you've got the law on your side, is that what you're saying?"

"I'm saying that sometimes, through no fault of his own,

a man winds up on the wrong side of trouble. When that happens, friend, the smartest thing for him to do is minimize the damage. At least that way you can live through it." Garrard took a cigar from his vest pocket. "Tell you what I'll do. To make it up to you, there won't be any charge for your hotel room tonight or for stabling your horse. You can ride out of here in the morning without owing any money."

"What if I don't want to leave in the morning?"

"Then I think you'd find that my hospitality—and my patience—have limits." Garrard put the cigar in his mouth and clamped his big white teeth down on it.

Suddenly, Smoke laughed. The absurdity of the situation made him do it. He said, "So what you want is for me to stand still for a beatin' to appease these hardcases of yours, and in return for it you'll give me a free room in the hotel and a stall for my horse?"

"That's the deal," Garrard said around the cigar. "Take it or leave it."

"I don't even get to fight back? What sort of a ruckus is that?"

"Let him fight, boss," Thorn said. "It won't do him any good."

Garrard shrugged again. "You heard the man," he said to Smoke.

"One condition," Smoke said. He felt like a lobo wolf was running around inside him, trying to get out, but he kept it under control as best he could. He nodded at Dowler who had returned through the side door. "Dowler holds everybody's guns."

"Fine with me," Garrard said. He jerked a hand at Thorn and the others in a curt gesture. "Give Dowler your guns."

Thorn frowned. "What if it's a trick? What if this hombre slaps leather as soon as we're unarmed?"

Smoke's hand went to the buckle of his gunbelt. "I'll hand over my weapons at the same time."

"Sounds fair," Garrard said.

Dowler looked nervous as a cat in a roomful of rocking chairs, as the old saying went, while he collected the gunbelts and holstered revolvers from Smoke, Thorn, Ballew, and Harley. Smoke had a two-shot derringer tucked in the high top of his left boot, a double-edged dagger in his right. He suspected that Thorn and the others had hide-out weapons, too. He wouldn't use the derringer or the dagger unless he was forced to.

He was actually looking forward to settling this with fists. There was something particularly soul-satisfying about knocking the sneer off the face of an arrogant bastard like Mitch Thorn.

Smoke backed into the center of the aisle to give himself some room to move as the three men advanced slowly toward him, spreading out so that they could come at him from different angles. "All right," Jason Garrard said, clearly looking forward to what he thought he was about to see. "Have at it."

Chapter 14

"Let me have first crack at him, Mitch," the stocky hardcase in the tall white hat said.

"All right, Gus," Thorn said. That meant the man in the black chaps and vest who wore an ugly grin on his face was Earl Ballew. Thorn went on, "Just leave a little so Earl and I can have some fun, too."

Harley reached up, took his hat off, and tossed it aside as if he wanted to make sure it didn't get hurt during the fight. Then he lowered his head and charged like a bull, straight at Smoke.

Smoke didn't fall for it. Such an open, straight-ahead attack had to be a feint. He took a step to the side as if trying to get out of Harley's way, then stopped short as the big man suddenly veered in the same direction.

Harley had already shifted his weight and was going too fast to stop. His momentum carried him past Smoke, who pivoted smoothly and brought his clubbed hands down on the back of Harley's neck with stunning force. The blow knocked Harley off his feet. He went face-first into the ground, landing hard.

Earl Ballew hadn't waited. He was right behind Harley. Smoke bent to his right at the waist and brought his left leg up in a kick that buried his foot in Ballew's midsection.

Ballew grunted in pain as he doubled over and stumbled to one side. He clutched his belly with both arms and looked like he was about to pass out, throw up, or both.

Harley and Ballew were out of the fight for a few minutes, but dealing with them left Smoke open to Thorn's attack. He threw a bony fist at Smoke's face that Smoke couldn't avoid completely. It landed just above his left ear with enough force to knock him off balance.

He would have recovered in time to deal with Thorn, but at that moment Harley rolled over, blood from his smashed nose coating the lower half of his face, and drove a boot heel into the back of Smoke's right knee. The unexpected kick caused Smoke's leg to fold up underneath him, dumping him over backward.

Harley was waiting for him. He wrapped his arms around Smoke's neck and yelled, "I got him, Mitch! Kick him! Bust him up good!"

Thorn moved in, swinging his right leg in a vicious kick aimed at Smoke's ribs. Before the kick could land, Smoke heaved himself into a roll that took Harley with him. The toe of Thorn's boot dug cruelly into the small of Harley's back instead. Harley howled in pain.

Smoke cut him off mid-yell by smacking his elbow into Harley's mouth. Harley's arms fell away from Smoke's neck. Freed from the man's grip, Smoke rolled again, keeping Harley between him and Thorn.

But Thorn hurdled over Harley and tackled Smoke as he came to his feet. The gunman's arms went around Smoke's waist and bore him backward until Smoke crashed into one of the thick pillars that held up the barn's roof. Pain shot through him, and the impact drove the air out of his lungs, leaving him gasping for breath.

Thorn began hammering punches into Smoke's body, keeping him pinned against the pillar. Although Thorn appeared to be slender, even scrawny, his stringy muscles possessed plenty of strength. His knobby fists dug deep into Smoke's gut and prevented him from drawing a breath. Smoke was getting a little light-headed from lack of air.

He grabbed the back of Thorn's neck, head butted the gunman, and knocked him back a step. Smoke swung a left that landed solidly and sent Thorn stumbling away. Smoke dragged a deep breath into his lungs.

The break lasted only a second before Harley came at him, swinging a roundhouse right that would have taken Smoke's head off if it had connected.

Smoke ducked under it, and Harley's fist slammed into the thick wooden beam instead. He screamed as bones broke. Bending low, Smoke shot a right into Harley's stomach, then brought a left uppercut from the ground. It landed under Harley's chin and lifted him completely off the ground. By the time Harley came crashing down on his back, he was out cold.

Ballew landed on Smoke's back and wrapped a chokehold around his neck. "Get him, Mitch, get him!" he yelled with his mouth next to Smoke's ear. Smoke smelled the raw whiskey on the man's breath.

He spun around and rammed Ballew into the wall of a stall. The horse inside the stall reared up in fright and pawed at the air with its hooves as it let out a shrill whinny. There was quite a racket and most of the horses in the barn were spooked. As Smoke twisted out of Ballew's grip, he caught a glimpse of Garrard and Dowler watching the battle. Dowler looked excited, like he was caught up in the heat of combat, but Garrard appeared worried. He hadn't expected Smoke to be able to hold his own against the three hardcases.

Smoke chopped the hard edge of his left hand against the spot where Ballew's neck joined his left shoulder. Ballew sagged, momentarily paralyzed by the blow. Smoke sent a right jab into his face that rocked his head back. Ballew was barely on his feet. He was on the verge of passing out when Smoke sent him over the edge with another punch that drove him to the ground. Ballew lay there, breathing harshly, unable to move.

"You son of a bitch!" Thorn yelled. Smoke looked around in time to see the gunman yank a revolver from a holster in the armload of weapons that Hoyt Dowler held. As Thorn whirled toward him and the gun came around, Smoke's right hand dipped to his boot and came up with the dagger. He sent it flying toward Thorn with a swift, underhand throw.

The blade pierced Thorn's forearm, going all the way through so that the bloody tip stood out on the other side. Thorn screamed and staggered back a step as his suddenly nerveless fingers opened and the gun thudded to the ground. Smoke saw that it was one of his own .44s.

He scooped it up and covered Thorn, who stood cradling his bleeding arm and cursing. "Fight's over," Smoke announced curtly.

"You had to use a weapon," Garrard pointed out. "You didn't abide by the terms of the agreement."

"Thorn grabbed a gun first. If you're worried about our deal, I'll pay you for the damn hotel room and the livery charge."

Garrard glared at him for a couple seconds, then suddenly laughed. "Forget it," he said with a wave of his hand. "Your stay in Buffalo Flat is on me, West. In fact, I'll go you one better. I'll offer you a job."

"A job?" Thorn repeated in disbelief. "Boss, what are you talking about?" He held up his injured arm and winced in pain. "Look what the bastard did to me!"

"Yeah, I see," Garrard said. "I also know that you and those other two are supposed to be tough. But they're out cold, and you've got a knife through your gun arm. West is still on his feet." Garrard shook his head. "I think I've been paying the wrong people."

Thorn turned to look at Smoke with hate and fury burning in his eyes. He took hold of the dagger and pulled it out of his arm. Blood welled from the wound. For a second,

Smoke thought that Thorn was going to throw the dagger at him, but the gun held rock-steady in Smoke's fist still covered him. Thorn flung the dagger onto the ground.

"You'll be wasting your money if you hire him, Garrard," he said. "Because I'm gonna kill him."

"Your arm will have to heal up first," Garrard said. "Well, how about it, West? You'd do well to hire on with me, because before I'm through, this whole corner of Wyoming Territory is going to belong to me."

Smoke felt a moment of nausea. When he looked at Jason Garrard, he saw the same sort of greed and arrogance that drove Richards and Potter and Stratton. They ran everything in Bury, no matter who got hurt, and Garrard aimed to run everything in Buffalo Flat the same way.

But Smoke was damned if he'd help the son of a bitch do it.

"Take your job and put it where the sun don't shine, Garrard," he said in a low, dangerous voice. As Garrard paled in surprise and anger, Smoke went on, "Take your hotel and your livery stable and everything else you own and cram them in there, too. I don't like any part of you or any of the rest of it."

"You'd best tread carefully there, boy," Garrard warned.

"No, you'd best tread careful," Smoke snapped back. "I've had my fill of men like you and your cheap gunhands." With an effort, he brought his temper under control and said to the hostler, "Sorry to trouble you, Mr. Dowler, but it looks like you're gonna have to bring my horse back out. I'll stop by the hotel and get my gear, then find some place else to stay."

Dowler sighed. "All right. But I sure was lookin' forward to havin' that Appy around for a while."

"You're making a bad mistake, West," Garrard said.

"I don't think so," Smoke said.

"I own the only hotel in town. Where are you going to sleep?"

"I'd sleep on a trash heap before I'd spend a night in your hotel, mister. Figure the smell would be better. Now that I've been around you and Thorn, it'll take a while to get the stink out of my nose."

"Oh, you really are a dead man," Thorn said.

"Reckon we'll see about that."

"We sure as hell will."

Dowler led Seven back up the aisle from the stall where he'd put the Appaloosa earlier. He had buckled Smoke's gunbelt and hung it from the saddle horn. As he handed over the reins, he said, "I'll get your two bucks."

"I'd tell you to keep 'em for your trouble, but my poke's a little light right now."

Dowler gave him the two coins. Smoke pocketed them, then picked up his dagger and backed toward the double doors. From the corner of his eye, he saw that Harley and Ballew still lay motionless on the ground. They would probably be waking up soon, but for now they were still out cold.

"Last chance to come to your senses," Garrard called as Smoke reached the doors. "You got caught up in the excitement and said some things in the heat of the moment. I can understand that. I can even forgive it."

Smoke shook his head. "Not a chance in hell, Garrard. And if you're thinkin' that you'll send those three after me, you'll wind up having to replace them anyway, because next time I'll kill them."

"Maybe you'd better not find another place to stay. Maybe you'd better just ride out of Buffalo Flat tonight and keep going."

Smoke had considered that very idea, but two things were stopping him. If he left town, Garrard and Thorn would think he was running because he was scared. He couldn't allow that. For another, there was still Sandor, or Little Bear or whatever the hell his name was, to consider. Smoke had decided he would stay there long enough to see the young man safely on the stage, heading for Casper and points east, and he hated to change course once he'd made up his mind.

"Don't get your hopes up," he told Garrard with an icy smile. "I'll be around for a while yet."

With that, he turned and walked away into the darkness that had fallen over the street. He kept the Colt in his hand and listened intently, in case any of them tried to follow him.

None of them did, not from the livery barn, anyway. But as he passed the stagecoach office, he thought he saw movement on the porch. He kept going, and after a few yards he was sure of it. He heard light footsteps behind him.

When they closed in, he stopped short and turned, moving fast as he brought the gun up. His thumb was looped over the hammer and his finger was taut on the trigger, but he held off on firing as he heard a startled gasp from the shadowy figure behind him.

Unless he was mistaken, the voice belonged to a woman.

Chapter 15

"Blast it, ma'am," Smoke said as he carefully lowered the Colt's hammer. "You almost got your brains blown out. Didn't anybody ever tell you not to sneak up behind a fella like that?"

"I-I'm sorry, Mister . . . West, isn't it?" She had a good voice, young and strong, and in the faint light that came from nearby buildings, he saw that she stood straight and slender, as graceful as a deer.

"How do you know me?" Smoke asked.

"I heard my father and those other men talking to you, there in the barn."

"Your father's Jason Garrard?"

"That's right."

Smoke immediately felt a little uncomfortable. If the young woman had heard what went on in the barn, then she had heard the things he'd said to her father. He had meant every word he'd told Garrard, but he would have preferred the man's daughter hadn't heard them.

As if sensing his discomfort, the woman went on, "Don't worry, Mr. West, I'm not upset with you. I can't stand those awful gunmen who work for my father. I'm glad they didn't hurt you." She held out her hand. "My name is Robin Garrard."

Smoke hesitated. He had never been that easy around women to start with, at least not until he'd met Nicole. Her death had left him devastated, and although months had passed since then, the pain hadn't dulled. Only the hatred he felt for the men responsible kept it at bay. There was no room in his life for something as gentle as the touch of a woman.

Yet, he'd been raised to be a gentleman. He didn't want to hurt Robin Garrard's feelings. So before that moment of hesitation stretched out long enough to be awkward, he shifted the Colt to his other hand, took her hand, and held it for a second. He couldn't help but notice her skin was cool and smooth, and her fingers were strong.

"Buck West, ma'am."

"I'm pleased to meet you, Mr. West."

"Pleasure's all mine, ma'am."

She laughed, and with a directness that told him she had spent some time in the West, whether or not she'd been born and raised there, she said, "Not hardly. I took great pleasure in seeing you wallop Mitch Thorn. He's my father's right-hand man, and he's got it in his head that he'll be even more than that someday by marrying me."

"I take it that's not gonna happen?"

"Not in a million years," Robin said. "I know that you're looking for a place to stay . . ."

She wasn't going to invite him to her home, was she? Smoke knew Garrard wouldn't stand for that. He didn't want it, either.

"If you'd like, there's a little storage room in the school you can use," she went on. "It's not much, but there's a cot in there and it's fairly comfortable. The children sometimes use it to lie down if they don't feel well. I've napped on it before, too."

"You're the teacher?" Smoke asked.

"That's right. There's also a shed out back where you can put your mount. Some of the children have to ride in from out of town, and they put their horses there."

"I'm obliged for the offer, ma'am, but why are you doing this? To get back at your pa?"

"My father and I disagree on many things, Mr. West, but I love him," Robin said. "I won't let that stand in the way of helping someone I think has been treated unfairly." She paused. "If I just wanted to annoy Father I'd make sure he knew what I was doing, but to tell the truth, I'd prefer he didn't find out about this. He's so wrapped up in his businesses he never comes near the school, so I don't think there's much chance he'll know."

Something about the whole setup rubbed Smoke the wrong way, but at least it was an answer to his problem. He could have camped somewhere out of town—he had spent the vast majority of his nights sleeping on the ground the past few years—but if he did he wouldn't be able to keep an eye on Sandor as well.

So he said, "All right. I appreciate it, Miss Garrard. I'll get my gear from the hotel. Where's the school?"

"On the northern end of town, set back to the left from the trail. I'll go up there now and light a lantern, so you'll be able to find it without any trouble."

"I'm not sure a lady should be wandering around after dark by herself like that."

"I'll be fine," she said with a crisp note in her voice. "I'm used to taking care of myself."

"All right," Smoke agreed. It was her business, not his.

They parted company, Smoke heading up the street toward the hotel while Robin crossed it at an angle. When he reached the hotel, Smoke holstered the Colt and buckled on the gunbelt again. He took the dagger, which he had tucked behind his belt, and replaced it in the sheath sewed into his boot top.

The clerk greeted him by saying, "Hello, Mr. West. Did you find the livery stable all right?"

"Yeah, but I won't be stayin'," Smoke replied. "I'll have to ask you for my money back."

The man looked surprised. "I'm not sure we can do that . . ."

he began. The look in Smoke's eyes made him swallow, nod, and go on, "But of course since you didn't make use of our accommodations, it wouldn't be fair to charge you."

He returned the money Smoke had given him earlier. As Smoke put it away, he said, "I'll go upstairs and get my saddlebags and rifle, then I won't trouble you anymore."

"It's no trouble, Mr. West, I assure you."

Smoke nodded and went up the stairs. He collected his Henry rifle and saddlebags from room 3, then went back down to the lobby.

The clerk indulged his obvious curiosity by asking, "Are you leaving town so soon?"

"Nope, just got a better offer on a place to stay." Smoke left it at that. He was sure the clerk would report his conversation to Garrard later. Let Garrard wonder where that better place was.

As he stepped out onto the porch, his instincts warned him, and the sound of a gun being cocked somewhere nearby confirmed the danger. He dropped the saddlebags and threw himself forward, landing on his belly at the edge of the porch as a revolver roared on his left. Smoke rolled away from the shot, even as another blast sounded and a slug chewed splinters from the planks near him. He worked the Henry's lever as he rolled, and when he came to a stop he fired at the spot where he'd seen muzzle flashes, aiming a little to the left and below them.

A rifle cracked from the entrance alcove of a darkened building across the street. Smoke heard the bullet whistle past his head and thud into the hotel's front wall. He swung the Henry in that direction and fired twice, squeezing the trigger as fast as he could work the rifle's lever. The large pane of glass in the building's door shattered in a million pieces as a body hurtled back into it.

Smoke rolled again, under the elevated railing that ran along the edge of the porch, dropping to the street between the hitch rail and the porch. Seven and a couple other horses tied there gave him some cover. Not wanting to endanger the animals by staying where he was, he powered to his feet and raced to the corner where a water trough stood. A six-gun roared a couple times, somewhere in the night, but the bullets didn't find him. He threw himself down behind the water trough, confident that its thick walls would stop any slugs that came his way.

He was sure he had wounded at least one of the bush-whackers, and since their attempt to kill him had failed, he didn't think they would hang around for very long. Already people were starting to venture cautiously out of some nearby buildings and shout questions as they tried to determine what all the shooting was about.

Smoke stayed where he was. The gunfire had stopped, which didn't surprise him. After a couple minutes, he heard Marshal Thad Calhoun's loud, angry voice demanding, "What the hell's goin' on here? Who's doin' all that shootin'?"

Smoke spotted the lawman coming along the street, a shot-gun clutched tightly in his hands. Without rising from behind the water trough, he called, "Over here, Marshal. Take it easy with that Greener. The ruckus seems to be over."

Calhoun swung the double-barrel in the direction of Smoke's voice. "Who's there? Speak up, damn it, or I'll dust your hide with buckshot!"

"It's Buck West, Marshal." That new name of his was getting quite a workout this evening, Smoke thought.

"Who?"

"The fella from Hammond's store this afternoon."

"The one who stuck up for that redskin?"

"That's right."

"What kind of trouble are you causin' now, West?"

Smoke kept a tight rein on his temper. "I'd just stepped out of the hotel when a couple of hombres started shootin' at me, Marshal. I don't think it was exactly me who caused the trouble."

"You hit?"

"No, but you might look in the doorway of that building across the street. I think the fella who was over there went through the glass in the door when I tagged him with my Henry."

"Stand up where I can see you," Calhoun ordered.

Smoke did so. Even if one or both of the bushwhackers were still lurking close by, he doubted if they would try to kill him with the marshal standing right there. Though he could be wrong about that, he thought as he remembered Calhoun worked for Jason Garrard more so than he did for the town. Smoke kept his rifle ready in case he needed it.

Calhoun trained the twin muzzles of his shotgun on the doorway across the street as he walked toward it. When he got there, he called over his shoulder, "Glass is busted out, all right. Scattered all over the boardwalk. I don't see no wounded bushwhacker, however."

"I guess he wasn't hurt bad enough to keep him from crawling away," Smoke said.

Calhoun lowered the Greener and thumbed a match to life. "Blood on the floor inside," he announced. "Some of that might be from gettin' cut up by the broken glass. Guess he could have gone out the back."

Smoke walked in front of the hotel toward the spot where the other man had lain in wait for him. As he passed the front window he saw the clerk looking goggle-eyed at him. Smoke gave the man a grim smile.

He fished out a match and lit it like the marshal had, then used the light from it to study the ground at the corner of the building. He saw a number of footprints in the dust, but dozens of people had walked along there during the day. The tracks were just a muddled mess. Smoke didn't see any blood on the ground, so he assumed the hurried shot he'd sent in that direction had missed.

It seemed to have come close enough to make the bushwhacker take off for the tall and uncut, though.

Calhoun came over to Smoke and said, "I'd ask you if you

knew who took those shots at you, West, but you're such a troublesome gent it probably could have been anybody."

"Or maybe it was Gus Harley and Earl Ballew," Smoke snapped.

"Couldn't have been. Those boys were with me just a little while ago when the shootin' started." Calhoun smirked in the light that came through the hotel's big front window. "They were filin' a report about how you assaulted them and tried to kill Mitch Thorn with a knife. I'd be justified in takin' you in and lockin' you up right now for attempted murder."

"So that's how it is, is it?"

"Yeah." Calhoun shifted the shotgun a little, and Smoke knew the marshal would use it if he gave the lawman an excuse. "That's how it is."

"Well, then," Smoke said quietly, "you just go ahead and try to arrest me, Marshal."

He was sick and tired of it. If he had to kill the corrupt badge-toter, so be it. Calhoun was just another of Garrard's hired gunmen, and the badge on his vest didn't change that. Maybe it did in the eyes of the law, but at the moment Smoke was too fed up to care about that.

After a few tense seconds, Calhoun said, "Those fellas ain't said for sure yet if they want to press charges, so we'll let it go for now. Might be a wise thing for you to get out of town while the gettin's good."

"Folks keep telling me that," Smoke said, "and I keep on not paying any attention to it."

Calhoun grunted. "Suit yourself. Whatever happens is on your head."

"That's fine with me," Smoke said.

The marshal turned and stomped off down the street toward his office. Smoke watched him go, then turned to the hitch rail and jerked Seven's reins loose. He swung up into the saddle and rode north. Anyone keeping an eye on him might think he was leaving town.

When he reached the outskirts of the settlement, he turned

to look for the lamp that Robin Garrard had said she would light for him. Spotting a yellow glow in some trees, he headed for it and came up to a long, whitewashed building in a clearing. The door was open, letting the lamplight spill through it, and in its glow Smoke saw a large bell hung from an iron post. That would be the school bell, he thought with a faint smile. Robin would ring it every morning to summon her students to class.

He dismounted, wrapped the reins around the post, and went up the two steps to the open door. As he looked through it, he saw that two people were in the school at the moment, both of them standing by the desk at the front of the room. They were so engrossed in what they were doing they must not have heard him ride up, he thought.

They were in each other's arms, mouths pressed together in a passionate kiss.

Smoke cleared his throat, and the couple broke the kiss and sprang apart guiltily. He got his first good look at Robin Garrard, who was in her early twenties and very pretty, with waves of red hair around her head and a dusting of freckles across her nose.

Smoke got a good look at the man who'd been kissing her, but it wasn't the first time he had seen the hombre. Sandor/Little Bear stared at Smoke in surprise and said, "Buck! What are you doing here?"

Chapter 16

"Oh, Sandy," Robin said. "I hadn't had a chance to tell you yet."

Smoke chuckled. "Sandy," he repeated. "That's a good name for you."

The young man flushed a darker red than his usual coppery hue. "Tell me what?" he said to Robin.

"That Mr. West is going to stay here tonight, too," she said.

"He is? Why?"

"Because he got in a big fight with Mitch Thorn and his cronies, and then my father threatened him. You can't blame Mr. West for not wanting to stay at the hotel."

"No, I suppose not," Sandy said. He looked at Smoke and went on, "You had trouble with those three again?"

"Again?" Robin echoed.

Sandy nodded. "Buck here is the one who stepped in when Thorn and the others threw me out of Mr. Hammond's store this afternoon. I thought there was going to be a gunfight then and there, but Thorn backed down."

"That must have stuck in his craw," Smoke said. "He and the other two caught up to me later on at the livery stable."

"Father set all three of them on Mr. West," Robin said, frowning in disapproval. "He told them to give him a good beating. But it was them who wound up taking the beating!"

Sandy looked like he had a hard time believing that, but Smoke was standing right there in front of him as proof. "You should be careful," the young man said. "They will want to settle the score with you."

"Reckon they already tried that," Smoke said.

Robin's hand went to her mouth as she gasped in alarm. "Those shots a little while ago! They tried to kill you!"

"I figure Harley and Ballew did, anyway. Thorn's gun arm was hurt during that fight at the stable. I don't think he could have even handled a rifle."

"But you weren't hurt?"

Smoke shook his head. "No. I'm pretty sure I winged one of the men who bushwhacked me outside the hotel and may have wounded the other one, too, but they both got away. Marshal Calhoun claims it couldn't have been Harley and Ballew because they were with him when the shooting started, but I don't think he's telling the truth."

"You're right to feel that way," Robin said. "He's a terrible excuse for a lawman. He just does whatever my father tells him and lets Thorn and the others get away with doing anything they want."

Sandy turned to Robin and put his hands on her shoulders. "You should come back east with me," he told her. "This is no place for you, whether your father is here or not."

His words obviously affected her. She looked emotionally torn as she said, "He's all the family I have left, Sandy. I . . . I can't just desert him. Anyway, if I left Buffalo Flat, who would teach the children?"

"The town could get another teacher! If you came with me, we wouldn't have to hide the way we feel about each other." Sandy shot a wary glance at Smoke. "You probably disapprove, too."

"It's none of my business one way or the other," Smoke said with a shrug. "The best friend I ever had was an old mountain man who had plenty of Indian wives and a passel

of kids by them. I don't see anything wrong with it bein' the
other way around."

"I don't want a lot of Indian husbands." Robin smiled.
"Only one. A big family might be nice, though."

"We can talk about that after I've gotten my education,"
Sandy said stiffly. "I want to be able to provide properly
for you."

"I'd go and live in the Crow village with you, if that's what
you wanted. I've told you that."

Sandy shook his head. "No, you deserve better than that."

"What could be better than being with the man I love?"

A bitter taste rose in the back of Smoke's throat. Seeing the
two of them like that, so obviously in love, reminded him too
much of the all-too-brief time he and Nicole had shared. They
had barely even gotten to know their son when tragedy struck.

He hoped Sandy and Robin never had to go through something like that, but given the opposition bound to plague their
marriage, they might have all sorts of trouble.

Smoke was a long way from being their guardian angel.
They would have to work out their problems for themselves,
like everybody else. The one thing he could do was see to it
that Sandy didn't get killed before he left Buffalo Flat for
the east.

"Might be wise for the two of you not to do your courting
in a well-lit room with an open door," he advised. "You'd
better blow that lamp out before you leave, Sandy."

"I'm not leaving," the young man replied. "Robin said I
could stay here at the school until the stagecoach arrives day
after tomorrow."

Smoke looked at Robin and raised an eyebrow.

"I know," she said. "I'm sorry. When I asked you to stay
here, Mr. West, I didn't think about the fact that I'd already
promised the cot to Sandy."

"Don't worry about it," Smoke told her with a wry smile.
"You said there's a shed out back?"

"That's right."

"Has it got any hay in it?"

"Yes, it does."

"Then that's where I'll spread my bedroll. It'll still be more comfortable than the hard ground."

"Are you sure you don't mind?"

"It'll be fine," Smoke told her. "I've slept in plenty worse places."

"All right. I am sorry, though." She turned to Sandy. "I have to go. Father will be getting home soon, and he'll wonder where I am. We don't want him coming down here to look for me."

"No, we don't," he agreed. He glanced at Smoke.

Trying not to chuckle, Smoke shifted his saddlebags on his shoulder and said, "I'll take my horse and go on around back. Good night, you two."

He went back out the front door of the school, pulling it closed behind him. As he led the Appaloosa toward the rear of the building, he said, "Looks like we'll be bunkin' together tonight, as usual, Seven. Far be it from me to stand in the way of young love."

The first part of the night Smoke's dreams were haunted by images of blood and death. Eventually he fell into a deep sleep, and if he dreamed any after that, he didn't remember it when he awoke the next morning. As he stretched, he heard rustlings in the hay on which he had spread his blankets and knew the rats that had spent the night with him were scurrying back into their hidey-holes.

He would rather spend the nights with furry, long-tailed rats than human ones like Garrard, Thorn, Harley, and Ballew, he reflected as he sat up. At least the four-legged ones were honest about being vermin.

He hated to think of Robin's father like that, since she seemed like a nice young woman, but facts were facts. Garrard had already seized a lot of power in the town and intended to have more before he was through. Smoke hadn't forgotten Garrard's comment about forcing Luther Hammond's general store out of business. Once he'd succeeded in doing that, Garrard would move on to whatever struck his fancy next and try to close his iron fist around that as well. He would keep going until someone stood up to him and tried to stop him.

When that day came, Smoke wondered, would Garrard have Thorn and the other gunmen kill whoever opposed him? Smoke didn't think it was beyond the realm of possibility.

He got to his feet. As was his habit, he had woken early. The sun wasn't up yet, although the eastern sky was rosy with its approach. He saw a pump behind the school with a bucket hanging on its handle. It would feel good to dump a bucket of cold water over his head. Nothing like it to wake a fella up properly in the morning, he thought.

He buckled on his gunbelt before he stepped out of the shed. Even groggy from sleep, he was careful.

He walked over to the pump and took the bucket from the handle. Holding it under the spigot, he began working the handle up and down. Water ran into the bucket.

Smoke had it almost full when a scream sounded from inside the school building.

He dropped the bucket, letting the water he had pumped into it splash on the ground. By the time the bucket landed, Smoke's first leap had carried him halfway to the school's rear door. He drew his right-hand Colt as he reached for the latch on the door and slapped it back. He jerked the door open.

No lamps had been lit yet. Smoke hadn't even known that Robin was already there, but the front door stood wide open, letting dawn light the big main room. Robin struggled in the grip of a tall man with his right arm in a black sling. Smoke recognized him as Mitch Thorn.

Wherever Thorn was, Harley and Ballew were usually close by. The two men had hold of Sandy. Harley held the young man's arms while Ballew stood in front of him, hammering punches into Sandy's midsection.

"Beat the damn 'breed to death!" Thorn ordered, raising his voice to be heard over Robin's cries. "He tried to molest Miss Garrard!"

"No!" Robin said. "That's not what happened! He and I—"

Thorn had only one good arm, the left one, but it was wrapped around Robin's throat. He tightened it and jerked her harder against him. "Shut up, you little slut!" he told her as he choked off her protests. "I know damn good and well what was going on here, but the rest of the town doesn't have to. We'll kill that bastard, and nobody else'll have to know that you were degrading yourself with a filthy redskin!"

Smoke drew his other Colt and eared back the hammers on both guns. "The only ones who are gonna die here are you and your friends if you don't let those folks go, Thorn," he warned, his powerful voice filling the schoolroom.

"It's West!" Ballew yelled. As he turned to face Smoke, the cuts and scratches on his face came into view, as did the bloodstained bandage wrapped around his upper left arm. When Smoke saw those things, he knew that Ballew was the one his bullet had knocked through the glass in the door across the street the night before. That left Harley to be the other bushwhacker. He didn't appear to be wounded, so Smoke figured again that his shot had missed.

Thorn turned hurriedly, hanging on to Robin so that she had to come with him. That put her between him and Smoke.

"It takes a mighty yellow son of a bitch to hide behind a woman," Smoke growled.

"You just don't know how to keep from sticking your nose into things that are none of your business, do you, West?" Thorn said. "What is it? You want this tramp for yourself, now that the Indian's through with her?"

Smoke didn't dignify that question with an answer. Instead, he said, "I'm gonna take particular pleasure in killin' you, Thorn."

"How are you gonna do that? I can't draw on you. You ruined my gun arm, remember? Only way you can kill me is by murdering me, and you'll hang for that."

Smoke shook his head. "Garrard's little tin badge of a marshal won't ever arrest me."

"No? You gonna kill him, too? You want to spend the rest of your life looking over your shoulder while every lawman in the West hunts you? Because that's what'll happen once word gets around that you gunned down a peace officer. The rest of the star packers won't know what really happened here. They'll just know that Buck West murdered a fellow lawman."

In that case, Smoke thought, he would just forget about Buck West and come up with some other name. But his description might follow him, and sooner or later Thorn's prediction might well come true. Smoke could find himself facing an honest lawman, or a whole posse of them, and might have to choose between death and becoming a real outlaw.

"Let Miss Garrard go," he said. "Your grudge is with me, not her or Sandy."

"The hell it is! I've been after this tramp for months to marry me, or at least to let me court her, and she always says no! But then I come in here this morning and find her letting that dirty Indian put his hands all over her. No, sir. She owes me, and she's gonna pay up."

"She doesn't owe you a damn thing," Smoke insisted.

Thorn backed toward the front door, dragging Robin with him. Harley still had hold of Sandy and was using him as a human shield, and Ballew was staying behind both of them with his gun drawn. Smoke couldn't get a shot at any of them without risking Robin or Sandy being hit.

"Earl, get the horses," Thorn ordered. "We're getting out of here."

Ballew was the closest to the door. He ducked out through it, and Smoke still wasn't able to get a shot.

Thorn sneered over Robin's shoulder. "You want her, you'll have to come after her, West. And we'll be ready for you this time. You won't ride away, you bastard."

"Not until I've killed all three of you," Smoke said.

"Big talk for a man who doesn't hold any cards."

Smoke heard hoofbeats outside and knew that Ballew had brought up their mounts. If Thorn and Harley made it outside, they could get away with their prisoners before Smoke could stop them.

But he couldn't fire without risking the lives of those prisoners. He seethed with rage and frustration and looked for some way to turn the tables on Thorn.

Suddenly, Thorn lunged back through the doorway, taking Robin with him. She managed to get a muffled scream past his choking arm, but that was all. Sandy was still stunned from the beating they had given him, so he wasn't able to put up a fight as Harley leaped after Thorn and Robin.

Smoke raced along the aisle after them.

Ballew popped in the doorway, the gun in his fist blasting out shots. Smoke weaved and fired, saw Ballew jerk under the impact of the lead and stagger to the side. Ballew managed to stay on his feet, and emptied the revolver at Smoke, who was forced to dive behind one of the desks as bullets whistled around his ears.

Ballew ran back outside. Smoke scrambled up and went after him. He reached the door in time to see that Thorn and Harley were already in the saddle. Since Thorn had only one good arm, Robin sat on the back of Harley's horse in front of him. He had an arm wrapped around her waist. Sandy was stumbling around nearby, still half-senseless, while Ballew, wounded again, was trying to climb onto his horse.

Smoke took all that in instantly, just as Thorn yelled, "Kill the redskin!"

The gun in Harley's free hand came up and roared. Blood flew in the air from Sandy's head as the bullet smashed into it. Robin let out a wrenching scream as she saw him fall.

Smoke opened fire at Thorn, but just as he pulled the trigger, Ballew finally made it into the saddle and his horse lurched to the side. That put Ballew in the path of Smoke's bullet. It punched into the man's right ear and bored on through his skull into his brain. Ballew toppled off the horse, his foot hanging in the stirrup. He was dragged along the ground as the animal bolted in fear from all the gunshots and the smell of powder smoke and blood in the air.

Thorn and Harley galloped off to the north as Smoke leveled his guns at them. He grimaced as he realized the horses' initial burst had already put them out of handgun range. But he didn't think they could outrun Seven. The Appaloosa had speed and stamina to spare.

As Smoke holstered his Colts and turned, intending to run behind the building to the shed and throw his saddle on Seven, he heard Sandy groan. Smoke had seen the young man shot in the head and assumed he was dead. Sandy was still alive, but he might not be for very long, without help.

Smoke glanced in the direction where Thorn and Harley had disappeared with Robin. Dust still hazed the air as it settled from being kicked up by their horses' hooves, but that was the only sign of them.

He could track them, Smoke thought. Preacher had taught him plenty about how to follow a trail. Although the two men were opening up a lead, Smoke knew he could find them.

And when he did, they would die.

He ran to Sandy's side and dropped to his knees to see what he could do for the wounded young man.

Chapter 17

Smoke took hold of Sandy's chin and turned the young man's head so that he could see the wound. Blood covered the whole right side of Sandy's face, but when Smoke parted the thick, dark hair above the ear, he saw that the slug had torn a gash in the scalp instead of penetrating. Wounds like that always bled like crazy, so they looked bad, but Smoke felt confident Sandy would live. The bullet had knocked him out and he would have a hell of a headache when he woke up, but other than that he ought to be fine.

The shots had drawn some attention in town, even at that early hour. Smoke heard heavy footsteps hurrying toward him, and when he looked up he saw Marshal Calhoun about twenty feet away, shotgun in hand.

Calhoun's eyes locked with his. The marshal yelled, "You've killed him!" and moved to swing the Greener up. Smoke doubted if Calhoun was aware of what Thorn and Harley had done. But it didn't matter. Smoke saw in Calhoun's eyes he was going to take the opportunity to kill him.

Before Calhoun could do more than start to make his move, the Colt in Smoke's right hand snapped up and roared. Calhoun came to a sudden stop as the .44 slug ripped through his right arm. He yelled in pain, dropped the shotgun, and staggered back a step as he clapped his left hand over the wound. His face contorted with hate as he let go of his right arm and tried to make an awkward grab for his holstered pistol with his left hand.

Smoke already had his revolver's hammer eared back again. "Don't do it, Marshal," he warned. "I don't want to kill you."

"You . . . you can't get away with this, damn you!" Calhoun said. He took his hand away from his gun, and used it to clutch his wounded arm again. "You shot me!"

"Figured that was better than letting you splatter me all over with that Greener," Smoke said coolly. "Anyway, if you'd cut loose at me, you would've killed Sandy here, too."

"The Indian? He ain't dead? He's got blood all over his face!"

"He's just creased and knocked out," Smoke explained. "Now, Ballew over there is dead."

Calhoun sneered. "I suppose you didn't kill him, either."

"Actually, I did," Smoke admitted. "It was sort of an accident, though. I was trying to kill Mitch Thorn, and Ballew's head got in the way of my slug. Those other wounds are from when he tried to kill me last night and then again this morning."

"Why were you tryin' to kill Thorn?"

"To stop him and Gus Harley from kidnapping Miss Garrard."

Calhoun's eyes opened wide with shock, confirming Smoke's hunch that the actions of Thorn and his companions at the school had been unplanned, spur of the moment things. Calhoun didn't know about them.

"Miss Garrard?" Calhoun repeated huskily. "The schoolteacher? Mr. Garrard's daughter?"

Smoke straightened to his feet. "That's right. They threw her on Harley's horse and took off with her, heading north."

"Son of a *bitch*! When Garrard hears about that—" Several of the townspeople had come up behind Calhoun. One of them turned and took off at a run, obviously going to spread the news of Robin's kidnapping. Calhoun heard the rapid footsteps, turned his head and saw the man, and yelled, "Hey! Come back here!"

The townie ignored the command. Jason Garrard was a powerful man, probably the most powerful man in town, and naturally some of the citizens would be eager to curry favor with him.

"All hell's gonna break loose now," Calhoun said with a sigh. "You'd better tell me what happened here, West."

"Save it for when Garrard gets here," Smoke said. "Right now, this young fella needs a doctor."

"The redskin?" Calhoun sounded like he thought it was ridiculous to waste medical attention on Sandy.

"Where's the doctor's office?" Smoke asked, his voice as hard as flint.

Calhoun sighed. "Pick him up and bring him along. I'll show you. Got to go there myself, to have the sawbones see about this arm of mine you ventilated."

"You wouldn't have gotten hurt if you hadn't lost your head, Marshal." Smoke holstered his Colts and bent to slip his arms around the still unconscious Sandy. He lifted the young man without much effort.

Because he didn't trust Calhoun he kept a close eye on the lawman as Calhoun led him along the main street to a neat cottage with a sign out front indicating that Dr. Peter Neal practiced medicine there.

Dr. Neal was a slender man in late middle-age, with a shock of white hair and spectacles that perched on the end of his long nose. He checked both wounds quickly once Smoke had carried Sandy into his surgery and Calhoun followed along behind.

"The head wound is slightly more serious," he decided, "so I'll treat it first. You'll have to wait your turn, Marshal. Try not to bleed too much on my floor."

That didn't sit well with Calhoun, but he just grumbled a little about it as he sat down to wait.

Jason Garrard burst in a couple of minutes later while Neal was cleaning the wound on Sandy's scalp. "Someone told me you'd come in here," he said with a wild look in his eyes. "What's this about Thorn carrying off my daughter?"

"Reckon it's true, Mr. Garrard," Calhoun said. He nodded toward Smoke. "West there can tell you about it."

Garrard glared at Smoke. "You! What's your part in this, West?"

"I just happened to be there at the school early this morning when Thorn, Harley, and Ballew burst in and attacked Sandy," Smoke said.

"Who?"

"The redskin," Calhoun put in.

"What was he doing there with my daughter?"

Smoke didn't try to sugar-coat it. "I imagine he was kissing her, from the way Thorn was so upset about it."

Garrard turned to stare with murderous fury at Sandy. "Why, the damn, dirty savage! I'll see that he hangs for molesting Robin!"

"He didn't molest her, you damn fool," Smoke snapped, out of patience with the whole thing. "The two of them are in love, and I reckon they have been for a while. That's one reason Sandy was goin' back east for a white man's education, so he'd feel worthy of marrying Miss Garrard."

"Marrying?" Garrard repeated in a voice that trembled from the depth of his rage. "That Indian wanted to marry my daughter?"

"And she wanted to marry him. In fact, she said she would go and live in the Crow village with him if that's what he wanted."

Garrard's hands clenched into fists as he took a step toward Smoke. "That's a lie!" he roared.

"I'll let you get away with callin' me a liar, Garrard . . . once," Smoke grated. "What I just told you is the truth, and you'd damn well better get used to it."

Garrard stared at him for a long moment, then with a visible effort choked out, "What about Thorn?"

"He wanted to marry Miss Garrard, too, but she wasn't interested."

Garrard snorted. "I never would have let her marry a cheap gunman, either."

"I don't know what the three of them were doing at the school so early," Smoke went on. "Maybe Thorn knew that Miss Garrard showed up there early to get ready for the day and wanted to see her. But they caught her and Sandy together and Thorn went loco. He told Harley and Ballew to beat Sandy to death. There's no tellin' what he had in mind for your daughter, Garrard, but when I took a hand, he made her a hostage and dragged her out with him. Harley shot Sandy, I shot Ballew, and Thorn and Harley got away with Miss Garrard. That's the whole story."

Garrard digested it all for a moment, then angled his head toward Calhoun. "How'd the marshal get shot?"

"I did that in self-defense because he was about to cut loose at me with a shotgun without finding out what was going on first."

"So you admit shooting a lawman? You'll go to prison for that, West."

Calhoun spoke up, saying, "Maybe you better think twice about that, Mr. Garrard. With this bullet hole in my arm, I ain't gonna be in any shape to go after Thorn and Harley."

Garrard's bushy red eyebrows rose in surprise. "Are you suggesting that I turn to this . . . this gunfighter for help?"

"West might be the only one in these parts who can handle Thorn and Harley. Even wounded like he is, I reckon Mitch Thorn's as dangerous as a cougar. And he's got Miss Garrard as a hostage, to boot."

Garrard's nostrils flared as he drew in a deep breath. He glared at Smoke and said, "I can't believe I'm doing this . . . but how about it, West? Will you go after those bastards and get my daughter back? I'll pay you any price you ask."

"I told you once before what you could do with your job offers, Garrard."

The man's face mottled with rage. "Damn it, West—"

Smoke held up a hand to stop him. "I'll go after them," he said, "but not because you asked me to. You don't know it, but I met Miss Garrard last night. She heard that ruckus at the livery barn and offered me a place to stay. I slept in the shed behind the school last night. That's how come I was there this morning when the trouble started."

Garrard looked like he couldn't believe it. "Sometimes Robin meddles in things that are none of her business," he growled. "But I guess all that really matters is that somebody is going after her."

"I'll come with you once I get this wound bandaged up, West," Calhoun offered. "I can deputize you, and since the kidnappin' took place here in town, that'll make it legal for us to go after Thorn and Harley."

The offer surprised Smoke. He wasn't sure he wanted Calhoun's help. It was doubtful that the marshal would prove to be of much assistance, with that wounded arm. But Calhoun's attitude toward him seemed to have shifted, and he supposed it wouldn't hurt to have some legal standing.

Calhoun would be mighty surprised, though, if he knew he was offering a deputy's job to the notorious Smoke Jensen, gunfighter and outlaw.

"All right," Smoke said, "providing the doc here can get you patched up pretty quickly so we can get started trailing them."

Dr. Neal glanced around. "I'm almost finished with the young man. I've cleaned his wound and checked for damage to the skull. There doesn't seem to be any. I'll put a dressing on there, and then I can tend to Marshal Calhoun."

Garrard said to Smoke, "What can I do to help? You need guns, ammunition, any other supplies? Anything Hammond has in his store, I'll buy it."

"How about you promise to leave Hammond alone and not try to put him out of business?"

Garrard's mouth tightened in response to Smoke's suggestion. "You can't dictate to a man how he's supposed to do business."

"You can if you're plannin' to risk your life trying to rescue his daughter from outlaws," Smoke said.

Garrard glared at him again, but then gave him a curt nod. "It's a deal. Bring Robin back safely to me, and I won't open a store to compete with Hammond. You have my word on it."

Smoke didn't know how good Garrard's word was, but he had to accept it for the time being.

Dr. Neal got to work on Calhoun's arm. The wound was a shallow one. The bullet had missed the bone, so all Neal had to do was swab out the hole and bind it up.

Smoke left the doctor's office, intending to return to the school and saddle Seven for the pursuit of Thorn and Harley. Garrard followed him. They found a large crowd waiting for them outside.

"Is it true that Miss Robin's been kidnapped?" a man called.

Garrard nodded. "It's true. But Mr. West here and Marshal Calhoun are going after the men who did it and bring her back."

Several men stepped forward. One of them said, "If you're puttin' together a posse, Mr. Garrard, we'd be happy to come along. Everybody in town thinks mighty highly of Miss Robin."

"That's right," a woman put in. "She does a fine job teaching the children."

Garrard looked over at Smoke. "What do you think, West?"

Smoke shook his head and said, "I appreciate the offer, folks, but we're just after two men. A posse would complicate things more than it would help. The marshal and I will handle this."

"You don't reckon those two varmints would just give up if they saw a big bunch after them?" a man asked.

"I think if they saw that, they'd be more likely to go ahead and kill Miss Garrard so she couldn't slow them down while they made their getaway," Smoke said bluntly. He turned to Garrard and went on, "Get a couple boxes of .44s, enough supplies for several days and meet me back here. Tell Calhoun to get his horse ready. We'll ride in about fifteen minutes."

Garrard nodded. "All right. West . . . I can't thank you enough for—"

"Save it," Smoke said. Garrard might be sincere in his gratitude, but Smoke didn't want to hear it. The man still reminded him too much of his old enemies Richards, Potter, and Stratton. Smoke had told the truth when he said he wasn't doing it for Garrard. He was doing it for Robin, pure and simple, and maybe a little for Sandy, too.

They would have trouble, now that their romance was out in the open, but Smoke couldn't do anything about that. His only worry was bringing Robin back safely to Buffalo Flat. Once he had done that, and settled things with Thorn and Harley, he intended to ride on without wasting any more time.

His destiny still waited for him in the rough frontier town of Bury, Idaho.

Chapter 18

Smoke and Calhoun left from in front of Dr. Neal's house a quarter of an hour later and rode to the schoolhouse to pick up the trail.

"That Injun woke up while the doc was tending to my arm," Calhoun said. "When he found out that Thorn and Harley carried off Miss Garrard, it was all the doc could do to hold him down. He wanted to come with us. Doc said that'd be too dangerous for him with a head wound like that. He gave the redskin somethin' to make him sleep."

Smoke nodded. "That was probably best. We don't need a wounded man to look after any more than we need a posse tagging along."

"Yeah, you're right about that. You ought to be able to handle two men, especially when one of 'em is wounded. You're pretty slick when it comes to handlin' a gun, ain't you, West?"

Smoke shrugged. "I'm still here."

"Yeah, that's sort of what you have to go by, ain't it?" Calhoun paused. "You know, West, I'm sorry we got off on the wrong foot the way we did. You may not believe it, but it's important to me that I keep the peace in my town. I've been around long enough to know trouble when I see it . . . and mister, you got it writ all over you."

"I don't go looking for trouble," Smoke said. That was stretching the truth a little, because in one special case, he was definitely looking for trouble.

"You don't back away from it when it comes callin', though, do you?"

"The Good Lord didn't put much back-up in me when He made me," Smoke admitted.

"See, that's just what I mean. I took one look at you and knew things'd be more peaceful in Buffalo Flat if you just kept ridin'."

"More peaceful for Jason Garrard, you mean."

"Mr. Garrard's the most important man in town, and I won't apologize for lookin' out for his interests. The more successful he is, the better off the town is."

"That's one way of looking at it," Smoke said. "Other folks might not see it that way."

They had reached the school. Earl Ballew's body was gone, having been carted away by the local undertaker. Smoke swung down from the saddle and hunkered on his heels to study the hoofprints on the ground in front of the building. The children's feet had worn the grass away and it was easy to see the prints in the dirt.

Every set of horseshoes had its own distinctive array of nicks and scratches that showed up in the tracks it left. Smoke was able to pick out the prints left by Thorn's and Harley's mounts, and he committed them to memory so that he would know them when he saw them again.

"They were headed north when they left here," he told Calhoun when he was back on the Appaloosa. "Got any idea where they could have been headed in that direction?"

Calhoun shook his head. "No, but if they curved west, that'd put them in the Big Horns, and there are plenty of places to hide up there."

"The Crow village is in that direction, isn't it? And Bannerman's ranch?"

"Yeah," Calhoun said, "but they could avoid those places easy enough. It's a big mountain range."

Smoke had been over some of it with Preacher and knew that the marshal was right. If they lost the trail, they might never find Thorn and Harley. They didn't have any time to waste.

"We'll be pushin' pretty hard," he warned Calhoun. "You'll have to keep up, wounded arm or no wounded arm."

"You just do what you have to do, West. I'll stick, don't you worry."

Smoke wondered why Calhoun's attitude had changed so dramatically. He wasn't sure he trusted the man and resolved to keep an eye on him. Of course, he would have done that anyway, since he didn't trust anybody all that much since Preacher was dead.

"You never did deputize me," he reminded Calhoun as they rode.

"No, I sure didn't. Forgot all about it. You swear to uphold the law?"

"I do."

"Then I hearby appoint you a deputy marshal of Buffalo Flat, Wyomin' Territory. That good enough, you reckon?"

"It'll do," Smoke said.

Calhoun hadn't really predicted that Thorn and Harley would head for the mountains, just suggested the possibility, but it turned out to be true. The farther away he and Smoke got from town, the more the trail they were following angled toward the Big Horns.

By midday, when Smoke called a halt to study the tracks again, he thought they had narrowed down the lead somewhat, but their quarry was still quite a ways in front of them. Smoke glanced narrow-eyed at the foothills looming closer.

"We won't be able to stop them before they reach the mountains," he told Calhoun.

"Will you be able to find 'em once they get there?"

"Do my best," Smoke promised. Not for the first time, he wished Preacher was still with him. The old man could follow a gnat through a hurricane. His tracking abilities bordered on the mystical, at least as far as Smoke could tell.

"I sure don't want to go back to town and have to tell Mr. Garrard we couldn't find his gal."

"I don't want that, either, although I don't give a damn about Garrard," Smoke said. "Miss Robin struck me as a mighty nice young woman."

"She is," Calhoun agreed. "For the life o' me, I can't see somebody like her mixed up with a dirty Injun. Half-breed, at that. I heard tell old Crazy Bear's squaw is a gypsy woman."

Without responding to the lawman's comments Smoke swung up into the saddle again and took up the trail once more.

They reached the foothills around mid-afternoon and started climbing. Smoke's keen eyes were able to pick up enough signs so they didn't lose the trail, but following it was becoming more difficult. Thorn and Harley hadn't been trying to conceal their tracks. They'd been interested in putting as much distance as possible between them and the settlement. Smoke could tell that had changed and they were trying to throw off any pursuit.

Late that afternoon, the hoofprints merged with the tracks left by half a dozen more horses. Smoke reined in and pointed them out to Calhoun.

"An Injun war party, maybe?" Calhoun suggested nervously.

Smoke shook his head. "No, those mounts were shod. They weren't Indian ponies. From the looks of it, Thorn and Harley joined up with them on purpose."

"Who could that other bunch be? And how'd Thorn know they were up here so he could rendezvous with 'em?"

"I don't know," Smoke said. "I reckon the odds against us have just gone up."

"Maybe we should've brought that posse with us after all."

"No, it's better this way. The others might've blundered into a trap if we'd brought them with us."

It was harder for the riders in the larger group to hide their tracks. Smoke didn't have any trouble following them until the sun dipped behind the mountains and dusk began to settle down over the rugged terrain. He called a halt. "We'll have to wait until morning and pick up the trail then."

"They'll have a whole night to gain on us," Calhoun warned.

"No, they won't," Smoke replied with a shake of his head. "They'll have to stop and camp for the night. It's too big a risk to go blundering around in these mountains after dark. You might fall into a ravine or something like that."

"I hope you're right, West."

Smoke found a place to camp in a small depression. Since full dark hadn't fallen yet, he built a tiny, almost smokeless fire that he used to boil a pot of coffee and fry some bacon. When they were finished with the sparse meal, Smoke put out the fire.

"Need me to change the dressing on that arm?" he asked.

"You'd do that?"

Smoke gave a grim chuckle. "I put the hole there," he said. "I might as well tend to it."

"I'd be obliged," Calhoun said. "Doc Neal told me I needed to change it at least once a day, and I hadn't quite figured out how I was gonna do that. I can fire a gun just fine with my left hand, but it ain't much good for little stuff."

Smoke had noticed Calhoun had replaced his regular holster with a crossdraw rig that he still wore on the right side, so he could use his left hand to draw the gun. "Where'd you get the holster?" he asked.

"Hell, I got a whole drawerful of different kinds of holsters in the office. When Buffalo Flat first got started, it was rough as a cob for a few months. Hombres would get themselves in gunfights and wind up dead, and whatever was left over from their gear that the undertaker didn't claim for plantin' 'em usually wound up bein' confiscated by the marshal." Calhoun grinned. "That'd be me."

Smoke grunted. Calhoun was different from most lawmen he'd run into. He almost seemed to take pride in his low-level corruption.

"You don't think much o' me, do you?" Calhoun went on as if he had read Smoke's thoughts.

"I think the citizens of Buffalo Flat could find themselves a better marshal," Smoke said bluntly.

"Really? Did you see how fast the town was growin'? Did you hear any commotion from the saloons last night?"

"No, but I was up at the school. I might not have been able to hear it."

Calhoun snorted. "There wasn't nothin' to hear. Even Bannerman's wild Texas cowboys behave themselves when they're in town. That's because of me, West. They know I won't stand for any foolishness."

"Except from Garrard's men."

"I told you, Garrard's the biggest man in these parts. If it wasn't for him, the town wouldn't have enough money to pay my wages. Damn right I'm gonna look out for him and his men." Calhoun waved a hand dismissively in the gathering shadows. "Ah, hell, forget it. You and me ain't ever gonna see eye to eye on anything except wantin' to get Miss Robin back safe and sound. Let's let it go at that."

"Sounds good to me," Smoke agreed. "Would you rather stand first watch or second?"

"Second's fine by me."

With that settled, Calhoun turned in, rolling up in his blankets. Smoke sat down with his back against a rock and his rifle across his knees. He worked the Henry's lever so the chamber had a cartridge in it, ready to fire if needed.

The night was quiet enough that Smoke heard the whisper

of wings as an owl glided overhead in search of prey. He peered into the darkness and wondered what else was out there looking for something to kill. He was a predator, too, he thought, a man who lived only for the deaths of other men, three in particular.

Yet that wasn't completely true. He was risking his life by going after Robin Garrard. If he died tonight, tomorrow, or the next day, the job of avenging Nicole, Arthur, and Preacher would never be finished. Did he have any right to take a chance on that?

Would he have a right to call himself a man if he didn't?

He couldn't answer those questions, and he wasn't the sort of hombre to sit around brooding about them—especially when he heard a small noise somewhere near the camp. It was a faint rustle in the grass, but enough to tell him that something—or someone—was out there.

They were coming closer, he realized when he heard the sound again a moment later.

In utter silence, Smoke came to his feet. His finger curled around the trigger of his rifle.

Convinced it was a person, not an animal, he waited, motionless, as whoever it was approached.

A shadowy shape loomed up in the darkness and stepped past him. The intruder didn't even know he was there, Smoke realized. Moving once again in complete silence, he set the rifle on the ground at his feet, then drew his right-hand Colt. He stepped forward, looped his left arm around the intruder's neck, and jerked him backward. At the same time, he pressed the revolver's barrel against the side of the man's head.

"No!" the man exclaimed before Smoke's arm across his throat cut off any more sound. The voice was familiar, and when the muzzle of Smoke's gun prodded against something soft—like a thick bandage—he realized who it was he had grabbed.

"Sandy," Smoke said disgustedly, "what in blazes are you doing here?"

Chapter 19

Smoke's voice awakened Calhoun. The marshal thrashed from his blankets and reached for his gun. "What the hell!" he exploded.

"Take it easy, Calhoun," Smoke said, making his voice sharp so it would penetrate Calhoun's confusion. "You don't need to draw." He let go of Sandy and stepped back. "We've got an unexpected visitor, that's all."

Sandy rubbed his neck where Smoke had grabbed him. "You didn't have to try to choke me," he said.

"You're lucky I didn't wallop you with my gun," Smoke told him. "On top of that bullet graze, it might've been too much even for that thick skull of yours. How'd you manage to follow us out here?"

"I'm a Crow warrior, remember? Well, half of one, anyway. My father taught me how to follow a trail when I was young. Plus I had a pretty good idea Thorn and Harley would head for the mountains. When I got close enough, I just followed the smell of the coffee. I didn't know if I was closing in on your camp, or that of Thorn and Harley."

"If it had been their camp, you would have walked right in there and gotten yourself killed. That would have done Robin a whole heap of good."

"You don't understand!" Sandy protested. "I love her. I'd run any risk for her."

Smoke understood, all right, a lot better than Sandy gave him credit for. But he said, "Those two bastards have joined up with another group. I don't know who they are, but the odds went up by half a dozen."

"Not exactly," Sandy said. "I'm here to help now."

Smoke rolled his eyes, though it was dark and Sandy couldn't see him. He said, "I don't think it's gonna make that much difference. You're wounded."

"So is Marshal Calhoun. I can handle a gun—a rifle, anyway. I've never been much good with a pistol."

"Kid's got a point," Calhoun said, surprising Smoke a little. "I don't care much for redskins, but he'd be an extra gun. You *did* bring a gun with you, Injun?"

"It's on my horse," Sandy said. "I left it tied to a bush a couple hundred yards east of here."

"What good was a rifle going to do you if it's back there?" Smoke asked. It wasn't a question that required an answer. "Go get it," he went on. "We can't take you all the way back to Buffalo Flat, and I don't want you wanderin' around out here by yourself. That might wind up causing us more trouble. I reckon you'll ride with us, but you'll have to keep up."

"Of course," Sandy replied. "I'll fetch my horse."

He came back a few minutes later leading the animal. Smoke asked, "Did you bring any supplies with you?"

Sandy hesitated before saying, "Well . . . no. I left the settlement in such a hurry after slipping out of Dr. Neal's house, I didn't think about it."

"How'd you get out, anyway?" Calhoun wanted to know. "I saw the doc give you somethin' to put you to sleep."

Sandy shook his head. "The powder he mixed up in water didn't work. It must have been old and lost some of its potency. It made me a little drowsy for a while, then wore off. When he stepped out of the room, I left through the window." He put his hand to his bandaged head. "I have quite a headache, but that's all. And that doesn't matter a bit, compared to Robin's safety."

"All right, we've got some jerky you can have," Smoke said. "That'll have to do, because I'm not lighting a fire again. Too much chance the varmints we're after might spot it."

"I understand. Thank you."

Smoke grunted. "No thanks necessary. You'll carry your weight when the time comes."

"I hope so."

"So do I," Smoke said, "because if you don't, we may all die."

Sandy hadn't brought a bedroll with him, either. It wasn't too cold at that time of year, but in the mountains the night air always held a chill. Smoke loaned the young man an extra blanket. Sandy rolled up in it and soon went to sleep. Calhoun turned in again, too.

The rest of Smoke's watch was uneventful. When he judged by the stars that the night was a little more than half over, he nudged Calhoun's shoulder with the rifle barrel.

"Wake up, Marshal," he said. "Your turn to stand guard."

Calhoun grumbled and sat up, shaking his head in an effort to get rid of the cobwebs of sleep. "I'm awake," he said. He threw his blankets aside and climbed to his feet, awkwardly because of his wounded arm. He sat down on the rock where Smoke had been leaning earlier.

"If you hear anything, don't hesitate to wake me," Smoke told him.

"Sure, sure."

Smoke slipped into his bedroll and placed the Henry on the ground close beside him. Using his saddle for a pillow, he lay there with his eyes slitted for a while, watching Calhoun. He didn't know the lawman well enough to trust that he would stay awake.

But Smoke wasn't relying totally on Calhoun. If anyone came lurking around, Seven would notice and make a racket. The Appaloosa was a good sentry.

Half an hour later Calhoun was still alert, looking around and standing up from time to time to roll his shoulders and shake his head. Smoke had to have some rest, so he chanced closing his eyes.

He fell into a light sleep. During his time with Preacher he had mastered the ability to come awake instantly, fully aware of his surroundings, ready to move fast, if anything disturbed him. He owed the old mountain man a debt greater than he could ever repay, even if Preacher had lived. Smoke knew he wouldn't be there if not for Preacher's help and teachings.

The sound of a soft nicker and a stomped hoof from Seven brought Smoke out of his slumber sometime later. A glance at the eastern sky showed him the black night had faded to gray. He heard deep, regular breathing and looked toward the rock. Calhoun had slid down it and sat on the ground. Slumped against it, he was sound asleep. Smoke reached for his rifle.

The ominous sound of a gun hammer ratcheting back stopped him.

"Go ahead," said a voice he recognized as Mitch Thorn's. "I'd like nothing better than to blow you all to hell and gone."

Without turning his head, Smoke cut his eyes toward the voice. In the dim, pre-dawn light, he saw Thorn's booted feet about five feet away. Smoke's gaze traveled up Thorn's legs to the man's body. Thorn had his wounded right arm under the twin barrels of a shotgun, bracing it while he gripped the stock with his left hand. The Greener's barrels and part of the stock had been sawed off, making the weapon short enough that Thorn could handle it mostly one-handed. The recoil would be hard on his left wrist, but if he touched off both barrels, the blast would be so tremendous it would wipe out anybody in front of him for ten yards or more. He wouldn't need to reload and fire again.

At the range he was from Smoke, the double charge of buckshot wouldn't leave enough to recognize as human.

Seven whinnied again as more men moved in from the chilly gloom. A couple covered Sandy, while one man reached down and plucked the revolver from the crossdraw rig worn by Marshal Calhoun. The lawman came awake then, sputtering and cursing. He lunged up, but one of the intruders planted a boot in his chest and shoved him back against the rock.

"Stay put, mister," the man ordered. "Nobody'll get hurt as long as all of you cooperate."

The voices woke Sandy. The young man started to sit up, then reacted with shock as he saw the men pointing their guns at him. He exclaimed something in his gypsy mother's language. At least Smoke assumed that was what it was. The words certainly weren't in English or Crow.

Thorn sauntered forward, still covering Smoke with the sawed-off shotgun. "Now that we got you boys' attention, listen up," he said. "This is how it's gonna be. We're gonna take your horses, your guns, and all your supplies."

"And then leave us out here?" Calhoun asked. "Hell! We'll never make it."

"Well, then, maybe we should just go ahead and kill you right now," Thorn said with a smirk.

Smoke said, "Take it easy. You've got the upper hand, Thorn, so keep talking."

Thorn shrugged. "There's not much more to say. I've told you the deal."

"There's more to it than that," Smoke replied with a shake of his head. "Who are these other hombres? How'd you come to meet up with them? And how did you find us?"

Thorn considered for a moment, then shrugged again. "Might as well indulge your curiosity, I suppose. That last question is the easiest. I figured you were stubborn enough to come after us, West, so we sent a man circling around to keep an eye on our back trail. He spotted you, and when he knew where you'd camped, he came and told us. Then it was just a matter of waiting for that lump of lard who calls himself a marshal to fall asleep. I knew he wouldn't be able to stay awake."

"You got no call to be talkin' about me like that," Calhoun complained. "I covered up for you and Harley and Ballew a whole heap of times, Thorn, and kept you out of trouble when most star packers would've thrown you behind bars!"

Thorn sneered at him. "And you were well paid for it, too. You were never a real lawman. You were just Garrard's lapdog."

"Same thing's true of you," Calhoun said.

"Not hardly. I always had my own plans. Garrard just didn't know about them. That's why I sent for these fellas and had them wait up here in the hills for me until the time was right."

Smoke guessed, "You were going to double-cross Garrard, raid the town, and loot it."

"No, you're wrong, West. I could only do something like that once. But Garrard's making money hand over fist, and it's been piling up in the safe in his office. He plans to ship it back to the bank in Casper before much longer because there isn't a bank in Buffalo Flat yet."

"Your gang was going to hit the stagecoach when Garrard's money was on it," Smoke said as he began to understand.

"That's right. They'd make it look good, too, before I drove them away and saved the money. Garrard would have been so grateful to me for saving his money that he'd convince Robin to marry me."

Sandy burst out, "She would never marry you, you . . . you . . ." More curses in the gypsy tongue came from the young man.

"Shut up that jabbering, redskin," Thorn said. "She wouldn't have had much choice in the matter. After all, I'd be the man who saved her father from being ruined."

Smoke put the rest of the plan together in his head. "Then once you were married to her, Garrard would've had some sort of fatal accident . . . leaving you in charge of the whole town."

"That's right," Thorn said. "We'd have bled it dry, too, and left there as rich men." His face contorted with anger and hate. "But you and this filthy Indian ruined all that, West. Now it'll never happen."

"You mean you ruined it for yourself when you lost your head yesterday morning," Smoke said.

"Well, what the hell would you do if you walked in and found the woman you loved bein' pawed by a dirty 'breed?" Thorn demanded.

Smoke smiled grimly. "You didn't count on fallin' in love with her, did you, Thorn? She was just supposed to be part of the plan, a means to an end. Now you've risked everything because you fell in love with her."

"Shut up!" Thorn lifted the sawed-off greener. "Just shut up, West. I've changed my mind. We're not going to let you bastards live. The only way we can salvage anything is by looting the town, the way you said, and I'd just as soon not have you behind me somewhere while I'm doin' that."

"So you're going to kill us?"

Thorn smiled. "That's the new plan."

"Where's Robin?"

"Don't worry about her. She's close by. I've got a man keeping an eye on her."

"You'll have to kill her, too, you know."

"No!" Sandy cried.

Thorn shook his head. "No, she'll come with us. She'll understand that's the only thing she can do. Might take her a while, but she'll come around."

"Why don't you bring her in?" Smoke suggested. "At least let her say good-bye to Sandy here?"

"Why the hell would I want to do that? Let this redskin slobber on her some more? I don't think so."

The sun wasn't quite up, but it was high enough so that reddish-gold light flooded the sky. Smoke looked around, his eyes searching intently over the hills that surrounded the campsite. He smiled again.

"It's a beautiful morning," he said. "A good day to die."

Thorn's lips pulled back from his teeth in a savage grin. "That's one way for you to look at it," he said.

"Nope, not me," Smoke said. "You're the one who's going to die, Thorn."

The grin became a snarl. "We'll just see about that!" Thorn said as he swung the shotgun up, his finger tightening on the trigger.

Chapter 20

Before Thorn could fire, one of the men covering Sandy suddenly gave a choked scream, staggered to the side, and dropped his gun so he could use both hands to paw at the shaft of the arrow that seemed to have sprouted like magic from his throat. The man with him whirled around, and as he did so, another arrow drove deep into his side.

Thorn's head jerked in their direction, and as it did, Smoke rolled the other way as fast as he could. He could have drawn his Colts with blinding swiftness and plugged Thorn, but the man might have been able to jerk the Greener's triggers, even as he was dying. At such close range, it would prove fatal to Smoke.

At the same time, Calhoun threw himself in a diving tackle at the legs of the man guarding him. The man's gun roared as Calhoun knocked him down, but the shot went wild into the trees.

Smoke came up on his feet and leaped out of the way as Thorn jerked the sawed-off's triggers. The explosion was like a huge clap of thunder. Smoke felt a fiery sting on his leg and knew one of the pellets had creased him, but the rest of the buckshot missed.

His guns—in his hands without him even having to think

about it—bucked against his palms as he fired at Thorn who had ducked away and was running for his life.

He might have gotten away if he hadn't strayed too close to Sandy. The young man lunged forward as Thorn passed him. His arms went around the outlaw's legs and brought him down. The empty scattergun flew out of Thorn's hand as he crashed to the ground.

"You son of a bitch!" The yell came from Smoke's left.

He whirled in that direction, but not in time to avoid Gus Harley's rush. Harley's weight barreled into Smoke and knocked him backward. Smoke landed on the rock where Calhoun had been sitting earlier. The rough stone dug painfully into his back, and as Harley bent him over it, Smoke felt like his spine was about to crack.

Before he could wallop Harley with a Colt, the man's weight suddenly vanished. Harley let out a startled yell. Smoke looked on in amazement as the biggest Indian he had ever seen in his life lifted Harley into the air. Harley was no lightweight, but with one hand clamped around his neck and the other around a thigh, the Indian handled him like a child's doll.

Smoke knew he was looking at the legendary Crazy Bear, Sandy's father, chief of the Crow . . . and the man Smoke had spotted sneaking up on the camp a few moments earlier, prompting his comment to Thorn about it being a good day to die.

With the sound of numerous bones breaking, Crazy Bear hurled Harley to the ground with incredible force. Harley didn't even moan. He just lay there, limp.

Smoke straightened, whipped up his left-hand gun, and fired. The outlaw standing behind Crazy Bear and drawing a bead on the Crow chief doubled over as Smoke's lead punched into his gut. Crazy Bear glanced over his shoulder, then nodded at Smoke in gratitude.

Calhoun had gotten the upper hand over the man he was wrestling with. The marshal was on top of his opponent, hammering his left fist into the man's face again and again. That fight seemed to be well under control, Smoke saw.

When he looked toward the spot where Sandy and Thorn
had been struggling, he realized that Thorn was gone. Sandy
lay curled up on the ground, gasping.

"He . . . he got away from me," Sandy said as Smoke
leaped to his side. "He'll go after . . . Robin!"

Smoke glanced around. There was one other outlaw unaccounted for, as well as the man Thorn had left guarding
Robin. That made three of the enemy still on the loose.

"Don't worry," he told Sandy. "I'll find her and bring her
back."

A huge hand closed on Smoke's shoulder, and a voice like
an avalanche said, "My son . . . he is all right?"

Smoke didn't see any blood on the bandage around Sandy's
head. "Yeah, he's not hurt any worse than he was before. He
was just too weak to stop Thorn from getting away."

"Then come. You and I will follow those men."

Smoke glanced around and saw that Calhoun had knocked
his man out and staggered to his feet. "Marshal! Keep an eye
on Sandy!"

"Yeah," Calhoun said. "Go get Thorn!"

Crazy Bear pointed. "This way."

They ran up the wooded slope. Smoke figured the man
guarding Robin had the horses with him. If Thorn and the
others got away with her, Smoke would have to chase them
down again. He didn't want that.

He wanted to end it, on that beautiful crisp morning.

As he had told Thorn, it was indeed a good day to die.

Smoke had to hurry to keep up with Crazy Bear's swift,
long-legged strides. He heard crashing in the brush up ahead
and knew they were closing in on their quarry.

Suddenly, a gun roared. Smoke heard the wind-rip of the
bullet as it sizzled through the air past his ear. Instinctively,
he fired back, blasting out shots from both .44s. The man who
had fled with Thorn reeled from the bushes where he had
hidden to ambush them and collapsed as blood welled from
the bullet holes in his chest. The outlaw had hurried his first

shot . . . and with Smoke Jensen facing him, he'd never gotten a second one.

Crazy Bear bounded ahead, his great bulk clearing a path through the brush. He didn't seem to feel the briars and branches clawing at him.

Smoke couldn't keep up. He ran past the man he'd killed and hurried along as best he could. Through a gap in the growth that the massive warrior had left behind him, Smoke caught a glimpse of horses moving around in a clearing and knew they had reached the spot where Thorn had left Robin.

Another gun boomed, but Crazy Bear never slowed down. Smoke ran into the clearing in time to see him lift the outlaw guarding Robin into the air by his neck. Crazy Bear shook the guard like a dog shaking a rat. The man's arms and legs flopped around like a rag doll's limbs. Smoke knew that his neck was surely broken—he was probably already dead.

Robin screamed, and Smoke twisted to see Thorn standing over her aiming the sawed-off shotgun one-handed at Crazy Bear's back. Instantly, Smoke thumbed off two rounds, one from each Colt. The slugs drove into Thorn's chest and knocked him back a step. The scattergun drooped in his hand.

Then he steeled himself with a visible effort and swung the barrels toward Robin. From the expression of pure evil on the man's face, Smoke knew that Thorn realized he was done for. He was going to kill Robin before he died. With his finger already on the trigger, Smoke couldn't stop him.

A figure rushed out of the brush, and lunged forward to grab Thorn's wrist. The white bandage around the man's head told Smoke that Sandy had caught his breath and come after them. The young man might not have been able to stop Thorn earlier, but now, seeing the woman he loved being threatened, he summoned up from somewhere deep inside, the speed and strength needed to twist the barrels of the Greener up, just as Thorn's finger closed spasmodically on both triggers.

Again the thunderclap sounded. The double charge of buckshot caught Thorn in the chest and face and under the chin, and the devastating impact flipped him over backward and literally blew his head off. When his body thudded to the ground among the spooked horses, there was nothing left above his shoulders but a bloody stump of neck.

Sandy bent and grabbed hold of Robin, lifting her from the ground and pulling her into a desperately tight embrace. "Robin, Robin!" he panted. "Are you all right?"

"I-I'm fine," she told him. "Sandy! You're alive! That's impossible! I-I saw Harley shoot you!"

"He just grazed me." Sandy kissed her, hard, then said, "We're alive, Robin! We're both alive!"

Calhoun came up behind Smoke, breathless. "Couldn't . . . keep the kid from chasin' after you," he said. "Looks like . . . it's all over."

"Yeah," Smoke said, thinking of Jason Garrard. "Until we get back to Buffalo Flat, anyway."

As they were riding toward the settlement later, having left the bodies of Thorn and his men for the buzzards and the wolves, Calhoun brought his horse alongside Smoke's and nodded toward Crazy Bear, who was riding well ahead of the others.

"I saw you talkin' to that big ol' Injun earlier," the marshal said. "Did you ask him how he managed to find us and show up like he did?"

"He followed Sandy," Smoke said.

"The kid?"

"Yeah. One of the men from the Crow village was in town yesterday morning when all the ruckus happened."

"Is that right?" Calhoun shrugged. "They come into town ever' now and then to pick up shells for their rifles at Hammond's store. Folks don't like havin' 'em around much— they're naturally a mite scared of redskins, after all—but the Crows and the whites get along pretty good most of the time. Some of 'em even scout for the army."

"You're not telling me anything I don't already know,"

Smoke said. "Anyway, this fella heard that Sandy had been hurt and hustled back up to the Crow village to tell Crazy Bear, who headed for town to see about his son. On the way there he spotted Sandy trailing us and decided to tag along after him. He figured that Sandy was going after Thorn to try to rescue Robin, so he came along to lend a hand if he needed to. And of course, he wound up saving our bacon, or helping to, anyway."

Calhoun shook his head and looked back over his shoulder at Sandy and Robin, who were riding side by side about twenty yards behind them. "Mr. Garrard's gonna be damn glad to get his daughter back safe and sound, but he ain't gonna like the gal bein' sweet on that boy."

"He may have to get used to it," Smoke said. "Some things a man can't do much about." But he agreed with Calhoun, that there might be trouble when they got back to Buffalo Flat. If there was, he would deal with it when the time came.

It was late afternoon when they rode into the settlement. The first man to see Robin was with them let out a cheer and took off at a run toward the stage line office, obviously intending to convey the good news to Garrard. Other citizens fell in alongside the riders and called questions to them, which were ignored. Smoke led the way to Garrard's office, and by the time they got there, quite a crowd had gathered around them.

Jason Garrard was waiting in the doorway, a huge smile on his face. As Robin reined in, he rushed forward to help her dismount. Then he pulled her into his arms and hugged her tightly.

"Are you all right?" he asked in a voice choked with emotion.

"I'm fine," she told him, "thanks to Sandy and his father." Garrard's face darkened. "The Indians?"

"And Mr. West and Marshal Calhoun, too, of course," Robin went on. "They all risked their lives to save me."

"That ain't all we saved, Mr. Garrard," Calhoun said. "Mitch Thorn was playin' us all for fools. He was gonna marry your daughter, murder you, and take over the whole town."

Garrard stared at the marshal in obvious disbelief. "How in the world do you know that?"

"Thorn admitted the whole thing when he thought he was about to kill us," Calhoun said.

Robin nodded. "The marshal's right," she told her father. "He said the same things to me when he was gloating about his plans. Of course, they were all ruined as soon as he lost his head and kidnapped me."

"I don't believe it," Garrard said as he rubbed his heavy jaw. "I knew Thorn was a pretty shady character, but I never figured he'd try to double-cross me."

Robin stepped over to Sandy's side and linked her arm with his. "It's true. So you see, you owe Sandy and Crazy Bear quite a lot. Not just my life, but maybe even your own."

Garrard's mouth twisted. "Get away from that—"

Crazy Bear straightened to his full height and squared his massive shoulders.

Wisely, Garrard stopped before he finished his sentence.

Smoke spoke up, saying, "Listen to me, Garrard. This is none of my business, but I reckon you'd be better off if you'd open your eyes and accept what's goin' on here."

"I don't have to accept anything I don't want to," Garrard snapped.

"Is that so? How do you figure to change it? You can't bully or buy off love."

"I can kill that young buck," Garrard said, so angry not even Crazy Bear's murderous glare made him hold back his words.

"And if you did, Robin would still love him. She'd just hate you, to boot."

Garrard maintained his stubborn stance for a long, tense moment. Then, slowly, he drew in a deep breath. His shoulders slumped a little in acceptance.

"I don't like it," he said to Robin, "and I'm going to do

everything in my power to talk you out of it, but I suppose West is right. I can't *force* you to feel differently than you do."

"That's right," she said quietly. "I'll always love Sandy."

"You're picking a mighty tough row to hoe, girl."

Her chin came up in defiance. "It's my decision to make."

And it was their problem to work out, Smoke thought as he tightened his grip on Seven's reins and led the Appaloosa toward the livery stable. Robin and Sandy were safe, and that was all he cared about in Buffalo Flat. He had his own tough row to hoe still ahead of him.

Calhoun came up alongside him. "Where are you headed, West?"

"The livery stable, right now. I'm going to see to it that this horse of mine gets a good rubdown, plenty of hay and water, and a night's rest. I'll be riding out in the morning."

"You sure about that?"

Smoke glanced over at him. "What do you mean?"

"Well, I was thinkin' . . . I could use a deputy here, the way the town's growin' and all."

Smoke managed not to laugh. "You want me to work for a crook like you?"

"Maybe I ain't quite as big a crook as you think I am," Calhoun said, bristling. "Maybe I see some things a mite differently now."

"I hope you do, Marshal, but it's none of my business, one way or the other. I'm leaving first thing in the morning."

"You sound like a man in a hurry to get somewhere."

"Maybe I am," Smoke said.

He had lingered long enough. The spirits of his wife and son and the old man who had been almost like a father to him called out their need for vengeance. Smoke had been sidetracked for a couple days in Buffalo Flat, but it was time he settled the score for Nicole, Arthur, and Preacher.

Come sunup, he was heading for Idaho.

Lord help his enemies when he got there.

Interlude

"Yeah, you settled the score for me, all right," Preacher said, "even though it turned out I weren't quite dead after all!"

"That was before I realized you're too blasted ornery to die," Smoke replied with a grin. He peered through the loophole. Lew Torrance and the rest of Bannerman's hired guns hadn't ventured out of the trees again since their last ill-fated attempt. Obviously, they had decided to be patient and wait for nightfall, which wasn't far off.

Already the light outside had begun to fade. Soon, it would be dark, and the gunmen would be able to approach the cabin without being seen.

"What happened to that corrupt Marshal Calhoun?" Matt asked. "I was in Buffalo Flat less than a year ago, and the town had a different marshal."

"Calhoun was killed a few years later in a shootout with some bank robbers," Smoke explained. "Garrard started a bank of his own in Buffalo Flat so he wouldn't have to send his money to Casper or Cheyenne. Calhoun had turned into a fairly honest lawman by then, and did his duty. He managed to stop the robbers when they hit the bank, but he was fatally wounded in the process."

Preacher snorted. "If you ask me, he was just tryin' to protect that skunk Garrard's money. Calhoun was suckin' up to Garrard right to the end."

"Obviously, Garrard never took over the whole town," Matt commented. "When I was there, I saw his name on the livery stable and the stage line, but that's all, as far as I can remember."

"And the bank," Smoke reminded him. "But yeah, after nearly losin' his daughter, I reckon he decided some things are more important than money and power. He's still a mighty successful businessman in Buffalo Flat, but there are bigger men in this part of the territory. Reece Bannerman, for one."

Preacher said, "Bannerman bided his time and increased his spread and his other holdin's until he was the *biggest* hombre in these parts. It ain't enough for him, or he wouldn't be after the land the Crows have been claimin' for so long."

"The problem is, the Crows never claimed it legally," Smoke said.

Preacher snorted. "What the hell's a piece o' paper mean to an Injun? I'll tell you what it means . . . not a damn thing. That's Crow land because they been livin' on it and huntin' on it for years, and there's nothin' some pasty-faced clerk in Washington or Cheyenne can do to change it!"

"I hate to say it, but that's where you're wrong, Preacher," Matt said. "The way the government works—"

"Don't talk to me about no damn gov'ment! There's the gov'ment way o' doin' things, and then there's the right way, and most o' the time, the two ain't the same!"

"Settle down," Smoke said. "Matt and I stopped in Denver on the way up here. The governor there is a friend of Matt's, and I have some good lawyers there on retainer."

"Last time I checked, Denver was in Colorado, not Wyomin' Territory," Preacher drawled. "Don't see what good it's gonna do to talk to the governor down there."

"Politicians usually have some influence over each other," Matt said. "The governor of Colorado agreed to write a letter to the territorial governor in Cheyenne urging him to investigate the situation up here and Bannerman's claim to the land.

Smoke's lawyers are coming up here to carry out their own investigation."

"Lawyers," Preacher repeated scornfully. "Fancy word for crooks, if you ask me."

Smoke smiled. "Sometimes it comes in handy to have the crooks on your side. We'll have to wait and see about that. In the meantime, it's up to us to protect Crazy Bear and his people from Bannerman's hired gunslingers."

"We ain't protectin' anybody, penned up in this ol' cabin," Preacher said. "It ain't gonna be long until those bastards out there got all the advantage on their side."

"Maybe not," Smoke said. "There's one thing I reckon they haven't considered."

"What's that?" Matt asked.

"Once it gets dark, we may not be able to see them, but they can't see us, either."

"What good is that going to do us? They've got a solid ring around us. We can't slip out through them while they're closing in on us."

"Speak for yourself, youngster," Preacher said. "Remember, the Injuns used to call me Ghost-Killer. I could sneak right into a village and out again without anybody knowin' I was there until it was too late."

"No offense, but I'm not sure you're that spry now, Preacher."

"Not that spry!" Preacher took offense—even though Matt had told him not to. "Why, you young pup, I'll have you know—"

"We're not sneaking out," Smoke broke in. "I'm starting to get another idea, but it'll have to wait until dark. We might as well settle down until then. I don't think they're gonna charge us again."

"No, neither do I," Preacher agreed. He looked over at Matt. "You said you was in Buffalo Flat a while back? What were you doin' in these parts?"

"Just drifting, as usual," Matt replied with a shrug. "Seeing what's on the other side of the hill."

Preacher sighed. "I know the feelin'. Been doin' the same thing for nigh on to sixty years."

"I'm starting to wonder," Matt went on, "if this area is jinxed or something. The two of you rode right into trouble when you came through here, and so did I . . ."

BOOK THREE

Chapter 21

The sudden crackle of gunfire somewhere nearby made Matt Jensen haul back on the reins and bring his big sorrel mount to a halt. "Hear that, Spirit?" he asked the horse. "Sounds like there's a ruckus going on."

Spirit turned his head to look back at Matt as if he were saying *Oh? Really?* Running into trouble was something the two of them did all too often.

Matt's Stetson was cuffed back on his shock of blond hair. Humor sparkled in his pale blue eyes at the moment, but under the right circumstances, those eyes took on a blue-gray tint that made them look like chips of ice. They were about as cold as ice, too, when Matt was angry.

He sat there for a moment, listening to the popping of gunfire. It seemed out of place in such idyllic surroundings. The heavily timbered slopes of the Big Horn Mountains loomed around him, forming a majestic backdrop for the lush valley through which he was riding. Off to his left, a creek ran clear, cold, and swift bubbling over its rocky bed as it traced a course between banks dotted with cottonwood and aspen. Several such creeks watered that valley, which explained the lush grass in the meadows that provided ample graze for the cows Matt had seen.

The Circle B brand was burned into the hides of the

animals. Matt hadn't heard of that particular spread before, but he knew the cattle industry had been growing rapidly in Wyoming Territory over the past decade. Texas cattlemen had headed north and established ranches all over the territory during that time. The Circle B cows that Matt saw were fat and sleek, so he assumed the ranch was a successful one.

Rifles continued to crack, and he heard the popping of six-guns, too. As he pondered whether to get involved in whatever was going on, he realized the decision might not be in his hands. The shots were coming closer.

A lone rider suddenly burst out of some trees about three hundred yards ahead of him. The man's horse was galloping at full speed, with the rider leaning over the animal's neck urging it on. Folks hardly ever rode that fast unless they were running away from something, Matt knew, and sure enough a few seconds later half a dozen more riders emerged from the trees. Powdersmoke puffed from their guns as they continued firing at the man they were chasing.

Matt glanced to his right. A clump of boulders offered shelter and concealment. He pulled on the reins and heeled Spirit into motion, sending the sorrel into the cluster of big rocks.

He wanted to know more about the game before he took a hand in it. The most likely explanation for what he'd seen was that some of the ranch hands who rode for the Circle B were chasing a rustler they had caught red-handed at his nefarious work.

But that wasn't the *only* possible explanation. Matt swung down from the saddle and climbed up a giant slab of rock that was tilted against another boulder. He took off his hat and stretched out on the stony slope, giving him a good view of the chase.

The lone rider being pursued was closer. Matt saw that he wore buckskins and was hatless, which was somewhat unusual on the frontier. The man's hair was as dark as a raven's wing.

The rider swept past, close enough to the rocks so Matt could see with a shock that he had made a mistaken assumption. That midnight-black hair was twisted into a pair of braids that hung far down the rider's back. The fringed buckskin shirt clung to curves that definitely didn't belong to a man.

The rider was a woman.

The men who were after her continued blasting away at her as they closed in. Matt got a good look at them, as they galloped past the boulders. They had the hard-bitten, beard-stubbled features of gunmen rather than regular ranch hands. Maybe they rode for the Circle B, but if they did, they hadn't been hired for their skill at working with cattle.

They were killers, plain and simple.

The pursuit rushed by so fast Matt didn't have time to think about what he was doing. He stood up on the steep slope, clapped his hat back on his head, then slid down and pushed off the rock. The leap landed him in the saddle on Spirit's back. His feet found the stirrups and he sent the sorrel racing out of the rocks.

The men chasing the woman in buckskins were about a hundred yards ahead of Matt. He called out, "Trail, Spirit!" and the stallion leaped forward, stretching his legs. The ground flashed past beneath him as Matt leaned forward, like the buckskin-clad woman. He tugged his hat down tight to keep the wind from blowing it off his head.

A Winchester .44-40 rode snugly in a sheath strapped to the saddle. Matt drew the rifle and worked its lever, jacking a round into the chamber. He lifted the weapon to his shoulder, steadied it, and fired.

The hurricane deck of a racing horse was no place for accuracy. Matt wasn't trying to hit any of the men. He wanted to come close enough to spook them and make them veer off from their pursuit of the woman.

But no sooner had the rifle cracked and kicked against his

shoulder than one of the riders ahead of him threw up his arms and slumped forward. The man would have toppled out of the saddle if one of his companions hadn't reached over to grab his arm and steady him. The riders hauled back on their reins and brought their mounts to skidding halts that raised some dust.

Those who weren't wounded turned their horses and opened fire on Matt. He saw flame spurt from the muzzles of their rifles. A couple of slugs whined past, close enough for him to hear them. Still shooting, the men charged him.

On second thought, Matt mused, maybe getting mixed up in the affair had been a mistake after all. "Come on, Spirit!" he told the sorrel as he whirled around. "Let's get back to those rocks!"

The boulders were the closest place where he could fort up. They offered good protection from gunfire, except slugs often ricocheted and bounced around. Dangerous or not the boulders were Matt's best hope, so he headed for them as fast as Spirit could carry him.

Shots continued to blast behind him, but none found him or Spirit. The rocks loomed ahead of him. He could hold off the gunmen for a while, but eventually they would spread out and come at him from different directions, making it impossible for him to stop all of them.

At least he had given the woman the chance to get away, he told himself. That chivalrous act might cost him his life, but if it did, so be it. He had already figured out the drifting life of adventure he led probably meant he wouldn't die of old age, surrounded by his grandchildren. Smoke Jensen, his mentor and adopted older brother, had taught him to do what was right, no matter the cost.

Saving a lone woman from six varmints bent on killing her was the right thing to do, no matter how you looked at it, Matt thought.

When he reached the rocks, he dismounted quickly and slapped his hat against Spirit's rump, sending the sorrel deeper into the clump of boulders. Then, carrying the Winchester, he ran back up the sloping slab of rock he had used as a vantage point a few minutes earlier. Throwing himself down on his belly, he thrust the rifle barrel over the top of the rock and lined his sights toward the onrushing gunwolves.

The rifle cracked as Matt squeezed the trigger. One of the riders jerked and slewed halfway around in the saddle before he caught hold of the horn and steadied himself—wounded—but not out of the fight yet. Nor was the first man he had winged, who had regained his strength and was trailing the others, firing a revolver toward the rocks.

Matt wasn't worried too much about handgun fire from that range, but the men with rifles continued shooting as they spread out. Slugs thudded into the rocks and chipped dust from them. He began to hear the high-pitched whine of ricochets, as he had expected. It wouldn't take long for his refuge to turn into a deadly hornet's nest.

He continued to fire, cranking off several rounds toward the men as they split up. The swiftness with which they had launched into the tactic told him they were professionals. Although he hated to do it, he shifted his aim and sent a bullet into the chest of one of the horses. The animal's forelegs folded up underneath and it crashed to the ground. The rider was thrown out of the saddle and landed hard, rolling over and over.

Matt was ready when the man came to a stop. He had the Winchester's sights lined up and squeezed the trigger. As the gunman tried to get up, Matt's slug ripped through his body and drove him back to the ground. He didn't move again.

One dead, two wounded, he thought. He was whittling the odds down, but not fast enough. The gunman had reached cover—three in a grove of trees, and the other two in a gully that zigzagged down to the creek. Those were the ones who worried Matt the most, because they could work their way up that gully where he couldn't get a shot at them until they were behind him.

The men in the trees had a pretty good angle on him, too. Their shots were coming closer. A bullet tugged at the sleeve of his faded blue bib-front shirt and bounced off the rock next to him.

Matt swung his rifle toward the trees, determined to go down fighting. As he peered over the barrel one of the gunmen staggered out from behind a tree, in plain sight. Something stuck out from his shoulder, and after a second Matt realized it was an arrow. Another man yelled in pain or alarm or both. Something brown flashed through the trees, moving too fast for Matt to be sure what it was.

He'd wager a guess it was a buckskin-clad form . . .

A bullet whipped past his head from behind. The men in the gully had flanked him. He turned and slid down the sloping face of the rock, firing three times as he did so at the place where the gully snaked behind the boulders. Not knowing if he hit either of the men he thudded to the ground at the base of the rock. He had been forced off the high ground. The rocks were little more than a deathtrap.

He whistled for Spirit, and as the sorrel rushed up, Matt grabbed the horn and swung himself into the saddle. He dug his heels into the horse's flanks. Spirit burst out through a gap between the rocks and charged toward the gully.

Matt rammed the rifle back in its sheath and drew his Colt. The gully was about twenty yards away and maybe a dozen feet wide. Spirit covered the distance in only a few bounds. Matt heard guns roaring, but the sorrel never faltered. He didn't slow down, and as Matt called "Up, Spirit!" the horse launched into a leap that carried them soaring into the air above the gully.

The gunmen hadn't expected that. They stared up in shock as Matt and the sorrel passed over their heads. Matt fired right, then jerked the Colt left and thumbed off another round.

A second later, Spirit's forehooves hit the ground, dug in, and kept them plunging forward.

Matt pulled back on the reins, slowing and turning the sorrel. He caught sight of both men moving fast back along the gully, heading for the spot where they had left their horses. One was clutching a bullet-shattered arm. The other appeared to be unharmed, but obviously had lost interest in the fight.

Matt holstered the revolver and pulled his rifle again. He sent a couple of shots after the men to hurry them on their way, then heeled Spirit into motion and rode in a big circle to the left around the boulders. He wanted to find out what had happened in those trees on the other side of the rocks.

Was it possible the woman he had intervened to save had doubled back to save him?

As he reached a point where he could see the trees, he spotted three horses and riders on the other side of the creek, moving fast toward the mountains. A moment later, off to the right, he saw the two he had chased out of the gully also mounted, also hurrying. The horse he had killed still lay where it had fallen, but the man was gone. Either his companions had taken his body with them, or he wasn't dead after all and had managed to grab a ride with one of the others.

What mattered was the echoes of the gunshots had faded away and silence had fallen over the landscape. The would-be killers were gone, and from the looks of the way they had taken off for the tall and uncut, they didn't have any intention of coming back soon.

That left the woman in buckskins unaccounted for. Matt jogged the sorrel toward the trees, holding the Winchester across the saddle in front of him so that it would be handy if he needed it.

He reined in and called, "Hello! Are you in there?"

At first there was no response from the timber. Suddenly a figure stepped out from behind one of the trees about a dozen feet away, and Matt found himself looking at an arrow nocked on a pulled-taut bowstring. All it would take to send that arrow flying into his body was a slight movement of two fingers.

Matt stiffened in the saddle, not wanting to do anything to spook the woman. He said calmly, "Take it easy, ma'am. I'm a friend. I'm the one who helped you back there."

For a moment it seemed that his words didn't penetrate to her brain, and he wondered fleetingly if she spoke his language. He could tell from her black hair and her coppery skin that she was an Indian.

Then, slowly, she lowered the bow and arrow slightly and said in perfect English, "I know what you did. What I don't know is why, and until I do, I'm not going to trust you."

He wasn't sure what surprised him more: the way she had come back to help him, the way she dressed like a warrior, the way she talked . . .

Or the fact that she was the most beautiful young woman he had seen for quite some time.

Chapter 22

Dark, luminous eyes dominated the lovely face. They had a slightly odd cast that made them look a little different from the eyes of other Indian women he had seen. She was armed with the bow in her hands, a quiver of arrows slung on her back, and a pair of sheathed knives, one on each hip. She wasn't pointing the arrow directly at him anymore, but the wariness in her eyes and the tenseness in her stance told Matt that she could raise the bow and let fly in the blink of an eye.

He could swing his Winchester up and fire faster than she could loose an arrow, but instead he said, "I don't have any interest in hurting you, ma'am. I saw those men chasing you and shooting at you, and I stepped in to stop them."

"Why?" She put the question to him sharply. "Why would you risk your life to help a stranger?"

"Well . . . you're a woman, for one thing. But I reckon I'd have taken a hand even if you were a man. I never did like six-to-one odds. They don't hardly seem fair."

"Fair?" she repeated. "You helped me because my plight offended your sense of fairness?"

"You could put it like that," he said with a shrug. *If you want to be all high-falutin about it,* he added to himself.

"Who are you?" she asked after a moment.

"Name's Matt Jensen."

"Jensen . . ."

The name seemed to mean something to her. She might have heard of him, Matt thought, but more likely she recognized the name because of Smoke, who was much better known on the frontier.

"What are you doing in this valley, Matt Jensen?" she went on.

"Just riding," he said. "I've been up in Montana Territory and thought I'd drift south for a while, before the colder weather moves in. Is there a settlement in these parts? It probably wouldn't hurt if I picked up some supplies."

"Buffalo Flat is about ten miles south of here," the young woman said. "You should be careful, though. Reece Bannerman doesn't like strangers riding across his range."

Matt grunted. "Bannerman, eh? As in the Circle B?"

She nodded. "Yes. That's his ranch."

"We're on his range now?"

"He runs his cattle on this land," she said, the sharpness back in her voice. "That does not mean he owns it."

"I see," Matt said, although he didn't, not fully. Since the woman had lowered the bow and arrow farther and seemed more relaxed, he ventured another question. "I've told you my name, but you haven't told me yours. What do they call you?"

After hesitating a moment, she said, "Starwind."

He nodded. "Starwind. It suits you." He studied the beadwork and markings on her buckskins. "You're a Crow?"

"That's right. My father's village is near here." She frowned at him. "You've said nothing about my clothes."

Matt shrugged. "I reckon folks have a right to dress however they want."

"Or the fact that I fight like a man."

"Well, that came in mighty handy when you ventilated one of those fellas with an arrow."

"Two of them," she corrected.

"I thought I heard somebody else yell in those trees," Matt

said with a smile. "If you hadn't turned around and come back to help me, there's a good chance they would've kept me pinned down in those rocks until a ricochet got me. So I owe you just as much as you owe me."

"We are square, as the white man says."

Matt nodded. "Yep. We're square. I'm curious, though . . . why were those varmints chasing you? Do they work for this fella Bannerman?"

"I don't know," Starwind replied with a shake of her head. "I was searching for . . . something . . . when they saw me and began shooting at me. If my pony was not so swift, they would have killed or captured me."

"What were you looking for?" Matt asked, still indulging his curiosity.

She didn't answer. Instead, she finally unnocked the arrow and slid it back into the quiver slung over her shoulder.

"Will you come with me to the village of my people, Matt Jensen?" she asked.

Matt didn't have any place he had to be. He knew the Crow were usually friendly toward whites and thought he could count on their hospitality. And he was still mighty curious. It seemed to him that the beautiful young woman called Starwind was being deliberately mysterious.

"Sure, I can do that," he told her. "I appreciate the invitation."

"Follow me, then." She turned her head and whistled, and the paint pony she had been riding earlier came out of the trees. She vaulted lithely onto its back. The buckskin trousers made it easy for her to ride astride.

And the way they hugged the curves of her hips wasn't half-bad, either, he thought.

Matt let her lead the way. Starwind headed west, her course winding through the lush valley between the rugged, heavily timbered mountains. They crossed the first creek, then another stream half a mile farther on. Turning south they followed the second creek. A few minutes later, Matt spotted a tendril of gray smoke twisting upward into the blue sky.

"My father's village," Starwind said, nodding toward the smoke coming from a cooking fire.

When they reached the village, Matt saw that the lodges were scattered along a plain beside the creek, with woods nearby for firewood. It was a good-sized village, housing probably a couple hundred people, he estimated as he and Starwind approached. Dogs came running out to greet them, barking loudly. The commotion drew plenty of attention. Men, women, and children emerged from the lodges. Warriors holding rifles or bows stepped forward, forming a protective line in case there was trouble. Matt wondered a little why they were so defensive.

An air of tension definitely hung over the entire village. Some of the women and children looked frightened. The warriors glared at Matt, and he was glad that Starwind was at his side. If she hadn't been there to indicate by her presence that he was a friend, he might have been risking his life by riding into that village, he realized.

Something had happened that had everybody spooked.

Matt spotted someone striding forward, behind the line of warriors. The man was easy to see, because he stood head and shoulders above the others. The line parted to let him through. Matt's jaw tightened as he got his first good look at the tall, broad-shouldered Indian.

The man's face was scarred and misshapen, and yet it bore a powerful dignity that slightly lessened the impact of his ugliness. His dark hair was heavily streaked with gray, but that was the only real indication of his age. The lines left by the years didn't show on his ravaged face, and his body seemed as powerful and vital as that of a younger man. He had to be the chief of the band. The way he carried himself, he could be nothing less.

"Starwind!" he said. "I feared that you had disappeared, too." The man looked at Matt and scowled. "Who is this?"

Starwind slid down from the back of her pony. The chief towered over her. "He says his name is Matt Jensen."

"Jensen!" The massive Indian seemed as impressed by the name as Starwind had been. He peered at Matt and asked, "You share the same blood as the one called Smoke Jensen?"

"Not exactly," Matt said. "He's my adopted brother. Or I reckon I should say he adopted me, since he saved my life, took me in, and pretty much raised me into a man. I took his name when I went out on my own, in tribute to him."

"Not blood, but blood brothers, then."

Matt nodded. "That's the way I feel about it."

The Indian clenched a ham-like fist and held it to his chest. "I am Crazy Bear. Years ago, Smoke Jensen did a great kindness for my family, and I have never forgotten him. Come. You are welcome here."

Matt relaxed, as did the warriors who were lined up behind Chief Crazy Bear. The crowd began to break up. Matt dismounted, and as he did so, Starwind reached for his reins.

"I will see to it that your horse is cared for," she said.

"Thanks. His name is Spirit."

Crazy Bear ushered Matt toward one of the lodges. "You will be my guest," he said. "Has Smoke spoken of his time here?"

"Not that I recall," Matt said. "It might have been after he and I went our separate ways."

"He called himself Buck West then. I learned his true name later."

Matt nodded. "Yeah, that was after we split up, after his first wife was killed. I heard about it from him later on, but I wasn't around when it happened. I'd like to think things might've been different if I had been."

An older woman waited in front of the lodge that was Crazy Bear's destination. She had gray in her hair, too, but she was still very attractive. Something had upset her. Matt saw pain and worry in her dark eyes.

"I thought there might be news of Moon Fawn," she said.

Crazy Bear shook his head. "No, but our daughter has come home. This man was with her. His name is Matt Jensen, blood brother to Smoke."

The woman came closer, and Matt realized that she wasn't an Indian. He had taken her for one at first, because of her coloring and her buckskin dress. Her features had a distinctly European look, and he knew that was what he had noticed about Starwind without really understanding it. The young woman was a mixture of the two cultures.

"My name is Mala," she said.

Matt took his hat off and nodded politely to her. "I'm pleased to meet you, ma'am. I just wish it was under better circumstances."

She stiffened. "What do you know of the circumstances?"

"Nothing, really, only that your daughter was being chased by gunmen because they caught her looking for someone else who has disappeared, someone named Moon Fawn." He had put that together quickly in his head from things that Starwind, Crazy Bear, and Mala had said.

Mala drew in a breath sharply. "Starwind was in danger?"

"I stepped in to help her," Matt explained, "and then she helped me when those hardcases turned around and came after me. I guess you could say we got each other out of trouble."

Crazy Bear looked past Matt and rumbled, "Starwind! Where did you go?"

The young woman walked up, having cared for her pony and Matt's sorrel. Her chin held a defiant tilt as she said, "I went to look for my niece. Someone has to find her before it's too late."

"We have searched from one end of the valley to the other."

"Not Bannerman's line camps or the headquarters of his ranch," Starwind shot back at him.

Crazy Bear frowned. "The truce between us is too easy to break. If we go near the line camps or Bannerman's house, there will be trouble."

"Why should we worry about trouble with Bannerman and his men when Moon Fawn is missing?"

Mala snapped, "You think I care about Bannerman when my granddaughter is gone? But your father is right . . . the peace is a fragile one. And Bannerman has no reason to be interested in Moon Fawn."

"He runs his cattle on land that has always been our hunting ground! He cannot be trusted!"

Crazy Bear said, "I do not trust him. But one little Indian girl means nothing to him."

Mala moved between Crazy Bear and Starwind. She said to Matt, "My apologies, Mr. Jensen. All this means nothing to you. The most important thing right now is that we owe you our gratitude for the help you gave our daughter. Please, accept our hospitality. We can feed you well and give you a good place to spend the night before you ride on to wherever it is you're going."

"I appreciate that, ma'am," Matt told her, "and I'll sure accept your kind invitation . . . but only on one condition."

"What condition is that?" Crazy Bear asked, not sounding too happy about Matt's response.

"That you tell me everything you can about what's going on here. You see, I'd like to help you get your granddaughter back safe and sound if I can."

Chapter 23

For a long moment, Crazy Bear didn't say anything, and his craggy face became impassive and unreadable.

Then he jerked his head in an abrupt nod and said, "It is to be expected that the blood brother of Smoke Jensen would make such an offer. Come into my lodge, Matt Jensen. We will smoke a pipe, and my wife will prepare a meal."

With the formality that he knew was expected at such a moment, Matt said, "I accept your hospitality, Crazy Bear."

A few minutes later, they were seated cross-legged inside the tepee on bearskin rugs near the fire pit. Crazy Bear prepared a pipe, packing it full of tobacco, then lighting it with a twig from the fire. After he had puffed it into life, he offered the pipe to Matt, who took it with a solemn expression on his face and puffed several times. Meanwhile, Crazy Bear's wife Mala began preparing a meal on the other side of the tepee.

Starwind hadn't followed them into the lodge. Matt glanced toward the entrance, where the hide flap that usually covered it was thrown back.

"If you look for my daughter, do not expect her," Crazy Bear said. "She will not help my wife with the meal. She says that is woman's work."

"No offense, Crazy Bear, but I figured Starwind was a woman, and a mighty pretty one, at that."

Crazy Bear grunted. "She says she should have been born a warrior. She has no interest in woman's ways. She would rather ride and fight."

"I saw her skill at both those things with my own eyes, earlier today," Matt said. "Did you teach her how to use a bow?"

"Someone had to." Despite his massive size, Crazy Bear sounded as if he had meet an irresistible force in his daughter's determination.

They passed the pipe back and forth again, then Matt said, "Tell me about the girl who's missing."

"My granddaughter, Moon Fawn."

"Not Starwind's daughter?"

Crazy Bear shook his head. "My daughter has no husband, no children. Moon Fawn is the child of my son Little Bear and his wife Robin."

Mala turned her head and added, "My son is also known as Sandor, Mr. Jensen. He has gypsy blood in his veins."

"And his wife is a white woman," Crazy Bear went on. He sighed. "There is much madness in my family."

Matt smiled. "It doesn't sound like your children are mad, just that they know what they want. This is a good thing, isn't it?"

"That's what I try to tell him," Mala said. "But tradition is important to him."

"I understand that, too," Matt said. "What about Moon Fawn?"

"My son and his wife have traveled east to the city called St. Louis. They left Moon Fawn here with us while they are gone. Little Bear wants to establish a school for Indians, and he thinks he can persuade some of the wealthy people in St. Louis to pay for it."

"Sounds like an admirable goal," Matt said with a nod. "How old is the little girl?"

Mala answered the question, and her voice broke slightly as she did so. "She has seen . . . seven summers."

Matt felt a chill go along his spine. For some reason, he'd

thought they were talking about a somewhat older girl. Moon Fawn was just a little kid, and on the frontier, a lot of dangerous things could happen to a child out on her own.

"Was she alone when she disappeared?"

Crazy Bear nodded. "Moon Fawn has always looked up to her father's younger sister. She wants to be like Starwind, who thinks nothing of taking a pony and riding through the valley by herself. Two days ago, Moon Fawn slipped away, took a pony, and went riding. She never returned."

"Good Lord," Matt murmured. "Did you find the pony?"

"It came back to the village that evening . . . alone."

Mala said, "There was no sign of Moon Fawn or Gregor."

"Who's Gregor?" Matt asked. "I thought you said she was alone."

"Her . . . her doll." Mala's voice choked with emotion. "She named it. She always carried it with her."

"I'm sure you went looking for her."

"Of course," Crazy Bear said. "Everyone in the village helped. We searched that night, and we searched again yesterday. No one found her. Today I went to Buffalo Flat, to ask for help from those in the settlement. When I got back, Starwind was gone, too, and no one knew where."

"She was east of here, and a little north."

Crazy Bear's face darkened. "On the land that Bannerman claims is his."

"You don't get along with Bannerman?"

"When he first came to the valley and brought his cattle, my people and I tried to be his friends. The Crow have fought the white men in the past, but the time for war is long since finished. It is a time for peace now." Crazy Bear made a sweeping gesture with an arm as big around as a sapling. "The valley is big. Plenty of room for all. But Bannerman takes more and more. Now he wants our hunting ground. This cannot be."

Matt felt a pang of sympathy for the Crow chief. Crazy Bear's story was one that had been repeated all over the West, and the situation was one that would probably continue to be repeated. Legally, the land didn't belong to the Indians anymore. As the country expanded and civilization marched across the frontier, they were being pushed back into smaller and smaller corners. Matt felt sorry for them, but he didn't see any way to stop what was happening.

"This fella Bannerman . . . would he stoop so low as to kidnap your granddaughter to make you go along with what he wants?"

"Of course he would," Starwind said as she appeared in the lodge's entrance and ducked low to come inside. "I told Moon Fawn never to ride alone on the other side of Badger Creek. There are too many of Bannerman's men over there. That's where I was today when those gunmen jumped me. I was nosing around one of their line camps."

"You know I have forbidden it!" Crazy Bear said.

"I also know that Moon Fawn might not be missing if she hadn't wanted so much to be like me," Starwind shot back, and Matt heard the pain in her voice. He realized that she blamed herself, at least in part, for her niece's disappearance. "I will find her, Father, if it is the last thing I do."

Mala said, "If it is the last thing you do, then I will have lost a daughter as well as a granddaughter."

Matt felt uncomfortable being in the middle of all the anger and tension between family members. He let the silence go on for a moment, then said, "Hold on. Even if Bannerman has Moon Fawn, surely he wouldn't do anything to hurt her. She's just a little girl. He's probably just letting you stew a little, Crazy Bear, if the two of you have clashed in the past."

"I do not trust him," Crazy Bear said.

"I don't blame you. But here's an idea . . . why don't you let me search for her?"

"You cannot know this valley any better than my people and I do."

"No . . . but I can ride over to the Circle B and see if Bannerman's hiring. If I can get a job with him, then I can look around without him knowing what I'm doing. He or one of his men might let something slip around me that would lead me to Moon Fawn."

"This is a good idea," Starwind said, adding, "I will come with you."

"You must not have been listening," Matt told her. "The idea is that Bannerman won't know I've got any connection to you folks."

"But I want to help!"

Mala said, "I think you have done enough, Starwind."

The young woman's face tightened. Anger darkened her features, and tears shined in her eyes. She came quickly to her feet and left the lodge before she let herself cry in front of her parents and their visitor.

Crazy Bear looked intently at Matt and asked, "How do we know we can trust you, Matt Jensen?"

"I'm blood brother to Smoke," he replied with a shrug. "If that means as much to you as it does to me, then you know you can trust me."

"Very well. If you can help find Moon Fawn and return her safely to us, you will be as much a friend to the Crow as Smoke Jensen is." Crazy Bear glanced through the entrance flap. "But the day grows short. Stay here tonight. You can ride to Bannerman's ranch tomorrow."

Matt nodded. "All right." Something had occurred to him. "I may have to go to Buffalo Flat first. That's the name of the settlement near here, right?"

"Yes. What do you need there?"

"If the men who were after Starwind today work for Bannerman, they got a look at me when I was trading shots with them. I don't reckon they ever saw my face very well, but they might recognize my horse and my clothes. I think I need to go to Buffalo Flat and get a new mount and some new duds."

Crazy Bear thought about it and then nodded slowly. "You are a smart man, Matt Jensen."

"I try," Matt said with a grin.

"I hope you are smart enough to find my granddaughter . . . and bring her home."

Matt ate supper with Crazy Bear and Mala, a savory stew that tasted good, so he didn't ask any questions about what was in it. After the meal, he checked on Spirit and found the sorrel was being well taken care of. Then Crazy Bear took him to a tepee that would be his to use for the night. A fire burned low in the center of the lodge, casting flickering shadows on the hide walls as Matt took off his hat, unbuckled his gunbelt and coiled it. He sat down on the bear robe that served as his bed to take off his boots.

The flap over the entrance was shoved aside suddenly, and Starwind stood there, glaring at him. She stepped farther into the tepee, let the flap fall closed behind her, reached down to the bottom of her buckskin shirt, and lifted it up and over her head, peeling the garment off her body so that she was nude from the waist up.

Matt took a deep breath. With an effort, he lifted his gaze from her firm, round, dark-tipped breasts so he was looking into her eyes instead. "What are you trying to do, girl?" he asked. "Get me killed? Anybody finds you here like that with me, I don't care how peaceable a man your father is, he'll have my hair."

With her jaw set angrily, Starwind lifted the shirt and held it in front of her, which was a little bit of a relief, anyway.

"I am a woman!" she said.

"Well, yeah, I kind of got that idea," Matt said.

"My father told you that I refuse to do woman's work and that I ride and fight like a man, and these things are true. But that does not mean I am like some women who . . . who refuse to have anything to do with a man!"

"I didn't really think it did," Matt told her. "To tell you the truth, I didn't even think about that."

"Someday I will have a husband and children, but not now."

"Good, because I'm not proposin' to you. And I sure as hell didn't make any sort of deal with Crazy Bear to buy you."

"Oh!"

In her anger, she flung the shirt at him, smacking his face. He caught it before it could drop into the fire and stood up to toss it back to her. He tried not to notice how breathing hard made her chest heave.

"I think you should put that back on and leave," he told her.

"Take me with you when you search for Moon Fawn."

"I told you, I can't. Having you along would ruin the whole plan."

"You saw what I can do. You know I can take care of myself."

"I also know I can't fool Bannerman into thinking I don't know your folks if I have their daughter tagging along with me."

She continued to glare at him, but after a moment, her sleek, bare shoulders rose and fell slightly. "I suppose you are right."

"I know I am. Now, uh . . ."

She lowered the hand that held the shirt in front of her and stepped closer to him. "You would kiss me, Matt Jensen?"

"I would if I wanted to be tortured and burned at the stake," he said. "Now, dadgum it, Starwind—"

During the ruckus that afternoon, he had seen how fast she could move when she wanted to, but she still surprised him. She dropped the shirt at her feet and had her arms around his neck before he could stop her. She had inherited some of her father's height, which meant she didn't have to stretch much in order for her mouth to reach his. Involuntarily, his arms went around her bare torso.

They stood like that, their lips working together, before Starwind pulled back and whispered, "I told you I am a woman."

"I, uh, never doubted it," Matt said.

Before he could kiss her again or say anything else, she slipped out of his arms. Moving as swiftly and gracefully as a deer, she picked up the shirt, pulled it over her head, and went to the entrance. She threw the flap back but paused to look over her shoulder at him. Her face wore a triumphant smile and her eyes sparkled as she said, "Now you will never forget it." Her expression grew solemn as she added, "Find my niece."

"I will," Matt promised.

Then Starwind was gone.

Chapter 24

Matt slept well that night, although it took him a while to doze off after Starwind's visit. He kept thinking about the warmth of her mouth and her body.

The next morning he ate breakfast with Crazy Bear and Mala. When Matt asked where Starwind was, the Crow chief shook his head despairingly.

"She has ridden out again. I do not know where she goes. Most fathers would say they have no daughter were she to treat them with such disrespect."

"You are not like most fathers," Mala pointed out. "You are a powerful man, Crazy Bear. You don't need to prove that power by punishing your children."

Matt managed not to smile. He figured that Crazy Bear had probably won every argument he'd ever had . . . except the ones with his wife and daughter. In that respect he was no different than most of the men Matt had met. Smoke's wife Sally could always get him to do what she wanted. The fact that Sally was nearly always right helped matters.

After breakfast, Matt saddled up Spirit and got ready to ride. Crazy Bear stood watching him and said, "Be careful, Matt Jensen. Reece Bannerman is a bad man, and some of the men who work for him are even worse."

"Hired killers, I imagine," Matt said.

Crazy Bear nodded gravely. "Yes. Men with cold eyes who care nothing for anyone but themselves."

"I'll be careful," Matt said as he tightened the cinch on the saddle. "I've come up against hombres like that before, Crazy Bear, and I'm still alive and kickin'." He slid his rifle into the boot. "If I can find Moon Fawn, I'll bring her back here. If I need help, I'll get word to you."

Crazy Bear slapped Matt on the back with a huge paw, and the impact staggered Matt a little, as if he had been swatted by a real bear. "May the spirits watch over you, my friend," the chief rumbled.

Matt swung up into the saddle and rode out of the village. He could feel numerous eyes watching him and knew that word had gotten around about him trying to find the missing Moon Fawn. He had the hopes of a lot of people riding with him.

Crazy Bear had told him how to get to Buffalo Flat. He crossed the first creek and swung south, riding down the valley between the two streams. He would bypass the Circle B, although it was possible he might run into some of Bannerman's stock along the way, and where there were cows, there would likely be cowboys. Matt kept his eyes open. He didn't want to be seen until he'd had a chance to change clothes and switch horses.

He approached the settlement at mid-morning. Smoke had been there a number of years earlier, not long after Buffalo Flat was founded. Matt paused on a hillside overlooking the settlement taking note of the big, well-established town so different from then. The main street ran for six blocks and was flanked by two more streets lined with businesses. The cross streets had businesses on them in the downtown area, and were crowded with residences beyond that.

He took a pair of field glasses out of his saddlebag and studied the town through them, locating a livery stable and a general store. He saw that he could approach the establishments on one of the less-traveled side streets, then cut into an alley that ran behind both businesses. That would be best, he decided, in case any of the men he'd clashed with the day before were in Buffalo Flat. He didn't want to be spotted and recognized.

Ten minutes later, he led Spirit into the livery stable through the rear doors, which were open to allow circulation through the barn from the front doors. A stocky man in late middle age was forking some fresh straw into one of the stalls. He stopped and leaned on the pitchfork when he saw Matt come in.

"Howdy, mister," he said. "That's a fine-lookin' sorrel you got there. Need to put him up here for a while?"

"That's right," Matt said. "And I'd like to rent another saddle horse, if you've got one."

The hostler frowned. "Oh, I got one. Several good horses, in fact. But none any better than the one you already have. Pardon me for bein' nosy, but why would you want to rent another horse?"

"We've come a far piece," Matt explained, using the story he had thought up on his way into town. "I'm going to be around here for a while, so I thought it might be a good idea to let this big fella rest and use another mount."

"Well, I reckon that makes sense," the liveryman said. "Not that it's any of my business anyway. Name's Hoyt Dowler, by the way. Used to run Jason Garrard's livery stable for him, but I saved up my money and finally bought a place of my own."

Matt could tell the man was waiting for him to introduce himself. He could also tell that Dowler was the garrulous sort and might keep him there all day if he could, talking to him about anything and everything.

"Call me Matt," he said curtly, not giving his last name and not allowing enough friendliness into his voice to encourage Dowler.

"All right, Matt," Dowler said, evidently getting the message. "You passed the corral with the horses I have for rent out back as you came in. See any that struck your fancy?"

"There was a big, rangy dun that looked like a pretty good horse."

A grin wreathed Dowler's weathered face. "You got a fine eye for horseflesh, youngster. Most folks'd look at that dun and not want it 'cause it's ugly, and it's got a mean cast to its eye. Well, it is mean, and it is ugly, but that son of a gun can run all day."

Matt loosened the cinches on Spirit's saddle. "I'll get my tack on him, then."

"Why don't you let me do that?" Dowler suggested. "I'll switch the saddle for you, then put the sorrel in a stall and see that he's got plenty of grain and water. When do you want the dun ready to ride?"

"I have to go down the street to the store, but I'll be back in twenty minutes or so."

Dowler nodded. "The dun'll be ready," he promised.

Matt left the barn through the rear doors. Dowler would likely wonder about that, but Matt couldn't very well explain his actions to the man. He didn't know what connection there was, if any, between Dowler and Reece Bannerman.

The back door into the general store was locked, so Matt had to go along the narrow passage between buildings to the street, step up onto the porch, and enter the store through the front door. He saw a couple women standing in one of the aisles, looking through some bolts of cloth, and stepped to the side so he could move down another aisle to the rear of the store, where a clerk stood behind a counter.

Along the way he picked up a pair of dark brown whipcord trousers, a fringed buckskin jacket, and a broad-brimmed, flat-crowned brown hat. He could wear his own butternut shirt with the jacket over it.

"That do you?" the clerk asked as Matt put the clothes on the counter.

"Reckon so."

"Nice duds," the clerk said. He stuck the tip of his tongue in the corner of his mouth as he picked up a stub of pencil and added up the prices on a ragged piece of butcher paper. "That'll be eleven dollars and twenty-five cents."

Matt opened his poke and counted out the money. "Got a back room where I can change?" he asked.

"You bet." The clerk swept the bills and coins across the counter. "Follow me."

When Matt came out of the back room a few minutes later, he had donned the new trousers and, different from normal, had tucked the legs inside his high-topped boots. He wore the buckskin jacket and the brown Stetson, and carried his old trousers wrapped around the hat he'd been wearing. When he caught a glimpse of himself in a mirror near the counter, he knew he looked considerably different than he had the day before during the shootout with the men who'd been chasing Starwind.

"I'm obliged," he said with a nod to the clerk. When he left the store, he walked right past the women who were still looking through the bolts of cloth. He was aware that they studied him pretty thoroughly, and he grinned as he heard a faint giggle behind him. Sounded like he met with their approval.

Hoyt Dowler seemed not to recognize him at first when he walked back into the livery stable, through the double doors in the front, then said, "Oh, you're the fella who brought in that sorrel a little while ago. Matt, ain't it? I got your saddle on that dun. He's ready to go."

"Thanks," Matt said. He gave the man a ten-dollar gold piece and the trouser-wrapped hat. "That enough to take care of the bill for a few days, including hanging on to this gear for me?"

"Sure is. You'll be around town?"

"I don't really know. I heard they might be hiring out at the Circle B. Thought I might try to get me a job."

"Circle B, eh?" Dowler's eyes dropped to the well-worn walnut grips of the .44 holstered on Matt's right hip. He didn't sound quite as friendly as before as he went on, "Yeah, I reckon Bannerman might hire you."

"You have a problem with Reece Bannerman?"

"No, no problem," Dowler said, a little wary. "It's just that he's the biggest cattleman in these parts . . . and he knows it. If you get a job out there, you'll come back for your sorrel and your gear?"

"Yeah, in a few days. Soon as I get the chance."

Dowler nodded. "I'll take good care of him until then. Nothin' I like better than takin' care of a good horse. Lemme fetch that dun."

He led out the mouse-colored horse, which had a dark stripe down the center of its back. The dun gave him a baleful stare but didn't shy away as he mounted up.

"So long, Mr. Dowler," Matt said as he turned the horse toward the doors. "I'll be seeing you."

He rode out of the barn and paused in the street. Under other circumstances, it would have been nice to take a look around Buffalo Flat and see what the town had to offer. It was getting on toward the middle of the day, and Matt would have liked to find a café and have a good meal.

But he couldn't forget there was a seven-year-old girl out there somewhere, probably mighty scared and uncertain about what was going to happen to her. It was a strong possibility that Reece Bannerman had her and Matt knew he had to find out the truth, one way or another. He knew if Crazy Bear's granddaughter remained missing long enough, it was bound to lead to trouble between the Crow and the white settlers who had moved into the valley. An Indian war would mean blood and suffering.

So Matt turned his back on Buffalo Flat and rode north, toward the Circle B. He didn't know what he would find there . . . and he wasn't sure what to hope for.

Chapter 25

He forded the easternmost of the two creeks—Badger Creek, Starwind had called it—and continued working his way up the valley. He began seeing quite a few cattle, and when he rode closer to them, he saw the Circle B brand burned into their hides. He was on Bannerman range, all right.

The sudden sound of a shot made him rein in. The gun had gone off somewhere nearby, but hadn't come too close to him. As he looked around, searching for the origin of the shot, three riders emerged from a stand of timber to his right and galloped toward him.

They charged straight at him but he didn't turn and run. Not wanting to give them an excuse to come after him, he stood his ground, sitting calmly in the saddle as he watched them approach. He held the reins with his left hand, and his right rested lightly on his thigh, not far from the butt of his Colt.

The men spread out and rode up in front of him, reining in so there were about five yards between each of them. It was a smart move. If things came to gunplay he'd have a hard time downing all of them before they could get lead in him.

Matt didn't intend to let that happen. He smiled faintly and nodded to the men. "Howdy," he said. "I reckon one of you fired that shot I heard a minute ago?"

"That was a warning shot, mister," the man in the middle said. He was stocky, with a thick black mustache drooping over his mouth. "This is Circle B range, and people don't ride here unless they're invited."

Matt glanced at the other two. The one to his right was tall and skinny, with hair like straw sticking out from under a battered gray hat. The man had an ugly grin on his face. The one to Matt's left was stoic and dark-complected, wearing a cowhide vest and a black hat. He was so bland-looking, the sort of man you'd glance at once and then forget, Matt figured he might be the most dangerous of the three.

"Sorry if I'm intruding," he said. "I'm not looking for trouble. I was passing through Buffalo Flat, heard about your ranch, and thought you might be hiring."

"It ain't *my* ranch," the spokesman said. "It belongs to Mr. Reece Bannerman. My name's Jud Talley, and I'm the foreman."

"Matt West," Matt introduced himself, picking the name out of his memory. Smoke had called himself Buck West when he visited the same valley years ago. Matt had already taken the name Jensen; he figured he might as well adopt part of Smoke's old alias, too.

"You don't look like a cowhand, West," Talley said.

"I've punched cows," Matt replied with a shrug, "but I've done other things, too."

"What sort of things?"

"Rode shotgun on a stage line out of Lordsburg, scouted some for the Army down in Arizona Territory, panned for gold over in Idaho. Some other jobs here and there."

"Are you any good with that gun?"

"Good enough," Matt said.

The straw-haired gent on the right spoke up. "That's big talk!" he said. "You want to prove it, mister?"

Talley snapped, "Take it easy, Hennessy."

The man leveled his left arm at Matt. "I don't like the way he looks at me, like he thinks he's better'n me! Lemme kill him, Jud. Lemme plug the son of a bitch!"

Matt saw what was going on. Hennessy was trying to goad him into a fight. If he drew on Hennessy, then the third man would kill him. A man couldn't beat the odds if he fell into a trap like that.

The trick was to not fall for it. Instead, Matt smiled again and said, "If you reach for your gun, Hennessy, I'm gonna kill this hombre over here on my left first thing. I'm betting you're slow enough that I can ventilate him and still have plenty of time to put lead in you."

Hennessy went slack-jawed with surprise. Talley's face darkened with anger. The third man's expression remained unreadable, except for a tiny sparkle of amusement in his eyes.

"Hennessy's right, you're full of big talk!" Talley said. "What's to stop me from killin' you while you're takin' care of these other two?"

"Not a thing, if *you're* fast enough," Matt said. "But I've got a hunch that I can blast you out of the saddle, too, before I cross the divide."

"Jud, we cain't let him talk to us like that," Hennessy protested. "We just cain't!"

The third man finally said something. "Hennessy, shut your mouth, you damn yokel. This hombre didn't ride out here by mistake, and he's not the sort of man you want to trifle with." The man moved his horse slightly closer. "My name's Lew Torrance, West. Maybe you've heard of me."

Matt nodded. "Reckon I have."

"You're not looking for a regular cowhand's job, are you?"

"Not particularly."

"You must've heard that Bannerman's looking for fighting men."

Matt shrugged. It was fine with him if Torrance believed that, although it wasn't true.

"Come on to headquarters with us," Torrance invited. "You can talk to the boss. No guarantees that he'll hire you, though."

"Fair enough," Matt said.

Talley burst out, "Wait just a damn minute here! I'm still the ramrod of this crew."

"Not this part of it," Torrance drawled. He inclined his head in the direction of the ranch headquarters. "Come on, West."

Matt rode past Talley and Hennessy and fell in alongside Torrance. He watched the other two men from the corner of his eye as he passed them. He didn't think they would make a try for him, but he was ready if they did.

He didn't much cotton to the idea of having Talley and Hennessy behind him, but he caught the warning look and the slight shake of the head that Torrance gave the men. Torrance was telling them to lay off, at least until they reached headquarters.

"You know anybody that I might know?" Torrance asked as they rode along. From the sound of the question, he was just making idle conversation, but Matt suspected there was more to it than that.

"I've crossed trails a time or two with Smoke Jensen," Matt said. No lie there.

Torrance grunted. "Jensen, eh? The two of you friends?"

"I wouldn't say that." True again, because Smoke and Matt were much closer than just friends. They were as close as brothers. "You know him?"

"Never met the man," Torrance replied blandly. "I've heard of him, of course. Supposed to be mighty fast on the draw."

"That's what I've heard, too."

A faint smile tugged at the corners of Torrance's mouth. "Maybe one day we'll find out who's faster, eh?"

"Could be."

"What about Frank Morgan?"

"The one they call The Drifter?" Matt asked.

"Yeah."

"Never met him, never even seen him."

"I did, once," Torrance said. "We were on opposite sides of

a little dustup in Kansas. I rode away from it alive. Some of the boys I was with didn't."

"It's a hard life," Matt said.

"But when you don't know anything else, it's tough to get away from it."

"Yeah," Matt agreed with a world-weary air that belied his youth. To a certain extent, it was a pose, but he was also beginning to understand the truth of it.

Torrance fell silent. If he had been trying to get a feel for Matt, evidently he was satisfied. About half an hour later, they came to the ranch headquarters.

Set on a long bench of land between the creek and a rugged bluff, the headquarters of the Circle B gave ample evidence the spread was a successful one. The sprawling, two-story, whitewashed house was the centerpiece, but it was surrounded by a couple barns, a series of corrals, a long, low bunkhouse, small cabins for the married hands, a smokehouse, a blacksmith shop, and several storage buildings. Pines grew close around the ranch house, and the contrast between the dark green needles and the whitewashed walls was striking. There were covered verandahs on three sides of the house.

Matt saw quite a few men moving around the ranch, mostly from the bunkhouse to the barns and back again, or from the barns to the corrals. Bannerman had a pretty big crew working for him. Most of them would be regular cowhands, but some would be like Torrance, recruited for his skill with a gun, not because he could handle a rope and a branding iron. If Bannerman was intent on grabbing more and more range for himself, he would need more men who could shoot. Matt was counting on that.

There was one similarity between the Circle B ranch and the Crow Indian village. Several dogs bounded out, barking loudly, as the men rode up. The commotion was bound to draw the attention of anyone in the house, so Matt wasn't surprised when the front door opened and a man stepped out onto the porch.

From the man's staight-backed, arrogant stance, Matt knew he was looking at Reece Bannerman.

The cattleman was around fifty. He was only medium height, but at first glance he appeared bigger because of the leashed power in his muscular body. He had big hands, and the calluses and knobby knuckles showed that he had done plenty of physical work in his life. His jaw thrust out defiantly. He had lost most of his hair except for a sandy fringe around his ears and the back of his head. He wore boots, a pair of canvas trousers, and a brown vest over a white shirt.

"Who's this, Jud?" Bannerman's voice lashed out like the crack of a whip.

"We found him ridin' on Circle B range south of here, boss," Talley replied. "Says his name's Matt West. Claims he's lookin' for a job."

Bannerman glared at Matt. "When I need to hire cowhands, West, I go looking for them. I don't give jobs to any grub-line rider who comes along."

"I wasn't exactly looking for that kind of job, Mr. Bannerman," Matt said. "I hear that you're looking for men who don't mind a little trouble."

The rancher's gaze moved over to Torrance. "What about it, Lew? You know this hombre?"

"Never heard of him," Torrance answered. "But I like the way he carries himself."

Bannerman made a curt, dismissive gesture. "You can't tell anything by that. You have to see a man in action to really know what he can do. Hennessy!"

The tall, straw-haired puncher had brought his horse up next to Matt's. As Bannerman barked out his name, Hennessy left his saddle in a sudden diving tackle that sent him crashing into Matt. Taken by surprise, Matt toppled off the dun and fell heavily to the ground in front of the porch, landing with Hennessy on top of him slamming bony fists into his face.

Chapter 26

Matt's surprise didn't last long. His instincts took over. He thrust his left arm up to block the punch descending toward his face, then brought his right fist up in a short but powerful jab that landed on Hennessy's nose. The cowboy howled in pain as blood spurted over Matt's knuckles.

Matt rolled and heaved, throwing Hennessy off to the side. Their horses were dancing skittishly around the struggling men, and Matt knew he had to get clear or risk being stepped on. He reached up, grabbed a dangling stirrup, and used it to brace himself as he surged to his feet.

Hennessy had made it upright as well. He charged toward Matt, swinging his long arms in wild, windmilling blows. Matt ducked and let a sweeping punch go harmlessly over his head. He stepped in and hammered a right and a left to Hennessy's midsection. The straw-haired puncher bent over and staggered back a step, putting him in perfect position for the hard right that Matt threw. His fist landed cleanly on Hennessy's jaw. The impact slewed Hennessy's head around and sent him crashing to the ground, out cold.

But Matt's troubles weren't over. The fight had drawn the attention of the other cowboys who were around the ranch headquarters, and as Matt tried to catch his breath, Bannerman made another gesture that sent a couple of the punchers charging at him from behind.

Hearing the rush of footsteps, Matt swung around and set himself for the attack. He dodged the initial punch from one man, but that brought him within reach of the other. The second man's fist raked along the side of Matt's head, above his right ear. He fought off the pain of the blow, grabbed the man's arm, and twisted at the waist, pivoting to throw the man over his hip in a wrestling move Smoke had taught him years before.

That move allowed the first man to grab him from behind. The man's arm went around Matt's neck in a choke hold and jerked him backward. Matt drove his elbow into the man's belly, which caused the man to grunt in pain but didn't loosen his grip enough for Matt to pull free.

The cowboy's forearm pressed into Matt's throat like an iron bar. Unable to breathe, cut off from air, Matt's head began to spin and his vision blurred. He reached back with both hands, knocked the man's hat off, and tangled his fingers in the man's hair. Bending forward sharply at the waist, Matt hauled as hard as he could with his arms. The man came off his feet and with a wild yell tumbled over Matt's back and crashed down in the dust.

Matt didn't get any respite. Back in the fight the second man tackled Matt from behind, knocking him to the ground. He tried to drive his knee into the small of Matt's back, but Matt twisted aside in time to avoid being pinned. He swung around and chopped a sidehand blow against the spot where the man's neck met his shoulder. It landed with paralyzing force. Matt followed it with a left jab to the man's belly, then slugged the cowboy with his right fist. The man's eyes rolled back in their sockets and he went limp.

Matt put a hand on the ground to brace himself and shoved upright. He was battered and breathing hard but still had plenty of fight left in him.

"Got any more, Bannerman?" he snarled at the rancher. "Or are you done?"

A smile appeared on Bannerman's hard-planed face. He waved away the other men who were closing in around Matt.

"That's enough," he said. "You're quite a battler, aren't you, West?"

"I don't back up when trouble comes at me, if that's what you mean," Matt snapped.

"That's exactly what I mean." Bannerman jerked his head toward the door. "Come on in. You, too, Lew."

"What about me, boss?" Talley asked as Torrance started up the steps to the porch along with Matt.

"You go on about your chores," Bannerman said dismissively. Matt glanced at Talley and saw the anger and resentment in the man's eyes. Talley might run the regular ranch crew, but it was clear that he didn't have any authority over Torrance and the other gunmen.

Matt filed that knowledge away. He might not ever need it, but you never could tell when something like that might come in handy.

Bannerman led the way into a large room furnished with heavy furniture, woven Indian rugs on the floors, and numerous sets of antlers from moose, antelope, and elk mounted on the walls. A huge stone fireplace dominated one wall. It was a dark, masculine room that looked like it had never known the touch of a woman.

"Want a drink?" Bannerman asked Matt.

"I could use one after that tussle."

Bannerman went to a sideboard, uncorked a bottle of whiskey, and splashed liquor into three glasses. He handed one to Matt, another to Torrance, and took the third one for himself.

"Sorry I had to do that. A lot of men claim to be tough, but then fold up when it comes to trouble." Bannerman paused, then added significantly, "You didn't." He lifted his glass in salute.

Matt returned it, then downed the slug of whiskey as Bannerman and Torrance drank theirs. It was good stuff, potent but smooth. Matt wasn't surprised. Bannerman didn't strike him as a man who would settle for second best in anything. It was why the cattleman had his eye on the entire valley, including the land that had been used for years as a hunting ground by the Crow.

"So you want a job," Bannerman went on.

"If the pay's right," Matt said.

"Ask Torrance," Bannerman said with a nod toward the bland-faced gunman. "He can tell you that you'll make more money working for me than for any other rancher in this part of the territory. For one thing, by the time I'm finished those other spreads will have gone under and been absorbed by the Circle B."

"You intend to grab all the range around here, is that it?"

Bannerman's face tightened with annoyance. "It's not a land grab when the strongest man winds up with the range. It's the way things were meant to be! Do you believe in destiny, West?"

The sudden question took Matt a little by surprise. "I suppose so."

"Well, it's my destiny to be the most powerful man in Wyoming. It's all well and good to be senator or governor, but I'm going to be the man who pulls *their* strings. There's a lot of money and power up for grabs, and I intend to have the lion's share of it." Bannerman reached for the bottle. "There's enough so that you and Torrance and the other men who work for me can have a share in it, too."

Matt shook his head when Bannerman proceeded to pour more whiskey into his glass. It was only the middle of the day, and Matt hadn't eaten since breakfast in the Crow village that morning.

"That sounds mighty good," he said. "What do we have to do to get our share?"

"It's simple. You do anything I tell you." Bannerman looked intently at him. "Anything."

The man expected some sort of reaction. Matt shrugged and said, "Fine. Like I said, as long as the money's good . . ."

"That's what I like to hear. I like a man who understands the true value of money. Lew, get West settled in. You can tell him what his job will be."

Torrance nodded. "Sure, boss."

Bannerman lifted his glass again, which he had filled half full of whiskey. "Good to have you with us, West."

"Same here," Matt said.

That was a lie, of course. He thought Bannerman was repulsive and didn't doubt for a second that the man would use a scared little girl as leverage to get what he wanted.

But Matt didn't have any proof, and more importantly, he didn't know where Bannerman might be holding Moon Fawn, if indeed he had her.

Starwind had been nosing around the line camps north of there when those gunmen jumped her, Matt reminded himself. He needed to get a look at that area as soon as he could.

Torrance took him back outside and said, "You can put your horse in the corral, West, then I'll show you where you'll sleep in the bunkhouse."

"If it's all the same to you, Torrance, I'd just as soon get started on the job."

Torrance smiled. "Eager, eh? We can find something for you to do this afternoon. But it's almost time for lunch now. Come on."

Matt led the dun into the corral Torrance pointed out and unsaddled the horse. Torrance looked the animal over and said, "That is one ugly horse."

"Yeah, but he's got plenty of sand," Matt said as he carried the saddle into the barn. He hoped that statement was true. He had only Hoyt Dowler's word for it, since he hadn't really had to put the dun to the test on the way out there.

As they walked toward the bunkhouse, Matt went on,

"What were you and Talley and Hennessy doing down on that south range this morning? No offense, Torrance, but you don't strike me as the sort of hombre they send out looking for strays."

"We ride regular patrols around the whole spread," Torrance explained. "The boss likes to keep people off his range. And right now the Indians who live a ways west of here are all stirred up about something."

"I didn't know there was Indian trouble in these parts."

"Usually there's not. Those Crows are just one step above blanket Indians. They don't give trouble. But some little girl is missing, according to what I've heard in town. The chief's granddaughter or something. If they get upset enough about it, they're liable to go on the warpath. That's another reason the boss wants scouts out all the time, keeping an eye on things. If you ask me, the thing to do is ride over there and wipe out that redskin village. I don't like waiting around for trouble to happen. I'd rather nip it in the bud."

Several things about those comments bothered Matt. For one, he thought that Torrance's derogatory opinion of the Crow was dead wrong. Just because Crazy Bear and his people preferred living in peace with the white men didn't mean they had lost their courage or given up their dignity for a mess of blankets, like some tribes had done.

For another, Torrance acted like he didn't know what had happened to Moon Fawn. Torrance seemed to be the ramrod of Bannerman's hired guns. Wouldn't he be aware of it if Bannerman had the girl?

Matt didn't think asking a question would make the gunman too suspicious, since they were discussing the subject anyway. He said, "You have any idea what happened to the girl?"

Torrance shook his head. "For all I know, she wandered off and fell in a ravine or a mountain lion got her."

As far as Matt could tell, Torrance sounded completely sincere. He pushed matters a little farther, saying, "Has there been any trouble with the Indians? Anybody on the crew been hurt?"

"No, not so far. It pays to be careful, though."

Matt didn't understand that at all. If it had been Bannerman's men who attacked Starwind the day before, several of them had been wounded and maybe even killed in the ruckus. Torrance should have mentioned that.

If they *weren't* Bannerman's men, why had they attacked Starwind when she started searching the area for her niece?

Matt didn't have an answer for that. Crazy Bear had made it sound like he and his people had searched the entire valley for the missing girl, except for the Circle B. That meant Moon Fawn had to be on the ranch somewhere, didn't it? That reasoning was why Matt had gotten the job with Bannerman in the first place.

The mystery had deepened. Matt still felt the answers lay in the area where Starwind had been attacked the day before. As soon as possible, he wanted to get up there and have a look around for himself.

Doing so might be the same thing as painting a big target on his back . . . but it wouldn't be the first time he had done such a thing, he told himself wryly as he followed Lew Torrance into the bunkhouse.

Chapter 27

After lunch, which was served in a mess hall attached to the bunkhouse, Torrance told Matt, "Reckon the first thing we need to do is get you acquainted with the range you'll be patrolling. The spread's too big to ride all the way around in one day, but I can show you part of it this afternoon. We'll take a *pasear* [walk] up north a ways."

Matt nodded without showing his true reaction to the gunman's words. That was the area he wanted to have a look at. Unfortunately, having Torrance along with him would limit the amount of searching he could do.

"I don't mind exploring it on my own," he offered, but Torrance shook his head.

"No, I'll go with you. Wouldn't want you running into any trouble by yourself on your first day."

They saddled their horses and set out from the ranch headquarters. Matt glanced back at the big whitewashed house, wondering suddenly what the chances were that Moon Fawn was locked up somewhere in there. Eventually he might have to figure out a way to have a look around inside the house.

He still wasn't sure what Reece Bannerman would have to gain by kidnapping the little girl. If Bannerman intended to use Moon Fawn as a bargaining chip to force the Crow to give up their hunting ground, he would have been in touch with Crazy Bear and given the chief his demands already, wouldn't he?

Matt sensed something else was in play, something he didn't know about yet.

Within a couple hours after leaving the ranch headquarters, Matt began to recognize the area where he had rescued Starwind from those gunmen the day before. He said, "Bannerman's range comes this far north?"

"Well . . . not the part he's actually filed on, I suppose," Torrance answered. "But this is open range country, West, you ought to know that. A man can graze his cattle wherever he wants to, as long as he's strong enough to hold the range."

"As long as somebody else hasn't filed on it," Matt said.

Torrance snorted. "Nobody's filed on this range. There aren't any spreads up here except for Circle B. The Indians seem to think they have some claim to this area because they're used to hunting on it, but you know good and well they never filed on it. Indians don't believe that anybody can *own* property. It's all just there for them to use."

Matt knew that was true. The concept of land belonging to somebody was foreign to the Indians, which was one reason they had had so much trouble adjusting to the white man's ways.

They rode past a small, stone-and-timber cabin. Matt nodded toward it and asked, "Is that a line shack?"

"Yeah. The boss sends men up here during the summer, when all the stock is moved to this end of the range. There are half a dozen of them built at intervals along the edge of the foothills. Nobody's using them right now. The regular crew won't start pushing all the cattle up here for another month or so."

"Maybe not," Matt said, "but somebody's in that cabin. Look at the chimney."

"What do you mean? There's no smoke coming out of that chimney."

"No, but you can see the heat still rising from it. The fire may be out now, but it was burning just a few minutes ago and the ashes are still hot."

Torrance's eyes narrowed as he looked at the little ripples of heat in the air that Matt had spotted first. "Son of a bitch," he said. "You're right. Nobody's supposed to be there."

"Maybe we'd better check it out."

Torrance shook his head. "We ride straight up there, we're liable to get blasted out of the saddle. We'll go on past, then once we're out of sight we can circle back around through the trees and come at the cabin from behind. Something's going on here, and I want to know what it is."

So did Matt, since he felt the chances were pretty good it had something to do with the missing girl.

The two men hadn't given any indication they were paying undue attention to the supposedly empty line shack. Not in any hurry they rode on—past the cabin. Matt felt eyes on him, watching him, and figured whoever was inside the cabin was peering out through the chinks and loopholes. He thought again about having a target painted on his back, feeling it more than ever before.

Matt and Torrance continued riding north, and within a few minutes, the cabin had disappeared from sight behind them. When they were sure they were out of sight, Torrance jerked his head toward the trees on the hillside.

"Let's go," he ordered.

They urged their horses to a faster pace and loped into the timber. Since Torrance knew the country better, he led the way as they circled back toward the cabin. It didn't take long to reach the vicinity of the line shack.

Torrance reined in and motioned for Matt to do likewise. They swung down from the saddles, and Torrance said, "We'll go ahead on foot from here."

Leaving their mounts ground-hitched, the two men moved forward through the trees and underbrush. Matt's hand moved toward the butt of his Colt as he heard movement up ahead. He relaxed as he recognized the sounds as horses shifting around and blowing air through their noses.

Matt and Torrance stepped into a clearing a moment later and found six horses there, contained in a crude rope corral. "Check their brands," Torrance whispered. "I don't think they're Circle B stock. I don't recognize any of them."

Matt moved closer and looked at the marks burned into the horses' rumps. All the brands were different, and none of them were Circle B.

That didn't necessarily mean anything. The gunmen who hired on to ride for Bannerman could have drifted in from anywhere, and their horses would naturally bear different brands. But at least the fact that they hadn't come from the Circle B remuda wasn't a direct indictment of the rancher.

Matt wondered if the men who'd attacked Starwind the day before were inside the cabin. Torrance motioned to go around the corral and close in on the cabin.

They came out behind it. Both men dropped into crouches and parted the brush carefully so that they could study the place. No one moved around the cabin, but a thin plume of smoke curled from the chimney. Whoever was inside had rekindled the fire.

Torrance put his mouth next to Matt's ear and said quietly, "Whoever those bastards are, they don't have any right to be in there. I want to draw them out. You up for it?"

"What do you want me to do?" Matt asked.

"See that stack of firewood next to the cabin? We'll split up. I'll go left, and you go around to the right where that firewood is. Grab a chunk of it and throw it up on the roof. They'll have to come out to see what the hell made the noise."

Matt thought about it for a second and then nodded. The plan sounded like it would work, and as far as he could tell, Torrance meant what he said and wasn't trying to set up some sort of trap for him. Both men drew their guns, then emerged from the brush and catfooted toward the cabin, moving fast but quietly.

Matt reached the rear corner and pressed his back against the wall for a second, listening. He heard the low rumble of men's voices inside the cabin. Then he stole along the wall to the stack of firewood and picked up a good-sized piece. He stepped away from the wall far enough so that he could heave the chunk of wood into the air above the cabin.

It landed on the roof with a solid thud, then bounced and rolled off, making even more racket. A man inside the cabin let out a startled curse, and another one said in a loud voice, "What the hell's that?"

Moving quickly to the front corner, Matt waited, gun in hand. The door of the cabin was thrown open, and three men stepped out to look around. One held a Winchester slanted across his chest, and the other two gripped revolvers in their fists.

Matt had hoped all six men would come out of the cabin, then he remembered he had probably killed one of them and at least two of the others had been wounded, no telling how badly. The three who showed themselves might be the only able-bodied ones left in the bunch, and one of them had a bloody bandage tied around his arm.

"Spread out!" one of the men ordered when they didn't see anything on top of the cabin. "Head around back!"

There was no point in waiting any longer. Matt stepped into view and leveled his Colt at the men, and he saw that Torrance had done the same thing on the other side of the cabin.

"Hold it!" Torrance ordered. "Drop those guns and put your hands up!"

He and Matt had the element of surprise on their side, and for a split-second, Matt thought the men were going to comply with the order.

But the man with the rifle whipped the barrel toward Torrance, who fired before the man had time to pull the Winchester's trigger. The bullet smacked into the man's chest and knocked him back a step.

At the same time, one of the other men jerked his gun toward Matt, who shouted, "Don't do it!"

The man ignored the warning, so Matt had no choice. The Colt roared and bucked in his hand. A black hole appeared in the man's forehead where the .44 slug bored through his skull and into his brain. He dropped like a rock.

Torrance blasted a second shot into the man with the rifle, and the man went down. That left one man on his feet, and he fired wildly as he made a dash for the cabin door. Torrance dropped him on his face with a well-placed shot that ripped through his body.

Matt saw movement inside the cabin's dim interior and yelled, "Look out!" Torrance threw himself aside as a great gout of flame erupted from both barrels of a shotgun. He rolled to the corner, out of the line of fire, and Matt drew back to the other corner.

The man inside bellowed, "I don't know who you bastards are, but I'll kill this little girl if you don't move out where I can see you and throw your guns down!"

An icy finger traced a path down Matt's spine as he heard the harsh-voiced threat. Moon Fawn was in there, all right, and her life was in deadly danger.

Torrance called, "You've got that little Indian girl who's missing?"

"That's right, mister, and I'll kill her if you don't do exactly what I say!"

"How do we know that?"

A second later, Matt heard a sharp cry from inside the cabin, then a wail of fear that trailed off into sobs.

"I didn't hurt her . . . much," the man said. "But next time I will."

"Take it easy," Torrance said. "If you hurt that little girl, you're liable to set off an Indian war that'll have this whole valley running red with blood."

"Well, then, that'll be on your head, not mine," the man

shot back. "Now get out there where I can see you, damn it, and throw down your guns!"

Matt and Torrance exchanged glances. Both of them knew that if they went along with what the man wanted, he'd just gun them down as soon as he had the chance. And they couldn't get to him in the cabin, especially not as long as he had the little girl for a hostage. They had to draw him out some way.

"You got me with that buckshot, you bastard," Torrance said. He put a note of strain in his voice, as if he were in pain. "My leg's shot to hell. I can't move."

"Throw your gun out where I can see it, then. And your partner still needs to step out there in the open."

Torrance nodded to Matt, telling him to go along with what the man wanted. That was an easy decision for Torrance to make, Matt thought. He wasn't the one who was going to be staked out like a judas goat.

"All right," Torrance said. "Here comes my gun."

He tossed his Colt into the doorway where the man inside could see it.

"Now you, mister," the man ordered. "The one to the right of the door."

Matt took a deep breath and threw his revolver onto the ground next to Torrance's. "All right," he said. "I'm stepping out."

"Keep your hands where I can see 'em, damn it!"

Holding his hands away from his body at shoulder height, Matt moved away from the cabin, angling forward so that he was in front of the open door. The man loomed up out of the shadows inside the cabin. He held Moon Fawn in front of him with one arm around her waist. Her feet dangled in the air. She looked terrified as she clutched a doll to her. The man's other hand held a gun pressed into her side.

Torrance had drawn a hide-out gun, a small pistol that had been holstered at the small of his back, under his vest. Before Torrance could fire, the kidnapper twisted so that Moon Fawn shielded him. At the same time, he took the gun away from her side and leveled it at Matt.

"You son of a bitch," he said to Torrance. "You ain't hurt. You lied to me."

Torrance smiled coldly. "I'm not going to lose any sleep over lying to a man who'd kidnap a little girl."

"Drop that gun, or I'll shoot your partner."

"Go ahead," Torrance told him. "I never even met the hombre until today." He glanced at Matt. "Sorry, West . . . but this ends here."

As the kidnapper's face twisted in a snarl and his finger whitened on the trigger, Matt knew it was going to end, all right . . . one way or another.

Chapter 28

Matt heard a faint fluttering sound just before the gun blasted. He was already throwing himself forward, hoping to dive out of the way of the bullet, when he saw the man's head writhe backward on his neck. The man gave a gurgling scream and dropped both Moon Fawn and his gun as he started to paw at the shaft of the arrow that pierced his throat. Blood spurted out around it.

Matt scooped up his gun, but he didn't need it. Torrance held his fire as well, as the wounded man staggered around in a wild, grotesque dance of death. Finally, as blood continued to pour like a river down the front of his shirt, he collapsed. The way he landed drove the arrow the rest of the way through his throat, so that the head stuck out the back of his neck. He twitched a time or two and then lay still.

Up on one knee Matt leveled his Colt at the doorway, but no one else appeared in it.

"Cover me," Torrance said. "I'll check inside."

Matt nodded. Torrance ducked through the door, moving fast and crouching low in case anybody in there took a shot at him. Matt didn't hear anything from inside. A few moments later, Torrance reappeared, shaking his head.

"Nobody in there but some hombre who was already dead," he reported.

One of the men who'd been wounded the day before hadn't made it, Matt knew, and his companions hadn't gotten around to burying him. He must not have been dead long.

Matt holstered his gun as he stood up. He moved quickly to Moon Fawn's side and knelt again to pick up the little girl.

"It's all right," he told her, not knowing if she spoke English. He tried to make his tone comforting enough that she would realize he was a friend, even if she didn't understand the words. He went on, "You're safe now, and I reckon there's somebody here you know."

He stood up with Moon Fawn in his arms and turned to look around.

"Starwind!" he called. "You can come out now. It's all over."

"What the hell?" Torrance asked.

"Where do you think that arrow came from?"

With a slight rustling of brush, Starwind appeared and came striding out of the trees. She had another arrow nocked, and she cast a wary eye toward Torrance as she approached.

"West, you son of a bitch," the gunman said. "You were in with the redskins all along. That business about looking for a job was a lie."

"Well, it's not like we were pards for a long time before you found out the truth," Matt said dryly. "After all, we just met this morning, like you told that hombre when he was threatening to shoot me, remember?"

"I wouldn't have let him kill you," Torrance protested. Matt didn't believe that for a second.

Matt had his left arm supporting Moon Fawn. He kept his right hand close to his gun. He didn't fully trust Torrance. Not even close.

"You can put that arrow away, Starwind," he told the young woman.

She glared at Torrance and said, "This man works for Bannerman."

"Yes, but he didn't know anything about Moon Fawn's disappearance. He even helped rescue her. You must know that if you've been trailing me." Matt smiled faintly and shook his head. "I should have expected as much when you were gone this morning. You were just waiting for me to leave the village so you could pick up my trail, weren't you?"

"You never knew I was there." Starwind's voice held a note of pride.

"That was because I never expected to be followed. Now that I think about it, though, I reckon I should have expected it, because I knew how blasted stubborn you are."

Moon Fawn was starting to squirm in Matt's grip. She held out her arms toward her aunt and called, "Starwind!"

That appeal helped Starwind make up her mind. She took the arrow and slid it back in the quiver, then stepped over to Matt and held out her arms to take her niece from him. She drew the little girl into a tight embrace.

"That's touching as all get-out," Torrance said, "but who the hell are you really, West? That's not even your name, is it?"

"Name's Matt Jensen," Matt said.

"Jensen!" Torrance's lips drew back from his teeth in a snarl. "We were just talking about Smoke Jensen a while ago. Are you any relation to him?"

"We're brothers. Adopted, I reckon you'd say. Look, don't get a burr under your saddle, Torrance. All I was trying to do was get that little girl back safe and sound to her family."

"Then why did you lie about who you are and get a job with Bannerman? You thought he'd kidnapped that kid, didn't you?"

Matt shrugged. "She didn't seem to be anywhere else in the valley." He inclined his head toward the cabin. "And this *is* one of Bannerman's line shacks."

"That doesn't mean a blasted thing! None of us knew those varmints were here, and we sure didn't know they had the girl. Hell, West—I mean, Jensen—I was as surprised as you were."

"Do not believe him, Matt Jensen," Starwind warned as

she held Moon Fawn and patted the child on the back. "He works for Bannerman. He cannot be trusted."

"He killed two of the kidnappers," Matt pointed out. "I reckon that's got to count for something."

Torrance snorted in disgust. "Damn right it does. I risked my neck for that kid, and I don't appreciate some squaw shooting her mouth off about me."

Matt saw the flare of anger on Starwind's face and knew he had to intervene before things got out of hand.

"We'll take Moon Fawn back to the village," he told her. "While we're doing that, Torrance can go back to the Circle B and tell Bannerman what happened." Matt looked at the gunman. "Is that all right with you?"

"I suppose," Torrance answered in a surly voice. "Then if I were you, I'd make myself scarce in these parts, Jensen. I don't cotton to being lied to. Next time we see each other, it won't be as friends."

"Don't reckon we ever were friends," Matt said, his own voice soft with menace. He was getting tired of Torrance being so prickly. It would have been fine with him if the man wanted to have it out right there . . . except for the fact that Matt wanted to see Starwind and Moon Fawn back safely in the Crow village with Crazy Bear.

Torrance jerked his head in a curt nod and headed for the timber where they had left the horses. Matt and Starwind waited until the gunman had emerged from the trees on his mount and trotted off toward the Circle B headquarters. Then Matt fetched the dun while Starwind went to get her pony.

"What about them?" Starwind asked with a nod toward the dead men sprawled on the ground on front of the cabin.

"They're the Good Lord's worry now," Matt said. "Or more likely, *El Diablo's*."

"You look different," Starwind commented as they rode toward the Crow village. "And that is not the same horse."

"Nope, it's not," Matt agreed. "I figured there was a chance some of the men we tangled with yesterday might work for Bannerman, and I didn't want them to recognize me when I rode out to the Circle B to look around."

"See? You thought they worked for Bannerman, too!"

"It seemed to be the most likely explanation. But from the looks of what happened today, the fellas who had Moon Fawn weren't Bannerman's men, even though they were using one of his line shacks for a hideout. Torrance explained to me that Bannerman's hands haven't started moving all the stock up here for the summer yet, so there wouldn't be many people around. If those men were careful, they could avoid being seen."

Starwind leaned over to talk to the little girl riding in front of her on the paint pony, clutching the doll she clearly hadn't let go of since the ordeal began. "Moon Fawn, how did you come to be with those men?"

She shook her head, clearly not wanting to talk about it.

"You have to tell us," Starwind urged. "We have to know what happened."

Fighting back tears, Moon Fawn said, "You . . . you are angry with me."

"No! No one is angry. We were just frightened for you, that's all. Now, can you tell us how they captured you?"

Moon Fawn swallowed. "I . . . I was riding up the valley . . . like you do, Starwind."

Without letting the little girl see her, Starwind grimaced. Matt saw the reaction and knew that Starwind was still blaming herself for what had happened, at least a little.

"They came out of some trees and asked me who I was," Moon Fawn went on. "I didn't want to talk to them, but I was afraid not to. When I told them, they said I had to come with them. I tried to get away . . . I made my pony run . . . but I was not fast enough. They caught me and took me off my pony and carried me back to that place where you found me."

"Did they hurt you?" Starwind asked softly.

"No." Moon Fawn fought back a sob. "They just scared me. But they gave me food, and they didn't beat me."

"I reckon that's good," Matt said, "or else Crazy Bear might've found some way to torture them even though they're already dead." He smiled over at the little girl. "Moon Fawn, can I ask you a question?"

She returned his smile tentatively and nodded.

"Did you hear the men talking much?" Matt asked. "Did you hear them say why they took you to that cabin, or who they worked for?"

"No. They said that since they had me . . . my grandfather would have to tell them where it was."

"It?" Matt repeated.

Moon Fawn nodded solemnly.

"They didn't say what this *it* was? Did they say what they were looking for?"

"No. But they sounded like it was very important, and they wanted it very much."

Matt and Starwind exchanged puzzled glances. The young woman gave a little shake of her head, indicating that she had no idea what Moon Fawn was talking about. Neither did Matt.

But they could figure that out later, he supposed. The important thing was that Moon Fawn was safe, and they were nearly back to the Crow village. In fact, the dogs had started to bark a greeting.

That brought people out to see what was going on, and as soon as they spotted Moon Fawn riding in front of Starwind, shouts of excitement and joy filled the village. Crazy Bear ran to meet them, his long legs carrying him swiftly over the ground. He wasn't the proud chief of the Crow at that moment; he was a loving grandfather filled with relief that his granddaughter was all right.

He plucked her off the back of Starwind's pony, held her high above his head, and the smile that wreathed his face transformed the grim, ugly visage into something almost beautiful.

"Moon Fawn," he said in a voice choked with emotion, "you have come back to us!" He looked at Matt and Starwind. "Your aunt and our good friend have brought you back to us."

Mala caught up to him then, took the child from him and hugged Moon Fawn, too. Crazy Bear turned to Matt, who had dismounted. The chief held out his hand.

"Thank you, Matt Jensen," he rumbled. "Like your blood brother before you, you have proven to be a good friend to the Crow."

Matt shook with him. Matt's own hand wasn't small, but Crazy Bear's paw swallowed it up almost like it wasn't there.

"I'm just glad I came along when I did and was able to lend a hand," Matt said.

"Where did you find her?" Suspicion suddenly turned Crazy Bear's face back into something savage. "Bannerman had her!"

"No, she was being held in one of Bannerman's line shacks—"

"I knew it was him!"

"But he didn't have anything to do with it," Matt forged on. "In fact, it was one of Bannerman's men who helped me rescue Moon Fawn. He risked his life, too, Crazy Bear."

The chief frowned. "How can this be? Bannerman is the enemy of the Crow. He wants our hunting grounds for his cattle."

Matt shook his head. "That's not the way it looks. Those men used the Circle B line shack because they thought no one would be around. They planned to use Moon Fawn to force you to tell them where something is."

That puzzled Crazy Bear. "What something?"

"That's what we don't know. They never said what it was while Moon Fawn was around. Do you have any idea what the thing could be? Obviously, it's something valuable, and it's hidden somewhere."

Crazy Bear could only frown and shake his head. "I have

nothing valuable except my home and my family. I do not understand—"

A sudden shout from one of the men cut short the celebration. Matt turned and saw the warrior pointing across the grassy meadows. A large group of riders was coming toward the village. Matt recognized the man in the lead as Reece Bannerman.

So did Crazy Bear. "Bannerman!" he exclaimed. "He comes to make war!"

That seemed unlikely to Matt, but he couldn't think of any other reason for Bannerman and a bunch of the Circle B hands to be approaching the Crow village. Bannerman had at least some of his hired guns with him. Matt spotted Lew Torrance among the horsemen.

Crazy Bear shouted orders in the Crow tongue. The warriors raced to their lodges to get their rifles or bows and arrows. If Bannerman wanted a fight, the Crow would give him one.

A lot of blood would be spilled on both sides if that happened. Matt wanted to head off trouble if he could. He reached for the dun's reins and told Starwind, "Go with your father."

"I will go with him," she said, "and I will fight at his side!"

"There's not gonna be a fight," Matt muttered as he swung up into the saddle.

He hoped he was right about that. Bannerman had at least thirty heavily-armed men with him. They were outnumbered by the Crow warriors, but their superior firepower made the odds roughly even. Even enough that quite a few men might die, Indian and white alike.

Matt heeled the horse into a run that carried him toward Bannerman. He met the cattleman and the other men while they were still a couple hundred yards from the village and held up his left hand in a signal for them to stop.

Bannerman reined in with obvious reluctance, and his men followed suit.

"Get out of the way, West, or Jensen, or whatever the hell your name is!" Bannerman snapped. "I've got business with those redskins."

"Why don't you tell me what your business is?" Matt suggested.

"You speak for them now, is that it? You're that big of an Indian-lover?"

"If you'd seen that sweet little squaw he's friends with, boss, you might understand a little better," Torrance drawled. "She could make any man an Indian lover."

Matt felt a flush of anger. He hadn't actually liked Torrance, but he had felt a certain amount of respect for the man. That was common when you fought side by side with someone. But Torrance's crude comment had put an end to that.

"Just tell me what you want, Bannerman," Matt said.

Bannerman glared at him but said, "All right, I will. I want to make sure Crazy Bear understands that I didn't have anything to do with what happened to his granddaughter. I'd like to tell him that I'm glad she's back home safely."

That took Matt by surprise. He wouldn't have expected such a sentiment from Bannerman. The cattleman looked and sounded sincere, so Matt said, "If that's all you want to tell him, you can do it without thirty guns at your back."

Bannerman sneered. "If you think I'm going to ride into a village full of savages by myself, you're crazier than that chief of theirs."

"You won't be by yourself," Matt said. "I'll ride in with you. Your men can stay right here where they can see everything that's going on. You'll be in plain sight the whole time."

"Don't let this lying bastard tell you what to do, boss," Torrance urged.

Bannerman frowned as he thought over Matt's suggestion. After a long moment, he finally nodded and said, "All right, Jensen. I'll come with you . . . alone." Bannerman looked over at Torrance. "But here's what I want you to do, Lew. If anything happens to me, if there's any kind of double-cross . . . kill Jensen first."

Torrance grinned. "Happy to."

Matt looked at the gunman and shook his head a little, sad that it had come to that. He said to Bannerman, "Come on."

They rode toward the Crow village, and when it became obvious the rest of the men were staying where they were, Crazy Bear strode out from the village to meet them. Matt and Bannerman reined in when about ten feet separated them from the chief.

"Bannerman's got something he wants to say to you, Crazy Bear," Matt said.

Crazy Bear crossed his arms over his massive chest and waited in silence.

Bannerman rested his hands on his saddlehorn and leaned forward a little. "You and I have never really spoken, Crazy Bear." He glanced over at Matt. "He does speak English, doesn't he?"

"I speak the white man's tongue," Crazy Bear answered for himself.

"Well . . . good. That makes it simpler. My man told me about what happened earlier today. Crazy Bear, I want you to know I'm glad your granddaughter has been returned to you safe and sound. I also want to tell you that I had nothing to do with what happened to her. Those men who kidnapped her didn't work for me. I give you my word on that."

Crazy Bear's face was as impassive as ever, but Matt thought he saw a flicker of surprise in the chief's eyes. He had felt the same way at first.

"We want different things, you and I," Bannerman went on, "but I would never harm or threaten a child. When I fight, it's against another man. I don't make war on women or children."

"Nor do I," Crazy Bear said.

"All right." Bannerman nodded. "Just so you understand."

Crazy Bear returned the nod, slowly.

Bannerman looked at Matt. "I'm done here," he said.

"Then take your men and go."

Bannerman hauled his horse around and put the spurs to it. He galloped back to his men and didn't slow down as he passed them. They fell in behind him, riding fast away from the Crow village.

"Did he speak the truth?" Crazy Bear asked Matt.

"I don't know. Seemed like it. Why come all the way over here just to tell you a lie?"

"He is a white man," Crazy Bear said, as if that explained everything.

"So am I," Matt pointed out.

"No. You are Crazy Bear's friend. That makes you different." The chief suddenly smiled. "Now, come. Join us. We celebrate the return of Moon Fawn. There will be feasting and dancing."

Matt thought about Starwind. It would be nice to be able to spend time with her when she wasn't shooting arrows at folks or taking her shirt off.

Although . . .

Matt pushed that thought out of his head and smiled. He dismounted and led the dun as he said, "It would be an honor to join you and your people in your celebration, Chief."

Crazy Bear grinned and slapped him on the back. "You are the next best thing to a Crow, Matt Jensen!"

A high honor indeed.

Interlude

"I wound up staying in the village for a while," Matt concluded his story. "I spent quite a bit of time in Buffalo Flat, too, and got to know some of the people there before I started feeling fiddle-footed again."

Dusk had settled over the landscape outside the cabin. Inside, it was almost completely dark. Into that darkness, Smoke said, "Wait a minute. You said Lew Torrance helped you get Moon Fawn back from the men who'd kidnapped her?"

"That's right," Matt said. "Why? Do you know Torrance, Smoke?"

"Never met him, but I've seen him a couple of times." Smoke paused meaningfully. "The last time was out there with those gunnies who are tryin' to kill us."

"So Torrance still works for Bannerman. Can't say as I'm surprised."

"Wait just a gol durned minute," Preacher put in. "You never did found out how come those rannies grabbed the little girl?"

"No," Matt replied. "I don't know if they were working for themselves or for somebody else, either. I asked around, but I never discovered anything connecting them to Bannerman. And he seemed to back off after Moon Fawn was kidnapped.

He quit trying to take over the Crow hunting grounds, and as far as I know, there was peace between him and Crazy Bear."

Preacher grunted. "Until lately. That letter his boy writ for him said that Bannerman's started pushin' his stock across both creeks, and his punchers have been shootin' at any Crows they see."

"Yeah, if there was a truce, Bannerman's decided to end it," Smoke agreed. "From the way those varmints jumped us, they were just waiting for somebody to show up and try to give Crazy Bear a hand. They didn't want us to get to the village."

Matt peered out one of the loopholes. "The light's just about gone. They'll be coming after us again before long."

"We'll be ready for them," Smoke said. "We just need for it to get a little darker. We'll make our move before the moon rises."

Preacher said, "Reckon you better tell us what this here plan o' yours is, Smoke?"

Feeling a surge of affection for the old man who had been his friend for so long, Smoke grinned in the darkness and said, "Matt and I are gonna leave you down here as bait while the two of us slip out of the cabin."

"Hmmph! Should'a knowed it," Preacher said with a snort. "You youngsters always cut and run when the goin' gets tough."

Smoke didn't take offense because he knew Preacher didn't mean that. The old mountain man was just joshing them. Smoke went on, "We're gonna get up on the roof and be ready when Bannerman's men start throwing torches up there. We'll catch the torches and throw them right back at the varmints. That'll give us enough light to shoot by."

"That could work," Matt said. "It'll be tricky catching those torches out of midair, though."

"We'll just have to be quick enough to do it."

"How you gonna get out the door and climb on the roof without them bastards seein' you?" Preacher asked. "It's pretty dark out there, but they still are liable to notice if the door opens up."

"That's why we're going up the chimney," Smoke said.

Preacher didn't respond for a moment, but then a hearty guffaw came from him. "Up the chimney, like some bass-ackwards Santy Claus! Lordy, if that ain't a hoot!"

"It's gonna be a close fit, Smoke," Matt warned. "I'm not sure our shoulders will go through there."

"We might lose a little hide," Smoke said with a shrug, even though the other two couldn't see the gesture. "But it's our best chance of gettin' out of here alive."

"Well, I can't argue with that," Matt said. "I've been thinking, and I sure haven't come up with any better ideas."

Smoke moved over to the fireplace and leaned his rifle against the wall beside it. "No point in putting it off. I think it's dark enough outside now that they won't notice us crawling out of the chimney."

"Just don't get stuck," Matt said.

Smoke took his hat off and bent down to work his head and shoulders into the fireplace opening. Luckily, there hadn't been a fire there for a while, so it was cold. He twisted, sat down on the hearth, and raised his arms to put them into the chimney first. He pulled in his shoulders, narrowing them as much as he could.

There were enough tiny gaps between the rocks that formed the chimney to give him fingerholds. He dug in his grip and pulled himself up until he was standing in the fire-place with most of his body in the chimney. His shoulders scraped against the walls. As Matt had warned, it was a very tight fit, but he was able to wedge himself through. If he could make it, he thought, Matt ought to be able to as well. Matt was an inch or so taller than Smoke, but his shoulders weren't quite as broad.

"Gimme a stirrup," he called down to Matt. "Preacher, keep an eye out for anything goin' on outside."

"Damn straight," Preacher replied. Matt knelt in front of

the fireplace, reached into the opening to lace his hands together, and formed a stirrup. Smoke put his foot in Matt's hands. Matt grunted with the effort as he lifted. Smoke planted his other boot against the chimney wall and shoved, pushing himself higher.

He tipped his head back and looked up to see stars in the opening above him. He needed to climb another few feet before he could reach up and get a hand on the lip of the opening. Matt couldn't help him anymore. He had to accomplish it through sheer strength, on his own.

The rough walls dragged painfully on his shoulders as he pulled with his fingers and shoved with his toes, and slowly worked his way higher. The good thing about it being such a tight fit was he wasn't likely to slip and fall. His back was pressed against one side of the chimney, his hands and feet against the other. He grunted and shoved, and his head rose another few inches. A couple more feet would do it, he told himself.

He climbed some more, then stretched his right arm above his head, reaching as high as he possibly could. His fingertips touched the lip of the opening at the top of the chimney. Another shove with his toes, and he was able to get a good grip on it.

From there it was easier, and once he got both hands on the edge, he pulled himself up and out of the chimney. His shoulders smarted where his shirt had been worn to tatters and the flesh was scraped raw, but that was nothing to worry about. He put his head back down the opening and called softly to Matt, "Come on. You can make it."

Matt made the climb even quicker, helped by Smoke, who reached down and grasped Matt's upraised hand to lift him. Within minutes, both men were on the cabin roof, sitting with their backs against the chimney. Their clothes, hands, and faces were smeared with soot, which served as camouflage and made them a lot harder to see against the roof.

"You reckon we got out . . . without them seeing us?" Matt asked, a little breathless from the climb.

"I reckon. They're not shootin' at us."

"Now we wait for them to make their move?"

"Yeah."

They didn't have to wait long. Less than five minutes later, Preacher called up the chimney, "I see somebody stirrin' around out yonder. You boys be ready."

Smoke crouched against the stone chimney at the end of the cabin. "We're ready, Preacher," he told the old mountain man.

Light suddenly flared, both in front of the cabin and behind it. Men had scratched matches into life and held the flames to kerosene-soaked rags wrapped around broken tree limbs. As the torches blazed, the men rose behind the tree stumps they were using for cover and threw the flaming brands high into the air above the cabin.

Preacher's rifle roared inside the cabin as he took several swift shots at the gunmen. Smoke and Matt didn't have time to see if any of Preacher's shots found their targets. "You take the back, I'll take the front," Smoke snapped. They leaped to their feet, being careful on the sloping roof, and watched the torches wheeling through the air toward the cabin. They had to judge it perfectly.

Smoke's right hand shot out. His fingers closed around the end of the torch that wasn't burning and snatched it out of the air just before it hit the roof. Instantly, he whipped it back toward the gunmen who ringed the cabin. As it whirled through the air, he palmed out both .44s and opened fire.

Behind him, Matt's Colt began to blast as well, so he figured Matt had been successful at grabbing a torch and throwing it back. Inside the cabin, Preacher's rifle continued to crack. As Smoke's revolvers roared, he saw several of the gunmen fall.

The move had taken Bannerman's men by surprise, but they were professional fighting men and adapted quickly.

They began firing at the roof, and as slugs whistled around his head, Smoke crouched and used the chimney for cover as much as he could. He slammed out several more shots. One man on the ground doubled over, and another fell backward to land with his arms and legs splayed out.

Whooping like a crazy man, Preacher burst out of the cabin. He had left the rifle inside and filled his hands with a pair of revolvers. He took the fight to the gunmen, charging forward as the guns in his hands gouted flame.

"Let's get off of here!" Smoke told Matt. He slid down the roof and dropped to the ground, landing with superb athletic grace. No sooner had his boots hit the ground than he was firing again, picking his targets. More shots blasted behind the cabin from Matt.

The torch lying on the ground in front of the cabin still burned, revealing the bodies that littered the ground between the cabin and the trees. Smoke and Preacher had laid waste to Bannerman's gun-wolves. Smoke didn't see any more of the hired killers still on their feet, so he holstered his left-hand gun and began reloading his right-hand Colt as he ran around the cabin to see how Matt was doing.

Matt crouched behind one of the stumps on that side, returning the fire of two men who had him flanked. Smoke took out one of them just as Matt downed the other. Another man loomed up, firing a Winchester. Matt's .44 was empty, so with eye-blurring speed he drew his Bowie knife and sent it speeding toward the man. The killer dropped his rifle and staggered back as the knife thumped into his chest, the cold steel of the blade burying itself deeply. He fell to the side, dying.

Hoofbeats filled the air as the thunderous echoes began to fade. Preacher came around the cabin to join Smoke and Matt. He was reloading as he said, "A couple of 'em lit a shuck. I reckon they was the only ones left."

Smoke and Matt joined the old-timer in thumbing fresh cartridges into their guns. Smoke said, "We'd better check the bodies and make sure none of them are still alive."

Preacher holstered his guns and drew his knife. "I can do that," he volunteered.

Smoke started to say something, then stopped and shrugged. If Preacher cut a few throats, it wasn't going to be any great loss to the world. Bannerman's men were all hired killers.

"We'd better find our horses and head for Crazy Bear's village," Matt suggested. "If Bannerman's got an army of gunmen patrolling the valley, there's no telling what might happen."

"His army ain't as big as it was before he jumped us," Preacher said.

"No," Smoke agreed, "but I'm betting the odds against us are still high enough that we've got some whittlin' ahead of us."

BOOK FOUR

Chapter 29

Matt's sorrel came when he whistled for it, and Smoke's and Preacher's horses followed. The three men mounted up and rode away from the cabin where they had been besieged, leaving the dead men who had worked for Reece Bannerman behind them. The rest of Bannerman's crew of gun-wolves could retrieve the bodies later, if they were of a mind to, or leave them there for the scavengers. The three men they had tried to murder didn't much care either way.

Preacher had the most unerring instincts of the three, so he took the lead. Despite the darkness and the fact that it had been a long time since he'd been in the valley, but he headed straight for Crazy Bear's village.

They splashed across both shallow creeks that ran through the valley. A short time later, Preacher said, "We're gettin' close now. If the Crows been havin' as much trouble as Crazy Bear claimed, they're liable to be pretty jumpy. We better keep our eyes open. We don't want to get shot full o' arrows so's we look like pincushions, just 'cause they mistook us for some o' Bannerman's bunch."

They rode slowly and warily through the darkness. Because he was alert, Smoke was able to control the impulse to reach for his guns when a dozen or more shadowy figures suddenly appeared all around them. Ahead of him, Preacher reined in and said, "Whoa there, Horse."

Smoke and Matt followed suit and halted their mounts as well. Smoke's keen eyes made out the bows and arrows in the hands of the men surrounding them, and he felt relief that they had found the Crow, or maybe it was vice versa and the Crow had found them. Either way, the task facing him and his two companions was to convince the warriors they were friends.

"We come in peace," Preacher said in the Crow tongue. "We are friends of Crazy Bear and the Crow people."

One of the warriors lowered his bow slightly, but the others didn't budge. The man stepped forward and asked, "Who are you who claim to be our friends?"

"Preacher," the old mountain man replied. "And Smoke and Matt Jensen."

For a moment, the Indian didn't react. Then he spoke sharply and the other warriors pointed their arrows at the ground. "Preacher," the man said in English, his voice breaking a little. "Smoke. Matt. Thank God."

"Sandy?" Smoke asked. "Is that you?"

The last time Smoke had seen Crazy Bear's son, Sandy had been wearing white man's clothes. Now he was in buckskins and had a feather in his hair. It looked like the clash with Bannerman had caused the young man to turn back to his father's ways.

Smoke, Matt, and Preacher dismounted. Sandy threw his arms around Smoke and hugged him, slapping him on the back, then shook hands with Matt and Preacher.

"We're not far from the village," he said. "Ever since the trouble started, my father has made sure there are guards out night and day, and warriors who are ready to move in a hurry if there's any trouble threatening. One of our sentries came to the village and said three white men on horseback were headed our way, so we were ready to defend ourselves."

Preacher nodded and said, "Thought it mighta been

somethin' like that, son. That's why we were takin' it sorta careful-like."

"We'll escort you to the village. Crazy Bear will be glad to see you."

"How is your pa?"

Sandy hesitated, then said, "He's been shot."

"Shot!" Preacher thundered. "What in tarnation happened?"

"How bad is he hurt?" Smoke asked.

"He claims he'll be all right," Sandy said, "and as strong as he is, he probably will be. He was wounded in the side, but it's just a deep graze. He lost a lot of blood, and he's weak. Plus it's a real struggle to keep him lying down so he can rest."

"When did it happen?"

"This afternoon. He was out watching the creek and saw some of Bannerman's punchers pushing cattle across, onto our land. He should have gone for help and not tried to stop them by himself, but . . ." Sandy's voice trailed off. He didn't have to explain. All three of the white men knew Crazy Bear. He didn't have any more back off in him than they did.

"Maybe you should take him to town and let a doctor look at him," Matt suggested.

Sandy shook his head. "Crazy Bear wouldn't go along with that. Anyway, my mother says she can take care of him as well as any doctor could. Between the Crow ways of healing and the things she knows from being a gypsy, she claims she can cure just about anything."

"She's probably right." Smoke said with a chuckle. "How are Robin and that little girl of yours?"

"They're fine, thank goodness."

"Does Moon Fawn still carry around that doll of hers? What was its name? Gregor?"

"She's never without it," Sandy said. "Now, we'd better get moving."

Smoke, Matt, and Preacher led their horses instead of riding.

Some of the warriors remained behind on guard. The others accompanied Sandy and the three white men to the village.

The smells of wood smoke and bear grease were familiar, as were the dogs that greeted the group with barks and wagging tails. Sandy asked some of the men to take care of the horses, then took the visitors directly to the large tepee that belonged to Crazy Bear and Mala.

"Our friends are here," Sandy announced as he pushed aside the hide flap over the entrance and stepped into the tepee. Preacher, Smoke, and Matt followed him into the lodge.

"Preacher!" Mala cried. She was sitting next to Crazy Bear, who lay stretched out on a pile of bearskin robes. She got quickly to her feet and hugged the old mountain man. "You're still alive."

"O' course I'm still alive," he said gruffly. "Accordin' to these disrespectful young'uns I'm travelin' with, I'm just too cantankerous to die."

Crazy Bear started to sit up. "Old friend," he rumbled.

Mala turned toward him and knelt to put a hand on his shoulder. "I want you to lie there and rest," she admonished. "Preacher can come over here and talk to you."

Crazy Bear wanted to argue, but he sighed and went along with what his wife told him. Preacher hunkered on his heels beside Crazy Bear and gripped the chief's hand. "Old friend," he said.

Crazy Bear waved for Smoke and Matt to come closer. They gathered around him. Crazy Bear had a thick pad of moss bound to his side where he'd been shot. It worked as well or better than anything for stopping the bleeding and drawing poison out of a wound.

"I did not know if you would come, or even if you were still alive," Crazy Bear said. His normal voice, which was reminiscent of an avalanche, was noticeably weaker than usual. He looked over at Smoke and Matt. "Now that all three of you are here, I know things will be all right."

"Durned right they will," Preacher said.

"We ran into a little trouble along the way," Smoke said. "We went around Buffalo Flat because we wanted to get here as quickly as we could, and when we were cutting across Bannerman's northern range, some of his hired killers jumped us."

Sandy said, "You must have gotten away from them. You don't appear to be wounded. Just . . . covered with soot?"

Smoke grinned. "Yeah, we had to fort up for a while in one of Bannerman's line shacks, and Matt and I wound up climbing out through the chimney." He waved a hand. "It's a long story. But we're all right—"

"And about a dozen o' Bannerman's gun-totin' rannies ain't," Preacher finished.

"Good," Crazy Bear said. "But he has more killers working for him."

"Many more," Sandy put in. "I've heard rumors that he may have as many as sixty gunmen on that ranch."

"That's only twenty-to-one odds for the three of us," Matt said with a grin. "We can handle that."

"My people will fight with you," Crazy Bear said. "Bannerman wants war. If he tries to force the Crow off our land, he will get it."

Matt thumbed his hat back on his blond hair and looked serious again as he said, "I don't reckon that was really a truce that started last year after Moon Fawn was kidnapped. Bannerman was just letting things cool off a little. Biding his time, I guess you could say."

"And using that time to recruit more gunfighters," Smoke said. "I'm startin' to wonder if he had something to do with that little girl being captured, after all."

"Of course he did," Sandy said. "I think he hired those men specifically to kidnap Moon Fawn and didn't tell the rest of his crew about it because he didn't want anything connecting him to them in case something went wrong and"—his voice caught, but he forced himself to go on—"Moon Fawn wound up dead."

"You could be right," Matt said. "But what in blazes was he after? What was that mysterious something the kidnappers wanted to find?"

"That's easy," Sandy said. "Bannerman was after the proof that our people really do own those hunting grounds. He can't push his cattle across the creek because that range legally belongs to the Crow."

Crazy Bear lifted his head to frown at his son. "What are you saying, Little Bear?"

Sandy smiled. "I'm saying that the law is on our side, because I filed on the entire upper section of the valley on this side of the creek eight years ago in the name of Sandor Little Bear."

Chapter 30

Smoke and Matt chuckled while the others in the tepee looked at Sandy in thunderstruck surprise. Finally, Crazy Bear asked, "How could you do this thing?"

"I sent the papers to the Department of the Interior in Washington while I was on one of my trips back to St. Louis," Sandy explained. "I knew Congress had just modified the original Homestead Act so people could acquire larger tracts of land, so I put in my claim and it was first. The next time I went to St. Louis, the deed to this part of the valley was waiting for me."

"No!" Crazy Bear pushed himself up on an elbow, ignoring Mala's efforts to keep him lying down. "I mean, how could you betray your people that way?"

Sandy drew back, a look on his face like his father had just struck him. "Betray my people?" he repeated. "Why do you think I've betrayed the Crow?"

"You use a white man's trick to claim the land we have hunted for many moons is now yours!" Crazy Bear's voice shook with angry accusation. "You would steal the land of your own people! You are worse than a white man!"

"Crazy Bear, stop it," Mala urged. "Lie down. You're going to make your wound worse."

"No worse than the wound my son has just dealt me,"

Crazy Bear growled. But he stretched out on the robes again and glared at Sandy.

"Listen to me," the young man said. "I'm not stealing anything. I'm protecting the land for the Crow. This was the only way to do it. You have to understand . . . Times have changed. Things are different now."

"We will protect our land the same way we have always protected it," Crazy Bear said. "With arrows and knives and tomahawks . . . and with our blood!"

"It doesn't work that way anymore," Sandy argued. "This way we have some legal standing."

Smoke spoke up, asking, "Was it the deed that Bannerman was after?"

"Of course," Sandy replied with a nod. "He thought he could trade Moon Fawn's life for it."

"How did he know about it in the first place?" Matt asked.

"I'm not sure, but I suspect that he tried to file on the land, too, and found that someone had beaten him to it." Sandy shrugged. "A man with Bannerman's wealth and influence wouldn't have much trouble finding some minor bureaucrat who would tell him what he wanted to know. I figure that's how he found out I own the land."

Crazy Bear made a disgusted noise deep in his throat and looked away, as if he couldn't stand the sight of his son.

Smoke rubbed his jaw in thought. "If you've filed a claim on the land, then it isn't open range anymore," he said to Sandy. "You could take Bannerman to court if he ran his cattle on it."

"Yes, but could I win?" Sandy made a gesture that took in his buckskins. "An Indian trying to convince a jury to favor him over a rich, powerful white cattleman?" He shook his head. "I hate to say it, Smoke, but that's pretty unlikely."

"Then why doesn't Bannerman just take you to court and get it over with?" Matt asked.

Smoke answered the question. "Because he doesn't want

to take the chance that Sandy *might* win, even if it's a slim one. But if he could get his hands on that deed and destroy it, then it would be simple for him to bribe some clerk back in Washington to . . . misplace, I guess you'd say . . . the copy that's on file back there."

"And if I were dead, it would clear the way for him completely," Sandy said.

Smoke nodded. "Yeah, that, too."

Preacher looked impatient as he burst out, "You young fellas yap as much as them danged dogs! The question is, what in blazes are we gonna *do* about this?"

"The first thing we're going to do is move Bannerman's cattle back across the creeks," Smoke said. "The longer we let them stay over here, the worse it'll look in court."

"Then you *do* think we should take the matter to court?" Matt asked.

Smoke nodded. "I do. If we can establish Sandy's legal ownership of the land, Bannerman might back off. He wouldn't just be going against Crazy Bear's people, he'd be going against the United States government, too."

Preacher made a disgusted noise and shook his head. "What in tarnation's happened to you, boy? Was a time you'd've just rode over to the Circle B and shot it out with Bannerman and his bunch, and to hell with the law and the gov'ment! You don't set the law on a hydrophobic skunk. You just kill it!"

"There's a good chance it's gonna come to that," Smoke said with a nod. "But Sandy's right, Preacher. Whether we like it or not, times have changed. If we get it on record that we're defending Sandy's rightful claim to the land, then the law won't be as likely to charge us with murder once the killin' starts."

Preacher continued to glare, but after a moment he shrugged and said, "All right. I'll go along with them crazy notions for now. But if that don't work, I'm settlin' things with old-fashioned law. Powdersmoke law!"

* * *

After the three visitors had been fed bowls of an excellent stew full of chunks of venison and wild onions, Crazy Bear asked Preacher to stay in his tepee, and the old mountain man agreed. Smoke and Matt were taken to lodges they could use as long as they were staying in the Crow village.

Matt was tired from the strain of the afternoon-long siege in the hot cabin. He was looking forward to stretching out on the thick bearskin robe and getting some sleep. He had taken off his hat, gunbelt, and boots and was unbuttoning his shirt when the entrance flap on the tepee was pushed back and a buckskin-clad figure ducked inside.

"Well," Matt said as a smile slowly curved his lips. He unfastened the last button and peeled off the garment. "I seem to remember another time when you burst in unannounced like that. You were the one who took off your shirt that time, though."

Starwind looked intently at him, her breasts rising and falling as she breathed hard. After a few seconds she said, "Then it is true. You have come back to help us, Matt Jensen."

Matt grew more solemn as he nodded. "That's right. Preacher and Smoke and I are all here to do what we can to keep Bannerman from forcing your people off their land. It won't happen if we have anything to say about it."

"People have been wounded, including my father."

Matt nodded again. "We talked to Crazy Bear, and to your brother Sandy." He paused. "Did you know he'd filed papers with the government claiming this whole part of the valley?"

Starwind nodded. "He told me . . . and I told him he was mad! No white man's court is ever going to say an Indian owns land another white man wants."

"I wouldn't be so sure," Matt said. "Anyway, Sandy is only half Crow, just like you."

"You truly think the fact that my mother is a gypsy will

help? According to her, in many places her people are looked down on and scorned, just like the Indians."

"Well, that may be true," Matt admitted. "But the law is the law. Not only that—and I'm not boasting here—Smoke and I both know some folks who might be able to help us. The governor of Colorado has already called on the territorial governor up here in Wyoming to launch an investigation. Smoke's been in touch with his lawyers in Denver, and he can call in favors from some of those railroad barons if he needs to. He's given them a hand in times past."

Starwind shook her head. "All this talk of politicians and lawyers . . . it means nothing where Bannerman's hired killers are concerned."

"Smoke and Preacher and I will deal with them if we have to," Matt said softly.

"Three men against fifty or sixty? What can they do?"

"Depends on who the three men are, I reckon."

Her dark eyes studied him as another moment of silence went by. Then she said, "You mean to do this, don't you? To risk your lives for my father and his people?"

"We've already done that. We had a run-in with Bannerman's gunnies this afternoon. We've already taken cards in this game, Starwind. There's no choice now but to play it out to the end."

"Even if it costs you your lives." The words weren't a question, but a statement. She stepped closer to him, rested the fingertips of one hand against his bare chest. "Matt . . ."

He put his arms around her and drew her to him. Their mouths met as their bodies strained against each other.

Outside, firelight flickered on the tepee, obscuring the shadows that moved inside it.

The next morning, Smoke, Matt, and Preacher rode across a broad meadow covered with lush green grass so tall that in places it brushed the bellies of their horses. About half a mile ahead of them twisted a line of trees that marked the course of the creek.

Between them and the creek were close to a hundred cattle. Though Smoke wasn't close enough to see the brands, he would have bet money each of those cows wore the Circle B.

"We'll split up and start the gather," Smoke said. As the owner of his own ranch, he had more experience at that sort of thing than either of the other two.

Preacher grumbled. "I never set out to be no dang cowpuncher," he said. "It ain't a fittin' job for a real man."

"That's right," Matt agreed with a grin. "Working cattle ties you down in one place too much. I'd rather drift on whenever the notion hits me."

"That's fine for a couple of irresponsible hombres like you two," Smoke said. "But where would the world be if everybody felt like that?"

"It'd be a damn sight less complicated, I can tell you that," Preacher insisted.

Smoke chuckled. "Keep your eyes open. Bannerman would be a fool not to have any riders up in these parts."

The three men spread out as they approached the cattle. The herd was scattered over a half-mile. Smoke, Matt, and Preacher began pushing them together, gathering the animals so that they could be driven back across the creek in a more compact group. Despite the protests voiced by Preacher and Matt, each of them had done enough similar work they were able to cover their section and get the cattle moving without too much trouble.

The cattle began to bawl. They didn't like being bothered when they could be standing around enjoying the rich graze. The men hooted and hollered and swung their hats in the air and the cows began trudging in the direction the men wanted them to go. It was noisy work, and Smoke knew he might not be able to hear hoofbeats of approaching horses. For that reason he kept his eyes moving all the time, searching the landscape around them for any sign of Bannerman's men.

He saw the four riders coming when they were still several hundred yards away on the other side of the creek. The cattle were all converging, and Smoke could see Preacher in the middle. He turned his horse and galloped toward the old mountain man.

As Smoke rode up and fell in alongside Preacher, he saw Matt coming from the other direction and figured that the younger man had spotted their impending company, too.

"I see 'em," Preacher said before Smoke could say anything. "More o' Bannerman's gun-wolves, you reckon?"

"Maybe not all of them," Smoke said. "A couple could be regular punchers. But I'm bettin' the other two are gunhands. We can't ignore the cowboys, either. They're probably plenty tough, and if they ride for the brand, they'll likely fight to defend it."

Matt rode up on Preacher's other side. "Looks like trouble coming," he said.

"I'm ready for it." Preacher leaned to the side and spat on the ground. "Hell, it's been more'n twelve hours since anybody shot at me."

Smoke grinned. Sally wouldn't like it, but he felt pretty much the same way.

The cattle stopped when they reached the creek, clumping up along the bank and bawling. Smoke, Matt, and Preacher rode around the herd to the north and reined in at the edge of the stream. The four men on the other side of the creek rode toward them and halted on the opposite bank.

"What the hell do you think you're doin'?" one of them yelled. "Those are Circle B cows! You ain't got no right to move 'em!"

"You're right about them being Circle B cows," Smoke replied. He didn't raise his voice, but his deep, powerful tones carried across the creek without any trouble. "And they don't have any right to be over here on Crow land."

"Crow land! What in blazes are you talkin' about? This is

open range. And even if it wasn't, it sure don't belong to no damn redskins!"

"That's where you're wrong," Smoke said. "You're gonna have to push these cattle back across to the other side of Badger Creek. The upper section of the valley, from Turtle Rock north and west of Badger Creek, belongs to Sandor Little Bear, son of the Crow chief Crazy Bear, and is being held in trust for the entire band of Crow led by Crazy Bear."

The spokesman for the four riders stared at Smoke for a couple seconds, then exploded, "You're outta your damn mind! Injuns can't own land!"

"You're wrong about that," Smoke said. "Just because most of them don't doesn't mean they can't."

During the tense conversation, Smoke had been studying the men on the other side of the creek. Just as he had guessed, two of them had the hardbitten look of hired gunslingers, while the other two men seemed to be common cowboys. As Smoke had said to Preacher, those cowboys couldn't be ignored. They were armed, just like the two gunmen, and they looked eager to fight.

The four men glared across the creek in angry silence for a moment, then the spokesman sneered and said, "So the redskins have hired themselves some gunnies."

Smoke shook his head. "We're not working for the Crow. They're our friends. We're just trying to help them do what's right."

"I'll tell you what's right," the gunman blustered. "You get the hell away from them cows and leave 'em be, that's what's right!"

Smoke's voice was dangerously mild as he said, "You can move them, or we'll finish the job we started. Up to you."

"What the hell kind of man takes up for a bunch of filthy Injuns?" the gunman demanded.

"Name's Smoke Jensen," Smoke said quietly. "That's Matt Jensen, and the old-timer is Preacher."

"You mighta heard tell of us," the old mountain man put in with a savage grin.

The two cowhands suddenly glanced at each other, and their eagerness to fight ran out of them like water from a cup. One of them said, "Maybe we better go back to the ranch and tell Mr. Bannerman about this, Ketchum."

"Go back and admit we turned tail and let these bastards move the boss's cattle?" The gunman called Ketchum shook his head. "Hell, no. You two can back down like lily-livered cowards if you want, but I ain't gonna."

The other cowboy said, "You can call me all the names you want, Ketchum. I'd rather stay alive. I'm headin' for the Circle B." He turned his horse and spurred it into a run.

"You yellow son of a bitch!" Ketchum yelled after him.

"Sorry," the first cowhand muttered. Then he hauled his mount around and headed after his companion.

"That leaves the odds three to two," the other gunnie said nervously to Ketchum.

"Don't worry about that," Preacher said. "I'll be glad to back off and let these young sprouts do the work." He lifted his reins. "Come on, Horse."

Smoke felt impatience growing inside him. "What'll it be?" he said to Ketchum and the other gunslinger. "These cattle are crossing the creek. You can get out of the way . . . or they'll go over you."

"Go to hell!" Ketchum yelled, and his hand streaked for his gun.

Chapter 31

The other gunman slapped leather, too. Both men cleared their holsters. They were fast.

But not fast enough.

The shots fired by Smoke and Matt blended into one roar. They hadn't had to discuss what they were doing. Smoke took the man on the left, Matt the one on the right. And both gunnies rocked back in their saddles as lead smashed into them.

The one Matt had shot dropped his gun and grabbed at the saddlehorn as his horse leaped around skittishly. His fingers slipped off the horn and he toppled out of the saddle. The horse bolted, dragging the man by a foot that had caught in one of the stirrups.

Ketchum managed to get a shot off even though blood was bubbling from the hole in his chest, but his arm had sagged and the bullet went into the ground. Smoke saw the gunman struggling to lift the revolver and fire again. A second shot blasted from the Colt in Smoke's hand. The .44 slug smacked into Ketchum's forehead, bored into his brain, and flipped him backwards off his horse, which stampeded away after the other gunman's mount.

Out of habit, Smoke and Matt slipped fresh cartridges from the loops on their shell belts and replaced the rounds they had fired. Powdersmoke still curled from the muzzles of the weapons.

Preacher sat on Horse a few yards away and chuckled. "Them boys was damned fools, but you tried to tell 'em," he said.

"I'm glad those two punchers lit a shuck," Smoke said as he holstered his Colt. "I didn't particularly want to kill them, too. They may work for Bannerman, but they weren't hired guns."

"Are we gonna push these cows on across the creek?" Matt asked.

Smoke nodded. "And across Badger Creek as well. We won't stop until they're back on Bannerman's usual range."

Despite what he had told Ketchum about the cows going over him, Smoke dismounted and moved the dead gunman's body out of the way. If he had left Ketchum's body where it had fallen, the herd's hooves would have pounded it into the ground until there was nothing left. Nothing that was recognizable as human, anyway.

Once that was done, the three of them got the cattle moving again, prodding the beasts into splashing across the shallow creek. It was half a mile from that creek—if it had a name, Smoke had never heard it—to the slightly larger Badger Creek that marked the eastern boundary of the Crow hunting grounds. The herd covered that distance fairly quickly.

Smoke had a hunch that Reece Bannerman would gather up as many of his crew as he could and come galloping up there as soon as those two cowboys reached Circle B headquarters. Bannerman would want to see for himself what was going on.

He would find his stock back on the eastern side of Badger Creek, because once Smoke, Matt, and Preacher drove the cows across the stream, it was doubtful that the animals would ford it again on their own. Bannerman might find the bodies of the two hired guns, as well, if he searched for them.

Smoke wished it hadn't come to killing so soon, since the

Crows' claim to the land hadn't been established in court yet, but Ketchum and the other gunslinger had called the tune. Smoke and Matt had acted in self-defense . . . but they didn't have any proof of that. There had been a time when an honorable man's word about such a thing was sufficient, but sadly, that had changed.

Oh, well, he had been an outlaw before, Smoke thought. He supposed he could be again.

Bannerman and his men hadn't shown up by the time Smoke, Matt, and Preacher finished driving the cattle across Badger Creek. "We'll leave these cows here and see if we can find more on the wrong side of the creek," Smoke said.

"In other words, we'll try to hunt up some more trouble," Matt said.

"That all right with you?"

Matt grinned. "Sure. Bannerman's gonna have a small army up here before you know it."

"We'll deal with that when and if it happens."

Preacher said, "Lemme find a good high spot, and me and that Sharps o' mine will settle this problem once and for all."

"Killing Bannerman like that won't solve anything," Smoke said. "Anyway, Preacher, you're not a bushwhacker."

"Well . . . maybe not," the old-timer grumbled. "Sometimes it sure is temptin', though."

They crossed Badger Creek and began working their way north along the strip of land between the two streams. Several times, they found small jags of cattle that weren't as big as the first herd and drove them back across Badger Creek.

By the middle of the day, Smoke felt like they had made enough of a start on the job. He said, "Let's head back to Crazy Bear's village."

"That sounds good to me," Preacher said. "Mala makes a mighty fine pot o' stew, and I could use some more of it right about now."

"I'd like to see Starwind again, too," Matt commented.

That brought a big grin to Preacher's whiskery face. "Ol'

Crazy Bear's gonna have another young'un marryin' up outside the tribe, if he don't watch out."

"Marry? Me and Starwind?" Matt shook his head. "Not hardly. She doesn't have any interest in getting married, and neither do I. It'll be a long time before I'm ready to be tied down like—"

"Like me?" Smoke asked with a laugh as Matt cast a glance at him. "Do you see me sittin' in a rockin' chair on the front porch?"

"Well, Smoke, if I can say it, you're not a normal man, and Sally's not exactly a typical woman, either."

"I can't argue that with you, especially that last part about Sally—" Smoke abruptly stopped what he was saying, reined in, and stood up in his stirrups to peer off to the south. "Looks like trouble coming."

The keen eyes of Matt and Preacher had spotted the riders in the distance at the same time as Smoke had. What looked like at least thirty men were coming fast up the valley. The three of them knew that many men had to be Reece Bannerman's bunch.

"Do we stand and fight?" Preacher asked, sounding eager to do so.

"Against ten to one odds?" Smoke said.

"Wouldn't be the first time."

"No, but there's a lot riding on us, and we can't afford to get ourselves killed this soon." Smoke wheeled his horse. "Come on. We'll make a run for it."

"Back to Crazy Bear's village?" Matt asked as he turned his sorrel.

Smoke shook his head. "No, we don't want a pitched battle, and that's what we'll get if Bannerman follows us all the way to the village, as mad as he must be right now. We'll lead him away from there."

He put his horse into a gallop, cutting east across the valley. Matt and Preacher wondered what he had in mind, but didn't ask any questions as they followed Smoke.

The three men rode hard, barely slowing down when they came to Badger Creek a couple minutes later. Water flew high in the air and hung there momentarily in sparkling droplets as the horses splashed across the stream. Then they were back on solid ground and running fast toward the foothills that rose a mile away.

Smoke glanced over his right shoulder and saw that the other group of riders had angled in the same direction and crossed the creek as well. They were trying to cut Smoke, Matt, and Preacher off from the hills, and if they did that, Smoke knew that he and his companions wouldn't stand much of a chance. They would be surrounded and gunned down. They would put up a fight, no doubt about that, and some of Bannerman's men would die, but in the end the result would be the same.

If they could make it to more rugged terrain, they might be able to slip away from their pursuers. That's what Smoke was counting on. That and the speed and stamina of the three fine horses he, Matt, and Preacher rode.

It was going to be a close race. Bannerman and his men had the angle, but the three of them had less ground to cover. As they neared the hills, Smoke heard the pop and bang of shots, and when he looked toward the large group of riders, he saw puffs of powdersmoke from their guns.

At that range, handguns didn't pose any real threat. The shots were more out of anger and frustration than they were out of any hope of hitting their targets. A wooded ridge loomed in front of Smoke, Matt, and Preacher. They called on their mounts for more gallant effort and sent the horses up the slope.

Smoke heard a bullet whistle past his head, close enough to be worrisome. He looked back and saw that several of the pursuers had reined in, dismounted, and were aiming rifles at the three men.

"Split up!" Smoke called. "We'll rendezvous at the base of that big bluff!"

The rocky bluff was visible in the distance above the trees, shouldering a good hundred feet in the air.

The three of them veered apart as more rifle slugs sizzled hotly through the air around them. The trees were getting thicker, and in moments, Smoke couldn't see Matt and Preacher anymore. He would have preferred that they stuck together, but they made too tempting a target that way. Also, if Bannerman wanted to pursue all three of them, he would have to split his force.

Smoke continued making his way through the timber and up the slope. He reached the top of the ridge and cut north along it, away from Matt and Preacher. He thought it was best that they remain apart for a while. Smoke would have worried about anyone else in the world facing a horde of gunmen alone, but he figured Matt and Preacher had a better chance of pulling through than anybody else.

An intense silence descended on the rugged hills. The shooting had scared off all wildlife, so the usual sounds of animals weren't there. Smoke slowed his horse to a walk and started up a gully. Thick brush clawed at both him and his mount, but it didn't stop them.

He heard noises off to his right. Something big moving, he thought. Horses, more than likely. Bannerman's men were searching for him. They didn't shout back and forth, and they seemed to be moving warily. They weren't amateurs. Far from it, in fact. Bannerman had spent the money necessary to recruit first-class fighting men.

Smoke dismounted and left his horse in the gully. He scrambled up the bank and pressed his back against the thick trunk of a pine. The searchers were coming closer. He took off his hat, edged an eye around the tree trunk, and had a look. He saw three men moving past, about twenty feet away.

They didn't see him, and the wind was wrong for their horses to scent his. As they moved past, Smoke knew he could draw his Colts, step out of cover, and gun down all three of them before they knew what was going on. But that would be cold-blooded murder—something he wouldn't do.

But he couldn't pass up the chance to whittle down the odds against him, though he knew the sound of shots would draw more of the pursuers to him. He drew back behind the tree again, put his hat back on, took a deep breath, and stepped out into the open.

"Lookin' for somebody, boys?" he drawled.

The three gunmen wheeled their horses frantically, clawing at their guns as they did so. Smoothly, Smoke drew both of his .44s. The right-hand gun blasted, and the one in his left hand spoke less than a heartbeat later. Two of the men fell. They had cleared leather but hadn't gotten a shot off.

Fate stepped in as Smoke triggered a shot at the third man. The gunslinger's horse, terrified of all the gun thunder, reared up and got in the way. Smoke's bullet tore into the luckless animal's throat. Blood spurted as the horse screamed and thrashed to the side. Its rider went flying.

Smoke snapped another shot at the man in midair but missed. The gunnie landed and rolled over and came up firing. Smoke felt the hammerblow of the bullet against his left arm. The impact knocked him halfway around. He stayed on his feet, and slammed out two more shots. The gunman came up on a knee and fired again, but his bullet went wild because Smoke's slugs had already driven into his chest and knocked him backward. He landed in a scattering of fallen pine needles and cones. His bloody chest heaved a time or two and then stilled.

Gritting his teeth against the pain, Smoke looked down at his wounded arm. He saw that the bullet had plowed a bloody furrow on the outside of his arm about halfway between his shoulder and elbow. It wasn't a serious wound, just gory and painful, and it would keep him from using that arm for a while. Though he still gripped the gun in his left hand, he couldn't raise it to put it back in the holster. He had to pouch his right-hand iron first, then reach across his body and take the other gun from numb fingers and slide it back into leather.

It wasn't the first time Smoke had been wounded. He took off his bandanna and wrapped it around the wounded arm. Using his good hand and his teeth, he tied it tightly so that it would slow down the bleeding, maybe even stop it. Reloading was awkward, but he managed to fill the chambers of his right-hand Colt before he went back to the gully and found his horse waiting where he had left it.

He swung up into the saddle and got moving again, listening for the sound of shouts or horses moving in the brush. He heard the latter behind him as he reached the upper end of the gully. He rode into a field of boulders that stretched for half a mile before he came to another timber-covered hillside. There had been a fire there in the distant past, and a lot of deadfalls littered the slope. Smoke let his horse have its head, and the animal picked its way through the debris. Smoke heard a distant shout, then a sudden spattering of gunfire.

He hoped that when he finally made it to the towering bluff that was his destination, Matt and Preacher would be there, waiting for him.

Chapter 32

Preacher sent Horse up a slope consisting of loose shale. The animal struggled quite a bit. That Horse was a good mount, but not a patch on some of the other Horses he'd ridden over the years.

He wished he could find a good Dog. A man in the wilderness needed a dog. Of course, there wasn't really that much actual wilderness anymore. Too damn many towns, too many people, stagecoaches, railroads, and telegraph wires every damned place you looked.

And nobody left who knew what it had been like in the Shining Times. Nobody who remembered how it felt to stand on a mountaintop and look out over the country and know that you were the only white man within a hundred miles or more, and you might even be the only man, period, within fifty miles. Nobody but him. Maybe there were some other old-timers still out there who shared memories like that, but if there were, Preacher didn't know them. He had lived past his time.

But that was all right. It sure as hell beat the alternative, he thought. As long as a fellow could still get around a little, it was better to be old and breathin'. He'd have plenty of time to rest when he was dead.

The sound of a bullet whipping past his ear brought him out

of his reverie. Echoes of the shot rolled up the slope and washed over him. He jabbed his heels into Horse's flanks and sent the animal lunging over the top of the ridge. He heard the flat *whap!* of another slug as it went by him. Wheeling his mount around, he brought the Winchester to his shoulder and opened fire at the four men who had ridden up to the base of the slope.

They scattered as Preacher sprayed lead among them, but one of them was too slow. He threw his arms up and pitched out of the saddle as a round from the Winchester blew a big chunk of his head away.

While the rest of the varmints were busy hiding, Preacher turned Horse and rode hard along the crest of the ridge, hoping that the rangy gray had good footing. More bullets kicked up dirt and rocks behind him, but after a moment Preacher came to a place where he could get down the other side. Horse took the slope in a half-slide, half-run. Preacher swayed in the saddle, keeping his seat with the expert grace of a much younger man.

Just as he reached the bottom, two more men rode out of some trees just a few yards to Preacher's right. The old mountain man never slowed down. He angled straight toward them as he gripped the reins in his teeth, shifted the rifle to his left hand, and drew the .44 on his hip with his right.

Taken by surprise, the two men yanked their guns out and fired, but they hurried their shots. Preacher extended the rifle one-handed and fired when the barrel was almost touching the chest of the man on his left. The close-range blast blew the man out of the saddle and burning powder set his shirt on fire. At the same time, Preacher triggered the Colt and hammered two shots into the man on his right, sending him flopping lifelessly to the ground as well.

The old mountain man kept going, disappearing into the trees almost as if he had never been there, leaving behind the bodies of two dead gunnies to prove that he had been.

* * *

Matt caught glimpses of the tall bluff through the trees and kept working his way toward it. As a young man, he had learned from Smoke how to use every bit of cover he could find, and he put that talent to good use, dodging through gullies and around hills and along dry washes. He hadn't heard any sounds of pursuit for a while, and it was beginning to look like he had given Bannerman's hired killers the slip.

He knew he shouldn't think like that. It was bound to jinx things. And was the first thing that went through his head when the three riders came out from behind a boulder and blocked the trail ahead of him.

The second thing was the shock of recognition as he realized one of the men was Lew Torrance.

The other two reached for their guns, but Torrance called out sharply, "Hold it!"

The two hardcases looked surprised, but their hands froze on the butts of their guns.

Matt stiffened in the saddle and his muscles were tense with the urge to draw, too, but he held off. He waited to see what Torrance was up to.

"What's the idea, Lew?" one of the men demanded. "You know the boss told us to shoot these bastards on sight."

"Yeah, but this hombre and I have some history," Torrance said coolly. His eyes watched Matt intently and never strayed. "After that dustup last year, I didn't figure I'd ever see you again, Jensen."

"You saw me yesterday," Matt shot back, "when you and some of Bannerman's other hired killers chased Smoke and Preacher and me into that cabin and tried to kill us."

"Yeah, well, I thought that was you, but I wasn't sure." Torrance shrugged. "You shouldn't have come back to the valley. There are things going on here that are none of your business."

Matt shook his head. "I'm making them my business, and so are Smoke and Preacher."

The third gunman said, "Nobody told us that Smoke

Jensen was part of this, Torrance. From what I hear, that hombre's hell on wheels with a gun."

"Any man can be beaten," Torrance said. "Any man can be killed. If you're afraid of dying, Hobbs, you in the wrong line of work."

"Maybe I am," Hobbs said. "But I took Bannerman's money, so I guess I'll stick."

"How about you, Wick?"

The other man sneered at Matt. "I'm faster than this rana-han. I can tell that by lookin'."

Torrance nodded and said, "I reckon you'll have a chance to prove that, because I'm sitting this one out."

"What are you talking about?" Matt asked.

"I don't want to kill you, Jensen. We fought side by side, and I'd just as soon not be the one to send you to hell. So I'm going to ride away and leave you to these two boys. If by some chance you happen to survive . . . well, I reckon there'll be another day for the two of us to settle things."

"Count on it," Matt said, biting the words out hard.

Torrance smiled lazily and turned his horse. Matt was wary of a trick. Maybe Torrance thought he could pretend to withdraw from the fight and then make his draw while Matt was concentrating on the other two gunmen.

But Torrance spurred his horse into a gallop and rode off, disappearing down a wash. Matt sat there stiffly as the hoof-beats faded.

"Well," Wick said to his companion, "let's kill this son of a bitch and get it over with."

Their hands stabbed toward their guns.

Matt's Colt seemed to leap out of its holster by magic and rose with blinding speed. Five shots blasted out in a matter of two seconds, the explosions blending together in a rolling roar of gun thunder. Hobbs rocked back in the saddle as one of Matt's slugs punched into his chest, right where the tag from his tobacco pouch dangled from his shirt pocket. Wick hunched his shoulders and doubled over from the bullet that penetrated his mid-section. Matt fired again, knowing that Wick might still be capable of firing another shot. The final slug blew the gunman's brains out and knocked him to the ground.

Matt was untouched. Each of his opponents had gotten off a shot, but the bullets had whined past him, close but not close enough. Hobbs, shot in the heart, swayed for a second on his horse before toppling off. Like Wick, he was dead when he hit the ground.

After replacing the three shells he had fired, Matt holstered his gun and got Spirit moving again. He rode around the dead men and continued on toward the bluff. He had heard a few shots in the distance and figured they meant Smoke and Preacher had run into trouble, too. He hoped they were all right, but he didn't worry. Worrying didn't do any good. Either they were alive, or they weren't.

Knowing Smoke and Preacher the way he did, Matt would have bet a fine new hat they were still alive and kicking.

There was a broad clearing in the pines at the base of the bluff. Up close, Smoke could see the big seams and cracks that split the face of the rock, and at the bottom of it lay several giant slabs of rock that had broken off and fallen over the years. An hombre would have to think twice about getting too close up there, he mused. Having all that rock looming over him was bound to make him a mite nervous.

Smoke's mouth tightened when he looked around and didn't see Matt or Preacher. He reined in and studied the clearing. It was empty, sure enough. No sign that anyone had been there.

The hills were quiet. No shots had sounded for a while. Smoke hadn't seen any of Bannerman's men since the shootout with the three he had killed.

He shifted his wounded left arm to ease the ache in it. The numbness had worn off, which was a mixed blessing because while he could use that arm again, it hurt like blazes. He thought he could draw and fire with his left hand if he had to, but it wouldn't be fast.

Smoke thought about Sally, missing her as he always did whenever fate drew him away from the Sugarloaf Ranch. It seemed he could smell the fresh scent of her hair, taste the sweetness of her lips, feel the warmth of her body. One of these days, he told himself, he was going to settle down and not let the call of adventure lure him away from his home. Yes, sir, he vowed. One of these days.

He thought about his friends Cal and Pearlie. They'd had his back in more than one fight, and he would have given a lot to have them with him. But it was worth more to know they were back in Colorado, looking after the ranch and Sally. Not that Sally needed much looking after. She was a better shot than most men and wouldn't hesitate to use a gun if trouble came calling.

Movement in the trees on the other side of the clearing caught his eye. He pulled his horse back into the timber and drew his rifle from its sheath, relaxing as Matt rode into sight. Smoke moved into the open, and waved the Winchester over his head. Matt trotted the sorrel over to him.

"Man, it's good to see you, Smoke," the younger man said. "I figured you'd be here, but after hearing all those shots scattered over the hills, I'm glad to lay eyes on you."

"Same here," Smoke said. "Have you seen Preacher?"

Matt shook his head. "No, but I'm sure he'll turn up. That old-timer's made of whang leather and barbed wire. He'll still be around when you and I are pushing up daisies."

"I wouldn't doubt it," Smoke replied with a grin. "Still, it'll be good to see him—"

He stopped short as Preacher rode out of the trees behind him. "Go on," the old mountain man said. "Tell some more about how glad you'll be to see me. I was startin' to feel plumb sentimental. Want me to take my hat off so's you can plant a kiss on this ol' bald head o' mine?"

"As I was sayin'," Smoke went on, "it'll be good to see him because that way we'll know the old rapscallion hasn't gone and gotten himself in some sort of trouble we'll have to rescue him from . . . again."

Preacher bristled. "*You* rescue *me?* When was the last time you had to pull my bacon outta the fire, boy?" He rode closer and frowned as he looked at the bloody bandanna tied around Smoke's arm. "Hell, you're hurt."

"It's not much to speak of," Smoke said. "I ran into some of Bannerman's bunch, and one of them creased me with a lucky shot. It'll be fine."

Preacher reached into his saddlebags and pulled out a flask. "Best let me douse it with some panther piss. Matt, keep an eye out whilst I tend to doctorin' this stubborn young cuss."

"Since when did you become a sawbones?" Smoke asked.

Preacher snorted. "Since I started patchin' up my own bullet wounds nigh on to seventy years ago!"

Smoke knew that Preacher was right, but he couldn't agree with the old-timer without giving him a little amiable grief first. While Matt kept a lookout, Smoke and Preacher dismounted and the mountain man cleaned the wound on Smoke's arm. Then he bound a clean bandanna from Smoke's saddlebags around it.

"That'll do for now," Preacher pronounced.

"What's our next move?" Matt asked.

Smoke considered the question for a moment, then said, "Some of Bannerman's gunhawks are probably still between us and Crazy Bear's village. Instead of going back there, why don't we head for Buffalo Flat?"

"What're we gonna do there?" Preacher asked.

"I'd sort of like to see if any of those visits Matt and I made before we started up here have done any good. I've got a hunch that beating Bannerman is gonna take more than bullets."

Chapter 33

The telegraph lines had reached Buffalo Flat in the months since Matt had been there. It wasn't the only change in the town, which had grown quite a bit since Smoke had been there last, but it was the one that interested him the most at the moment. As soon as he spotted the telegraph office, he headed straight for it. He had told his lawyers in Denver that he could be contacted there if they had any news about their investigation into Bannerman's dealings.

Matt and Preacher stayed outside while Smoke went into the office. He had to wait while a man in a town suit talked to the clerk. He couldn't help overhearing when the man said, "Are you sure Mr. Jensen hasn't been in to check for messages?"

"Sorry, mister," the clerk said from the other side of the wicket. "I ain't seen the fella."

Smoke tensed when he heard the name Jensen. He didn't know whether the man in the suit was looking for him or Matt or some other Jensen entirely . . . although that last seemed unlikely. As the man turned away from the window with a scowl on his face, Smoke stayed right where he was, planted directly in the stranger's path.

"Excuse me," the man said. "I need to get by."

"No, you need to tell me which Jensen you're looking for," Smoke said.

The man regarded him coolly. He was wearing an expensive town suit, but he had a rough-hewn look about him, as if he hadn't always sported such fancy duds. He was tall and brawny, with a shock of red hair under his hat.

"What business is it of yours who I'm looking for?" he asked.

"Because my name is Jensen. Kirby Jensen, usually called Smoke."

The man took a deep breath—the only sign he gave of being surprised. "Mr. Jensen," he said. "My name is Halliday. I was sent up here from Denver by your lawyers to find you."

"You're an attorney?"

Halliday shook his head. "An investigator. I have some news for you regarding—" He stopped short and gave a curt shake of his head. "Not here. Can you come with me to my hotel room?"

Smoke glanced at the telegraph operator and thought quickly. If Halliday had news for him, it had to be something to do with Bannerman that he didn't want to discuss in front of the telegrapher. He was afraid the man might tell Bannerman about it, which was certainly a possibility. Bannerman was maybe the richest and most powerful hombre since Jason Garrard had given up his ambition to run everything in that corner of the territory.

"All right. Matt and Preacher are with me."

Halliday nodded, obviously knowing who Smoke was talking about. "Bring them along. All of you need to hear this."

Matt and Preacher looked puzzled when Smoke walked out of the telegraph office with Halliday. "Who's this hombre?" Preacher asked.

"Name's Halliday," Smoke explained. "He works for my lawyers down in Denver. Says he came all the way up here to tell us something, so I figure it must be important."

"It certainly is," Halliday said. "If you gentlemen will come with me . . ."

They left their horses tied in front of the hotel and followed

Halliday up to his room on the second floor. When they got there, the detective offered them a drink.

"Never mind that," Smoke said. "Just tell us what the investigation found out."

"Nothing good, I'm afraid," Halliday said as he hooked his thumbs in his vest. "The trail of Bannerman's connections runs all the way back to Washington."

"To the Department of the Interior?" Smoke guessed.

"Among others, including the Capitol. Gentlemen, Mr. Bannerman has some friends in high places . . . very high places. I'm talking about politicians, judges, bankers, railroad men . . . the sort of men who believe they actually run this country. Unfortunately, in most cases they're right. Have you heard of the Indian Ring?"

Smoke tensed. "I've heard of them. A bunch of damn crooks who took over the Bureau of Indian Affairs for a while. They had some high-powered political backing, but they were broken up several years ago, weren't they?"

Halliday nodded. "That's right. Some of the principals managed to avoid indictment, and they've never forgotten how much money there is to be made off the Indians. It appears they're trying to put together a new Indian Ring . . . and Reece Bannerman has been selected as their first standard-bearer."

Preacher frowned and said, "What in blazes are you talkin' about, mister?"

"He means that if Bannerman gets away with stealing the Crows' land, it'll just be the first step," Smoke said. "Members of this so-called Indian Ring will start grabbing Indian land all over the West, taking it by force if they have to."

"That's right," Halliday said with another nod. "Bannerman's landgrab is a test case, so to speak."

Preacher shook his head. "I still don't understand. Folks've been stealin' Injun land for years now, and they usually pretend that it's all legal-like because o' broken treaties and what not."

"Yes, but if the men behind this have their way, they won't even bother doing that anymore. They'll just take the land and dare anyone to do anything about it. I've heard rumors they won't stop there. The ultimate goal seems to be the destruction of all the Indian tribes west of the Mississippi."

The other three men stared at Halliday for a few seconds following that statement. Then Matt said, "That's crazy! They can't do that."

"They might be able to with the army backing them," Smoke said. "There are still some Indian wars going on in places."

"But we've never tried to wipe out whole tribes!"

Preacher said, "No, we just force 'em onto reservations where they might as well be dead." The old mountain man's voice held a bitter edge, and Smoke knew that was because Preacher had spent so much time with the Indians over the decades, sometimes living with them for years at a stretch.

"I reckon we can argue about whether or not they can get away with it all we want to," Smoke said, "but the important thing is that if they try, there'll be a hell of a lot of blood spilled along the way, no matter how things turn out."

"That's exactly right," Halliday said. "So the thing to do would be to deal them a setback right now, so they'll think again before they try anything else. However, that's not what my employers are advising, Mr. Jensen."

Smoke frowned. "What do they think we ought to do?"

"The firm has concluded that Bannerman and his associates are too powerful to oppose. Their official advice is that you don't try."

Preacher let out a loud snort of disgust. "Give up? What the hell kinda lawyers you got, Smoke?"

"It wouldn't be ethical of them to advise a client to go against his best interests," Halliday went on.

"What about the best interests of Crazy Bear and his people?" Smoke asked.

Halliday shrugged. "They're not clients."

"You said that was the official advice," Matt pointed out. "What about some unofficial advice?"

That brought a slight smile to Halliday's face. "Unofficially, I've learned that a federal judge is on his way here to Buffalo Flat even as we speak to rule on the matter of whether or not the Crow have a valid claim to the land. He should be coming in on tomorrow's stagecoach. Someone named Sandor Little Bear wrote and requested a hearing more than a month ago. He must have known this showdown was coming."

"What good will it do to have a hearing if everybody connected to Washington is on the side of the Indian Ring?" Smoke asked.

"Not everyone is. This particular circuit court judge isn't. He has a reputation as an honest man, and if he rules against Bannerman, it'll be a blow to the Ring. His name is Judge Errol Starr."

"Does Bannerman know about this?"

"He does. A lawyer sent out here by the Indian Ring came in on the same stagecoach I did a few days ago. He'll be representing Bannerman."

Smoke's brain struggled to make sense of all the dizzying new developments. He had believed it was a relatively clearcut case of a powerful rancher trying to grab more range for himself. What with Sandy's revelation that he had filed a legal claim on the land, followed by Halliday's information concerned the so-called new Indian Ring, the situation had taken on a lot more scope while at the same time becoming murkier. The clash between Crazy Bear and Reece Bannerman had national implications and might well involve the fate of the entire frontier.

"So what do we need to do?" Matt asked.

Smoke turned that question over in his head. As far as he could see, there were two things that needed attention.

"Matt, you and Preacher ought to head back out to Crazy Bear's village," he said. "Sandy's the one making the claim on the land, and if anything happens to him, the case will fall apart. Bannerman has to know that, so he's liable to take things into his own hands again and try to get rid of Sandy before the judge can get here. To do that, he's got to attack the entire village, so he may decide just to wipe it off the face of the earth and be done with it."

Preacher said, "He could prob'ly get away with it, too, if he's got such all-fired powerful friends."

"I don't know the man," Halliday said, "but based on what I've heard, I wouldn't put anything past him."

Matt said, "What about you, Smoke?"

"We've seen plenty of evidence that Bannerman doesn't want to take a chance on the case being heard by a judge. If he knows this fella Starr is on his way to Buffalo Flat, he might send some of his men to stop him. The judge can't rule against Bannerman if he's dead. So Halliday and I will ride out in the morning and meet the stagecoach to make sure it gets here safely."

Halliday grunted. "I don't recall volunteering my services, Jensen. How do you know I can even ride?"

"Well, can you?" Smoke asked.

"As a matter of fact, yes," Halliday replied with a shrug. "All right. It's not really part of my job, but I'll admit that I'd like to see Bannerman's face if the ruling goes against him."

"Then all we have to do," Smoke said, "is make sure that everybody gets to the hearing all right."

"The hearin' that Bannerman and all his hired guns are gonna be doin' their damnedest to stop," Preacher pointed out.

Smoke smiled. "Well . . . I never said it would be easy."

Chapter 34

As soon as they had gotten something to eat and let their horses rest for a while, Matt and Preacher left Smoke in Buffalo Flat with Halliday and headed back to Crazy Bear's village.

"We may have to dodge some of Bannerman's gun-wolves along the way," Matt commented as they rode out of the settlement.

"Might even have to kill a few of 'em," Preacher said. "Which would be just fine with me. That'll be however many it is we won't have to kill later."

"You still think it'll come to that if we manage to get that hearing to take place and the judge rules in favor of the Crows?"

"Them are a couple of mighty big *ifs*," Preacher said. "And yeah, even if both them things happen, I don't expect Bannerman to swallow 'em and let it go. I've seen greedy sons o' bitches like him before. When it comes down to the nub, he'll try to take what he wants, and everything else be damned."

Matt nodded. "You're probably right."

"I know I am," Preacher said.

They had gone several miles up the valley, following the no-man's-land that ran between the creeks, when they spotted half a dozen riders on their right, about three hundred yards away.

"Preacher . . ." Matt said warningly.

"I see 'em," the old mountain man said. "Probably spotted 'em before you did. You reckon they're some o' Bannerman's bunch?"

The men suddenly spurred toward them, urging their horses forward at a gallop.

"That's all the proof I need!" Matt said. "Let's go!"

They wheeled their mounts to the left and leaned forward in the saddles as they sent the horses racing across the grassy valley. The closest cover was at least half a mile away, where cottonwoods grew along the creek. If they could reach the trees, they would stand a chance of fighting off Bannerman's men.

Spirit and Horse both stretched out and ran, and while Preacher's gray stallion wasn't the equal of some of the horses he'd had in the past, he was almost as fast as Matt's sorrel. Matt held Spirit back a little so he wouldn't leave the old mountain man behind.

The faint crackle of gunfire reached their ears. Preacher looked over his shoulder and saw the orange winks of muzzle flame and the little puffs of smoke. He laughed.

"They ain't gonna hit us at this range!" he called over the pounding hoofbeats. "They ain't gonna catch us, neither!"

Matt saw that was true. It took only a few minutes to reach the creek. In that time, the pursuers had closed the gap slightly, but they were still well out of handgun range and they hadn't stopped and dismounted to use their rifles.

Matt and Preacher swung out of the saddles as their horses continued across the creek, splashing through the cold, clear water. The duo carried their rifles back to the trees and crouched behind the trunks.

Preacher had brought his Winchester instead of his Sharps. "Range is too short for that Big Fifty o' mine!" he said as he levered a round into the repeater's firing chamber. "I can make do with this piddlin' little Winchester."

Matt grinned as he worked the lever on his rifle and then lifted the weapon to his shoulder. "If everything was so much better in the old day," he said, "why don't you still carry a flintlock?"

"Don't think I ain't thought about it!" Preacher snapped. He pressed his grizzled cheek against the smooth wood of the stock, squinted as he sighted over the Winchester's barrel, then pressed the trigger. The rifle cracked wickedly as it kicked against his shoulder. One of the onrushing gunmen jerked in the saddle but managed to stay mounted as he slowed his horse and hunched over in pain. "When a ball from one o' them old muzzle-loaders hit you, you went down no matter where you was hit!"

Matt began to fire, too. The two men poured a steady stream of lead into their attackers for several moments, wounding at least a couple more of Bannerman's men. The gunnies reined in, turned their horses around, and fled in the face of that withering fire.

"Look at 'em turn tail and run!" Preacher whooped.

"Yeah, they'll be running right back to Bannerman to tell him that we're on our way to the Crow village," Matt pointed out. "We'd better get moving before Bannerman sends more men up here to cut us off."

They whistled their horses back to them, mounted up, and headed north again. They had asked a lot of their mounts. Spirit and Horse were getting tired. But it wasn't too much farther to Crazy Bear's village. Once they got there, the horses would be able to rest.

Matt was a little surprised they didn't run into any more of Bannerman's hired killers on the way, but he and Preacher reached the village late that afternoon without any more trouble. The barking dogs announced their arrival as usual. At least forty warriors appeared, some armed with rifles, the others with bows and arrows, just in case the visitors turned out not to be friendly. The men relaxed as they recognized Matt and Preacher.

Crazy Bear strode forward to greet them, flanked by Sandy and Starwind. "I see you're up and around again," Matt said to the chief, who still had bandages wrapped around his mid-section.

"Try making him rest for very long," Sandy said. "You'll see what an impossible job that is."

"Sort of like getting a federal judge to come in and rule on your claim on this land?" Matt asked as he swung down from Spirit's back.

Sandy's face lit up with excitement. "My request for a hearing has been granted?"

"Yeah. You didn't tell us about that."

"I would have. I didn't want to get anyone's hopes up in case it never happened. When is the judge supposed to get here?"

"Tomorrow, if all goes as planned," Matt said. "Smoke's going to see that it does. Then we'll be able to go into town and settle this."

Crazy Bear frowned in confusion. "I do not understand," he said. "Who is this judge you speak of?"

"He's a representative of the white man's government," Sandy explained. "He decides what's right and what's wrong."

"You mean he decides that the white man is right and the Indian is wrong," Crazy Bear rumbled.

Matt said, "According to what we were told, this particular gent doesn't think that way. He'll rule on the facts of the case and follow the law."

Crazy Bear shook his head. "When the moose grows wings and learns to soar like the eagle," he said.

"I'm with you, Crazy Bear," Preacher said. "I don't put no stock in any law but this." He rested his hand on the butt of his .44.

"Maybe it will come to that," Sandy said, "but there's nothing wrong with trying the other way first."

"Unless it gets you killed," Preacher said.

Matt said, "That's why we're here, to make sure that doesn't happen. We'll deliver you to that hearing tomorrow, Sandy, and see what the judge says. After that—"

"After that, devil take the hindmost," Preacher said.

Matt expected trouble. It wouldn't have surprised him if Bannerman launched an all-out attack on the Crow village during the night or first thing the next morning. Instead, the night passed quietly, and Matt spent some time with Starwind. Neither of them had any intention of settling down, but there was no doubt they enjoyed each other's company.

In the morning, Matt went to the lodge where Sandy lived with his wife Robin while they were in the Crow village. He knew the couple also had a house in Buffalo Flat and spent part of their time there, as well as making regular trips back to St. Louis where Sandy continued his efforts to secure funding for an Indian school and perhaps eventually a university on the frontier. There was talk of starting a state university in Laramie, and according to Sandy, that would be a good place for a privately supported Indian university as well. Whether that dream would ever come about was anybody's guess, but Sandy was working at fulfilling it.

When Matt called through the entrance flap, Sandy pushed it aside and emerged from the lodge dressed in his town clothes. His hair was cropped shorter than it had been the night before. Robin followed him from the tepee and hugged Matt. Moon Fawn was with her, clutching at her mother's skirts and smiling shyly at Matt.

Matt hunkered on his heels and grinned at the little girl. "Remember me?" he asked. She nodded. He pointed at the doll she carried. "How's Gregor?"

"He's fine," Moon Fawn said. "He wants to go to town."

"I'm sorry, little one," Sandy said. "I've told you that it's too dangerous for you and Gregor to come with me today. You and your mother have to stay here with your grandparents."

Robin said, "I don't like that, Sandy. If you're going to be risking your life, I should be with you."

"I'd rather have you here, so I don't have to worry about you," Sandy told her. "It's dangerous enough, the two of you staying here. We don't know what Bannerman will do. I'm hoping that he'll concentrate on what's happening in town today, rather than out here."

Robin put her arms around his neck and pressed herself to him. "Be careful," she murmured. "You know I couldn't stand it if anything happened to you."

"I'll be fine," Sandy said. "Matt and Preacher will see to that. Isn't that right, Matt?"

"Do my best," Matt promised.

Sandy kissed his wife, then knelt to hug and kiss his little girl. Moon Fawn clung to him for a moment. Then Sandy said, "Could I see Gregor for a minute before I go?"

"Do you want to tell him goodbye, too?" Moon Fawn asked.

"No, he's been keeping something for me, and I need to get it back from him."

Moon Fawn held out the doll.

Matt frowned as he watched Sandy slip a couple of fingers under the buckskin outfit the doll wore. There must have been a little slit in Gregor's body under there, because Sandy appeared to be fishing around inside the doll. A few seconds later, Sandy withdrew his hand, holding between his fingers a tightly folded piece of paper.

"What's that?" Robin asked.

Sandy gave Gregor back to Moon Fawn and straightened. He unfolded the paper and held it so Robin and Matt could see that it was some sort of official document. A grin began to spread across Matt's face.

"Is that the deed to your claim?" he asked.

Sandy nodded. "Yes. I thought that would be a safe place

to keep it, since Moon Fawn always has Gregor with her and no one would think to look inside a doll's stuffing."

"You mean she had it all along when those varmints kidnapped her?"

"That's right."

Matt laughed and shook his head. "They never knew that what they were looking for was right under their noses. But I reckon you were counting on that, weren't you?"

"Exactly." Sandy folded the document again and put it in a pocket inside his coat. "We should get going. We don't want to be late for that hearing."

The horses were ready, as was Preacher. The old mountain man had been deep in conversation with Crazy Bear while Matt was talking to Sandy, Robin, and Moon Fawn. As Matt and Sandy came up, Preacher said, "We best rattle our hocks. I don't know what time that stage is supposed to get to town, but I reckon we better be there when it does. That judge is liable to want to start the hearin' right away."

"I hope so," Sandy said. "The sooner this is settled, the better as far as I'm concerned."

"I reckon we all feel the same way," Matt said.

The three men mounted up. Preacher waved and called, "So long," to Crazy Bear. Matt nodded to Starwind, who gave him an encouraging smile. Then they rode out of the village, heading south toward Buffalo Flat.

Sandy wore a bowler hat to go along with his suit. With the slightly European cast to his features he had inherited from his mother Mala, he didn't look much like an Indian. That might work in his favor, Matt thought, although legally there wasn't any reason it should matter.

"Do you think we'll run into any trouble between here and town?" Sandy asked when they had gone a couple miles. He sounded a little nervous.

"I'd be mighty surprised if we don't," Matt said. "All along, Bannerman's been trying to keep this from ever going to court. He won't back off now."

"Maybe we should have brought some of the warriors with us," Sandy suggested.

"Maybe," Matt agreed.

Sandy frowned. "Well, then, why didn't we?"

"Best worry about that later," Preacher said, his voice sharp. "Look yonder!"

Matt glanced to his left, saw a group of riders emerging from a stand of trees. "They're over there, too," he said, inclining his head to the right, where more riders had just come over a ridge. "Looks like they've got us boxed in!"

Sandy groaned in despair. "What are we going to do?"

"Make a run for it!" Matt said. His eyes searched for the nearest cover. "Head for that knoll up ahead!" He nodded toward some rocks on the top of the little hill. They wouldn't provide much cover, but they were better than nothing.

And *something* was definitely better than nothing, Matt thought as he leaned forward in the saddle, heeled Spirit into a gallop, and heard the ominous sound of guns beginning to pop.

Chapter 35

The three men rode hard as they headed for the knoll. Their pursuers continued to close in from both sides, but Matt thought he and Preacher and Sandy stood a good chance of reaching the little hill in time. Luckily, nobody could aim very well from the back of a galloping horse, so it would be a fluke if any of them were hit.

Bad luck sometimes happened, no matter how well-prepared you were, and misfortune struck at that moment. Sandy's pony stepped in a hole and went crashing down in a welter of flailing legs. Sandy yelled as he was thrown off and flew through the air.

Matt reined in hard as he called to Preacher, "Cover us!" The old mountain man yanked Horse to a stop and whipped out his Winchester. He sprayed lead toward the onrushing riders as fast as he could work the rifle's lever.

Matt raced to the spot where Sandy had fallen. The young man had landed hard but didn't seem to be hurt. He was already scrambling to his feet. Matt extended his arm and leaned down from the saddle. Sandy grabbed Matt's wrist and swung up behind him.

"Can your horse carry both of us?" Sandy gasped.

"Hide and watch!" Matt replied as he heeled Spirit into a run again.

The chase was on once more. Preacher slid his Winchester back in its sheath and sent Horse pounding after Matt and Sandy. The delay had allowed the attackers to close in, making their fire more accurate. Bullets kicked up dirt around the hooves of the horses as they reached the knoll and started up the slope.

Matt drew his Colt and triggered several shots at the men on the right. Preacher's .44 blasted toward the men on the left. Slugs whined around them as they ran a gauntlet of lead toward the top of the knoll. They reached it untouched, and the three men leaped off the horses and flung themselves down behind the rocks. Matt yanked his rifle from its sheath as he hurriedly dismounted, and Preacher held on to his Winchester. Both of them fired from prone positions as they sprawled behind the low rocks.

"Keep your head down," Matt warned Sandy. "All we have to do is hold them off for a few minutes . . ."

"A few minutes!" Sandy repeated as he ducked while bullets whined over his head. "What's going to happen in a few minutes?"

A grim smile tugged at Matt's mouth. "You'll see."

Bannerman's hired killers had the knoll completely surrounded. They dismounted and hugged the ground behind rocks and hummocks of earth as they continued firing up at the three men atop the knoll. A couple minutes of fierce fighting went by, but neither side did any real damage to the other.

Then Preacher laughed and said, "It's about time!"

"About time for what?" Sandy asked.

"For your father to play his cards in this game," Matt said.

Dozens of Indian ponies suddenly appeared as if by magic, boiling up from the gully Matt had spotted earlier. He'd figured Crazy Bear would use it to approach the battleground and he was right. Whooping and yipping to demoralize their opponents, the Crow swept forward and charged into Bannerman's men. Some sent rifle slugs smashing into their startled enemies, others pierced them with arrows, and some of the gunmen were trampled under the slashing hooves of the ponies. Matt and Preacher continued picking off any of Bannerman's men they had good shots at, until dust swirled up around the base of the knoll and they could no longer see to aim.

The fighting was brief. The grim noises of battle faded away, and the dust began to settle. Matt stood up and looked down the slope to see that all of Bannerman's gunhawks were either dead, wounded, or captured. Preacher joined him and said, "Looks like that plan we hatched with Crazy Bear worked just fine."

Sandy stumbled to his feet. "You knew this was going to happen?" he demanded.

"We couldn't imagine that Bannerman would let you reach Buffalo Flat for that hearing without trying to stop you," Matt said. "So we figured to lure his men into a trap by starting out for town with just the three of us, while Crazy Bear and some of his warriors followed us and stayed out of sight."

"In other words, the three of us were the bait!"

Matt shrugged. "Call it what you want. We figured Bannerman would send most of his men out here to stop you from getting to town while the rest of them went after the stagecoach with that judge on it. We've taken care of this bunch, so I don't reckon we'll have any more trouble between here and Buffalo Flat." He turned and peered off toward the south, as if he could see across the intervening miles. "Now it's up to Smoke to get that judge there safe and sound."

Smoke and Halliday left Buffalo Flat early that morning, following the stage road that led south to Casper and ultimately on to Laramie and Cheyenne.

"There's an overnight stage stop down on the Middle Fork of the Powder River, close to where the river splits into three branches," Smoke said. "That's where the coach will be startin' from this morning, I imagine."

Halliday nodded. "That's the way it was when I rode it up here a few days ago." He was mounted on a horse rented from Hoyt Dowler and seemed to be a decent rider. He had traded his town suit for range clothes, and from the way he handled himself, Smoke suspected he'd done a little cowboying at some time in the past.

It was a beautiful morning with a deep blue sky overhead. The air was so clear it seemed like the snow-capped peaks of the Big Horns to the west were close enough to reach out and touch. On such a day, it was hard to believe anything could ever change, Smoke reflected.

Then he thought about how different the West was from the untamed wilderness Preacher had first ventured into nearly sixty years earlier. Who knew what would happen in the *next* sixty years?

The mountains would still be there, Smoke thought as he glanced toward the Big Horns. It was a considerable amount of comfort to know they would endure long after he and everyone else he ever knew were gone.

The two men kept their horses moving at a steady, ground-eating pace, and they covered quite a few miles by mid-morning. If the stagecoach driver had started on the last leg of the journey at first light, as usual, he and Halliday ought to be meeting the vehicle soon, Smoke told himself.

It was only a few minutes after that thought crossed his mind when he spotted a column of dust rising in front of them.

"That'll be the coach," Smoke told Halliday as he pointed out the dust. Then he stiffened in the saddle and rose in his stirrups, his eyes narrowing as he peered at a second cloud of dust not far behind the first one.

"What's wrong?" Halliday asked.

"Looks like somebody else is headed this way, too."

"Bannerman's men?"

"Could be," Smoke said. "Out on these flats, it's hard to set up an ambush because there's not enough good cover. But those gun-wolves could've gotten out of sight, waited for the

stagecoach to pass them, then tried to overtake it from behind.
I reckon that's what's happening right now."

"Then we'd better get a move on," Halliday said as he drew
his rifle from the saddle boot.

"That's just what I was thinkin'," Smoke said. He heeled
his horse into a run.

The men galloped hard along the trail. The gap between
them and the two clouds of dust closed rapidly. After a couple
minutes Smoke was able to spot the stagecoach itself at the
base of the first dust cloud, rocking and swaying on its thor-
oughbraces as it careened along the trail. The driver had the
team at a full gallop.

"You take the right, I'll take the left!" Smoke called to Halliday, who nodded in understanding. The two of them split up,
each veering to one side of the trail so the racing coach could
pass between them. Dust swirled, choking and blinding them
for a second as the big Concord stagecoach flew by. Smoke
heard gunshots and knew they came from the pursuers, but he
couldn't see to return the fire.

When the dust blew away and his vision cleared, he saw
eight men on horseback thundering toward him and Halliday,
who was drawing rein on the other side of the trail. Smoke did
likewise and raised the Winchester to his shoulder. He and
Halliday opened fire as the pursuing gunmen realized they
weren't chasing a defenseless stagecoach anymore.

The rifle's lever was a blur as Smoke blasted out all fifteen rounds as swiftly as he could. He swung the barrel from
left to right as he fired, and the hail of lead was rewarded by
the sight of three men toppling from their saddles. Halliday's shots were having an effect as well. Two more men fell
to his slugs.

That left three hired killers still charging toward Smoke and
Halliday, blazing away as they came through. Smoke rammed
the Winchester back in its sheath and drew both of his .44s.
The range was close enough for handguns.

Smoke emptied his right-hand gun first, since his wounded

left arm was still stiff and sore. One man rocked back in the saddle and then pitched to the side, either dead or badly wounded. More dust, raised by the hooves of the gunmen's horses, curled around him and, again, he couldn't see very well.

One of the remaining killers loomed up in front of him, only a few yards away. Smoke twisted in the saddle as the man fired. He heard the wind-rip of the bullet pass his ear as it narrowly missed. His left arm came up, slower than usual but fast enough for him to get a shot off before Bannerman's man could fire again. At the moment Smoke might be slower with his left hand, but he was just as accurate as ever. The gunslinger's head jerked back as the slug smacked into his forehead and killed him. His body thudded to the ground a second later.

Smoke heard other shots and knew that Halliday was swapping lead with the remaining hardcase. When the guns fell silent Smoke holstered his right-hand Colt, then took the other revolver from his left hand in case he needed to use it fast. As the dust settled he saw that Halliday was still on the rented horse and the last of the gunmen was on the ground, writhing for a second before stiffening as death claimed him.

"You all right?" Smoke called to the detective.

Halliday nodded. "Yeah. That was the hottest shootout I've been mixed up in for quite a while." A grin stretched across his angular face. "Brought back some memories . . . not necessarily good ones."

"I know what you mean," Smoke said as he began to reload. He had killed so many men over the years that he sometimes wondered if the killing was ever going to stop. Someday it would, he thought, when times were finally peaceful . . . but he might not be around to see it.

He looked over his shoulder and saw the stagecoach had come to a stop several hundred yards away. "We'd better go check on it," he said to Halliday. "Make sure that judge is still all right."

They jogged their horses toward the coach. Before they

got there, the door opened and a stocky, powerfully-built man stepped out holding a rifle. He wore a town suit, but his broad-brimmed tan Stetson and well-worn boots looked more like something a frontiersman would wear. He had a close-cropped dark beard shot through with gray and looked up at Smoke and Halliday with intense, keenly intelligent eyes.

"Judge Starr?" Halliday asked as he and Smoke reined in.

The man nodded. "That's right. Who're you?"

"Name's Halliday. Right now I work for a law firm in Denver." Halliday inclined his head toward Smoke. "This is Smoke Jensen."

Judge Starr's somewhat bushy eyebrows rose in surprise. "The gunfighter?"

"Some call me that," Smoke allowed. "The way I see it, I'm just a rancher."

Starr snorted. "A rancher with one of the fastest draws in the West, if not *the* fastest. I take it you gentlemen came out to meet me and escort me the rest of the way to Buffalo Flat?"

"That's right," Smoke said. "We knew there was a good chance Reece Bannerman would try to stop you from getting there and conducting that hearing."

Starr raised a hand to stop him. "I won't allow any testimony out here on the trail that might prejudice my judgment. Save that for the hearing, gentlemen."

Smoke frowned in irritation and said, "But those were Bannerman's men who were tryin' to kill you."

"That assumes facts not in evidence." Starr tucked his rifle under his arm. "Now, shall we go?"

Smoke bit back an annoyed curse and nodded. "Yeah, I reckon so." He watched as Starr climbed back into the coach and shut the door. The driver called out to the team, slapped the reins against their backs, and got them moving again. Smoke and Halliday fell in alongside the vehicle.

"Reckon he's a by-the-book judge, all right," Smoke muttered.

"That's just what you want," Halliday pointed out. "That

means he'll be more likely to rule in favor of your friend Little Bear if the claim is a valid one."

"I hope so. I don't want to wind up havin' to go against the government."

Halliday frowned over at him. "You'd do that?"

"If it means stopping Bannerman and his high-powered cronies back in Washington from getting away with the biggest, dirtiest landgrab in history . . . I'll do whatever it takes," Smoke said.

Chapter 36

Sandy's horse hadn't broken its leg in the fall, but it was lame, so Sandy traded mounts with one of the Crow warriors who had sprung the trap on Bannerman's hired killers. Accompanied by Crazy Bear and three warriors, Matt, Preacher, and Sandy rode on to Buffalo Flat. The Indians drew a bit of attention but didn't cause a panic as they rode down the street. Folks were used to seeing the Crow around there.

Jason Garrard emerged from his hotel and lifted a hand in greeting to Matt, who reined in and nodded to him. "Mister Garrard."

"That's Mayor Garrard now," the man said with a smile. "I've decided to go into politics." He looked a little less friendly as he nodded to his son-in-law. "Sandy."

"Hello, Mr. Garrard," Sandy said. "It's good to see you again."

From the looks of it, an uneasy truce existed between the two men, Matt thought. They had to get along with each other because of Robin, but they might not ever genuinely like each other.

Matt considered Garrard an ally of sorts. The man had put his shady dealings behind him and was working for the betterment of the entire community. Matt said, "A federal judge will be on the stagecoach when it comes in, Mr. Garrard. He's going to hold a hearing about Sandy's claim to the upper portion of the valley. Is there a place in town big enough to have a hearing like that?"

"Sure. You can use the lobby of the hotel. Should be plenty of room in there, and we can bring in chairs from the dining room, as well as a table for the judge."

"That would be fine. Thanks."

Garrard nodded to Crazy Bear and the three warriors. "Will the, ah, Indians be coming in?"

"I think that would be a good idea," Matt said.

"Well, all right. Maybe having some savages around won't spook my guests too much."

Matt glanced at Crazy Bear, knowing that the chief understood English. His face remained as impassively ugly as ever.

The men dismounted. Garrard said to Sandy, "How are my daughter and granddaughter?"

"They're fine," Sandy told him. "We'll be spending more time in town soon."

"I hope so. I want Emily to grow up knowing her grandpa."

It took Matt a second, then he realized that Emily was Moon Fawn's white name. She was a lucky little girl, he thought. She would grow up experiencing both worlds, Indian and white.

Preacher said, "You and Sandy go on inside, Matt." He inclined his head toward Crazy Bear and the Crow warriors. "Me and these fellas will stay out here. We ain't too fond of havin' hard roofs over our heads. Never quite got used to it."

Matt nodded. "All right. You keep an eye out for Smoke and that stagecoach."

Garrard enlisted the help of his desk clerk and began preparing the hotel lobby for the hearing. Matt and Sandy pitched in, and so did some curious traveling salesmen who were staying at the hotel. The drummers didn't know what was going on, but anything that broke up the monotony of their lives was welcome. Before long, they had the sofas that normally sat in the lobby moved out of the way and had set up several rows of chairs from the dining room.

"This may interfere with your business," Sandy said to his father-in-law.

"Not enough to worry about," Garrard replied. He smiled. "Besides, having such an important proceeding here might just increase business in the long run."

A short time later, Preacher stuck his head in the front door. "There's some dust comin' south o' town!" he called. "Could be the stagecoach."

They crowded onto the hotel porch and watched the vehicle come up the street flanked by Smoke and Halliday. The presence of the Indians and rumors of what was about to happen at the hotel had spread around town, and quite a crowd was gathering. The coach's driver slowed his team to let the townspeople get out of the way. The leather-lunged old jehu bellowed fiery curses that caused women to put their hands protectively over the ears of their children.

Smoke and Halliday dismounted and tied their horses at the hitch rail in front of the hotel. With a big grin on his face, Smoke bounded onto the porch, shook Matt's hand, and slapped Preacher on the back.

"You made it," he said. "Any trouble?"

"Oh, just a little dustup with about thirty o' Bannerman's boys," Preacher drawled. "Nothin' we couldn't handle."

Smoke nodded. "Glad to hear it." He turned to nod toward the bearded man climbing out of the coach. "Meet Judge Starr."

Garrard stepped forward. "Judge Starr!" he said. "Welcome to Buffalo Flat! Allow me to introduce myself. I'm the mayor of this community, Jason Garrard—"

"Don't bother with the political glad handing, Garrard," Starr snapped. "I'm here on legal business, and I don't have time for it."

Garrard blinked in surprise, but recovered quickly and

said, "Of course. Right this way, Your Honor. We have a courtroom set up inside."

"Much obliged," Starr said as he followed Garrard into the building.

"Did Bannerman make a try for the judge?" Matt asked Smoke.

"He sure did," Smoke replied. "He sent eight men to stop the coach, and I'm sure if they'd succeeded, they would have killed Starr."

"But they didn't, thanks to you and Halliday."

Smoke shrugged. "That was the plan. We carried it out."

"That leaves the hearing." Matt looked up and down the street. "I wonder where Bannerman is. You don't think he went with any of his men to carry out those attacks, do you?"

Smoke shook his head. "Not hardly. He'd want to be here in case his men failed to stop the hearing from taking place. He's probably been keeping an eye on the town, so I expect he'll show up soon."

A few minutes later, Smoke proved to be a prophet. A dozen riders entered Buffalo Flat from the north end of town and came slowly along the street. Silence gradually spread through the chattering crowd as the men rode past. Smoke, Matt, and Preacher watched them approach and recognized Reece Bannerman riding in the lead. Lew Torrance was just behind him and to his right. The other ten men were cut from the same cloth as Torrance: hardened gunfighters whose killing skills were for sale to the highest bidder.

"Looks like he saved the cream of the crop to come into town with him," Smoke commented.

"Or the worst of the worst," Matt said.

"That's 'cause he knows this is where the final show-down'll be, if there is one," Preacher said. "If the judge don't rule the way Bannerman wants him to, he'll try to kill ever'-body on the other side and scare the townspeople into backin' him up when the law comes in. He'll find a way to blame ever'thing on us and Crazy Bear. He'll say we went loco and killed that judge before they gunned us down."

"You think he'd really murder a federal judge?" Matt asked.

Preacher squinted at him. "I seen fellas like Bannerman before. They get to thinkin' they're above the law—man's law, God's law, any other kind of law—and if they got enough guns on their side, sometimes they're right. So, yeah, I think he'd try to wipe us all out, and if folks around here know what's good for 'em, they'd keep the truth to theirselves."

"Then it's up to us to make sure that doesn't happen," Smoke said. His face was set in grim lines. He hooked his thumbs in his gunbelt and stepped to the front edge of the hotel porch as Bannerman and the crew of gun-wolves pulled rein in the street.

"If you're lookin' for the hearing, Bannerman, this is it," Smoke said.

"Who're you?" Bannerman snapped.

"That's right, we haven't met, have we? Name's Smoke Jensen."

Torrance said, "I told you about him, Mr. Bannerman. He and the other Jensen are related somehow."

"What about that filthy old codger?" Bannerman asked as he glared at Preacher.

The old mountain man bristled instantly. "Filthy, am I?" he demanded. "Well, I'd rather be a mite dirty on the outside than rotten on the inside like you, Bannerman. As for who I am . . . they call me Preacher."

Several of the gunmen recognized the name and frowned in surprise. "Preacher?" one of them repeated. "That ain't possible. Preacher's been dead for years."

"Then I'm mighty spry for a corpse, sonny," Preacher shot back, his lip curling in a snarl. His hand hovered over the butt of his Colt. "Care to find out just how spry?"

"Stop it," Bannerman ordered his man. "We're here to attend a hearing, not to get in some fracas with an old lunatic." He dismounted and looped his reins around the hitch rail. "Come on."

Smoke moved to block Bannerman's path as the cattleman started up the steps. "You plan on bringing that whole bunch in with you?"

"They have a right to come in. A hearing like this is open to the public, isn't it?"

"Indeed it is," Judge Starr boomed from the front entrance of the hotel. "And I'd like to get started, so everyone come inside." He looked at Crazy Bear and the other three Crow. "Including you gentlemen."

"Wait just a minute!" Bannerman said. "No offense, Your Honor, but you can't mean to let those savages attend."

"They have a stake in the matter, and they're citizens, according to the Treaty of 1868 and subsequent judicial decisions."

Sandy stood behind Judge Starr and nodded. Clearly, he was familiar with the law regarding those matters.

"All right, blast it," Bannerman said. "But it seems to me letting them in is making a mockery of the legal system."

"I warn you, Mr. Bannerman, don't tell me how to conduct legal proceedings," Starr said.

Bannerman grimaced and said, "Sorry, Your Honor. I meant no disrespect."

Starr jerked his head. "Let's go."

Everyone filed inside. The chairs filled up quickly with spectators, but Smoke, Matt, Preacher, and Halliday weren't among them. They remained standing and arrayed themselves against a side wall where they could keep an eye on the entire room. Torrance and several of the gunmen took up similar positions on the opposite wall.

Bannerman consulted with a tall, slender man in an expensive suit. Smoke had never seen him before, but he recalled what Halliday had said about the Indian Ring sending a lawyer to represent Bannerman.

Sandy took a seat in the front row, as far as he could get

from where Bannerman and the Eastern lawyer were sitting at the other end. Crazy Bear and the three warriors stood in the rear of the room. Some of the spectators glanced around at the hostile forces on three sides of them and began to look a little nervous, as they realized maybe it wasn't such a good idea to sit in the middle.

Judge Starr walked behind the table that had been placed at the front of the room, and Garrard took it upon himself to call out, "All rise!", as if he were a bailiff.

Starr glanced at him and said with dry amusement, "Thank you, Mayor." Then he looked at the crowd in the room and went on, "Be seated."

The spectators sat down. Smoke and his companions, Torrance and the gunfighters, and the Indians all stayed on their feet where they could move fast if they needed to.

"Federal court for the Western District, Fifth Circuit, is now in session," Starr proclaimed. "In the absence of a bailiff, I'll just say it myself, modesty be hanged. The Honorable Errol Starr presiding. This is a special hearing regarding a question of land ownership and homestead rights. Is anybody taking this down?"

A man in the second row said, "I am, Your Honor. I'm the editor of the Buffalo Flat *Sentinel*."

"Newspaperman, eh? Well, I suppose that's better than nothing." Starr leaned over in his chair and reached into a carpetbag he had carried in from the stagecoach. He took out a gavel and rapped it sharply on the table in front of him. "Should've done that first. *Now* court's in session, The Honorable Errol Starr presiding, et cetera, et cetera. This hearing is to establish the validity of a land claim by one Sandor Little Bear. Is Mr. Little Bear present?"

Sandy stood up. "Yes, Your Honor, right here."

"You have documentation of the aforementioned claim, Mr. Little Bear?"

"I do, Your Honor. If I may approach the bench to introduce the deed into evidence?"

Starr nodded. "Come ahead."

Bannerman looked at the lawyer, who jumped to his feet and said, "Objection, Your Honor. My client and I have not had an opportunity to examine this so-called deed before it is entered into evidence."

"That's because *I'm* the one who'll examine it and determine its validity, counsel," Starr said. "Objection overruled."

The lawyer sat down but didn't look happy about it. Bannerman's neck was getting red, Smoke observed. Bannerman didn't like anything about the proceeding. His ambition was in the hands of a man he hadn't had a chance to bribe, bully, or murder, and he couldn't control what was going to happen.

Sandy took the deed from his coat, unfolded it, placed it on the table in front of Starr, and smoothed it out. He said, "You'll note, Your Honor, the dates on which the claim was filed, approved, and the deed drawn up. You can see as well, the official seal of the Department of the Interior granting provisional ownership of the land."

Starr took a pair of spectacles from his vest pocket, unfolded them, and put them on. He leaned forward to study the document intently. A minute dragged by and seemed longer in the silence that gripped the makeshift courtroom.

"Provisional ownership," the judge finally said, "dependent on certain conditions, such as making improvements. It's my understanding that this land is being used as hunting grounds by a tribe of Indians."

"A band of Indians, yes, Your Honor," Sandy said. "My father's people. He's Chief Crazy Bear."

"Then if the land is in an unimproved state, the conditions of this grant of land haven't been met."

Starr's words drew a fleeting grin of triumph from Bannerman before the rancher controlled his reaction.

"Your Honor, if you'll look at the dates again, you'll see that the term of the grant isn't up yet. In fact, I still have a year to fulfill them. In that time, I intend to have a house built for my wife and myself, a well dug, and a vegetable garden put in. I believe that will satisfy the conditions?"

Starr thought about it, then nodded. "It will. But what about the rest of the land?"

"My father's people . . . my people . . . will be free to live and hunt there as they always have," Sandy said.

The lawyer was on his feet again. "Your Honor, this . . . this is a perversion of the intent of the Homestead Act! It was meant to provide farms for civilized people, not some . . . some refuge for savages!"

"When you start speculating on the intent of the framers of a law, you venture onto shaky ground, counsel. The law says what it says, within reasonable interpretations, of course. And I see nothing in the law that denies what Mr. Little Bear is claiming."

"Your Honor, please—"

Starr motioned the lawyer back into his seat. "You'll get your turn in a minute." He looked at Sandy. "Do you have anything else to say, Mr. Little Bear?"

"Not really, Your Honor. That deed speaks for itself. The Department of the Interior wouldn't have attached its seal if my claim was not a valid one."

"Very well, if you have no other statement or evidence, you may sit down."

Sandy took his seat.

"*Now* it's your turn," Starr told Bannerman's lawyer. "I understand that your client is challenging Mr. Little Bear's claim to the land in question?"

"That is correct, Your Honor," the Easterner said as he came to his feet. "My client attempted to file a claim on the same land, only to be denied because there was already a spurious claim on file."

"Now, I'm sure the Department of the Interior didn't tell him the other claim was spurious," Starr said. "That's what we're trying to determine here."

"Your Honor, surely you're not saying that you would allow

a . . . savage to take precedence over my client, a successful, well-respected citizen who owns one of the largest ranches in the territory—"

Sandy stood up and said, "Your Honor?"

"What is it, Mr. Little Bear?" Starr asked.

"I'm not an attorney, but may I object anyway?"

"On what grounds?"

"Relevance, Your Honor. My *savageness*"—the word, coming from the articulate, well-dressed young man, brought appreciative chuckles from some of the spectators, and from Smoke and Matt as well—"has nothing to do with the matter at hand," Sandy went on, "nor does the success of Mr. Bannerman. I could be a Hottentot and Mr. Bannerman could be Cornelius Vanderbilt, and it wouldn't have anything to do with anything."

Starr smiled. "Point taken, young man. Your objection is sustained." He looked at the flustered Eastern lawyer. "Do you have any actual *legal* argument, counselor, or are you simply appealing to emotion here?"

"Your Honor, it . . . it's in the public interest for my client to have that range as grazing land—"

Starr smacked the gavel down on the table. "Putting up the so-called public interest as a false front for private business doesn't trump individual property rights, sir, and by God, I hope it never does! If that ever happens, this country can kiss its blessed liberty good-bye! Anything else?"

Bannerman looked furious. He glared at the lawyer, who seemed stunned that anyone would oppose him. He was used to rolling right over anybody who stood up to him, Smoke thought as he looked at the man. With all the political power and money behind him, he figured he and his clients were always going to get their way. He had run smack-dab into an honest man, and he didn't know what to do about it.

"No, Your Honor, I . . . I . . ."

Starr's gavel smacked down again. "In that case, I rule that Mr. Little Bear's claim is valid and there will be no interference with him during the term of his provisional claim, which of course can be revisited when said provisional period is up. Mr. Bannerman!"

"Yes?" Bannerman said between teeth clenched in fury.

"You understand that my ruling means you're to keep your cows off that Indian land and leave them the hell alone?"

"I understand," Bannerman grated.

"You understand what?" Starr prodded.

Bannerman got to his feet and clapped his hat on his head. "I understand this isn't over yet, damn it!" He stalked out of the hotel lobby, followed by Torrance and the other gun-slingers.

"By God!" Starr burst out. "I'm going to hold that man in contempt of court!" He pointed at Smoke. "You there, Mr. Jensen, is it?"

"Yes, Your Honor?" Smoke asked.

"I hereby appoint you and your three companions there as special federal deputies and empower you to arrest Mr. Ban-nerman."

"You know what that means, Judge?"

"Indeed I do," Starr said.

"All right. You and everybody else had better stay inside."

"Excellent advice." Starr rapped the gavel. "Everyone stay seated, but court's adjourned. Mr. Jensen, you and your friends go get that son of a bitch."

Smoke nodded and went to the door, Matt, Preacher, Hal-liday, Crazy Bear, and the three Crow warriors right behind him. As he stepped onto the porch, he saw Bannerman, Tor-rance, and the rest of Bannerman's gunhawks clustered across the street in front of the saloon. Word of what was about to happen had spread like wildfire through the town. The crowd that had clogged the street earlier was gone.

And with good reason, because no sooner had Smoke stepped through the door than Bannerman yelled, "Kill them! Kill them all!"

Chapter 37

Smoke shouted over his shoulder, "Everybody down!" as he threw himself to the left. Matt, directly behind him, went to the right, and Preacher and Halliday threw themselves flat on the porch as Bannerman's hired killers opened fire. Bannerman had a gun in his hand and snapped a couple of shots at Smoke.

Every bit of glass in the hotel's front windows shattered under the onslaught of lead. Inside the lobby, Judge Starr, Sandy, the Eastern lawyer, and all the spectators dived for cover. The lawyer, especially, was terrified, crawling under the judge's table and cowering there.

Outside, Smoke, Matt, Preacher, and Halliday returned the shots. Smoke rolled off the porch and dropped behind a water trough. Matt took cover behind a parked wagon. Most of the horses tied at the hitch rail jerked free and bolted to get out of the line of fire, except for a couple of luckless animals who went down screaming and thrashing as stray bullets ripped into them.

Bannerman turned to run into the saloon just as Smoke sent a slug whistling past his head. The ranks of the gunmen closed in, preventing Smoke from getting another shot at the ruthless cattle baron. A couple of the gunnies went down before they scattered so they didn't present as good a target. Within moments, both sides were engaged in a running gunfight up and down Buffalo Flat's main street as Smoke, Matt, and the others traded shots with Bannerman's men.

Crazy Bear and the other warriors joined in the battle. Arrows flew through the air and impaled gunmen. With one blow of his mighty fist, Crazy Bear crushed the skull of a man wielding an empty pistol. He didn't see a killer drawing a bead on him from behind, but Sandy, who had slipped out a side door in the hotel, did. The young man tackled the hardcase before the man could pull the trigger and send a bullet into Crazy Bear's back. Sandy grabbed the gun, twisted it out of the man's hand, and slammed the butt back and forth across the man's face, shattering his jaw.

As he looked down at the groaning, bloody, broken face of his opponent, Sandy said, "Maybe I *am* a little bit of a savage after all."

Bullets from Preacher's rifle drilled a couple of the gunfighters, and Halliday knocked down another one with a well-placed shot from his revolver. A few yards away, Matt dropped two of the gunmen as he fired from behind the wagon, then he took off at a run after Lew Torrance, who obviously had decided to get out while the getting was good. Torrance made a grab for one of the horses running free in the street.

Matt sent a bullet in front of Torrance's face that made the man jerk back. "Torrance!" Matt called. "You ready to settle this?"

"You're a damn fool, Jensen!" Torrance yelled over the roar of gunfire from down the street. "You and I ought to be on the same side again!"

"That'll never happen," Matt said.

Each man had a gun in his hand. Torrance brought his up with blinding speed, but Matt was just a hair faster. Flame spouted from the muzzles of both guns. Matt felt Torrance's slug pluck at his sleeve. Torrance took a sharp step backward and paled under the impact of the bullet that drove into his body. He opened his mouth to say something, but blood gushed from it he pitched forward onto his face. He still clutched his gun, but his fingers slowly relaxed and slid off the grips.

Back up the street, Smoke had surged to his feet with blazing irons filling both hands. The last of the gunmen spun off their feet in the face of that storm of lead. Smoke raced past them, the acrid tang of burned powder filling his nose as he leaped onto the boardwalk in front of the saloon. He pressed his back against the building's front wall as he holstered his left-hand gun and reloaded the right-hand Colt.

Then, holding the .44 ready, he called, "Bannerman! You hear me? Come on out and surrender! Your men are all either dead or out of the fight!"

"Go to hell!" Bannerman shouted back.

Smoke went in fast and low while the words still echoed in the place, which had emptied out quickly before the battle started. He rolled under the batwings as they shivered under the impact of Bannerman's bullets. Smoke could tell from the sound of the thunderous explosions that Bannerman was above him somewhere.

His eyes picked up a staircase at the back of the room and followed it up to a narrow balcony where Bannerman crouched, firing down at him. It took less than a heartbeat for Smoke to react. The barrel of his .44 tilted up and spewed flame. The bullet, traveling at an angle, caught Bannerman low in the belly and tore up through his gut before it shattered his spine and blew a hole out through his back. He screamed and toppled forward, crashing through the railing along the edge of the balcony. Turning over in midair, he plummeted and crashed onto the bar.

Smoke stood up and kept his Colt trained on Bannerman as he approached the cattleman. Bannerman was still alive, but his eyes were wide with pain and shock. His mouth opened and closed spasmodically without any sound. As Smoke reached him, Bannerman was able to gasp, "Damn . . .

you . . . Jensen! You'll be sorry . . . you messed with . . . me and my friends!"

"I'm already sorry you thought you were bigger than the law, Bannerman."

A grimace that might have been a smile pulled Bannerman's lips back from his teeth. "We . . . are!" he said. "You'll see . . . This isn't over . . . you fool . . ."

Then his eyes rolled back in their sockets and his head fell to his side. Smoke heard the grotesque rattle that was Reece Bannerman's final breath leaving his body.

Footsteps behind him made Smoke look over his shoulder. Matt and Preacher walked into the saloon, followed by Halliday, Judge Star, Crazy Bear, Sandy, and the Crow warriors.

"Is Bannerman dead?" Starr asked.

"I'm afraid so," Smoke said. "He didn't want to be arrested for contempt of court, Your Honor."

Starr snorted. "He didn't want to face the fact that he was beaten and looking at enough counts of attempted murder to keep him behind bars for the next thirty years." The judge shrugged. "But that's irrelevant now. The record will show that he was killed while resisting arrest, as were his men. What will happen to his ranch I don't know, but thankfully, that's a matter for a probate court, not me."

"You knew when you sent us after him that he'd fight," Smoke said.

"Of course I did. Just like I knew he'd try to kill us all and cover up his crimes if somebody didn't stop him. I was raised on the frontier, Mr. Jensen. I know Bannerman's type . . . men who have wealth and power but are really just two-bit desperados at heart."

"You've got some more just like him in Washington, from what I hear," Matt said.

"You're probably right," Starr agreed, "and I intend to look into that. For now, though, this case is settled." He turned to Sandy. "You and your father can go home now, Mr. Little

Bear, and live your lives. It would be a good idea for you to get those improvements made before the end of the year."

"Yes, Your Honor. I surely will."

Starr looked around the room, gave everyone a curt nod, and departed.

Preacher said to Sandy, "Your wife's pa is gonna have a heap o' cleanin' up to do around this town, since he's the mayor and all. Got dead gunslingers layin' ever'where, not to mention all the busted glass to replace and bullet holes to patch."

"Yes, but if anyone can do it, Jason Garrard is the one," Sandy said. "He's civilization personified, with all its virtues and its flaws, and you can't stop civilization."

"I know," Preacher said with a sigh. "Ain't it a damned shame?"

Smoke, Matt, and Preacher spent the next few days at Crazy Bear's village, visiting with their old friends and recovering from the violent clash with Reece Bannerman.

But Smoke missed Sally, and Matt got to worrying that maybe Starwind was more interested in settling down than she let on at first, and Preacher . . . well, Preacher hadn't let any grass grow under his feet for a long, long time, and he wasn't just about to start. The restlessness was inevitable.

So the three men said their good-byes, traded hugs and handshakes with Crazy Bear and his people, and mounted up. They rode off together down the valley, enjoying the magnificent beauty of the mountains around them.

Something nagged at Smoke, and after a while he said, "Bannerman was right, you know."

"About what?" Matt asked.

Preacher said, "This ain't over. That's what you're gettin' at, ain't it, Smoke?"

"That's right. Bannerman and this whole mess didn't really amount to much, not to those hombres back in Washington who think they can make their fortunes even bigger on the land and the blood of other folks. This was like the opening move in a chess game, that's all. They'll try something else, and it's liable to be worse next time."

"Well, then, we'll keep an eye out, and if they get up to any more mischief, we'll just stop 'em again," Preacher declared. "If you boys run into any of the varmints, give a holler and I'll come a-runnin' and lend a hand with the snake-stompin'."

"The same goes for me," Matt said. "Whatever they get up to in the future, I don't want them getting away with it."

Smoke nodded. "It's a deal. The West is a mighty big place, but I reckon as much as the three of us get around, and as many people as we know, we'll hear about it if the new Indian Ring tries anything again. Maybe we can keep it from getting as big and doing as much damage."

"In the meantime, I've sorta got a hankerin' to head out Californy way," Preacher said. "Been a while since I seen them big ol' redwood trees. I reckon you're headin' back to Sugarloaf, Smoke?"

A grin stretched across Smoke's rugged face. "That's right. It's been too long since I've seen a certain dark-haired beauty I happen to be married to. What about you, Matt?"

"I thought I'd stop by Dodge City and say howdy to Bat Masterson. He's the sheriff there now, and he promised me a deputy's job if I ever wanted one."

Preacher frowned at him and asked, "Now why in tarnation would you want to wear a tin star in a rip-roarin' hellhole like Dodge?"

Matt grinned. "I figure it'll be a lot more peaceful than hanging around with you two!" He lifted a hand in farewell and headed east, calling *"Vaya con Dios!"*

"So long, Smoke," Preacher said as he turned Horse to the west. "Be seein' ya."

"Count on it," Smoke told the old mountain man.

He rode on south toward home, knowing he would see both

of them again. More than likely all hell would be breaking loose at the time, but at least they would be together. The same blood didn't run in their veins, but that didn't matter, not one damn bit.

They were family . . . and always would be.

J. A. Johnstone on William W. Johnstone
"When the Truth Becomes Legend"

William W. Johnstone was born in southern Missouri, the youngest of four children. He was raised with strong moral and family values by his minister father, and tutored by his school-teacher mother. Despite this, he quit school at age fifteen.

"I have the highest respect for education," he says, "but such is the folly of youth, and wanting to see the world beyond the four walls and the blackboard." True to this vow, Bill attempted to enlist in the French Foreign Legion ("I saw Gary Cooper in *Beau Geste* when I was a kid and I thought the French Foreign Legion would be fun") but was rejected, thankfully, for being underage. Instead, he joined a traveling carnival and did all kinds of odd jobs. It was listening to the veteran carny folk, some of whom had been on the circuit since the late 1800s, telling amazing tales about their experiences which planted the storytelling seed in Bill's imagination.

"They were honest people, despite the bad reputation traveling carny shows had back then," Bill remembers. "Of course, there were exceptions. There was one guy named Picky, who got that name because he was a master pickpocket. He could steal a man's socks right off his feet without him knowing. Believe me, Picky got us chased out of more than a few towns."

After a few months of this grueling existence, Bill returned home and finished high school. Next came stints as a deputy sheriff in the Tallulah, LA. Sheriff's Department, followed by a hitch in the U.S. Army. Then he began a career in radio broadcasting at KTLD in Tallulah, Louisiana, that would last sixteen years. It was here that he fine-tuned his storytelling skills. He turned to writing in 1970, but it wouldn't be until 1979 until his first novel, *The Devil's Kiss*, was published. Thus began the full-time writing career of William W. Johnstone. He wrote horror (*The Uninvited*), thrillers (*The Last of the Dog Team*), even a romance novel or two. Then, in February 1983, *Out of the Ashes* was published. Searching for his missing family in the aftermath of a post-apocalyptic America, rebel mercenary and patriot Ben Raines is united with the civilians of the Resistance forces and moves to the forefront of a revolution for the nation's future.

Out of the Ashes was a smash. The series would continue for the next twenty years, winning Bill three generations of fans all over the world. The series was often imitated but never duplicated. "We all tried to copy *The Ashes* series," said one publishing executive, "but Bill's uncanny ability, both then and now, to predict in which direction the political winds were blowing, brought a dead-on timeliness to the table no one else could capture." *The Ashes* series would end its run with more than thirty-four books and twenty million copies in print, making it one of the most successful men's action series in American book publishing. (*The Ashes* series also, Bill notes with a touch of pride, got him on the FBI's Watch List for its less than flattering portrayal of spineless politicians and the growing power of big government over our lives, among other things. "In that respect," says collaborator J. A. Johnstone, "Bill was years ahead of his time.")

Always steps ahead of the political curve, Bill's recent thrillers, written with J. A. Johnstone, include *Vengeance Is Mine, Invasion USA, Border War, Jackknife, Remember the Alamo, Home Invasion, Phoenix Rising, The Blood of Patriots, The Bleeding Edge,* and the upcoming *Suicide Mission*.

It is with the Western, though, that Bill found his greatest success and propelled him onto both the *USA Today* and *New York Times* bestseller lists.

Bill's western series, co-authored by J. A. Johnstone, include *The Mountain Man, Matt Jensen the Last Mountain Man, Preacher, The Family Jensen, Luke Jensen Bounty Hunter, Eagles, MacCallister* (an *Eagles* spin-off), *Sidewinders, The Brothers O'Brien, Sixkiller, Blood Bond, The Last Gunfighter,* and the upcoming new series *Flintlock* and *The Trail West.* Coming in May 2013 is the hardcover western *Butch Cassidy, The Lost Years.*

"The Western," Bill says, "is one of the few true art forms that is one hundred percent American. I liken the Western as America's version of England's Arthurian legends, like the Knights of the Round Table or Robin Hood and his Merry Men. Starting with the 1902 publication of *The Virginian* by Owen Wister, and followed by the greats like Zane Grey, Max Brand, Ernest Haycox, and of course Louis L'Amour, the Western has helped to shape define the cultural landscape of America.

"I'm no goggle-eyed college academic, so when my fans ask me why the Western is as popular now as it was a century ago, I don't offer a 200-page thesis. Instead, I can only offer this: The Western is honest. In this great country, which is suffering under the yoke of political correctness, the Western harks back to an era when justice was sure and swift. Steal a man's horse, rustle his cattle, rob a bank, a stagecoach, or a train, you were hunted down and fitted with a hangman's noose. One size fit all.

"Sure, we westerners are prone to a little embellishment and exaggeration and, I admit it, occasionally play a little fast and loose with the facts. But we do so for a very good reason—to enhance the enjoyment of readers.

"It was Owen Wister, in *The Virginian* who first coined the phrase *'When you call me that, smile.'* Legend has it that Wister actually heard those words spoken by a deputy sheriff in Medicine Bow, Wyoming, when another poker player called him a son-of-a-bitch.

"Did it really happen, or is it one of those myths that have passed down from one generation to the next? I honestly don't know. But there's a line in one of my favorite Westerns of all time, *The Man who Shot Liberty Valance*, where the newspaper editor tells the young reporter, 'When the truth becomes legend, print the legend.'

"These are the words I live by."

TURN THE PAGE FOR AN EXCITING PREVIEW!

From NY TIMES *and* USA TODAY *bestselling authors*
William W. Johnstone** and **J. A. Johnstone

SUPPORT YOUR LOCAL DEPUTY
A Cotton Pickens Western

*Welcome to the peaceful little town of Doubtful, Wyoming,
which has more than its fair share of kill-crazy gunslicks,
back-shooters, and flat-out dirty desperadoes. . . .
It also has a sheriff named Cotton Pickens,
who tries his best to keep law and order without
getting his head blown off before breakfast.*

NOW DOUBTFUL'S GOT A NEW DEPUTY . . .
FOR THE MOMENT

Cotton Pickens got where he is by virtue of a quick draw
and a slow wit. He knows the difference between
lawbreakers you have to lock up . . . and the kind you
might as well just let go. Deputy Rusty Irons,
though, ain't the sharpest tool in the shed.
Someone kidnapped Rusty's mail-order bride. They were
probably doing Irons a favor, but a deputy in love is blind.

And as for the various carny barkers, medicine show
con artists, and revival-meeting fly-by-nighters who
pass through Doubtful . . . Cotton just tries to keep the
peace and keep the traveling hucksters moving.
But for one terrible moment in Doubtful, it all goes straight
to hell. That's when the town explodes in a frenzy of killing
and bloodshed. That's when a lawman like Cotton earns
his pay, saves his soul, or loses his life by looking evil
straight in the eye. And of course, there's also the matter of
keeping his new deputy alive and in one piece. . . .

SUPPORT YOUR LOCAL DEPUTY
A Cotton Pickens Western

On sale now wherever Pinnacle Books are sold.

Chapter I

My deputy, Rusty Irons, was as itchy as a man ever gets. We were at the Laramie and Overland stage station, in Doubtful, waiting for the maroon-enameled Concord stage to roll in. Rusty couldn't come up with proper bouquets, not in the barely settled cow town of Doubtful, Wyoming, but he managed some daisies and sagebrush he had collected out on the range.

Rusty was waiting for his mail-order brides. That's right, Siamese twins, joined at the hip, from the Ukraine. He ordered just one, but they sent him the pair. He'd gotten a hundred and fifty dollars reward, offered for Huckster Bob, wanted dead or alive. Rusty got him alive, and collected, and applied the money to getting himself a wife.

And now we were waiting for the stage to roll in. It was an hour late, and maybe more.

Well, my ma always said there's nothing worse than a sweating bridegroom, and Rusty filled the bill. He had sweat running down his sides. His armpits had turned into gushers.

"Well, you get to be best man," Rusty said.

"If I don't arrest you first for bigamy," I said.

"I looked it up; there's no law in Wyoming Territory against it."

"Well, I'll arrest you for something or other," I said. "You found a preacher who'll tie the knot?"

"No, but I'm going to argue that all he has to do is marry me to one of 'em."

"What'll you do with the other?"

"I can't auction her off," Rusty said. "So she gets to be the spectator."

"They speak English?"

"Not a word. They're from Lvov, Ukraine."

"Well, that's a good start," I said. "You won't get into arguments. My ma always said the best part of her marriage was when my pa was snoring."

"Well, you're the result," Rusty said.

I wasn't sure how to take that, but thought I'd let it pass without a fistfight. His armpits were leaking worse than ever and I didn't want his sweat all over my sheriff suit and pants.

"You figure they're joined facing the same way?" I asked.

"Well, I wouldn't marry them if one was facing backwards. Here," he said, pulling out a tintype.

The image of two beautiful blondes leapt out at me. It looked like they were side by side, except they had a single dark skirt.

"This one here's Natasha, and the other is Anna," Rusty said.

"You know which one you'll hitch up with?"

"We'll toss a coin. Or maybe they've got it worked out."

"What if one wants you and the other doesn't? Or you want one and not the other?"

Rusty, he just grinned. "Life sure is interesting," he said.

Word had gotten out, and a small crowd had collected at the wooden stage office on Main Street. Some of the women squinted at Rusty as if he was a criminal, which maybe he was. One man looked like he wanted to propose to the other.

But mostly they stared at Rusty, wondering what sort of twisted beast would want to marry Siamese twins. And now there were fifty of the good citizens of Doubtful, standing in clumps, whispering, pointing at Rusty as if he belonged in the bottom layer of hell.

Rusty, he just smiled.

"I'm glad you got me that raise," he said.

"You'll need it," I replied.

I'd gone to the Puma County Supervisors and talked them into raising Rusty's wage by five dollars, because of his impending wedlock, and his faithful service as my best and most useful deputy. That put him up just two dollars below my forty-seven a month sheriff's salary, but I didn't mind.

I saw Delphinium Sanders, the banker's wife, glaring as hard as she could manage at both of us. And George Waller, the mayor, was studying us as if we belonged in a zoo, which maybe we did. I sure didn't know how this would play out, or who'd marry whom, but it made a late spring day real entertaining there in the cow town of Doubtful.

Hanging Judge Earwig was there, too, and thought maybe he'd do the marrying if no one else would. Judge Earwig was broadminded, and didn't mind it if people thought ill of him. He might even marry both the twins to Rusty, seeing as how there wasn't any law against it. That'd come later, when the next legislature got moralistic. Or maybe Rusty could take his gals to Utah and find a Mormon cleric to fix him up, but I didn't put much stock in it. Utah had outlawed that sort of entertainment.

That stagecoach sure was late. Dry road, too. Dry spring, no potholes or mud puddles. The waiting was hard on Rusty.

"Hey, Rusty, you got a two-holer, or are they gonna take turns?" some brat yelled.

I went after the freckled punk, got an ear, and twisted it.

"Cut that out or I'll throw you down a hole and you'll stink for a week."

"Aw, sheriff, this is the best thing hit Doubtful in a long time."

"You're Willie Dickens, and your ma didn't raise you right. I let go of your ear, you promise to respect people?"

"Anything you say," Willie said, and yanked loose, smirking.

I let him go. This was turning into an ordeal for my deputy sheriff, instead of a moment of joy. It wasn't hard to tell what all of them good folks of Doubtful were thinking. This marriage would have a threesome in the bedroom.

And still no coach.

Then, about the time I was ready to head back to the sheriff office and look over the mail, we spotted the coach rounding the hill south of Doubtful, coming along at a smart clip, maybe faster than usual because them drays looked pretty lathered.

Jonas Quill, the jehu, pulled back the lines slightly, and the sweated horses gladly quit on him, while the coach rocked gently.

"Well, Rusty, here it comes," I said.

But Quill yelled at me, "We got held up, man."

"Held up?"

"Four armed men, masked."

By then the maroon door of the coach swung open, and six passengers emerged: four rumpled males, mostly whiskey drummers, and two frightened women, both gray-haired, in bonnets.

No Ukrainian Siamese identical female twins.

Rusty seemed to leak gas.

"Clear away from here," I yelled at the mob. "We got trouble."

"Where are they?" Rusty asked.

"Don't know, but we got business," I said. "Sheriff business."

"You passengers, stick close here. I'll want statements from all of you."

One woman looked annoyed and started off.

"You, too, Mrs. Throckmorton."

"I surrender to my fate," she said.

Rusty looked shell-shocked, so it'd be up to me. "Quill, tell me. What happened and what got took?"

"Nothing got took. Just the twins."

"My mind isn't quite biting this cookie, Quill."

"Three masked men on saddle horses, another in a chariot."

"A what?"

"A two-wheel chariot hung on two trotters. Man there was masked, too."

"A chariot like them gladiators used?"

"A two-wheel stand-up cart, with a lot of gold gilt and enameled red on it. They stop my coach, one has a scattergun aimed at me, and they open the door, and point at the twins, and say, 'Ladies, get out,' but the twins, they don't speak a word of English, so they prod the ladies out with their revolvers. That takes some doing, four legs, one skirt, but they get the Siamese twins out, get them into the chariot, and the man with the whip smacks the butts of those trotters and away they go, the three of them standing in that chariot."

"That's it?"

"The others wanted the twins' luggage, and they loaded it on a packhorse."

"And you didn't fight it?"

"They made us drop our weapons," one of the drummers said.

"What else did they take? The mail? Anything in a lock-box?"

"Nope," said Quill. "The foreign women and their bags."

"Did they give any reasons?"

"They said, 'Don't shoot,' we'd hit the women, and that was true. They headed due west, over some off-road route."

"Good, we'll have some tracks to follow," I said.

"Them were my brides," Rusty said.

"Real purty, they were," Quill said. "But sure hobbled up. I can see the direction your steamy little brain's taking, Irons," the jehu said.

This was getting a little out of hand.

"Rusty, you interview the male passengers, and I'll interview these women. Meanwhile, you people, clear out of here."

But no one moved. Half the town, it seemed, had flooded in.

Rusty and I got what we could from all those passengers. Nothing was taken except the Ukrainians. No one was forced to empty pockets. No valuables ended up in bandit pockets. The robbers were young, well masked, rode easily, wore wide-brimmed hats and jeans and dirty boots. They were all polite; no apparent accents. None of them offered reasons. The Ukrainian twins went peaceably, not understanding a bit of it. They were even smiling. They were treated courteously by the bandits.

"Were they hostages? Would they be returned for a reward?" Rusty asked the drummers.

"Nope, no sign of it," said one in a black bowler.

"Who'd want female Siamese twins?" Rusty asked.

"They were real lookers," another salesman ventured.

Rusty whipped out his tintype. "These the ones?"

They studied the black-and-white a while. "Not sure, but seems so," one said.

"Did these women seem in distress?"

"Nope, they thought this was all pretty merry."

The passengers had been detained long enough, so me and Rusty cut them loose, cut the jehu loose, and headed for Turk's Livery Barn. We had some hard riding in front of us.

Chapter 2

Rusty, he wanted a posse. He was plumb irate. Them was his brides got stolen, and he was rooting around, looking for ways to hang the wife-rustlers at the nearest cottonwood tree.

"Hey, cool her off," I said. "Go saddle up and take some fixings. I'll get Critter, and we'll get this deal shut down in no time."

"Who'll run the office?"

"I'll send Burtell," I said, referring to a part-time deputy.

"I want a posse. That was Anna and Natasha got took. I want plenty of armed men."

"This'll be the easiest kidnapping we ever solved," I said. "Where can they hide? We got some dudes in a red-and-gold chariot, kidnapping beautiful Siamese twins in one skirt, and they speak Ukraine, whatever the tongue is. We got 'em cold, Rusty."

He didn't want to believe it, and I didn't blame him. He got robbed out of two real pretty gals, and a lot of real fine nights once he got hitched to one or the other or both.

But my ma, she used to say that twins were double the trouble. She'd settle for twin cocker spaniels, but not any pair that would put her out some. In truth, if we got them joined-up twins back, I wasn't sure Rusty could handle the deal.

I headed for Turk's Livery Barn, fixing to saddle up Critter the Second. The first got his throat slit, and I looked hard before I found the Second, who was meaner than the first, so it worked out all right. I don't know what I'd do with a gentle horse. Horses are like women: If they don't buck when you're riding them, they're no good.

A while later me and Rusty met up at the livery barn, and fixed to ride out.

"Shouldn't we have a buggy or a cart?" he asked.

He was thinking about how to transport the Ukrainian ladies. You can't expect Siamese twins to climb up on a horse, but maybe a pair of horses would work if they crowded close.

I noticed he was armed to the teeth, with a saddle gun and a pair of mean-looking Peacemakers hanging from his skinny hips. He was gonna get his women back, even if he burned some powder.

"You got any idea why them gals got took?" he asked.

"It sure is interesting," I replied.

Critter was out in the yard, which wasn't good. He kicked down any stall he got put into, so Turk often put him outside. I got the bridle and went after him, and sure enough, he headed for a corner in the fence and waited for me, his rear hooves itchy to land on me. I tried moving along one rail and he switched that way, so I tried the other rail, and he switched that way.

"Critter, dammit, we're going to look for some women. Or one woman. I don't have it straight. So shape up," I yelled.

He turned and eyed me, and settled down and let me bridle and brush and saddle him without trouble. Critter was a philosopher.

"Dog food," said Rusty. "He needs to be turned into dog food."

"I won't argue with it," I said.

Turk spotted us. "You going after them stage robbers?" he asked.

"That's my woman they took," Rusty said.

"Double the feedbags," Turk said. "You sure got odd tastes."

That was my private opinion, but I wasn't voicing it. Rusty was the best deputy I had, and I didn't want to rile him up.

The town watched us ride out. Word spread through town like melted butter, and now they were all watching. Mostly watching Rusty, not me, because they were seeing Rusty in a new light. What sort of man would marry Siamese twins joined at the hip? Mighty strange. The women stood along Main Street with pursed lips, and I could read their every thought.

But soon we were trotting down the Laramie Road, heading for the ambush spot, so I could see what was to be seen, and we could see what the chariot wheels did to the turf. It should be easy enough to follow that cart, and with a little luck I'd have the bandits in manacles and heading for my lockup in a day or two.

Rusty, he sure was silent.

"What are you thinking, Rusty?"

"Maybe I won't marry after all. They'll be plumb ruined. I was marrying double virgins, and now look at it. It's a mess."

"You sure got big appetites, Rusty. Double everything— double marriage, double honeymoon, double household, double mouths to feed."

"Yeah, that's me," he said, a little smirky. Somehow he was seeing all this as proof that he was double the rest of us.

"What if they both expect babies at the same time, eh?"

Rusty was still looking smirky, so I didn't push it. Life sure was going to be interesting.

Critter loved to get out, and now he was pretty near popping along, and Rusty's nag had to trot now and then to catch up. We were riding through empty country, nothing but hills and sagebrush, and not worth anything except to a coyote. But that was Wyoming for you—ninety percent worthless, ten percent pretty fine.

It took us about three hours to reach the ambush place, well chosen to hide the ambushers behind a curve in the road. The jehu had given me a pretty good idea of it. There were signs around there, all right. Some iron-tire tracks, some hoof-prints, some handkerchiefs, and plenty of boot heel dimples in the dun clay.

Sure enough, the iron-tire tracks led straight west, off the road, over open prairie, so we followed them.

"We'll nail 'em, Rusty. How can we lose? Look at them tracks, smooth and hard."

But the tracks were gradually turning, and finally came entirely around and headed for the Laramie Road, maybe a mile south of where the ambush happened. And there they disappeared. Those clean iron-tire tracks vanished. We messed around there a while, widening out, looking for the tracks, and there weren't any. It was as if that chariot had taken off from the earth and rolled on up into heaven.

Rusty was having the same sweats as me. That just couldn't be. Big red-and-gold chariots didn't just vanish—unless through the Pearly Gates. I wondered about that for a while. Were them Ukrainian ladies taken on up?

The road had plenty of traffic showing on it, and we scouted it one way or the other, checking hoofprints, poking at ruts, and kicking horse turds, but the fact was, the kidnappers had ridden off into the sky, and were now rolling across cumulus, or maybe thunderheads, to some place or other.

"You got any fancy theories, Cotton?" Rusty asked.

He sure looked gloomy, like he had been deprived of a night with two of the prettiest gals ever born.

"We could ride on down to Laramie and see what's what," I said.

"Who'd want 'em?" Rusty asked.

"Some horny old rancher, I imagine," I said.

"Well, there's no man on earth hornier than me," Rusty said.

It was dawning on him that he'd lost his mail-order bride, or brides, I never could get that straight, and he was sinking into a sort of darkness. I thought it was best to leave him alone.

"I'll get ahold of the sheriff, Milt Boggs, and tell him what's missing, and to let us know if we got a red chariot and two hipshot blondes floating around southern Wyoming," I said.

"We catch them, what are you going to charge them with?" Rusty asked.

"Now that's an interesting question," I said. "My ma used to say people confess if you give them the chance."

"Well, she inherited all the brains in your family," Rusty said, just to be mean.

Truth to tell, my mind was on what might happen when we got back to Doubtful without two hip-tied blondes and a red chariot and a mess of crooks trudging along in front of my shotgun. They'd be telling me to quit, or maybe trying to fire me again. Seems every time I didn't catch the crook or stop the killer, they wanted to fire me. I've spent more time in front of the county supervisors trying to save my sheriff job than I've spent running my office.

Well, about dusk, we got back in, and all we raised were a few smirks. Like no one thought that kidnapping Siamese twins from the Ukraine was worth getting lathered up about. Especially when it was all Rusty's problem. He's the only one got shut out of some entertainment. So we rode in, by our lonesome selves, without a passel of bandits and bad men parading in front, and without those brides. People sort of smiled smartly, and planned to make some jokes, and maybe petition the supervisors to get rid of me, and that was that.

Me, I felt the same way. If Rusty hadn't mail-ordered the most exotic womanhood this side of Morocco, it never would've happened.

Turk showed up out of the gloom soon as we rode into his livery barn.

"Told you so," he said.

"Told us what?"

"That you'd botch another job again."

I was feeling a little put out with him, and if there were any other livery barns in town, I would have moved Critter then and there. Critter chewed on any wood he could get his big buck teeth around, and sometimes Turk sent me a bill for repairs, but I could hardly blame Turk for that.

Rusty unsaddled, turned out his nag, and disappeared. He was feeling real blue, and I didn't blame him.

"Hey," Turk said, "while you gents were out the Laramie Road, chasing Ukrainian women, a medicine show came up the Cheyenne Road and set up outside of town."

"Medicine show?"

"None other. Doctor Zoroaster Zimmer's Three-Way Tonic for digestion, thick hair, and virility. Three dollars the six-ounce bottle, thirty-five dollars a dozen. And you get to watch a juggler, belly dancer, an accordion player, and a dog and pony act, and then lay out cash for the medicine."

"Zimmer? Seems to me he's on a wanted dodger in my office. Whenever he hits town, jewelry and gold coins start vanishing, and dogs howl in the night. I think his tonic's mostly opium, peppermint, and creek water, but I'll find out."

"Yeah, sheriff, and guess what? I wandered over there to have a gander. He's driving a big red-enameled outfit with gold trim. But there's no chariots or Ukrainian blondes in sight."

Chapter 3

Doubtful, it had growed some, and was fixed in the middle of some of the best Wyoming ranch country around. So there were plenty of people in the Puma County seat, and also plenty more out herding cows and growing hogs and collecting eggs from chickens. There were even some horse breeders around town, most of them raising remounts for the cavalry.

And the town was half civilized. I knew the rough times were over when some gal named Matilda opened up a hattery. I don't know the proper name of a hat shop, but it don't matter. Hattery is what she operated, and she did nothing but sell bonnets and straw hats full of fake fruit to the town's ladies. And gossip, too. All the local gals went in there to gossip about the rest of us. Sometimes I got a little itchy about sheriffing in a halfway civilized town and thought I should pack up and head for the tropics.

But my ma, she always said don't shoot a gift horse between the eyes, and that's how I looked at my job. That eve, Rusty quit early on me, and headed off to his cabin to nurse his disappointment. He had his heart set on marrying the Ukrainian beauties, and never having to have a conversation with his women because he didn't understand a word they said. I thought it was a fool's dream, myself. What if they was saying mean things about him, in their own tongue, maybe even at night with the pair of them lying beside him?

The town was drawing everything from whiskey drummers to medicine shows these days, and I intended to get out to the east side to have a close look. Half the shows rolling through the country roads of the West were nothing but gyppo outfits, looking to con cash out of the local folks, while swiping everything that wasn't nailed down tight. And if they could get a few girls in trouble while robbing citizens and peddling worthless stuff, they did that, too, and smiled all the way to the next burg.

I'd wander over there. But first I'd patrol Doubtful, as I did every evening, wearing my badge, walking from place to place, rattling doors to see if they were locked, and studying saloons closely to see if there was trouble. Sometimes there was, and the barkeeps would be glad I wandered in at a moment when some drunken cowboy, armed to the teeth, was picking a fight.

So I did my rounds, seeing that all was quiet at Maxwell's Funeral Parlor, and no one was busting the doors at Hubert Sanders's Merchant Bank. I peered into Barney's Beanery, and saw that it was winding down for the eve, and peered into the dark confines of Leonard Silver's Emporium. I checked the office of Lawyer Stokes, and saw no one rifling his file cabinets. McGivers' Saloon was quiet, and so was the Last Chance, where I saw Sammy Upward yawning, his elbows on the bar, looking ready to close early.

There were a few posters promoting Dr. Zoroaster Zimmer's show. The man had a string of initials behind his name, but I never could figure out what all they meant, but the Ph.D. meant he was a doctor of philandery or something like that. The "KGB" puzzled me, but someone told me it was British and had to do with garters and bathtubs. You never know what gets into foreigners. At any rate, this Professor Zimmer had them all, and they followed his name like a string of railroad cars. I thought I'd like to meet the gent.

Denver Sally's place, back behind saloon row, looked quiet, the evening breezes rocking the red lantern beside her door. Most of her business came on weekends. The Gates of Heaven, next door, looked as mean as ever. Who knows all the ways a feller wants to get rid of his cash?

Doubtful was peaceful enough, that spring evening. So it was time to drift out beyond saloon row, east of town, and take a gander at this here medicine man show. There were a mess of these shows wandering through the whole country, setting up in dark corners of a little town, running an act or two across a stage set up on a wagon. Then the medicine man would step out and peddle his stuff, and when he gauged that he'd done all the selling he could, he'd pull up stakes and head for the next little town and do it all over again.

Sure enough, east of town, on an alkali flat, there were a couple of torches going, two fancy red-and-gilt wagons, a makeshift rope corral with some moth-eaten drays in it, and a lamp-lit stage on a wagon. There were maybe twelve, fifteen suckers watching some jet-haired woman in a grass skirt wiggle her butt and make her bosom heave. I'd never seen that, and it seemed entertaining, but I had sheriff business to do. Namely, look for a red-and-gilt chariot, and two blond Ukrainian women joined at the hip. I took a quick prowl around the rear of the place, and into the other wagon, to satisfy myself that no one was hiding a chariot or Siamese twins, blond or any other color. Whoever kidnapped the ladies, it wasn't this miserable outfit.

I spotted a gent smoking a cigar back there, and thought he might have some answers. He saw the glint of my badge even before we spoke. He sucked on his gummy cheroot, and knocked off the ash.

"You looking for something, sheriff?"

"Just keeping an eye on things. How many people you got in this outfit?"

"Six and the professor."

"Any women?"

He stared at me as if I were an idiot. "That's Elvira Smoothpepper out there. And we got Elsie Sanchez, the Argentine firecracker."

"No Ukrainian blondes?"

"You got eyes, dontcha?"

"Who else's in the show?"

"Sheriff, there ain't anyone with a wanted poster on him. There's me and another teamster. He's the accordionist, and there's a tap dancer named Fogarty, and the professor."

"What does the professor sell? What's his medicine?"

The gent smiled. "Try it sometime and come back and tell me."

"Any chariots around here?"

"Any what?"

"Oh, never mind."

"You all right, sheriff? Want to lie down? That second wagon, it's got bunks. Had a little too much?"

"Who's the professor?"

"He's whatever he is at any moment. Right now, he's a medicine man, and he's working the rubes for a few bucks."

"Yeah, well I'll go watch the show," I said.

"It beats pissing on a fence post."

Half of the crowd was cowboys, out from the saloons. I recognized a few, most of them the ones that hung out at Mrs. Gladstone's Sampling Room. They were tied up with the Admiral Ranch, other side of the county. But there were some locals, too, including the mayor, George Waller, who looked embarrassed when he saw me.

"I just came to view the competition," he said. Waller was a merchant, and any outfit that sold anything was competition, as far as he was concerned. "Maybe you should arrest the whole lot," he said.

"What for?"

"They're all crooks."

"Well, that's progress. You show me one act of crookery, and I'll pinch the person straight off."

Elvira Smoothpepper was making her belly roll and the grass skirts sway, and that was pretty entertaining. The accordionist got to wheezing away, and pretty soon the act creaked to a stop, and out came Professor Zoroaster Zimmer, in black silk top hat, tux and tails, and a grimy white vest that looked a little worse for wear.

I'd never seen the like.

He spotted me at once, and welcomed me. "Ladies and gents, here's the sheriff of, ah, what? Puma County, Wyoming. Come to see our little show, and maybe endorse my product, namely, the Zimmer Miracle Tonic, guaranteed to cure piles, insomnia, gout, St. Vitus Dance, and all bowel troubles. Welcome, Mr. Sheriff.

"Now, esteemed friends, I want to tell you about a product that should need no introducing, since it sells itself. You need only ask your neighbor, who has the remedy on his shelf, ready to use, and you'll see how effective it is. Mr. Sheriff, please come up."

"Me?"

"Of course, you. Step right up, my friend."

"I haven't got anything ailing me, doc."

"Oh, my friend, do you have restless nights? Toss and turn nights?"

"Naw, I sleep like a log."

"Do you ache after a long day on your horse?"

"Now, you're talking about Critter, the orneriest critter on four legs. Yes, I'll allow that I ache some after a long ride on that beast."

"Were you out on him today, sheriff?"

"Pretty near the whole blasted day, professor."

"Then you must feel weary, right down to the bone."

"Well, we were out looking for some blond Ukrainian women that got attached at the hip and plain disappeared."

That got mostly dead silence and a couple of snickers from some of them cowboys.

"I think you are very weary, sir, after a day of searching for blond Ukrainian women. Are you a bit worn?"

"I am done in."

"Well, perfect. I would truly like to have you sample Doctor Zimmer's Tonic, and report the results to all these fine folks."

"My ma, she used to say, one drink is enough."

"Oh, this is not drink, sir. This is an elixir to balm the soul, elevate mood, celebrate life, and rejoice in your own splendid body. Now how old are you?"

"I forget; past thirty, anyway."

"Ah, the shady side of thirty. Let me tell you, my friend, that is when Doctor Zoroaster Zimmer's Tonic works wonders the fastest. It works wonders at any age, sir, but especially after thirty."

The maestro of this here event reached for a bottle of the stuff, which was sitting on a little shelf, with a gold halo around it, so the bottle looked like a saint.

He sure was smiling. He grabbed that stuff, and pulled the cork, and poured a little into a tumbler, and handed it to me, while all them cowboys and Mayor George Waller watched.

I remembered what my ma used to say, no guts, no glory, and I downed the stuff in one gulp.

Well, it took a moment and worked through me, like a glow of a lot of fireflies, and then I plumb keeled over. The accordionist caught me going down.

SPECIAL BONUS!

Smoke Jensen.

*A mountain man who braved the harshest elements
nature could throw at him, fought hostile Indians
and outlaws, and blazed the trail for
generations of pioneers and homesteaders.*

Turn the page for Chapters Four, Five, and Six of

TRAIL OF THE MOUNTAIN MAN,

one of Smoke's earliest western adventures.

Trail of the Mountain Man

by William W. Johnstone,
today's most popular western storyteller

Chapter 4

As Smoke was riding out of the town, one of Tilden's men, who had been in the bar around the card table, was fogging it toward the Circle TF, lathering a good horse to get the news to Tilden Franklin.

Tilden sat on his front porch and received the news of the gunfight, a look of pure disbelief on his face. "Matt killed Red? What'd he do, shoot him in the back?"

"Stand-up, face-to-face fight, boss," the puncher said. "But Matt ain't his real name. It's Smoke Jensen."

Tilden dropped his coffee cup, the cup shattering on the porch floor. "Smoke Jensen!" he finally managed to blurt out. "He's got to be lyin'!"

The puncher shook his head. "You'd have to have been there, boss. Smoke is everything his rep says he is. I ain't never seen nobody that fast in all my life."

"Did he let Red clear leather before he drew?" Tilden's voice was hoarse as he asked the question.

"Yessir."

"Jensen," Tilden whispered. "That's one of his trademarks. Okay, Donnie. Thanks. You better cool down that horse of yours."

The bowlegged cowboy swaggered off to see to his horse. Tilden leaned back in his porch chair, a sour sensation in his stomach and a bad taste in his mouth. Smoke Jensen . . . *here*! Crap!

What to do?

Tilden seemed to recall that there was a murder warrant out for Smoke Jensen, from years back. But that was way to hell and gone over to Walsenburg; and the men Smoke had killed had murdered his brother and stolen some Confederate gold back during the war.*

Anyway, Tilden suddenly remembered, that warrant had been dropped.

No doubt about it, Tilden mused, with Smoke Jensen owner of the Sugarloaf, it sure as hell changed things around some. Smoke Jensen was pure hell with a gun. Probably the best gun west of the Mississippi.

And that rankled Tilden too. For Tilden had always fancied himself a gunslick. He had never been bested in a gunfight. He wondered, as he sat on the porch. Was he better than Smoke Jensen?

Well, there was sure one way to find out.

Tilden rejected that idea almost as soon as it popped into his mind.

He did not reject it because of fear. The big man had no fear of Smoke. It was just that there were easier ways to accomplish what he had in mind. Tilden had never lost a fight. Never. Not a fistfight, not a gunfight. He didn't believe any man could beat him with his fists, and damn few were better than Tilden with a short gun.

He called for his Mexican houseboy to come clean up the mess made by the broken cup and to bring him another cup of coffee.

*The Last Mountain Man

The mess cleaned up, a fresh cup of steaming coffee at hand, Tilden looked out over just a part of his vast holdings. Some small voice, heretofore unheard or unnoticed, deep within him, told him that all this was enough. More than enough for one man. You're a rich man it said. Stop while you're ahead.

Tilden pushed that annoying and stupid thought from his mind. No way he would stop his advance. That was too foolish to even merit consideration.

No, there were other ways to deal with a gunhawk like Jensen. And a plan was forming in Tilden's mind.

The news of the saloon shooting would soon be all over the area. And the small nester-ranchers like Nolan and Peyton and Matlock and Colby would throw in with Smoke Jensen. Maybe Ray and Mike as well. That was fine with Tilden.

He would just take them out one at a time, saving Jensen for last.

He smiled and sipped his coffee. A good plan, he thought. A very good plan. He had an idea that most of the gold lay beneath the Sugarloaf. And he'd have the Sugarloaf. And the mistress of Sugarloaf too.

Sally.

Sally had dressed in boys' jeans and a work shirt. Her friends and family back in New Hampshire would be horrified to see her dressed in male clothing but there came a time when practicality must take precedence over fashion. And she felt that time was here.

She looked out the window. Late afternoon. She did not expect Smoke to return for another day—perhaps two more days. She was not afraid. Whenever Smoke rode in for supplies it was a two- or three-day trek—sometimes longer. But those prior trips had been in easier times. Now, one did not know what to expect.

Or from which direction.

As soon as Smoke had gone, she had saddled her pony, a gentle, sure-footed mare, and ridden out into the valley. She had driven two of Smoke's stallions, Seven and Drifter, back to the house, putting them in the corral. The mountain horses were better than any watchdog she had ever seen. If anyone even came close to the house, they would let her know. And, if turned loose, the stallion Drifter would kill an intruder.

He had done so before.

The midnight-black, yellow-eyed Drifter had a look of Hell about him, and was totally loyal to Smoke and Sally.

Sally had belted a pistol around her waist, leaned a rifle against the wall, next to the door, and laid a double-barreled express gun on the table. She knew how to use all the weapons at hand, and would not hesitate to do so.

The horses and chickens fed, the cow milked, all the other chores done, Sally went back into the house and pulled the heavy shutters closed and secured them. The shutters had gun slits cut into them, which could be opened or closed. She stirred the stew bubbling in the blackened pot and checked her bread in the oven. She sat down on the couch, picked up a book, and began her lonely wait for her man.

Smoke put No-Name Town far behind him and began his long trip back to Sugarloaf. He would stop at the Ray ranch in the morning, talk to him. The fat was surely in the fire by now, and the grease would soon be flaming.

Some eight high-up and winding miles from the town, just as purple shadows were gathering in the mountain country, Smoke picked a spot for the night and began making his lonely camp. He did not have to picket Horse, for Horse would stay close, acting as watcher and guard.

Smoke built a small fire for coffee, and ate from what Sally had fixed for him. Some cold beef, some bread with a bit of homemade jam on it. He drank his coffee, put out the fire, and settled into his blankets, using his saddle for a pillow. In a very short time, he was deep in sleep.

In the still unnamed town, Utah Slim sat in a saloon and sipped a beer. Even though hours had passed since the shooting of Red, the saloon still hummed with conversation about Smoke Jensen. Utah Slim did not join in the conversations around the bar and the tables. So far, few knew who he was. And that was the way he liked it—for a time. When it was time for Utah Slim to announce his intentions, he'd do so.

He was under no illusions; he'd seen Smoke glance his way riding into town. Smoke recognized him. Now it was just a waiting game.

And waiting was something Utah was good at. Something any hired gun had better be good at, or he wouldn't last long in this business.

Louis Longmont stepped out of his canvas bar and game room and glanced up and down the street. A lean, hawk-faced man, with strong, slender hands and long fingers, the nails carefully manicured, the hands clean, Louis had jet-black hair and a black pencil-thin mustache. He was dressed in a black suit, with white shirt and dark ascot—the ascot something he'd picked up on a trip to England some years back. He wore low-heeled boots. A pistol hung in tied-down leather on his right side; it was not for show alone. For Louis was snake quick with a short gun. A feared, deadly gunhand when pushed.

Louis was not an evil man. He had never hired his gun out for money. And while he could make a deck of cards do almost anything except stand up and sing "God Save the

Queen," Louis did not cheat at poker. He did not have to cheat. A man possessed of a phenomenal memory, Louis could tell you the odds of filling any type of poker hand; and he was also a card-counter. He did not consider that cheating, and most agreed with him that it was not.

Louis was just past forty years of age. He had come to the West as a mere slip of a boy, with his parents, arriving from Louisiana. His parents had died in a shanty-town fire, leaving the boy to cope the best he could.

Louis had coped quite well, thank you.

Louis had been in boomtowns all over the West, seeing them come and go. He had a feeling in his guts that this town was going to be a raw bitch-kitty. He knew all about Tilden Franklin, and liked none of what he'd heard. The man was power-mad, and obviously lower class. White trash.

And now Smoke Jensen had made his presence known. Louis wondered why. Why this soon in the power-game? An unanswered question.

For a moment, Louis thought of packing up and pulling out. Just saying the hell with it! For he knew this was not going to be an ordinary gold-rush town. Powerful factions were at work here. Tilden Franklin wanted the entire region as his own. Smoke Jensen stood in his way.

Louis made up his mind. Should be a very interesting confrontation, he thought.

He'd stay.

Big Mamma O'Neil was an evil person. If one could find her heart, it would be as black as sin itself. Big Mamma stepped out in front of her gaming room and love-for-sale tent to look up and down the street. She nodded at Louis. He returned the nod and stepped back inside his tent.

Goddamned stuck-up card-slick! she fumed. Thought he was better than most everyone else. Dressed like a dandy.

Talked like some highfalutin' professor—not that Big Mamma had ever known any professor; she just imagined that was how one would sound.

Big Mamma swung her big head around, once more looking over the town. A massive woman, she was strong as an ox and had killed more than one man with her huge, hard fists. And had killed for money as well as pleasure; one served her interests as much as the other.

Big Mamma was a crack shot with rifle or pistol, having grown up in the raw, wild West, fighting Indians and hooligans and her brothers. She had killed her father with an axe, then taken his guns and his horse and left for Texas. She had never been back.

She had brothers and sisters, but had no idea what had ever become of any of them. She really didn't care. The only thing she cared about was money and other women. She hated men.

She had seen Smoke Jensen ride in, looking like the arrogant bastard she had always thought he would be. So he had killed some puncher named Red—big deal! A nothing rider who fancied himself a gunhand. She'd heard all the stories about Jensen, and discounted most of them as pure road apples. The rumors were that he had been a Mountain Man. But he was far too young to have been a part of that wild breed.

As far as she was concerned, Smoke Jensen was just another overrated punk.

As the purple shadows melted into darkness over the noname town that would soon become Fontana, Monte Carson stepped out of the best of the two permanent saloons and looked up and down the wide, dusty street. He hitched at the twin Colts belted around his waist and tied down low.

This town, he thought, was shaping up real nice for a hired gun. And that's what Monte was. He had hired his guns out in Montana, in the cattle wars out in California, and had fought

the sheep farmers and nesters up in Wyoming. And, as he'd
fought, his reputation had grown. Monte felt that Tilden
Franklin would soon be contacting him. He could wait.

On the now-well-traveled road for beneath where Smoke
slept peacefully, wagons continued to roll and rumble along,
carrying their human cargo toward No-Name Town. The line
of wagons and buggies and riders and walkers was now several miles long. Gamblers and would-be shop owners and
whores and gunfighters and snake-oil salesmen and pimps
and troublemakers and murderers and good solid family
people . . . all of them heading for No-Name with but one
thought in their minds. Gold.

At the end of the line of gold-seekers, not a part of them
but yet with the same destination if not sharing the same mo-
tives, rattled a half a dozen wagons. Ed Jackson was new to
the raw West—a shopkeeper from Illinois with his wife Peg.
They were both young and very idealistic, and had no working knowledge of the real West. They were looking for a place
to settle. This no-name town sounded good to them. Ed's
brother Paul drove the heavily laden supply wagon, contain-
ing part of what they just knew would make them respected
and secure citizens. Paul was as naive as his brother and
sister-in-law concerning the West.

In the third wagon came Ralph Morrow and his wife Bountiful. They were missionaries, sent into the godless West by
their church, to save souls and soothe the sinful spirits of
those who had not yet accepted Christ into their lives. They
had been looking for a place to settle when they had hooked
up with Ed and Peg and Paul. This was the first time Ralph
and Bountiful had been west of Eastern Ohio. It was exciting.
A challenge.

They thought.

In the fourth wagon rode another young couple, married

only a few years, Hunt and Willow Brook. Hunt was a lawyer, looking for a place to practice all he'd just been taught back East. This new gold rush town seemed just the place to start.

In the fifth wagon rode Colton and Mona Spalding. A doctor and nurse, respectively. They had both graduated their schools only last year, mulled matters over, and decided to head West. They were young and handsome and pretty. And, like the others in their little caravan, they had absolutely no idea what they were riding into.

In the last wagon, a huge, solidly built vehicle with six mules pulling it, came Haywood and Dana Arden. Like the others, they were young and full of grand ideas. Haywood had inherited a failing newspaper from his father back in Pennsylvania and decided to pull out and head West to seek their fortunes.

"Oh Haywood!" Dana said, her eyes shining with excitement. "It's all so wonderful."

"Yes," Haywood agreed, just as the right rear wheel of their wagon fell off.

Chapter 5

Smoke was up long before dawn spread her shimmering rays of light over the land. He slipped out of his blankets and put his hat on, then pulled on his boots and strapped on his guns. He checked to see how Horse was doing, then washed his face with water from his canteen. He built a small, hand-sized fire and boiled coffee. He munched on a thick piece of bread and sipped his coffee, sitting with his back to a tree, his eyes taking in the first silver streaks of a new day in the high-up country of Colorado.

He had spotted a fire far down below him, near the winding road. A very large fire. Much too large unless those who built it were roasting an entire deer—head, horns, and all. He finished the small, blackened pot of coffee, carefully doused his fire, and saddled Horse, stowing his gear in the saddlebags.

He swung into the saddle. "Steady now, Horse," he said in a low voice. "Let's see how quiet we can be backtracking."

Horse and rider made their way slowly and quietly down from the high terrain toward the road miles away using the twisting, winding trails. Smoke uncased U.S. Army binoculars he'd picked up years back, while traveling with his mentor, the old Mountain Man Preacher, and studied the situation.

Five, no—six wagons. One of them down with a busted back wheel. Six men, five women. All young, in their early twenties, Smoke guessed. The women were all very pretty, the men all handsome and apparently—at least to Smoke, at least at this distance—helpless.

He used his knees to signal Horse, and the animal moved out, taking its head, picking the route. Stopping after a few hundred twisting yards, Smoke once more surveyed the situation. His binoculars picked up movement coming from the direction of No-Name. Four riders. He studied the men, watching them approach the wagons. Drifters, from the look of them. Probably spent the night in No-Name gambling and whoring and were heading out to stake a gold claim. They looked like trouble.

Staying in the deep and lush timber, Smoke edged closer still. Several hundred yards from the wagon, Smoke halted and held back, wanting to see how these pilgrims would handle the approach of the riders.

He could not hear all that was said, but he could get most of it from his hidden location.

He had pegged the riders accurately. They were trouble. They reined up and sat their horses, grinning at the men and women. Especially the women.

"You folks look like you got a mite of trouble," one rider said.

"A bit," a friendly-looking man responded. "We're just getting ready to fulcrum the wagon."

"You're gonna do *what* to it?" another rider blurted.

"Raise it up," a pilgrim said.

"Oh. You folks headin' to Fontana?"

The wagon people looked at each other.

Fontana! Smoke thought. Where in the hell is Fontana?

"I'm sorry," one of the women said. "We're not familiar with that place."

"That's what they just named the town up yonder," a rider said, jerking his thumb in the direction of No-Name. "Stuck up a big sign last night."

So No-Name has a name, Smoke thought. Wonder whose idea that was.

But he thought he knew. Tilden Franklin.

Smoke looked at the women of the wagons. They were, to a woman, all very pretty and built-up nice. Very shapely. The men with them didn't look like much to Smoke; but then, he thought, they were Easterners. Probably good men back there. But out here, they were out of their element.

And Smoke didn't like the look in the eyes of the riders. One kept glancing up and down the road. As yet, no traffic had appeared. But Smoke knew the stream of gold-hunters would soon appear. If the drifters were going to start something—the women being what they wanted, he was sure—they would make their move pretty quick.

At some unspoken signal, the riders dismounted.

"Oh, say!" the weakest-jawed pilgrim said. "It's good of you men to help."

"Huh?" a rider said, then he grinned. "Oh, yeah. We're regular do-gooders. You folks nesters?"

"I beg your pardon, sir?"

"Farmers." He ended that and summed up his feelings concerning farmers by spitting a stream of brown tobacco juice onto the ground, just missing the pilgrim's feet.

The pilgrim laughed and said, "Oh, no. My name is Ed Jackson, this is my wife Peg. We plan to open a store in the gold town."

"Ain't that nice," the rider mumbled.

Smoke kneed Horse a bit closer.

"My name is Ralph Morrow," another pilgrim said. "I'm a minister. This is my wife Bountiful. We plan to start a church in the gold town."

The rider looked at Bountiful and licked his lips.

Ralph said, "And this is Paul Jackson, Ed's brother. Over there is Hunt and Willow Brook. Hunt is a lawyer. That's Colton and Mona Spalding. Colton is a physician. And last, but certainly not least, is Haywood and Dana Arden.

Haywood is planning to start a newspaper in the town. Now you know us."

"Not as much as I'd like to," a rider said speaking for the first time. He was looking at Bountiful.

To complicate matters, Bountiful was looking square at the rider.

The woman is flirting with him, Smoke noticed. He silently cursed. This Bountiful might be a preacher's wife, but what she really was was a hot handful of trouble. The preacher was not taking care of business at home.

Bountiful was blond with hot blue eyes. She stared at the rider.

All the newcomers to the West began to sense something was not as it should be. But none knew what, and if they did, Smoke thought, they wouldn't know how to handle it. For none of the men were armed.

One of the drifters, the one who had been staring at Bountiful, brushed past the preacher. He walked by Bountiful, his right arm brushing the woman's jutting breasts. She did not back up. The rider stopped and grinned at her.

The newspaperman's wife stepped in just in time, stepping between the rider and the woman. She glared at Bountiful. "Let's you and I start breakfast, Bountiful," she suggested. "While the men fix the wheel."

"What you got in your wagon, shopkeeper?" a drifter asked. "Anything in there we might like?"

Ed narrowed his eyes. "I'll set up shop very soon. Feel free to browse when we're open for business."

The rider laughed. "Talks real nice, don't he, boys?"

His friends laughed.

The riders were big men, tough-looking and seemingly very capable. Smoke had no doubts but what they were all that and more. The more being troublemakers.

Always something, Smoke thought with a silent sigh. People wander into an unknown territory without first checking out all the ramifications. He edged Horse forward.

A rider jerked at a tie-rope over the bed of one wagon. "I don't wanna wait to browse none. I wanna see what you got now."

"Now see here!" Ed protested, stepping toward the man.

Ed's head exploded in pain as the rider's big fist hit the shopkeeper's jaw. Ed's butt hit the ground. Still, Smoke waited.

None of the drifters had drawn a gun. No law, written or otherwise, had as yet been broken. These pilgrims were in the process of learning a hard lesson of the West: you broke your own horses and killed your own snakes. And Smoke recalled a sentiment from some book he had slowly and laboriously studied. When you are in Rome live in the Roman style; when you are elsewhere live as they live elsewhere.

He couldn't remember who wrote it, but it was pretty fair advice.

The riders laughed at the ineptness of the newcomers to the West. One jerked Bountiful to him and began fondling her breasts.

Bountiful finally got it through her head that this was deadly serious, not a mild flirtation.

She began struggling just as the other pilgrims surged forward. Their butts hit the ground as quickly and as hard as Ed's had.

Smoke put the spurs to Horse and the big horse broke out of the timber. Smoke was out of the saddle before Horse was still. He dropped the reins to the ground and faced the group.

"That's it!" Smoke said quietly. He slipped the thongs from the hammers of his .44's.

Smoke glanced at Bountiful. Her bodice was torn, exposing the creamy skin of her breasts. "Cover yourself," Smoke told her.

She pulled away from the rider and ran, sobbing, to Dana.

A rider said, "I don't know who you are, boy. But I'm gonna teach you a hard lesson."

"Oh? And what might that be?"

"To keep your goddamned nose out of other folks' business."

"If the woman had been willing," Smoke said, "I would not have interfered. Even though it takes a low-life bastard to steal another man's woman."

"Why, you . . . *pup!*" the rider shouted. "You callin' me a bastard?"

"Are you deaf?"

"I'll kill you!"

"I doubt it."

Bountiful was crying. Her husband was holding a handkerchief to a bloody nose, his eyes staring in disbelief at what was taking place.

Hunt Brook was sitting on the ground, his mouth bloody. Colton's head was ringing and his ear hurt where he'd been struck. Haywood was wondering if his eye was going to turn black. Paul was holding a hurting stomach, the hurt caused by a hard fist. The preacher looked as if he wished his wife would cover herself.

One drifter shoved Dana and Bountiful out of the way, stepping over to join his friend, facing Smoke. The other two drifters hung back, being careful to keep their hands away from their guns. The two who hung back were older, and wiser to the ways of gunslicks. And they did not like the looks of this young man with the twin Colts. There was something very familiar about him. Something calm and cold and very deadly.

"Back off, Ford," one finally spoke. "Let's ride."

"Hell with you!" the rider named Ford said, not taking his eyes from Smoke. "I'm gonna kill this punk!"

"Something tells me you ain't neither," his friend said.

"Better listen to him," Smoke advised Ford.

"Now see here, gentlemen!" Hunt said.

"Shut your gawddamned mouth!" he was told.

Hunt closed his mouth. Heavens! he thought. This just simply was not done back in Boston.

"You gonna draw, punk?" Ford said.

"After you," Smoke said quietly.

"Jesus, Ford!" the rider who hung back said. "I know who that is."

"He's dead, that's who he is," Ford said, and reached for his gun.

His friend drew at the same time.

Smoke let them clear leather before he began his lightning draw. His Colts belched fire and smoke, the slugs taking them in the chest, flinging them backward. They had not gotten off a shot.

"Smoke Jensen!" the drifter said.

"Right," Smoke said. "Now ride!"

Chapter 6

The two drifters who had wisely elected not to take part in facing Smoke leaped for their horses and were gone in a cloud of galloping dust. They had not given a second glance at their dead friends.

Smoke reloaded his Colts and holstered them. Then he looked at the wagon people. The Easterners were clearly in a mild state of shock. Bountiful still had not taken the few seconds needed to repair her torn bodice. Smoke summed her up quickly and needed only one word to do so: trouble.

"My word!" Colton Spalding finally said. "You are very quick with those guns, sir."

"I'm alive," Smoke said.

"You *killed* those men!" Hunt Brook said, getting up off the ground and brushing the dust from the seat of his britches.

"What did you want me to do?" Smoke asked, knowing where this was leading. "Kiss them?"

Hunt wiped his bloody mouth with a handkerchief. "You shall certainly need representation at the hearing. Consider me as your attorney."

Smoke looked at the man and smiled slowly. He shook

his head in disbelief. "Lawyer, the nearest lawman is about three days ride from here. And I'm not even sure this area is in his jurisdiction. There won't be any hearing, mister. It's all been settled and over and done with."

Haywood Arden was looking at Smoke through cool eyes. Smoke met the man's steady gaze.

This one will do, Smoke thought. This one doesn't have his head in the clouds. "So you're going to start up a newspaper, huh?" Smoke said.

"Yes. But how did you know that?"

"Me and Horse been sitting over there," Smoke said, jerking his head in the direction of the timber. "Listening."

"You move very quietly, sir," Mona Spalding said.

"I learned to do that. Helps in staying alive." Smoke wished Bountiful would cover up. It was mildly distracting.

"One of those ruffians called you Smoke, I believe," Hunt said. "I don't believe I ever met a man named Smoke."

Ruffians, Smoke thought. He hid his smile. Interesting choice of words to describe the drifters. "I was halfway raised by an old Mountain Man named Preacher. He hung that name on me."

The drifter called Ford broke wind in death. The shopkeeper's wife, Peg, thought as though she might faint any second. "Could someone please do something about those poor dead men?" she asked.

Dawn had given way to a bright clear mountain day. A stream of humanity had begun riding and walking toward Fontana. A tough-looking pair of miners riding mules reined up. Their eyes dismissed the Easterners and settled on Smoke. "Trouble?" one asked.

"Nothing I couldn't handle," Smoke told him.

"'Pears that way," the second miner said drily. "Ford Beechan was a good hand with a short gun." He cut his eyes toward the sprawled body of Ford.

"He wasn't as good as he thought," Smoke replied.

"'Pears that's the truth. We'll plant 'em for four bits a piece."

"Deal."

"And their pockets," the other miner spoke.

"Have at it," Smoke told them. "The pilgrims will pay."

"Now see here!" Ed said starting to protest.

"Shut up, Ed," Haywood told him. He looked at the miners. "You gentlemen may proceed with the digging."

"Talks funny," one miner remarked, getting down and tying his mule. He got a shovel from his pack animal and his partner followed suit.

"You live and work in this area, Mister Smoke?" Mona asked.

"One miner dropped his shovel and his partner froze still as stone. The miner who dropped his shovel picked it up and slowly turned to face Smoke. "Smoke Jensen?"

"Yes."

"Lord God Almighty! Ford shore enuff bit off more than he could chew. Smoke Jensen. My brother was over to Uncompahgre, Smoke. Back when you cleaned it up. He said that shore was a sight to see."*

Smoke nodded his head and the miners walked off a short distance to begin their digging. "How deep?" one called.

"Respectable," Smoke told them.

They nodded and began spading the earth.

"Are you a gunfighter, Mister Smoke?" Willow asked.

"I'm a rancher and farmer, Ma'am. But I once had the reputation of being a gunhawk, yes."

"You seem so young," she observed. "Yet you talk as if it was years ago. How old were you when you became a . . . gunhawk?"

"Fourteen. Or thereabouts. I disremember at times." Smoke usually spoke acceptable English, thanks to Sally; but at times he reverted back to Preacher's dialect.

*The Last Mountain Man

"He's kilt more'un a hundred men!" one of the miners called.

The wagon people fell silent at that news. They looked at Smoke with a mixture of horror, fascination, and revulsion in their eyes.

It was nothing new to Smoke. He had experienced that look many times in his young life. He kept his face as expressionless as his cold eyes.

Smoke cut his eyes to Bountiful. "Lady," he said, exasperation in his voice, his tone hard. "Will you please cover your tits!"

Smoke had seen the remainder of the rancher-farmers in the mountain area and then headed for home. He almost never took the same trail back to his cabin. A habit he had picked up from Preacher. A habit that had saved his life on more than one occasion.

Even though he was less than five miles from his cabin when dark slipped into the mountains, he decided not to chance the ride in. He elected to make camp and head home at first light.

He caught several small fish from a mountain stream and broiled them over a small fire. That and the remainder of Sally's bread was his supper.

Twice during the night Smoke came fully awake, certain he had heard gunshots. He knew they were far away, but he wondered about it. The last shot he heard before he drifted back to sleep came from the south, far away from Sally and the cabin.

He was up and moving out before full dawn broke. Relief ruled him when he caught a glimpse of the cabin, Sally in the front yard. Smoke broke into a grin when he saw how she was dressed . . . in men's britches. His eyes mirrored approval when he noted Seven and Drifter in the corral. As he rode closer, he saw the pistol belted around her waist, and the express gun leaning against the door frame, on the outside of the cabin.

Man and wife embraced, each loving the touch and feel of the other. With their mouths barely apart, she saw the darkness in his eyes and asked, "Trouble?"

"Some. A hell of a lot more coming, though. I'll tell you about it. You?"

"Didn't see a soul."

They kissed their love and she pushed him away, mischief in her hazel eyes. "I missed you."

"Oh? How much?"

"By the time you see to Horse and get in the house, I'll be ready to show you how much."

Fastest unsaddling and rub-down in the history of the West.

Passions cooled and sated, she lay with her head on Smoke's muscular shoulder. She listened as he told her all that had happened since he had ridden from the ranch. He left nothing out.

"See anyone that you knew in town? Any newcomers, I mean?"

"Some. Utah Slim. I'm sure it was him."

"I've heard you talk of him. He's good?"

"One of the best."

"Better than you?"

"No," Smoke said softly.

"Anyone else?"

"Monte Carson. He's a backshooter. Big Mamma O'Neil. Louis Longmont. Louis is all right. Just as long as no one pushes him."

"And now we have Fontana."

"For as long as it lasts, yes. The town will probably die out when the gold plays out. I hope it's soon."

"You're holding just a little something back from me, Smoke."

He hesitated. "Tilden Franklin wants you for his woman."

"I've known that for a long time. Has he made his desires public?"

"Apparently so. From now on, you're going to have to be very careful."

She lay still for a moment, silent. "We could always leave, honey."

He knew she did not wish to leave, but was only voicing their options. "I know. And we'd be running for the rest of our lives. Once you start, it's hard to stop."

In the corral, Seven nickered, the sound carrying to the house. Smoke was up and dressed in a moment, strapping on his guns and picking up a rifle. He and Sally could hear the sounds of hooves, coming hard.

"One horse," Sally noted.

"Stay inside."

Smoke stepped out the door, relaxing when he saw who it was. It was Colby's oldest boy, and he was fogging up the trail, lathering his horse.

Bob slid his horse to stop amid the dust and leaped off. "Mister Smoke," he panted. So the news had spread very fast as to Smoke's real identity.

"Bob. What's the problem?"

"Pa sent me. It's started, Mister Smoke. Some of Tilden's riders done burned out Wilbur Mason's place, over on the western ridge. Burned him flat. There ain't nothing left nowhere."

"Anybody hurt over there?"

"No, sir. Not bad, leastways. Mister Wilbur got burned by a bullet, but it ain't bad."

"Where are they now?"

"Mister Matlock took the kids. Pa and Ma took in Mister Wilbur and his missus."

"Where's your brother?"

"Pa sent him off to warn the others."

"Go on in the house. Sally will fix you something to eat. I'll see to your horse."

Smoke looked toward the faraway Circle TF spread. "All right, Franklin," he muttered. "If that's how you want it, get ready for it."

THE MOUNTAIN MAN SERIES BY
WILLIAM W. JOHNSTONE